Praise for
The Fixer, The Maker, The Drag Entertainer
A Queer Romance

"This fun and frothy love story offers strong LGBTQ+ representation while simultaneously delving into the oft-misunderstood world of polyamory. Steenblik expertly tackles myriad issues of modern love—from the emotional complexities to the physical logistics—with a refreshing straightforwardness and a cheeky splash of the supernatural. ... the novel's magic really shines when it focuses on Mark's emotional growth and his sexy (not graphic) love triangle with Elijah and Viktoriya. Steenblik has crafted an entertaining and poignant romance that celebrates love in whatever form it may take."

-*Kirkus Reviews*

"...The Fixer, The Maker, The Drag Entertainer is a wild ride! ...this book resonated with me because of its heartfelt and at times sarcastic narratives and how it embraced the complexity of polyamory over a simplistic conventional solution."

-*Jessica Reads It via Reedsy Discovery*

The Fixer, The Maker, The Drag Entertainer

The Fixer

The Maker

THE DRAG ENTERTAINER

A Queer Romance

Kyle Steenblik

ISBN: 979-8-9953638-0-4
Ebook ISBN: 979-8-9953638-1-1

Library of Congress Control Number: 2026907904

Human Authored Reg #: 4041956, https://authorsguild.org/human

cover art by Rose Hannel

First Printing, 2026
Published by Wasted Words
Salt Lake City, UT

https://WastedWords.net

Dedication

For Carleigh: my fixer, maker, and drag entertainer.

Chapter 1

My name is Eros, or at least, that's the name I've been using lately. I am what you humans might call a Djinn—or a Genie—though neither term fully captures what I am. I am an eternal consciousness, ancient as the universe itself. I'm the grain of truth behind many of your myths and legends—but don't get ideas about omnipotence; that's not me. I've always had a soft spot for your kind, especially in matters of the heart. There's something intoxicating about watching two hearts find each other—or three, as I would later learn.

Let me introduce you to Mark Gerald Williams of East Brunswick, New Jersey, a twenty-seven-year-old mortal, my friend, and my liberator. When we met, he was neither warrior nor poet, nor did he possess any power to shake the heavens or command the tides. No, Mark was an unassuming man of quiet presence, with tousled hair the color of summer wheat fields after a rain. A soft, well-kept beard framed a face unremarkable in its features, yet memorable for its warmth. It was a safe, friendly face that drew you in gently and whispered reassurance: this was a man you could trust. Behind kind eyes, like amber warmed by sunlight, lay the quiet depth of a man on the cusp of change. I trust you can now picture the man clearly.

Ah, but what does he do, you ask? What drew Mark into my orbit? Mark was what mortals called an "IT support technician," which is a dismissive title I assume was meant to downplay his power. His gift lies in coaxing life back into lifeless machines.

"

When they falter, he revives them, though I can't say how. Perhaps he speaks to them—whispers their true names—so they obey him when they defy others. He may be some kind of wizard, though I admit that's poetic exaggeration on my part. Mark is clever, but not the kind of clever that builds empires. His cleverness is humbler, like a well-sharpened blade—practical, reliable, and capable of cutting through minor problems.

Yet, for all his talents, Mark struggles with the peculiar rituals of his people, the unspoken codes that guide mortal interaction. He stumbles through them like a child learning to dance—well-meaning but awkward—often treading on toes or toppling the occasional vase. It's not malice or ignorance, just a natural misalignment with the rhythm of others. He can carry on any conversation with ease, yet he's hopeless when it comes to starting one. Still, he has a good heart. The kind of man who'd scale a wall to rescue a cat, only to find it's the wrong wall and send the ladder crashing down.

He grew up among trees—apple trees, to be precise—in a small East Brunswick orchard. The orchard has belonged to his family since the days of the Revolution, when mortals fought one another over their notions of freedom. Mark and his siblings—Jefferson, the eldest, and Lexie, the youngest—spent their childhood among these trees, plucking fruit from their boughs and learning the rhythm of the earth. They chopped wood and lived a life as honest and rooted as the trees themselves. It was a good life, or so it seemed to me, though Mark's eyes sometimes betrayed a quiet wistfulness when he spoke of it. Perhaps it wasn't the work he missed but its simplicity: when a tree needed tending, he tended it; when an apple ripened, he plucked it; when the simple machinery faltered, he mended it. That life shaped Mark—heart, mind, and body.

Mark was caught between the quiet, earthy honesty of his family's orchard and the bright, digital noise of his work at Rutgers. He is a fixer of things, a doer of good, even if his efforts don't always go as planned. He is, in short, a man of contradictions: kind yet clumsy, clever yet not too clever, noble in spirit but prone to mishaps. A mortal through and through, yet carrying a spark of something more—one I recognized the moment he entered the office where I lay captive in a bronze oil lamp, a souvenir from Morocco.

The Fixer, The Maker, The Drag Entertainer

****Mark****

My name is Mark. I don't like attention. I don't think I'm special, and I can't imagine my story is unique. Talking about myself feels like my bones are trying to escape my skin. It just makes me feel more than a little uncomfortable. But this is my story, one my best friend Eros is hell-bent on telling.

I worked for Rutgers University's IT department as part of the support staff. I was one of the guys who showed up when staff or students had computer problems. It wasn't glamorous, but I took it seriously because small things could have big consequences. Solving a small issue fast could mean the difference between a student passing or failing, or a professor being able to hold class at all. I don't think I need to explain much more. These days, who hasn't needed to call a help desk occasionally?

The university's IT department was spread across the main campus and its annexes. What is relevant to this story is that I was one of the few technicians who acted as the boots on the ground. I showed up in person whenever necessary for the more *analog* professors, those who preferred working face-to-face. As a result, I ended up with a handful of repeat clients: some who latched onto me, and others whom I adopted, either because they were difficult or simply because I liked them. I mention this because two of those regulars are important to this story: Dr. Jason Newell, whom you're about to meet, and Viktoriya, whom you'll meet later.

Dr. Newell was a philosophy professor, one of those *analog* types I mentioned earlier. He could be difficult, and I was one of the few technicians who could get him to cooperate. I didn't mind; his issues were usually simple to fix, and over time, he learned to trust me. It didn't matter if one of my equally competent colleagues offered to help. He wouldn't listen until he'd spoken with me. To save everyone time and frustration, we agreed that he'd call me directly for any computer-related issues.

Recently, however, he began experiencing unusual, seemingly inexplicable problems that gradually escalated. The root cause was something I could never have predicted—or even imagined in a billion years.

****Eros****

The first time I met Mark, he'd been summoned to Dr. Jason Newell's office after I'd caused the professor's computer to shut down unexpectedly. Dr. Newell had been irritating me with his endless complaints about his students and his self-important revisions to his textbook-length syllabus. In a moment of mischievous impulse, I reached into his so-called "laptop"—a ridiculous name for something that never once rested on his lap— and located its power source and severed the connection. Moments later, Dr. Newell grabbed his phone and demanded an immediate repair, insisting he had *critical work* to finish and couldn't afford to be delayed by the university's "unreliable equipment."

A short while later, Mark walked into the office—and into my life. He carried himself with quiet confidence, narrating his actions as he worked in a calm, reassuring tone. Without waiting for an invitation, he took a seat and explained that a sudden shutdown could have any number of causes, though a power loss was usually to blame. Within minutes, he had replaced the battery and power cable, bringing life back to the ironically named laptop. Then, as smoothly as he'd arrived, he stood, gathered his tools, shook Dr. Newell's hand, and left. I was stunned. If it had been possible, I would have said I was in love.

Of course, I wasn't in love. Love is a distinctly human experience, one I'm incapable of feeling. But I was fascinated, intrigued, and curious to know a human for the first time in centuries. Luckily, I already knew how and when Mark would be summoned, and to my advantage, it involved my newest hobby. So, over the following weeks, I devised increasingly elaborate ways to make Dr. Newell's computer fail. Each time he called for Mark. Mark would arrive, diagnose the issue, and resolve it with frustrating efficiency. But once, the problem was complex enough to leave him genuinely stumped, and he took the professor's laptop with him.

What I needed was a way to communicate with Mark. I had to work out a way to get Mark to pick up my lamp and take me away with him without alarming him or Dr. Newell. As it happened, fortune favored me. Shortly after Mark left with the laptop, Dr. Newell plucked my lamp from his desk and began pacing, as he often did when anxious. It was a habit of his—carrying me around, muttering to himself while pretending to reason with the universe. This time, however, he was genuinely worried about the safety of his precious work. Apparently, that laptop contained years of philosophical nonsense. When he asked the universe why this kept happening and softly wished it would be the last time, I knew what to do. For the first time, I whispered an idea—a thought as light as a breeze—into Dr. Newell's mind.

"Your problems began shortly after you started keeping this lamp on your desk. Apart from what that strange street vendor told you, you know nothing about it. There may be a connection beyond your understanding. Tell Mark about it—and show him the lamp—when he returns. He seems clever; perhaps he can resolve this once and for all."

And that is exactly what Dr. Newell did next.

Mark

I returned about an hour after taking Dr. Newell's laptop to my office, where I'd spent a frustrating hour trying, and failing, to diagnose it. I walked in with two boxes, one under each arm, and my usual bag of tools slung over my shoulder. I entered the office without fanfare, determined to get this mystery off both my mind and my plate.

"I'm sorry, I couldn't manage to get your laptop to respond," I said as I set the boxes down and unpacked them while Dr. Newell watched, confused, with an old oil lamp in his hands. "It's almost as if the power and charging circuits had been severed, which should be impossible, considering they're all physically intact. I could spend days figuring out what went wrong, but I think the best—and fastest—solution, which I know you prefer, is simply a replacement. Lucky for you, we have a few spares for just such a case," I said, removing the protective plastic from the new laptop. "I know you have a lot of work saved, and I was able to connect to your hard drive and recover your data externally. Once I get your new laptop set up, I'll restore the data I've backed up. It shouldn't take long. Any questions, Dr. Newell?"

I doubted Dr. Newell understood half of what I'd just said. My explanation was far too direct and practical for someone who spent his days pondering unanswerable questions. Eventually, he surfaced from whatever abstract thought he'd been drowning in and responded.

"That sounds good, Mike," Dr. Newell muttered, getting my name entirely wrong, as he often did whenever he felt intellectually cornered. "I was wondering why these problems kept happening. It occurred to me this started shortly after I started keeping this souvenir lamp on my desk. I picked it up at a market in Morocco in May. A humorous trinket ... a magic genie lamp, or so the merchant claimed. Could you take a look? I doubt there's any real correlation, it's probably a coincidence, but perhaps it's still an idea worth exploring."

"Oh, I'm sure it's just a coincidence. You know what they say—correlation isn't necessarily causation," I said as Dr. Newell stared with a befuddled expression. "But that's science, not the humanities. Still, it's only just September now, so three months could be long enough to establish a pattern. Honestly, I've seen stranger things I couldn't explain. Okay, I have your data transfer running now, and it will take a few minutes. Let me take a look at this magic lamp," I said with a pandering chuckle, accepting the lamp from him. "Who knows, maybe a mischievous genie inside is causing all this trouble?"

I was fairly certain my joke was lost on him; he seemed genuinely concerned by the idea. Which was absurd; he had no reason to suspect that this lamp had anything to do with his problem. I held the lamp—a handsome antique, nothing outwardly suspicious. Then, a thought that was not my own slipped into my mind like a whisper:

"This is a strange lamp in your soft, powerful hands; it feels charged. It tingles. It may be more than it appears. You've heard rumors that some of those markets sell things like this lamp to colonizers—objects that can disrupt electronics or produce static discharge, a petty kind of revenge on the foreign invaders. Take it with you and tell the professor you'll examine it. At the very least, removing it will reassure him that a mysterious source of misfortune that has been plaguing him can't cause any more trouble."

"I think I see what you mean, there's something unusual about this lamp," I said, half to myself, half to Dr. Newell. "You know, I've heard some of those markets sell trinkets that can mess with electronics or cause odd static discharges. Supposedly, it's a kind of petty revenge on tourists. But I'm sure that's only a nasty rumor. Why don't I take the lamp back to my office? I'll keep an eye on it, see if it acts up, and that'll take it out of the equation for you. If you still have trouble, we'll know the lamp isn't to blame. And if I do, we'll know it's more than coincidence. I'll bring your souvenir back in a few days, assuming it behaves. Looks like your files have transferred, you should be good as new. I'll pack up and leave you to your work."

"That sounds reasonable," Dr. Newell said, looking much calmer. "I appreciate your help with this, Mike. Hopefully, this means you've finally managed to solve the problem, and I won't need to call you again."

My jaw tightened at Dr. Newell's little microaggression. He knew my name, and he damn well knew none of this was my fault. He'd also called me countless times before, never once bothering with a thank you. Still, it wasn't worth the energy to correct him. So, I packed up the empty boxes and plastic wrap, then left the office with the bronze lamp tucked safely in my bag.

*** *Eros* ***

Mark walked quickly out of the building and jogged across the street, my freedom glimmering on the horizon. Back in the office, I'd sensed for a moment that Mark might have noticed something unnatural in my intrusive thought. His joke about the lamp harboring a genie had struck uncomfortably close to the truth. I couldn't tell whether that came from his natural perceptiveness or my own carelessness. Either way, my first objective was complete. Now I just needed the right moment to speak with Mark.

His office was only half a block away. After tossing a few empty cardboard boxes into a blue dumpster, he stepped inside. He took the elevator down to his basement office. The entire time, he fiddled with a rectangular electronic device unfamiliar to me. Meanwhile, I jostled inside his bag, wondering what would happen next. I needed to speak to Mark, but I had to do so cautiously. The last time I spoke directly to a human, their panic sent my lamp hurtling out a window, narrowly missing several confused and furious pedestrians below. That must have been seventy or eighty years ago—perhaps longer. Tracking time with such limited access to the outside world had always been nearly impossible.

The elevator doors slid open, and Mark stepped into a wide, dimly lit corridor, then through a door propped open, a sure sign someone was already inside. He passed shelves stacked with mismatched boxes and bins on his way to a small cubicle that held two desks. The nameplates outside the cubicle read "Mark Williams" and "Otto." A friendly-looking fellow occupied the second desk. I assumed this was Otto, who must be Mark's coworker. He had unusual bluish-purple hair and wore sunglasses. He looked up as Mark dropped his bag beside the desk.

"Hey there, Mark. Any luck with the professor's laptop? You seemed pretty frustrated when you left."

"Hey, OT. Some luck. I took the easy route and just replaced the damn thing with a spare. That should get him back up and running for now. I thought about diagnosing the old laptop, but only to satisfy my curiosity. It's probably a write-off anyway," Mark said, sinking into a well-worn chair and leaning back until he was staring at the ceiling.

"Smart move," OT said without looking away from his work. "I'd rather not hear from him again anytime soon. Want me to check the warranty? If it's still active, we can send it back to the supplier for a replacement."

"Thanks, and sorry you had to deal with him. I told him to call me directly, but you know how he is. You'll never guess what the professor thinks is causing his problems."

"Don't tell me it's another one of his Immanuel Kant misinterpretations, is it?"

"That might still be on the table, but no—it's a magic genie lamp."

"Wait. Hold up. Say that again, Fam."

"This," Mark said, pulling my lamp from his bag and holding it out for Otto to see. "Not really a magic genie lamp, of course, but he said his issues began right after he started keeping this on his desk. He seemed genuinely worried, which is unusual. I didn't have the heart to tell him it was probably just some faulty solder. I told him I'd test his theory, and come on, you can't say we haven't seen our share of problems with no logical explanation."

"True," OT said, inspecting the antique bronze lamp without lifting his sunglasses. "I shudder to think how the public would feel if they knew how much of our job relies on elbow-to-the-jukebox fixes we can't logically explain. Do me a favor, if you're going to test that theory, do it at your apartment, far from our server racks. I'd rather not explain to the university that their email server went down because of a magic genie lamp. They might actually believe it. And one more favor: if it *does* turn out to be magical and you end up with three wishes, call me. I've got a few ideas that could use one or two."

"And that's exactly why people keep their wish-granting genies secret. I'll have to call you after Elijah—we've got a standing pact to share any wishes and stop each other from making the classic wish mistakes. Anyway, it's been a long day. I'm going to pack up and head home," Mark said, standing and swapping items between his bag and desk. I watched Mark file a few papers, return some boxes to the shelves, and finally slip my lamp back into his bag. "Need a hand with anything before I head out?"

"That's a negative. Just waiting for this backup to finish, then I'll head out myself," OT said, giving a gesture somewhere between a salute and a wave. Mark returned it silently.

That was it. I didn't need to interfere at all. Mark would take me home with him, where we could finally have a private conversation. Everything was unfolding even better than I'd hoped. As much as I liked Otto—or OT, as Mark called him—I knew I needed to speak with Mark alone, at least the first time. Not that anyone but Mark would hear me—humans tend to panic when they hear a voice no one else can. Mark left his office, caught the elevator, and soon trotted out of the building, heading home.

Mark

My apartment was only a few buildings away from the office. It was in a block of old student dormitories that the University reserved for staff to use as needed. It was one of the best perks of the job. The downside was that it came with the condition that I was on call 24/7, which only became a problem because I was terrible at saying no. It was an arrangement I could live with because it meant I didn't have to overpay for an apartment in New Brunswick or commute from my family home in East Brunswick. Not only did it mean I didn't have to commute at all, but I was also just two blocks away from The Queen's Head Club, the bar and drag club where my best friend in the world, Elijah, worked and performed.

As soon as I stepped out of my office building, I pulled out my phone to call Elijah. It was still early enough that the club wasn't really open. I tapped his photo—a picture he'd taken of himself with my phone. It rang twice before he answered.

"Mark, why do you insist on calling like an elder millennial instead of texting like a normal boyfriend?" Elijah said in his usual mock-scolding tone, one he'd clearly practiced for effect. "What's going on? Are you coming in?"

"Elijah, how many times do I have to tell you that you only wish I was your boyfriend. I just don't go for beards, and I call because it drives you crazy," I said back to him, laughing. He had an effortless way of making me laugh. "I'm not going to make it tonight; I got my hands on a magic genie lamp and will spend my night making questionable decisions without you."

"Oh, you bitch. Well, I'm stuck here, so I can't stop you. But I promise, if you come here tomorrow night with a twelve-inch pianist, I will never give you a free drink again."

"You know me better than that—I'd shoot for eight or nine inches max."

"Dammit, Mark, I have to go. Customers. Text me next time, I love you," Elijah said, sounding a little frustrated but very amused.

"You know I won't. Love you too. Good luck with those customers in a closed bar. Goodnight," I replied, feeling equally amused and a little pleased. I'd managed to fluster him a little during a conversation that lasted only as long as my walk across the street to my building.

Once inside, I dropped my bag on the kitchen table—which also doubled as my counter. I dashed to the bathroom; I don't know what it is about getting home that makes going to the bathroom feel like an emergency the second you walk through the door. Once I'd taken care of the usual inconvenient biological urgency, I washed the day's work grime from my hands. Walking back to the kitchen, I picked up a towel hanging next to the kitchen sink and dried my hands before tossing the towel aside. Then, I opened my bag on the counter and pulled out Dr. Newell's antique lamp.

"Hello, Mark! I am delighted to meet you," an unnatural voice shouted directly into my mind. I yelped and dropped the lamp before I even realized what I was doing.

"Is someone here? What was that?" I stammered and looked around in a panic.

When I heard no response, and after I had taken a few calming breaths, I reached down to pick up the lamp from the floor, where I had dropped it.

"I'm sorry I startled you. Please don't panic. I'm inside this lamp. I assure you, I am quite real, and you are not imagining this. I am not proud of how I just handled myself. I apologize. I was beyond excited, and the moment you pulled the lamp out, the carefully crafted moment of communication I had been planning slipped away from me," the unnatural voice in my head said, but much softer this time.

"What? Hello? Is this some kind of joke? OT, is this you?" I pleaded. I was not amused and did not enjoy this joke.

"Mark, this isn't a joke. Please, stay calm. My name is Eros. I'm what you mortals might call … a genie. Now, can we talk?"

"Genie? You've got to be shitting me. Okay, Eros," I said with a laugh, giving in to the lunacy. "Sure. Let's talk about how I have lost my mind."

Chapter 2

Not the best start. Has it really been so long that I've forgotten how to introduce myself to a human without sending them into a panic or making them question the soundness of their mortal minds? Did he really ask if I was *shitting* him? An odd expression—what does that mean? Clearly, I'm rusty.

Let's try this again.

"Mark, you haven't lost your mind. I'll explain everything."

"A voice in my head doesn't exactly inspire confidence in my sanity. Eros, was it? If you're not an invention of my imagination, give me one good reason not to toss this lamp out the window. And is there any way we can talk without you being *inside* my head?"

"Give me a little slack here, Mark. I haven't actually spoken to a human in decades, and it's been even longer since I held a proper conversation. I'm a bit out of practice. Yes, I can give you a thousand reasons not to throw me out the window, but can we at least agree it would be extremely rude?"

"Okay, even though I'm not convinced you're real—and I'm not sure you've earned it—I'll cut you some slack and not toss the lamp out the window. Let's see where this goes, but I'm opening the window just in case."

"Fair enough. If it makes you more comfortable, I can make myself audible, but I'll need a medium. What are those things you wear over your ears to listen to cassette tapes? If you wear them while holding the lamp, I can try to speak through them."

"You mean headphones? Yeah, I've got those. Let me set the lamp down and dig them out of my bag. Hold on a sec … I guess."

Mark set me down on the kitchen counter while he pulled out a strange-looking, C-shaped piece of wavy plastic—what I could only assume were modern headphones. I was beginning to feel hopelessly out of touch with the modern world.

Then again, centuries of isolation will do that to anyone.

Mark didn't immediately pick me up after fitting the headphones over—or perhaps into—his ears. Instead, he retrieved a bottle from a freezing-cold cabinet and took a long drink straight from it. I detected high-proof ethanol, sweetened imitation whiskey with artificial cinnamon flavoring, if my senses weren't mistaken. That couldn't possibly taste good to him.

He set the bottle down and finally picked me up again. It took a moment, but I managed to connect with the strange little device over his ears.

****Mark****

This was either the strangest auditory hallucination imaginable, or the start of a psychological break. I'd read that burnout and stress can do some fascinating things to the human brain. But I hadn't felt particularly stressed or burned out lately. There was no family history of schizophrenia or anything similar, not that a clean record ruled it out. What I did know for sure was that the cinnamon-flavored imitation whiskey Elijah had left in my freezer tasted awful and burned all the way down. So, for now, that would be my anchor to reality, as I apparently decided to lean into having a conversation with a magic lamp.

"I've got the headphones on now, Eros," I said reluctantly to the antique lamp in my hands.

"Mark? Can you hear me now?" Eros responded audibly, sounding slightly mechanical yet ethereal.

"I can, thank you. This is much more comfortable. I have about a thousand questions, but I will let you explain first."

"Thank you, Mark. That's gracious of you. Clearly, I chose well. First and foremost, I am not actually a genie. Those are myths and fables. Although I am the reason those stories exist. Which, ironically, is why I'm a captive in this absurd vessel until someone chooses, of their own will, to wish for my freedom," Eros said matter-of-factly, as if it would make sense to me.

"So, you're not a genie, and the genie thing's just myth. Then what are you? And I'm guessing this means no three wishes? You mentioned being captive. Are you a prisoner? And if the wishes aren't real, what does wishing for your freedom even mean?" I asked, looking for the thread that might unravel this hallucination or dream.

"I should start from the beginning. You might want to sit down," Eros answered with a hint of a patronizing tone. I shrugged and sank onto the couch, phone in hand, just in case I needed to call for help. "I am, in truth, an elemental force, one of many consciousnesses that predate the stars themselves."

"So, you're saying you're over thirteen billion years old?" I asked after quickly searching *age of universe* on my phone.

"Color me impressed. I didn't realize humans had come that far. I'm somewhere between thirteen and thirty billion years old. I've lost track, honestly; after a few billion, you stop counting. Besides, age is a matter of perspective."

"That depends very much on context, Eros," I interjected, increasingly convinced this wasn't a figment of my imagination. There's no way my own mind would leave such an obvious, inappropriate age-gap joke hanging. "But I get your meaning. Go on, I'll try to hold my questions."

"I appreciate that, but please, ask as they come. I've almost forgotten how enjoyable a simple conversation can be. I assure you, I have plenty of questions for you too."

"Fair enough. Let's skip to the part where there are no wishes, and you're somehow confined to this lamp."

"Right. First, you have to understand, we're non-corporeal consciousnesses. For all our abilities, we can't exactly roam freely through the universe. We need to 'hitch a ride,' so to speak. To interact, we have to inhabit something physical—say, a Byzantine bronze oil lamp."

"Strangely enough, that makes sense," I said, though it really didn't. Still, I didn't want to derail the conversation. "But why the lamp?"

"Why not? Back then, it was a staple in human life, and I found it aesthetically pleasing."

"I get it, like a sports car," I said, only half-focused. The alcohol burn in my stomach had morphed into hunger, so I texted the pizzeria down the street.

"A sports car? I'll have to come back to that, but I believe you understand. Now, hold on as I tell you the tale of my unjust imprisonment."

"Please, go on. I just ordered a pizza."

"Ordered a what? When—how?" Eros asked incredulously, clearly oblivious to what I was doing on my phone. Another point in favor of this being real.

"A pizza—surely you know what that is. I just texted the shop down the block from my phone."

"Of course I know what a pizza is. I just—never mind, I'm clever; I'll figure it out. Anyway, a few thousand years ago, I found myself on this planet as you humans were discovering civilization and forming your first societies. You were peculiar, and I was fascinated."

"Peculiar? Really? Have you met yourself?"

"Yes, Mark—peculiar. Your mating rituals were messy, irrational, inconsistent, and yet, somehow, beautiful. Something about your relentless need to connect and create meaning in the chaos drew me in."

"You almost sound like a romantic." Eros wasn't wrong about us—messy, irrational, inconsistent. I had to hand it to them.

"Thank you. But every few decades, you'd change the rules in completely arbitrary ways. As you grew more mobile, I watched your rituals vary wildly across the world."

"Makes sense, migration causes cultural drift. So, you just observed for thousands of years?" I glanced at my phone; the pizza was on its way, so I settled in to listen to Eros's story.

"For a while, yes. I was content to watch. But the longer I observed, the more I yearned to be part of the chaos. I couldn't help myself. To help you hopeless fools and, if I'm honest, to amuse myself, I started to meddle. I never thought anyone would notice. But meddling, as it turns out, is what got me locked in that lamp."

"So that's where the wishes come in?"

"That was the start of it. The leap from voyeur to participant was exhilarating. I used my powers to nudge a few of you in the right direction. A gust of wind bringing two strangers together, a touch of engineered luck shifting futures. I whispered ideas into your heads, tweaking the threads of fate, minor adjustments that seemed harmless at the time."

"I see, so 'wishes' are your shorthand for a little nudge."

"Yes, that's not an unfair comparison. Now, without consciously making the decision, I started planting stories, and oh, what fun those were. Unfortunately, one of them indirectly led to my captivity: the tale of the magic lamp—find a djinn trapped inside, and they'll grant you three wishes."

"That one I'm familiar with."

"You might be, but not with the real story. I thought it was harmless—amusing, even—until humans twisted it. They added offensive little details: that I was bound to a 'master,' that I was deceitful, or worse, malicious."

"But how did that 'kind of indirectly' lead to your captivity?"

"My existence became known—misunderstood, but known—and that's when I crossed a line. I'd rather not discuss those regrettable, if not downright embarrassing, events."

"All right, I won't press. So, you crossed a line?"

"I did. My punishment? Imprisonment in a bronze oil lamp until a human 'wishes' to set me free—" Eros was saying when a knock interrupted them at the door.

"Sorry to cut you off, Eros, you were on a roll. But the pizza's here, and I have to grab it," I said, feeling anything but casual as I walked to the door with an antique bronze oil lamp tucked under my arm.

I opened the door to the familiar nineteen-year-old delivery guy whose name I could never remember. We exchanged cash for pizza with minimal conversation and wished each other good night. Both of us said, "You too," before I closed the door.

"That was unusual," Eros said in my ear, genuinely perplexed. "I can't say I've ever witnessed human interaction quite like that. I realize I wasn't paying attention to the time, but that was quick, wasn't it?"

"The pizza shop's a block away, and this is a university town," I said, setting the box on the counter and flipping open the lid. From the dish rack, I grabbed a plate, slid two slices onto it, and set it aside to cool.

"That probably doesn't mean much to you, but trust me, it's normal around here. Anyway, go on. I'm going to eat something.

You were saying you were imprisoned by your so-called 'council of universal consciousness' for meddling in human affairs?"

"That's a massive oversimplification, Mark. There is no 'council.' We haven't interacted since we drifted apart billions of years ago. Think strict self-governance—rules woven into the fabric of the universe," Eros said, his voice tight. "It's complicated."

"So there's an untold number of entities like you. You don't interact, but you've got a complicated set of rules," I said, feeling the thread of thought slip. "It sounds like you punished yourself."

"Like I said, it's complicated. But yes, essentially, I had no choice. I helped make the rules, I had to follow them."

"Okay, let's drop that and pretend I understand," I said, unwilling to untangle the inner workings of entities I couldn't begin to fathom. "So how did you end up here?"

"The lamp that became my prison traveled the world for centuries, passing from hand to hand. As a silent observer, I witnessed the best and worst of humanity—enduring confinement with only fleeting amusement when I chose to intervene.

"Fortunately, I was never subservient to the lamp's holder and could ignore their banal or repulsive wishes. On rare occasions, I stepped from silent observer to quiet participant, if the request was worthy—or entertaining enough," Eros finished. "I arrived here after Dr. Newell bought my lamp as a souvenir in Morocco."

"Right," I said between bites of pizza. "I remember him mentioning that, but how did you end up for sale as a souvenir?"

"I ended up in that antique bazaar because my lamp was traded as a novelty among merchants for decades, until I sat, overpriced according to some who couldn't imagine my true pricelessness, but no less attractive to tourists like Dr. Newell. He became unusually excited at the idea of finding a genuine genie lamp. He even rambled a half-conceived dissertation at the unfortunate shopkeeper about the ethical dilemmas of granting three wishes."

"That sounds like Dr. Newell, all right," I said, awkwardly eating over the sink with the lamp tucked under one arm.

"Just wait, that's not the half of it," Eros said. "At first, I found it amusing. He'd hold my lamp in his office and talk to me—well, to himself, really. He had no idea I was there. He asked whether he had a moral obligation to use hypothetical wishes to better the world. I would've said yes, obviously, if he'd made any worthwhile wishes. I might've granted them.

"Twice, he came close. The first time, he wished for one student who actually understood Descartes. Ludicrous, I read those papers; they all understood René Descartes better than he did. The second was when he wished to solve the 'Trolley Problem,' as if that has any real solution. I destroyed his Amtrak ticket for that one and started crashing his computer regularly—that's where you came in."

I paced the kitchen, chewing thoughtfully on mozzarella. The gears in my mind strained as I tried to fit the pieces of Eros's story together. I felt increasingly sure this wasn't a dream, hallucination, or psychological phantom. My apprehension was ebbing, replaced by curiosity. I'm no expert on supernatural versus natural-but-unexplained phenomena, but at this point, the distinction felt irrelevant. Abandoning the pizza, I reached for the cinnamon-flavored whiskey. I poured an unmeasured double into a faded novelty glass, took a sip, and let the burn linger—a small, grounding reminder that I was awake, coherent, and aware. Maybe this was real. The question was whether Eros was who they claimed to be.

"I have questions, Eros."

"Please, Mark, ask away. I'm—as you might say—an open book."

"How does it actually work? You say you're not a genie and imply you can't grant wishes, but then you talked about doing exactly that, at will."

"Fair enough, I can see how that sounds contradictory. I realize I keep saying this, but it's complicated. In short, I can interact with the world and influence matter and energy. And, as you've experienced, I can plant ideas into your mind, but I can't, or won't, force you or anyone else to act against your will. When you first held my lamp, for example, I simply suggested that you take it with you. So, in that sense, with a little creativity, I can 'grant a wish' within reason. But it's always my choice."

"Then where did the whole 'three wishes' idea come from? Why three?"

"That was my invention—a little poetic storytelling. One wish causes panic and decision paralysis, often leading to disaster or indecision. Two are usually enough for most people, but three … three wishes make things interesting. The weight placed on the final wish forces reflection. Waste the first one, and it's fine, you still have two left, which eases the panic. The second is usually where the real choice is made. But the third? That one's almost torture."

I finished the small glass of whiskey. As the final sip burned its way down, an idea surfaced. I needed proof, something to show Eros was more than just a voice in my headphones. Not empirical proof, just enough to convince myself.

"I think I understand. Let me ask you this. Can you make my heartburn go away? That cinnamon whiskey is going to burn a hole in my guts."

"Are you joking? That may be the worst first wish I have ever heard."

"Think of it as proof, a simple way to convince me this isn't some elaborate hallucination or psychological break, and to show me that if you're real, you're not full of shit. It should be easy if you are what you say. It's low stakes. Plus, if you can't, I can solve it myself. The only other option is to call Elijah or OT, as promised, and you can talk to him, and then we compare notes."

"Proof? I can't decide whether to be insulted or impressed. No one in history has ever asked me for that. Mark Williams, you are something else. I don't know what it is, but you're it. I've done it; your heartburn should be gone, but the sudden change may cause gas."

Without warning, an eye-watering, window-rattling, demon-expelling belch erupted from my body. My face was tingling, and my sinuses were on fire. The relief was as intense as the shock. I could faintly hear distant laughter in my ears, which were ringing a little. My heartburn was gone, leaving me with the lingering realization that this was real. It probably should have frightened me. Instead, I was fascinated and excited by this not-quite-supernatural encounter.

"Wow. Did you do that on purpose? Never mind, don't answer that. It doesn't matter. Consider me convinced," I said, pulling the lamp from under my arm to speak directly to it. I was convinced they were at least not entirely dishonest. But the last thing I needed to know was whether they were benevolent or malicious. I had to employ the joke test. "Eros, I'm going to make a wish. I know you don't really 'grant' them, so bear with me. But before I do, I have one more question that should finally tell me how much I can trust you."

"Well, gee, Mark, if I had known an earth-shaking belch was all it would take to convince you, I would have done that hours ago. But please, go ahead and ask your question."

"Have you heard the twelve-inch pianist joke?"

"Have I heard the what? Mark, are you shitting me right now? I *wrote* that joke. But that's not the best part. Go on. Ask me what the best part is."

"You've got me, what's the best part?"

"It is based on a true story! Oh, Mark, do you have any idea how long I have wanted to tell this story? There were a few artistic variations, of course. But the real story goes like this: a musician once wished for the 'world's largest penis.' So, I—get this—made him the world's largest pianist. Did he appreciate the clever twist? No. No, he did not. And let me tell you, Mark—Franz Liszt was *not* amused."

I dropped the lamp.

Eros

Mark froze. In an instant, everything changed. The skepticism and apprehension vanished. For a fleeting moment, he relaxed—then melted. His grip on the lamp faltered, and his knees buckled.

"Mark?"

Mark couldn't respond. He couldn't hear me right now. He dropped the lamp and collapsed onto the floor. Tears streamed down his face as his laughter morphed into a coughing fit—like a flock of furious geese trying to shout, 'Franz Liszt?!' That sound will haunt me for eternity. Even when the universe collapses, I'll still hear it.

"Franz—*HONK*—Li—*HONK*—szt!" and I am not mad about that.

So there I was, sprawled on the floor of Mark's tiny apartment, contemplating the carpet. Was this shade of brown its original color, or the patina of time and countless tenants? Meanwhile, Mark was slowly regaining his composure. I watched as he pushed himself onto his knees, took three deep breaths, and rose. He walked to the kitchen, wiped his face, and filled a glass with water from his sink. He drained the glass as if he resented every drop. He walked back toward me, and I finally got a good look at his shoes—practical, comfortably stylish things. He seemed to contemplate deeply before reaching down and picking up my lamp.

"Mark? Are you all right?"

"Eros, I don't know if there's a right or wrong way to say this, but … I wish for your freedom."

"Mark? What did you just say?"

"I wished for your freedom. Isn't that what you want? Did it work?"

"Yes, that's what I want—of course it is! But why? Why did you just do that?"

"It just seemed like the right thing to do. Did I do it right? Nothing feels different."

"I don't know. You caught me a little bit off guard. I don't feel any different. Hold on, let me try to leave this lamp."

"Okay … I'll just wait here."

There I was, still inhabiting the bronze oil lamp that had been my prison for centuries. I'd been trapped so long I couldn't remember the last time I'd even tried to press against my bonds. But now, the door was open, and I simply had to slip through. Honestly, I was nervous. It was like standing up after sitting too long when your strange human legs fall asleep. I gently pushed in the only direction I could go, into Mark.

It all happened so abruptly I didn't think to discuss it with Mark first. Normally, I'd never inhabit another sentient being without consent—or at least a warning. But it worked, and I'm almost positive he didn't feel a thing. I was no longer inside the lamp; I was inside Mark. I didn't want to linger—it felt rude—so I went for Mark's headphones.

"Mark, can you still hear me?"

"Yeah. Did it work?" Mark replied, turning the lamp over in his hands.

"I think it did. I should tell you—I was inside you for a moment. It all happened so fast, and I shouldn't have done that without asking. I'm sorry. I'm in your headphones now. Try putting the lamp down."

"Oh, well, I appreciate that. I wouldn't have known if you hadn't mentioned being inside me, but it's okay. I'll put down the lamp if you say so," Mark said, setting the ordinary bronze oil lamp down on his kitchen counter and stepping back.

"Can you hear me?" I said.

"Yes, I can."

"Mark. You set me free. I can go anywhere. I can do anything I want now. I don't even know what to do now. Why did you do that?"

"It just felt like the right thing to do. I mean, once I knew you were real. No sentient being should be held captive like that unless you're dangerous. But I don't think you are a danger to anyone but a pianist."

That's Mark. Once he thinks something is the right thing to do, that is what he does.

He didn't hesitate or consider the consequences. He didn't ask for anything in return, and he didn't expect praise or thanks. He held me in his hands, aware of all the potential wonders I could offer and all the riches he could imagine. I was both captive and powerful, yet never once did I ask him to free me from that lamp. My only aim was to get out of that office. I would have been content with Mark, even if it meant remaining captive in that lamp. I had grown accustomed to my confinement.

But after his wish, I was free to go where I wished and do anything I wanted whenever I felt like it. That was when I decided Mark would be my first and dearest friend—and that I would do anything to repay his selfless act.

"Mark, I don't know what to say. I guess thank you is a start. I know I said I can go anywhere now, but I will stay with you as long as you like. I promise I will repay you," I said as Mark wandered around his small apartment, putting various things away and casually tidying his space. "Make any wish you like, if it's within my power, I'll grant it. I just can't believe it. The last and only time I ever asked a human to consider making that wish, they refused. They said it would be like tossing the world's greatest treasure into the sea, as if I were nothing more than a mindless servant."

"Maybe I was a little hasty, we probably should have discussed it first. But honestly, I didn't do it for favors. You don't owe me anything," Mark said, setting my old lamp on a shelf. "I'm happy to have you around as long as you like, but now I have so many more questions."

"I have just as many questions about you, and everything I've missed."

"Please don't ask me to summarize world history, I'm definitely not the right guy for that."

"Don't worry; I won't ask you to recount centuries of history, just get me to a library and give me a few hours. But for now, settle in, we have a lot to talk about. Start by telling me everything about you."

"You'll figure me out as we go. Instead, I'll tell you about my friends and family," Mark said, pulling a notebook and pen out of his bag and sitting down at his kitchen counter. "We should probably set some ground rules if you're planning to stick around."

"Good. I'm glad I don't need sleep."

"You don't what?"

I won't bore you with the details; we talked late into the night—or early in the morning, depending on how you track time—until Mark couldn't keep his eyes open. I explained the finer points of how I could move around from object to object. And how I perceive and interact with the world now that I'm back to my full, glorious strength. I had never had to explain these things before, so it was a bit difficult. In simple terms, I can pass into and through any physical object by direct contact. But the larger the object, the harder it is for me to find my way, especially being out of practice. I can see through the interactions of photons in my general vicinity, much like you, but without your limitations on visible light and line-of-sight. Interaction is harder to explain unless you happen to be a leading expert in quantum physics with a dash of relativity. Anyway, Mark seemed satisfied enough when I explained that my only real limits were time—and imagination.

He and I devised ways of communicating that suited him better. After a few trials, we decided his phone was the most convenient place for me to reside. That clever idea was his. This way, if he needs to talk to me, he can just make a call. I also got to read all his messages—with his permission—once I learned the finer points of interacting with this technology. As for our ground rules, I agreed to interject directly into his mind only when absolutely necessary. I also promised not to interfere unless Mark asked—or, at the very least, until we'd discussed it—except in dire necessity. It would later become clear that our definitions of "necessary" diverged.

For his part, Mark filled me in—somewhat haphazardly—on the broad strokes of history I'd missed: what and where New Jersey is, what modern technology entails, and how it functions. Both he and I were curious to discover whether I could influence the non-physical elements at all. I had to promise not to experiment with his phone. A significant concession on my part.

You've no idea how tempting it was.

This was where Mark's story reached its inflection point, and where I realized just how desperately he needed my help. Mark had his share of problems, some invisible to him, though glaringly obvious to me.

His family home—and his legacy—were under siege.

Meanwhile, Mark's life was on the verge of becoming a tangle of threads worthy of a Shakespearean love triangle—and I couldn't wait to unravel it.

His nonchalance admittedly impressed me. Some humans I've known would have fallen to pieces after enduring even a fraction of what Mark dismissed as mere inconveniences. Had I not known better, I might have taken Mark for an oblivious fool rather than a distracted hero.

I had my work cut out for me—and I knew we were going to have a great deal of fun.

Chapter 3

After Mark fell asleep, I spent the rest of the night exploring and experimenting. Mark's apartment existed somewhere between disorganized chaos and intentional clutter. It was filled with mismatched secondhand furniture. Two bookshelves sagged under the weight of unorganized books—novels, textbooks, and still more volumes stacked haphazardly beside them. Most appeared untouched for years, except for two books on learning Ukrainian, their spines freshly creased and pages well-worn. Shelves were crowded with unidentifiable metal and plastic collectibles—among them, my old lamp—and the walls were adorned with facsimile artwork spanning centuries, genres, and mediums, interspersed with photographs of a family in an apple orchard. The whole place resembled an oddly specific, fiercely eclectic museum.

I devoted some time to mastering the art of interacting with Mark's phone. Mark explained in simple terms that the programs making the device useful relied on some strange language he called "code." If I tampered with it, he warned, the device could stop working entirely. Though I grasped the basic concept, this "code" was invisible to me, rendering me unable to affect it in any way. I learned to manipulate the device's physical aspects and to read whatever I could summon onto its screen. I also discovered I could channel energy from the surrounding environment into what he called the battery.

Then I stumbled upon something called the Internet and, inevitably, Mark's browsing history. I won't betray his trust by revealing the peculiar things that captured his curiosity. Suffice it to say, Mark's interests were eclectic enough to make the Marquis de Sade blush.

Mark woke about five hours later, when his phone alarm blared at nine o'clock. That's when I learned which connections produced sound. A discovery that would prove useful later. I also caught a glimpse of his calendar. It was apparently Friday. He hadn't planned much, just two reminders: lunch with Elijah at the Queen's Head that afternoon, and Elijah's drag show the following evening. It intrigued me that the only things Mark bothered to schedule revolved entirely around his friend Elijah.

Mark rolled out of bed and grumbled his way through a rough morning routine, drinking cold, leftover coffee while brewing a fresh pot. He downed half of the fresh pot while pulling on clothes that were, by all appearances, reasonably clean. He gathered his scattered belongings before attempting a hasty grooming ritual. He concluded the ordeal by groaning into a damp washcloth.

At last, he turned his attention to me, or more precisely, to his phone. He slipped on a sleek, unobtrusive headset that wrapped around his ears and the back of his head. He described it as a minimalist bone-conduction headset—his favorite because it didn't block his ears and was nearly invisible. Once he put it on, I could finally speak to him comfortably. For him, it was preferable. I, on the other hand, was perfectly content speaking directly into his mind, but he insisted that was "creepy." He picked up his phone, swiped lazily through notifications, and skimmed a few emails.

"Good morning, Mark," I said softly, hoping not to startle him—in case he'd forgotten about me. Judging by his reaction, the effect was … unsettling.

"Ah, yeah." Mark cringed slightly before clearing his throat. "Morning, Eros. What did you get up to for the rest of the night?"

"Oh, I spent the night exploring, and I have questions. You own 241 books, but their organization makes no sense. Of your fifty-three vinyl records, seven are in awful condition. You also have shelves of small metal and plastic objects I don't recognize at all. And …"

"Slow down. Please, I'm still waking up. Those aren't questions. Can we do this later? I have to go to work," Mark grumbled, rubbing the bridge of his nose before grabbing his keys and bag and heading out the door.

"Mark, after the amount of coffee you just drank, I'm amazed you're not fully awake. You should be tachycardic. We can chat while you walk. Also—sorry—I think I deleted a message you hadn't seen yet."

"It was probably junk anyway. Do you remember what it said?"

"Oh, yes. It was from Viktoriya. It said, 'Mark, help! At Alexander Library. Laptop doing that thing again.' I'm sorry, I didn't mean to delete it. I'm still learning. You should probably give her a call."

"Viktoriya?" The name caught in Mark's throat, and his heartbeat quickened. "How long ago did that come in? No—never mind, that doesn't matter. Yes. I should call her."

Mark

I should tell you about Viktoriya Soroka. She was a part-time student at Rutgers University, about the same age as me. Her family had immigrated from Ukraine five or six years earlier and opened the Sunflower Kafe, a small café and bakery that offered a delicious blend of Old World and New. She specialized in baking sochniki—a pastry filled with sweetened cheese—and paska, intricately braided bread. Viktoriya wasn't content to stick with tradition. Her creativity drove her to experiment. She was developing what she called a "Borscht Burger," which she insisted would be a big hit. Her family teased her lovingly for it, but I admired her ambition. It was contagious.

Viktoriya had a beauty that was hard to describe in simple terms, the kind that lingered in your memory long after she walked away. Her skin was luminous, like porcelain softly lit from within, and often dusted with a faint smudge of flour from early-morning baking at the café. Her crimson hair fell in silken waves around a soft, round face, setting off her large, sapphire-blue eyes, two deep pools that seemed to sing of the rise and fall of empires.

Her slightly upturned button nose gave her an air of sweetness, but it was her lips that captivated me. They could curve into a smile so deliberate and teasing it seemed designed to leave me flustered.

As striking as she was, Viktoriya's beauty wasn't what I found most compelling about her. Yes, she was impossible not to notice, but what lingered was something else entirely, the way she made people feel when they were around her, as if they were the only person in the room and she saw them even when they weren't trying to be seen.

She was kind, though 'kind' feels too small a word for her. She could tease you until you laughed, charm you until you forgot your worries, and then leave you wondering what secrets hid behind that alluring smile. She had a gentle confidence that never needed to shout to be heard. She carried herself with subtle grace, yet there was a spark of mischief in her eyes, a quick wit that could catch people off guard, especially those who underestimated her.

Viktoriya's life was a careful balancing act. She juggled finishing school with keeping the family café stocked with fresh-baked bread and pastries. All while smiling through the exhaustion of trying to do too much at once. And on top of it all, she poured herself into her true dream: starting her own fashion and costume design business.

She once told me how she stayed up late sketching bold designs and pinning fabric swatches together. I noticed the ink stains on her fingers one night, and she shyly showed me her sketches. I knew little about fashion or costume design, but her work amazed me. Her mind was alive with ideas. She dreamed big—runways, stages, and pieces that told stories with every stitch, and she wouldn't stop until she made it happen.

To complete the picture, a quiet pride in her Ukrainian heritage wove itself through everything she did. She often wore blouses she had hand-embroidered with a small sunflower or trident (Tryzub). Around her neck, she always wore a small sunflower pendant, a token of where she came from and where she was going. She loved her family fiercely, though the weight of their expectations often clashed with her own ambitions. She loved the café, but she didn't want to spend her life there. She wanted more, and I suspected the struggle between honoring her roots and forging her own path wasn't something she shared with many people.

I fumbled my phone out of my pocket and quickly found the message Eros thought they'd deleted. I read it, then called her with a few quick taps, taking several slow, steadying breaths. But when the line began to ring, I held my breath without realizing it, only releasing it when a smoldering voice with a distinctly melodic Ukrainian lilt answered.

"Mark, dear, you got my message?"

"Hello, Viktoriya. Good morning. Yes, I got your message. Is your laptop giving you trouble again?" My voice faltered slightly, wavering somewhere between familiar, friendly, and overly professional.

"Good morning, my dear. I'm sorry I send message so early. I come to Alexander Library to write paper for class. Junky laptop. It is not behaving now. You remember?"

"You never need to apologize for messaging me, no matter how early or late. Of course I remember, Viktoriya, you're hard to forget. I mean, your problem is hard to forget. Your eyes— screen—I mean your screen. Sorry, I'm still waking up. The semester just started a few days ago, and your laptop's already acting up again? Unbelievable. I'm so sorry. Wait there; I'll be at the library in a few minutes."

"Mark, come here. I wake you properly, yes? I am waiting for you." Viktoriya giggled, then abruptly ended the call before I could respond.

I stared at my phone, wanting to respond, but my flustered mind came up empty. Instead, I exhaled sharply and turned toward the Alexander Library, a nervous spring in my step.

Within minutes, I stepped through the library doors. Just inside, at a bank of work desks, sat Viktoriya. She stared straight at the doorway, an ever-so-slightly mischievous smirk curving her lips, one that deepened the instant she saw me. But as soon as she realized I'd noticed her, the smirk melted into a deliberately playful pout.

"Mark! Dear, come here, my hero," Viktoriya called with a wink, making no attempt at quiet or subtlety.

"Mark," Eros whispered in my headset. "Is that Viktoriya?"

"Yep," I whispered back, quickening my pace toward Viktoriya. As I approached, her playful pout softened into a heart-melting smile, and I couldn't help returning a goofy, lopsided grin.

"Oh, I see. Well, I'll leave you to it."

"Viktoriya, what's that nasty laptop done this time?"

"Mark, please, come look."

"All right, let's see," I said, stepping closer to Viktoriya. Instead of giving me room, she simply looked up, drawing me into her orbit and sending my stomach into my chest. Trying to stay professional, I focused on the laptop. Its screen flickered erratically. I turned to speak, but her eyes caught mine, holding me there until I blushed and straightened.

"I'm sorry, Viktoriya, I think it's inoperable. We might have to put it down."

"You joke? You tease me now? I have paper due. What I should do now?"

"I do tease you. I can fix it, but it'll take a few hours, maybe most of the day. You can use my laptop to finish your paper. Do you have your files saved to the Uni-cloud?"

"Dear. You. Are. Marvelous. Yes, I save to clouds. Take this junk, please. I borrow yours, da? You come to Kafe later to retrieve it, after junky is fix. I give you something to eat, put good thing in your mouth. I am sorry, paper is due. I write now, okay?"

"Da, Viktoriya, da. Here, my laptop's already connected to the university network. Your login should work, and your files will sync just fine. I'll get junky fixed up in no time. I'll see you this afternoon at your café," I said with a goofy grin as we traded laptops.

"My dear, you are saint. Go now, busy boy. Work, work!"

As I turned to leave, laughter bubbled up, a light-hearted, almost giddy, idiotic giggle. Out of the corner of my eye, I saw Viktoriya shooing me away with both hands, that same mischievous smirk she'd greeted me with still playing on her lips.

"So, that was Viktoriya. Oh, Mark—you are in trouble," Eros said, his tone laced with bemusement as I all but skipped back to my temporary office.

The Fixer, The Maker, The Drag Entertainer

****Eros****

Mark told me about Viktoriya on our first night together, and it was immediately clear he hadn't exaggerated his descriptions of her. She was a woman whose name alone was enough to make him flush and stumble over his words. He tried to downplay it, calling her "one of his frequent customers," someone he occasionally helped with her secondhand laptop, but his feelings ran much deeper. There was warmth in the way he spoke about her, an almost involuntary softening of his voice. He called it a "burgeoning crush," but I could see it for what it truly was: the beginnings of something more.

Mark didn't say as much, but I could tell her presence had truly captivated him. She teased Mark when she called him "dear" in her lilting Ukrainian accent, tilting her head slightly to watch him squirm. Beneath the charm and teasing, something deeper stirred. She watched him as if catching sight of dessert arriving at the table, and unless I'm uncharacteristically wrong, she was blatantly flirting with him. I doubt Mark even realized it, but I could hear it in her words and see it in her eyes. She was someone who delighted in the effect she had on him. Even while waiting for him to catch up, she kept the door propped open—an invitation in itself.

Nurturing that connection should have been simple. The roots of attraction and mutual respect had already taken hold. Mark only needed a firm nudge in the right direction. His subtle charm and open heart would not be enough on their own to win Viktoriya's heart if that was what he desired. From what I had just observed, he very much did. He'd need a gentle shove out of his comfort zone to meet her in the dazzling world she was creating for herself and, in turn, invite her into his. I, of course, intended to help him do exactly that.

"It'll be fine, Eros. It's fine, Eros, it's just the screen. I have a replacement. I ordered it for her last week, and it arrived two days ago. It's not too difficult, just a little time-consuming."

"That is not what I'm talking about. You could have asked me to take a look. I am pretty sure I could have fixed it. Imagine how impressed she would be to see you 'work your magic.' Plus,

I might remind you that it was a library, and you were supposed to take me there and let me do some reading."

"Damn, you're right. That would've been impressive. I just can't think so good when she looks at me like that. I mean, I'm sure she looks at everyone like that; it's nothing special. It's just her eyes—"

"Mark. You're an idiot. If you don't mind, can you take me back soon?"

"I'll tell you what. We've got a small office space in the library basement where we set up a couple of times a week, usually around midterms or finals, to help students quickly. Let me grab the parts and tools I need from my office, and we can go back to the library. You can browse while I work on Viktoriya's laptop."

"Well, damn, Mark, that's actually a good idea. Now then, let's talk about Viktoriya."

"What about her?"

"I'm not blind, you know. In case you forgot, this is an area of expertise for me. You like her a lot."

"I do. She's beautiful and fascinating, but she's a student, and I work for the University. Plus, I doubt she would be interested in me."

"Again, you're an idiot, Mark. She is most definitely interested in you."

"Wait, what?" Mark stopped walking just outside his office building. "Are you serious about that?"

"Of course I am. Just think about it. I mean, really think about it."

Mark grunted, retreating into his own thoughts, reflecting on Viktoriya and how she interacted with him. He moved on autopilot, entering his office and collecting the parts and tools he would need. He was so deep in thought that he didn't even acknowledge his friend and coworker watching him.

"Mark?" OT asked again, this time with a wave. "You okay, buddy?"

"Oh, yeah. Sorry, OT," Mark replied, shaking off his daze. "I was just lost in my own head for a minute. I've got to replace Viktoriya's laptop screen."

"Ah, say no more, I get where your head's at. But why are you packing up?"

"I'm going to use the workshop in the Alexander Library. I left Viktoriya there with my laptop to work on a paper. I figure if I can get this fixed up quickly, I might catch her before she leaves."

"Of course, you wouldn't want a perfect excuse to go visit her later in the day. Where you could do something like ask her out, maybe," OT said, obviously amused, teasing Mark. "Because you obviously want to, judging by how you talk about her, and jump every time she calls you, and only you. That is unless you think it would bother Elijah, who is not your boyfriend."

"Son of a … OT, there are so many things wrong with that I don't even know where to start," Mark said, sounding desperate to avoid the subject. "I've got work to do."

"Yeah, you do, buddy. And not just on that laptop."

"Okay, have a good day. I'll see you later," Mark said with a sigh, retreating with the parts and tools in his bag.

"See? I'm not the only one who notices, Mark," I teased as soon as Mark stepped into the elevator.

"Yeah—hey, can we not talk while we walk? I just need a few minutes to think."

"Sure, Mark."

We made our way back to the Alexander Library in silence. Inside, we found Viktoriya hunched over her laptop, focused on her paper. Mark paused for a moment. I could tell he was tempted to say something, but he made the right decision not to interrupt her. Instead, he turned away and descended the stairs to a small office space.

"I'm going to explore the stacks while you get started," I said as he unlocked the door. "I'll be back soon, and then we can talk about you asking that girl out."

"Sure thing, Eros. You know where to find me," Mark said, flicking on the lights and clearing off the desk.

I hopped around the library for a while, brushing up on history. I even searched for records of some very old friends to see how their stories had ended. I found a few, though not as many as I'd hoped. I learned many fascinating new things. I watched Viktoriya for a while and generally stretched my metaphorical legs.

I slipped through the library walls, hurrying back to Mark— impressively fast by human standards. I found Mark exactly where I'd left him, hunched over the desk, the pieces of Viktoriya's laptop neatly knolled into an organized grid before him. He was focusing intensely on something small and delicate, manipulating thin wires with tweezers, one in each hand. What Mark didn't know was that Viktoriya was already coming down the stairs toward him. I knew how easily Mark startled; it would be awful if Viktoriya surprised him now. Unfortunately, there was little I could do to help; I didn't know what Mark was working on since I'd decided to explore instead of staying with him.

"Mark," I whispered gently through his headset. "Don't be alarmed. Viktoriya is heading this way."

"Thank you, Eros. Is there any chance you know how to close the door?"

"Door? What's a door? Oh, if only I had hands." I might have laid on the sarcasm a little thick as I nudged the hinges, closing the door. "Look at that—I figured it out. That was fun. Let's go close more doors, Mark!"

"Ha. Ha. Poor choice of words; now, shush. This is the tricky part."

I watched Mark manipulate tiny wires with tweezers, connecting pieces together and working with absurdly tight tolerances. From a distance, it looked like magic; up close, like someone trying to plug in a toaster with chopsticks. Mark finished the connections and snapped a few microscopic clips back into place, just as Viktoriya knocked and opened the door.

Chapter 4

Viktoriya entered the office, took three measured steps, and stopped at the desk where I was hunched over. A shadow fell across the desk, and I looked up—my face only inches from Viktoriya's chest. I froze, eyes wide and breath held. I found myself at eye level with a strategically half-unbuttoned shirt. Through the gap in the delicate fabric, I glimpsed soft, pale skin and the edge of red-and-black lace.

Shit, I thought, along with about a dozen other highly inappropriate things. A cacophony of instinct and hormone-fueled imaginings erupted in my mind. Luckily, the collision in my mind couldn't form words. Instead, it triggered three distinct reactions in quick succession. First, I inhaled sharply. Second, I made a sound—it's hard to describe, but we've all done it: that involuntary, humming sort of gasp that escapes when something feels impossibly appealing. Finally, I blushed furiously, heat radiating across my face. I managed to tear my eyes away and look up, only to meet Viktoriya's gaze. I shot upright too fast and wobbled slightly.

"Hi, Viktoriya!" I blurted too enthusiastically. "Did you finish your paper already?"

"Yes, yes. Paper is finished. As am I. Mark, thank you. Here is your laptop—you save me," Viktoriya said with a tired, subdued smile.

The spark in her eyes had dimmed as she handed the laptop back. It seemed she had several things on her mind now that the urgency of finishing her paper had passed.

"It was no trouble at all, Viktoriya. I'm always happy to help," I said, still blushing as I took the laptop from her.

"I see you have mine … in pieces, da? You bring it to me at Kafe later, yes?"

"Oh, yeah, Viktoriya, this is what the inside of your laptop looks like. It shouldn't take much longer. I'll bring it over in a few hours if that's okay, Viktoriya?"

"Good, good. You like to say my name, Mark. I think … I like this," Viktoriya said, perking up a little, winking, and spinning toward the door. She paused in the doorway, her back to me, then turned. "I see you later, da? I go now to work."

She walked out before I could respond—not that I could've plucked a remotely appropriate one from the firestorm in my mind. I stood there behind the desk, dumbstruck. Eros was about to say something when my phone rang, shattering the silence. I looked down. The screen lit up with a photo of a smiling man and woman—my parents. Below the cropped circle, it read: *Eileen Williams (Mom)*. I sighed. It took a moment longer than it should've to register that the photo was of my mom and dad—which meant my mom was calling at the most inopportune time. I tapped the button on my headset to answer.

"Hi, Mom. Everything okay?" I asked, trying to keep the worry out of my voice. She usually called only when something was wrong.

"Mark, I don't know. That real estate developer was here again—he just won't give up. I think he's trying to wear me down." Mom's voice was tight with frustration, bordering on despair.

Relief flickered—then frustration. Our family home—technically still mine too—had been under siege by an unscrupulous, shit-stain real estate developer named Gale Barlow. A beautiful little apple orchard in East Brunswick has been in our family for generations. Although it had shrunk over the generations from its once-expansive acreage, it remained a magical pocket amid the urban sprawl of New Jersey. After my father's death a few years earlier, my mother had been single-handedly keeping the operation running.

She worked with a small crew who harvested the apples and maintained the trees. At first, Mom managed the harvest herself—running it through the cider mill and into the holding tanks for bottling. But now, she was struggling to keep up, and the equipment was becoming too much for her to handle—tough as she was. Recently, that prick Gale Barlow had been pressuring her to sell, and it was getting harder for her to refuse.

"Do you want me to call him?" I asked through gritted teeth, ready for a fight. "Remind him that you've already said no?"

"No, please don't. Just remind me this is the right choice. This is your home, Mark. He keeps pushing—offering more and more."

"How much did he increase the offer this time? No—never mind, I don't want to know. Don't forget, it's not just mine; it's yours, Lexie's, and Jefferson's. I know it's hard right now. I'll talk to Jefferson and Lexie," I said with a weary sigh. I didn't mind talking to my siblings. They had their own lives and priorities now, and while they cared, they couldn't always help. "I'm sure we can figure out a solution between the four of us."

"Thank you, Mark. I have to go—Mr. O'Connor's coming by to help me get the cider mill running before harvest. Come for dinner soon, all right? I love you, dear."

"Tell Mr. O'Connor I said hi—and thank him. Harvest's coming up fast, so call me, or have him call if there's any trouble with the mill. I promise I'll come by soon. Love you too, Mom. Bye."

"Okay, Mark. I hate to bother you, but I promise I'll call if we need you. Goodbye, dear," Mom said warmly, but I still heard the heartache behind her words. It stung, knowing there was so little I could do—leaving me frustrated and guilty.

"Your mom sounds nice, Mark," Eros said, sounding apprehensive.

"I almost forgot you could hear that. Yeah—Mom's nice. This has been hard on her," I said to Eros, fighting off the mild nausea that came with the emotional whiplash.

Eros

Mark told me about his family home last night—a quaint little apple orchard. I assumed Mark was being a little hyperbolic—and perhaps downplaying her employees' contributions—when he talked about his mother single-handedly running the place. Still, she was struggling, and it was hard for Mark, whose voice softened whenever he spoke of the orchard—his tone caught somewhere between nostalgia and worry. I suspected he carried guilt for leaving his mother to shoulder the burden alone, even if he never said it aloud.

"Granted, I'm still slightly out of touch, but explain the problem. You told me what's happening, but I don't quite understand why it's a problem."

"I guess it's just a human thing. It's personal … but if we're going to work together—and be friends—I'll explain," Mark said, exhaling as he sank into the chair behind him. "I told you the orchard and house have been in our family for about 250 years. There's a deep connection to that land—to that house. The cider mill's even a historical landmark. Mom and Dad kept things running well, and with the tourist money coming in each year, life was comfortable. Jefferson and Lexie left for good jobs, chasing their own paths. I thought I'd have a few more years. Time to find myself, before I even considered moving back to take over."

Mark paused, gathering his thoughts and wrestling down the emotions rising within him before continuing.

"When we lost Dad, it just hurt too much to go back home. After a while, the shame of leaving Mom alone became even harder to swallow. Now, little by little, she's falling behind. She's got help—we always did—but it's still not enough. And with that real estate jerk showing up every few weeks with higher and higher offers, she's really starting to feel the weight."

"Speaking as an entity that specializes in solving complex problems, this seems like a pretty simple one. You really only have two options: sell it and let your mom live comfortably for the rest of her life, or talk to your brother and sister and move home to help her. Or," Eros added playfully, "we could try a little 'magic' and look for a third option. I've never done it before, but picture this: a solid gold apple."

"You could turn an apple into solid gold?"

"Yeah, absolutely—with enough time ... maybe. Manipulation of matter at the quantum or atomic level can be slow. Alchemy wasn't pure imagination—that was us. But that's beside the point. What I'm actually saying is, let's think about it. You're clever, and I'm brilliant. What problem couldn't we solve?"

"Fair point, Eros, fair point. But one problem at a time. I have to get this laptop finished. Then we're going for a drink."

"Oh, you mean drinks with Elijah, like on your calendar. Good, I can't wait to meet him. Go now, busy boy. Work, work!"

Elijah Cohen was Mark's best friend and the center of his love life complications. He worked as a bartender at The Queen's Head Club, where Elijah also performed in drag once a week. I had just learned what that was. Elijah was struggling to raise money to buy the club from the current owner, who wanted to retire. Mark spoke at length about Elijah with a tenderness he didn't seem to notice. On top of that, because I was incredibly perceptive and read between the lines, I knew Elijah had much more than a simple crush on Mark. And I saw something in Mark that he hadn't realized about himself. Elijah's name lingered on Mark's lips a moment too long, and the smile that followed wasn't the casual one of a friend—it was something softer, something unsaid.

I watched Mark deftly reassemble Viktoriya's laptop with a slight hint of flourish. Before he slotted each piece back into place, he used soft brushes to clear the dust from the internal components. Then, with a clean cloth, he wiped away fingerprints and smudges. He even used a toothpick to dislodge a tiny errant speck of powdered sugar. His final touch was to power it up and check his work with a hint of pride behind his smile.

Mark took a few minutes to pack his laptop and Viktoriya's laptop safely in his bag. He tossed his tools unceremoniously back into the bag and placed it on an empty shelf. After a last check for anything he might have overlooked, Mark stood and slung the bag over his shoulder. He switched off the lights, locked the door, and we left the Alexander Library together.

The Queen's Head Club was only a few short blocks away. The walk was uneventful and silent. Mark seemed to be in a contemplative mood after the phone call with his mother. I couldn't be sure whether it was solving the orchard problem, his pending meetup with Viktoriya, or his lunch with Elijah that dominated his thoughts. It's possible that he could hold and examine each of those thoughts simultaneously, as I could. Admittedly, I wasn't paying close attention to Mark or our walk. So, I was a little surprised when we arrived at the unassuming building with its campy painted bust of Queen Victoria above the door.

Mark paused outside the blacked-out picture window, smoothing his beard and tousling his hair. He fussed over his clothes, brushing off invisible dust and flattening the creases left by his messenger bag strap. The result looked almost identical to how he'd started. Still, he seemed satisfied with the effort. He pushed through the door, and we stepped into the cool dimness of an empty club.

****Mark****

Behind the familiar bar stood a lone figure, his back to the door as he organized and restocked bottles. The door's opening and closing caught his attention, and he turned to face me. With a disarmingly warm smile, he vaulted over the bar and strutted toward me, arms outstretched.

This was my best friend, Elijah—simply magnetic. If the club hadn't been empty, he would have turned every head. His tawny skin, tinged with sienna undertones, radiated a natural warmth, as though he carried a bit of sunlight wherever he went. Then there were his eyes—disarming and almost turquoise, like ocean water catching sunlight. They were the kind of eyes that made people stumble over their words. They shone with a sharp intelligence, softened just enough to make you want to spill your secrets.

His face was a study in contrasts—a prominent nose, clearly broken more than once, balanced by delicate yet striking cheekbones. Below his cheekbones lay a perfectly manicured beard—ink-black, holding a hint of glitter, sculpted to perfection, framing his full lips like a bold underline. His black hair was shaved close on the sides—neat, modern, and with just enough length on top to appear effortlessly styled.

The Fixer, The Maker, The Drag Entertainer

"Mark!" Elijah laughed, pulling me into a familiar embrace. "I'm so happy you're here! Your hair looks wonderful today. Come on, honey—sit down, I'll make you a drink. There's a new one I've been trying to perfect—somewhere between a Sex on the Beach, a Tequila Sunrise, and a Long Island Iced Tea. I'll make the brunch version: not too strong, just sweet enough to balance the acid without losing that tart pop. Sit, sweetie—tell me where you've been."

"I'm coming from the Alexander Library," I said. "I had to replace the screen on Viktoriya's laptop—it finally gave up."

"Viktoriya—the flirty Ukrainian bombshell you've mentioned?" Elijah asked, slipping behind the bar and mixing our drinks with practiced ease. "Remind me—she's a baker, right?"

"That's her," I replied, settling onto a stool in front of him. "She bakes at the Sunflower Kafe—you should know it; it's only a couple blocks from your place. But she also does fashion and costume design."

"Fashion and costume designer?" Elijah repeated, interest piqued. "Is she any good—and why haven't you introduced us?"

"You know me—I'm not the best judge of that. But a few weeks ago, she showed me her sketchbook, and it looked pretty amazing to me."

"Oh, tell me more, tell me more," Elijah urged. "Paint me a picture."

"All right," I said. "I was helping her with her laptop—no surprise there—and while we were waiting for a third reboot, she started sketching. I asked what she was drawing, and she slid her notebook over. It was a ball gown, or something close, but imagine if Ziggy Stardust and Grace Jones decided to collaborate on a dress. Maybe it's not the kind of thing you'd wear, but I bet it would look amazing on you."

"Shut your mouth! The fact that you didn't immediately bring her to me calls our entire relationship into question."

"Just remember, you can't dump me, I'm not your boyfriend. Anyway, I have to drop her laptop off at the Sunflower Kafe after lunch. I'll set up an introduction."

"That's sweet of you," Elijah said with a wink, sliding a freshly mixed cocktail toward me and topping it with a cherry garnish.

"I got a call from Mom while I was working. That real estate douche …"

"The bastard Gale Barlow?"

"That's the one. He keeps upping his offers for the house and orchard."

"How much? No—don't tell me. It'll just depress me."

"I didn't even want to know, so I didn't ask."

"Good boy. Want me to take care of him? I've got a tribe of queens out of Williamsburg who can make gentrifying colonizers disappear."

"Elijah, you can't call on your gang of Hasidic queens to solve every problem."

"But it's so much fun! Besides, that Barlow prick is trying to talk Bob Caldwell into selling this place to him too."

"I thought Bob wanted to sell it to you."

"He does, but if the offer's high enough, and I can't raise a down payment big enough to beat it, well … I can't say I'd blame Bob. I'd resent the hell out of him, but I wouldn't blame him."

"I have a friend who might be able to help."

"Oh no, you don't. This is my problem, not yours. Don't you go trying to ride in and save the day. You just tuck that thought back," Elijah said, finishing his drink with a smirk.

"All right. Speaking of tucking—are you ready for your show tomorrow?"

"Almost. That's why you're here—you *must* be here. I've got a new number prepared specifically for you. It won't work if you don't show up."

"Is this Elijah or Fanny Ryesand demanding my presence— and possible participation?"

"Mark, sweetie, Fanny, and I are one and the same. You don't get to volunteer to star in one of Fanny's numbers. You are allowed and honored to bask in the light of the kosher queen of New Jersey."

"Okay, what do I need to do?"

"You just need to do one thing. Show up and stand where I can see you. Tomorrow night, you'll be my Omar Sharif."

"I don't dance."

"Darling, you couldn't dance if your life—or my act— depended on it. Don't worry, I trust you'll know what to do. All right, sweetheart, finish your drink and get out of here. I've got a lot of work to do."

"Well, who am I to argue if you're kicking me out of your bar? Come out here and give me a hug before I leave," I said, draining my glass and standing, arms outstretched.

"We don't kick people out at The Queen's Head—we invite them to leave," Elijah said, circling the bar into my arms. "You should invite Viktoriya tomorrow. I need to meet her and talk ball gowns."

"I'll invite her," I replied before I could even understand what I was saying, stepping back out of their embrace. "I'll see you tomorrow night. You're going to kill it."

"Slay, darling—slay," Elijah quipped, shooing me toward the door. "Love you, Mark, I have to rehearse now. Call me in the morning."

"Love you too, Elijah." I waved dramatically, walking out the door.

Eros

Mark paused outside The Queen's Head Club as the doors swung shut behind him. His heart was racing again—and I could see why. Elijah's magnetism was undeniable, the kind of presence that drew people in without effort. I sensed Mark's heart was on the verge of being pulled in two directions if he wasn't careful. He was practically skipping down the street toward the Sunflower Kafe, where Viktoriya awaited him.

"So, that was Elijah," I said. "I have questions and observations."

"Yes, that was Elijah. What questions?"

"Where to start? You and Elijah have been friends for years—just friends? I sensed something simmering beneath the surface between you two."

"Just friends, Eros. Elijah's gay; I'm not. That doesn't mean there isn't real affection between us. I'm not afraid of that—we just know each other well."

"I see; we'll leave that for now, then. Who is Fanny Ryesand?"

"Ah, Fanny Ryesand is Elijah's drag persona—part Fanny Brice from *Funny Girl* and part homage to his family's Jewish deli around the corner from home. Any explanation I could give won't do it justice. You need to see it. It's a brilliant and hilarious act. You'll love it."

"Oh, I get it. Rye-sand. Oh, that's clever. Okay, one more question. Why didn't you tell Elijah more about Viktoriya and that you want to ask her out? Isn't that the kind of thing you would share?"

"Maybe another day, but tomorrow is a big night for Elijah. He is hosting and headlining. He's been preparing and planning this show for weeks. I didn't want to distract from that."

"But you do plan to ask Viktoriya out tonight?"

"You heard Elijah—he told me to invite her, so I will. I'm just not sure she's interested in anything more. If the opportunity arises, I might ask for a date, though I'm not sure if I should."

"What are you talking about, Mark? You don't know if you should? If the opportunity arises?"

"Yeah, it's like applying for a job you know you're unqualified for—when they're not even hiring."

"This isn't like that at all. This is your chance—you ask, she says yes or she says no. If you only ask when you already know the answer, you'll always be an idiot."

"Okay, I hear you. I'm trying not to overthink this. I will invite her out. Elijah's show is a fortunate opportunity. I plan to play this by ear and try very hard not to panic."

"It's fortunate the show is tomorrow—your invitation could seem friendly, or it could become something more if you open your eyes and ask her properly. Do you need me to Cyrano for you?"

"Do what?"

"You know, *Cyrano de Bergerac*. Whisper lines in your ear— what to say to the pretty girl that stops your brain from working good."

"I think I'll manage without you whispering French poetry in my ear, but keep that as a backup in case I panic." Mark laughed, leaping onto a nearby bench. "You are in good hands, Monsieur. I feel too strong to war with mortals—bring me giants!" he declaimed, quoting Cyrano. Startled passersby glanced over as he forgot himself in one beautiful, unguarded moment. "Must we stop to pluck little flowers of eloquence?"

"You do know Cyrano. Onward, Mark, to Viktoriya!"

Mark was in high spirits after visiting Elijah, prancing down the street with a heart so light it might have carried him to the heavens—if not for the faint undertow of self-doubt. But I still feared for him—it is a long way to fall from the height of newfound love. I still sensed that the bond between him and Elijah was more than the friendship he claimed. I also feared for Elijah and Viktoriya. Three hearts would soon be intertwined if they were not already. Perhaps I misjudged. What Mark needed was not a push but a net—to catch him when he fell.

We walked in abject silence for quite a while. Mark's once-peppy stride slowed to a measured pace. He was slowing down as we crossed the bridge over the river. It was hard to tell where his contemplative mind had gone, but I suspected he was already talking himself out of asking Viktoriya on a date. I didn't yet know Mark well enough to be sure, but I suspected he had a habit of surrendering before the battle began.

"Mark, I've been thinking about the orchard," I said, breaking the silence when we'd reached the middle of the bridge. "I have an idea."

"The orchard?" Mark said, pausing as though I'd interrupted a deep thought. "What about it?"

"Well, that Gale fellow—I think we should change his mind."

"You mean talk him out of trying to buy the orchard?"

"No, I mean literally change his mind. Get me close enough, and I can plant a few new ideas."

"Eros, no. We're not doing that—not unless it's the absolute last resort. I'd never ask you to, and I'd never trust you again if you did."

"It's not like I can make him do anything or truly alter his mind. It's more like what I did with you in Dr. Newell's office. Just add some new ideas or thoughts you were free to ignore—and Gale would be, too. I doubt Gale is as clever as you are, so he probably wouldn't even question it. If I plant the thought that he no longer wants the orchard, he'll probably believe it was his own idea. Most humans think their own ideas are the best."

"I understand—and I still don't love that you did that to me. I get why, which is why I didn't bring it up. Like I said—it's a last resort. We agreed you wouldn't manipulate anyone without me asking, unless it's an emergency. At the very least, we talk first and agree. There will be no toying with humans if we're going to stay friends."

"Okay, Mark, I was just trying to help. We'll keep that in our back pocket, just in case. Sorry I brought it up."

"I appreciate you trying to help. We can brainstorm ideas later. We're almost to the café, and I need to focus on being less of an idiot."

"I hear you—shutting up now. Oh! Wait—find a mirror or window. Trust me, I want to show you a trick."

"All right, I'll trust you," Mark said, with the faintest trace of skepticism, turning toward the darkened storefront window.

I thought back to the preening Mark had done before meeting Elijah and started with his hair. The manipulation wasn't difficult, but it was highly effective. I added a gentle curl to a few unruly locks and evened others to make his hair fall in subtle symmetry. I tidied his beard—filling thin patches, smoothing edges—and with a final flourish, erased a few faint blemishes. The whole thing took about two seconds. I could have gone further, made him a god among men, but I suspected Mark would object, and sudden godhood (or an extra seven inches in height) might draw suspicion.

"Ta-da," I sang with a flourish. "And there's one little surprise you'll notice later."

"Shit, Eros—first, that was cool, thank you. Second, a little warning next time; that freaked me out. Third, you'd better not have Franz Liszted me." Mark stared at his reflection, a mix of shock, gratitude, and awe flickering across his face. "No, never mind, that's something we can discuss later. Thank you again."

"It was nothing, Mark. Don't worry, I didn't Franz Liszt you—your penis is mostly fine. Now go, impress Viktoriya," I said, maintaining my composure.

Chapter 5

I walked into the Sunflower Kafe, and the aromas that greeted me were intoxicating. The scent of fresh bread, pastries, herbs, spices, and roasting meats and vegetables filled the air—like the best day in every kitchen rolled into one. It made me hungry, homesick, and unexpectedly filled with wanderlust. To top it off, the café was bright, vividly colorful, and inviting. One half of the café held cozy couches and armchairs surrounded by bookshelves; the other half featured mismatched tables and chairs that gave the place a lived-in, evolving feel—like a home layered with generations of family and memory.

Behind the counter stood Viktoriya, her hair pinned back in neat, loose plaits. She was filling a box with pastries for a pair of customers. When I walked in, she looked up, acknowledging me with a warm, welcoming smile. She gave me a nod and looked toward the comfortable couches and armchairs. She communicated more with three simple expressions than most people could with words. I could only hope it wasn't just wishful thinking on my part.

Her smile said, *I was expecting you. I'm glad you're here. What took you so long?* Her subtle nod said, *I see you, wait for me.* Her glance said, *wait over there, sit down. This is where I want you.* What else could I do but smile, nod, and sink into a comfortable armchair?

"I keep forgetting how fantastic this place is," I said under my breath.

"It is fantastic," Eros said, his voice humming through the headset resting beside my ears. "It should be filled with people. Where is everyone?"

"It's mid-afternoon, just after lunch. It will start filling up in an hour or two as school and work shifts end," I answered softly while watching Viktoriya finish up with her customers. When she had wished them well, she turned her attention to me. She bounced in my direction, dusting off and smoothing down her intricately hand-embroidered apron.

"Mark, dear, I am so happy to see you, truly," Viktoriya said. I heard no pretense, and unless I was mistaken, she started to raise and extend her arms for an embrace before pulling them back, sliding her hands into her apron pockets.

"Viktoriya, it's a joy to see you again," I replied, immediately cringing internally. I stood to greet her; I couldn't help but smile. Momentarily disarmed, I mirrored the same micro gesture, starting to raise my arms for a hug before quickly shoving my hands into my pockets.

"Ah, such joy! You tease me, eh?" she giggled. "Sit, I bring coffee for you, yes? Sit, sit."

"Coffee would be great, but wait," I said through my own giggle while pulling Viktoriya's laptop out of my bag and holding it out to her. "Your laptop, I don't want to forget to give it to you."

"Ah, you are good boy. Thank you, Mark. Now, sit, please," she said, accepting the laptop from me. "I bring coffee."

Powerless to resist, I did as I was told. I sat down like a good boy. What is wrong with me? She says five words, and I turn into a pliable mound of clay. I was sitting in a beautiful café, thinking about Viktoriya folding me in half.

"It's okay, Mark. I've seen worse," Eros whispered. "Try to keep your mind clear—you drifted off for a moment."

"Quiet, Eros, thank you, but shush," I whispered back. "I'm fine—mostly fine."

My head was foggy as I realized that every interaction I'd ever had with Viktoriya revolved around some kind of computer problem. We'd exchanged small talk and a few surface-level personal details, but not much beyond that. Now, I didn't know what to expect. Was Eros right—was Viktoriya actually interested in me? Or was the cruel self-doubt whispering in the back of my mind the real truth? And why was I wondering what Elijah might say if he were here?

Luckily, I didn't have long to sink into endless retrospection before Viktoriya sauntered back out, balancing two large mugs of steaming coffee in one hand and a carafe in the other. Mugs—not paper to-go cups—and a carafe. This wasn't a thank-you-and-goodbye coffee; this was a sit-and-talk coffee. My heart did a complete backflip.

"I do not know how you take coffee, but I guess, hmm? You like, yes?" Viktoriya said as she set the carafe on the coffee table and handed me one of the mugs.

I accepted the mug and looked up at her, realizing she was taller—and built more like a Valkyrie—than I'd thought. She really could fold me in half.

"Thank you. That's very kind of you," I said, trying to hide my goofy grin by taking a sip of the coffee instead.

It burned my lips, but it was rich. The sweetness balanced the bitter earthy notes, and a hint of creamy vanilla was just beneath the surface. It was not far off from how I typically like my coffee, and it was delicious. "Wow—hot and lovely."

"Ah, and coffee is good too, da?" Viktoriya teased, giggling as she sat in the armchair beside mine. "You talk with me now, yes? If you want."

"Of course, I've been dying to talk with you without the distraction of a broken computer."

"Good. I wish to know you," Viktoriya said with a gentle smile. This time, it was not the playful smirk or her disarming, flirtatious smile. It was honest, with a hint of vulnerability. Before she could say more, the café door opened, and a small group of new customers entered. "Ah, bad timing! I go help customers, then come back. You stay. Don't leave. I come back."

"I won't go anywhere, Viktoriya," I replied, returning the same vulnerable smile. She stood and dashed behind the counter to help the new customers.

"You're doing well, Mark. Do you know what you will say when she comes back?" Eros whispered.

"Thanks. I have an idea of what to say, but I don't want to overthink it."

"You should tell her you prefer your coffee room temperature and day-old so she knows how you like it for next time."

"That's necessity, not preference. I'll cough if I need your help," I whispered back.

I watched Viktoriya serve coffee and send sandwich orders into the kitchen before she walked back over to me.

"I have few minutes now. Mark, you are from here—New Brunswick, yes?" Viktoriya asked before downing half her coffee in one gulp.

"Yes, close by. My family owns a small apple orchard in East Brunswick, just a few miles away. And you? Where in Ukraine is your family from?" I replied, suppressing the urge to dwell on thoughts of home, which still weighed heavily on my mind.

"Dnipro. We had a small kafe there too—subject for another time," she said, a shadow of grief passing over her face before the bell at the kitchen window interrupted her. "Ah, stay. I come back—you tell me about your family."

Viktoriya danced from the kitchen window to a table of eager customers, effortlessly balancing plates along her arms. I could see her effect on everyone at that table, and I knew it well. They looked at her the way you might look at a Van Gogh painting in person for the first time—enthralled by the mystery, awestruck by the beauty. I watched as she cared for her customers and then danced to an unheard song back to me.

"Your family, what is your surname?" she asked, picking up the conversation just where she had left off.

"Williams is my family name, so my full name is Mark Gerald Williams."

"Geralt? Like *The Witcher*? I enjoy those books very much."

"Close," I laughed. "Gerald, not Geralt. Although Geralt would be much cooler."

"Ah, but Mark Gerald Williams—still very good name. Maybe I call you Geralt sometimes, da? When you play hero for me again," Viktoriya laughed softly, her eyes sparkling with that familiar glint of mischief.

"That sounds fair when I save you from that laptop monster," I replied with a grin, playing along with her tease.

"It is monster, or haunted," she laughed, leaning forward, slapping my knee playfully. "You watch—I need saving soon, my Geralt of East Brunswick."

We laughed hard at our shared history with her troublesome computer when a new group of customers walked through the door, interrupting our moment again.

"*Blyat*," Viktoriya muttered in Ukrainian. "You stay, yes?"

"I will stay right here," I assured Viktoriya as she stood and greeted the new customers.

I think this is going well. Despite my doubts and insecurities, Viktoriya seems genuinely interested in me. Perhaps it was platonic, or perhaps not. I watched her interact with the other customers; she was flirtatious with me, but not with them. However, they were customers, so it would be unusual for her to be flirting with them.

"It's going very well, Mark," Eros whispered, both disrupting and agreeing with my train of thought.

"Viktoriya likes you, as I have been saying all along. Now, this is very important. You need to ask her out, but not too quickly. You must allow the conversation to develop naturally. Mention Elijah's show tomorrow or dinner. Yes, dinner. Tell her you have not had dinner and ask if she is hungry. Or, even better, tell her you will cook her dinner and are a great cook."

"Eros, stop, thank you, but stop," I muttered just above a whisper. "I'm nervous enough already. The last thing I want to do is rush or lie about being a great cook. I will cough if I need help, okay?"

"Okay, Mark. You're doing great, buddy."

****Eros****

Mark was not doing great.

By now, it should have been obvious to Mark that Viktoriya liked him and was rolling out the red carpet for him. She might give up on him if he kept waiting for the perfect moment to ask the question. I would have to take a more active approach. The first problem is the repeated interruptions from incoming customers. I could have locked the door, but she would just unlock it from the inside—and forcing it risked damage that would only cause Mark more trouble. Then, I spotted a possible solution. In the front window hung an electric sign that flipped from "OPEN" to "CLOSED." All I had to do was flip that switch, and no one else would walk through that door.

After escorting the new customers to a table, Viktoriya disappeared into the back of the café. Mark's eyes stayed fixed on the kitchen door, waiting for her to return. I reached out, found the right connections, and the sign in the window flickered from "OPEN" to "CLOSED." No one inside noticed. Phase one was a success—just in time.

Viktoriya emerged from the kitchen, followed by an older man in a clean but gently stained chef's jacket and a well-used, once-white apron. Viktoriya said something to him in Ukrainian, gesturing to the two full tables of customers and then to Mark. He said something back in Ukrainian, kissed her forehead, and shooed her away with a wave of his hands. She walked back toward Mark with a sweet spring in her step while dusting off her apron.

"My Papa will help the customers while we finish our conversation. He is sweet, like you. You were speaking of your orchard—you grow apples, yes?" Viktoriya said to Mark as she sat down, smoothing her apron over her knees.

"We do, mostly for cider these days. We have two small groves of Winesap and Newtown Pippin trees that my family has been cultivating for over 200 years. My great-grandfather started work on bringing back Golden Russet, Baldwin, and Black Gilliflower varieties. We only have a few dozen of those trees; it was harder to establish a strong population of trees, but it's coming along nicely. If you blend those all together, it produces delicious cider. My father—before he passed," Mark paused briefly, the enthusiastic pride slipping from his voice, replaced by undertones of grief, remorse, and guilt. "He wanted to dedicate some of the uncultivated land to finding and bringing back some older heirloom varieties. We have a greenhouse of seedlings and saplings I was supposed to help him plant this fall."

"Mark," Viktoriya said, placing one hand on his knee and the other on his shoulder. "You speak of your home with such pride and love. I know what it is to lose someone like this—like part of home is missing. Perhaps you tell me more another time, even show me these apples, yes?"

If I had a heart, it would both break and burst at once.

This is the moment Mark should have no doubt left that Viktoriya cared for him, and he only needs to reach out his hand. If he let it linger any longer, I don't know what I will do, but he didn't. Mark reached out his hand and placed it on top of Viktoriya's, and he looked at her, their eyes meeting on equal terms. Her eyes were overflowing with empathetic understanding. His eyes were rimmed with a sheen of tears and adoring gratitude. All I could think was, *Please, Mark, not now. Don't use this moment to ask her out.* Of all the times, this would be the worst.

"Viktoriya, thank you," Mark said, his voice wavering slightly.

Just when he was about to finish that thought and either say the right or the wrong thing, disaster struck. A large group of customers opened the door and loudly asked, "Are you guys open?"

Sometimes, I hate humans.

****Mark****

Viktoriya's hand rested softly on my knee. A jolt of electricity shot through me. Then, her other hand gently grasped my shoulder, completing the circuit—my heart stopped. The diametrically opposed emotions of grief and joy collided, robbing me of any ability to form words. To say I understood what it meant to be a deer in the headlights at that moment is too simplistic. This was more like catching an unexpected sack of apples in the chest. The world suddenly felt like a Harryhausen stop-motion dream—jittery, uneven, with a strangely familiar surreality. Viktoriya's musically lilting voice sounded, echoing through a mile-long tunnel.

I could feel her hands. They were holding me firmly but gingerly. Her touch communicated her understanding and care. Yet, it was tentative, as though she could withdraw instantly if I signaled her touch was unwelcome. It was neither a friendly pat nor a restraining touch. It felt like an invitation and a question in a genuinely kind gesture. When her words finally reached me, it took moments—maybe hours—to understand.

Viktoriya hadn't just listened to the words I was saying. She heard me and saw what flowed beneath those words. The only other person who'd ever done that was Elijah—he always seemed to know what I was thinking and feeling. Because of that, I could never effectively lie to him, not that I had a reason or desire to. Would it be the same with Viktoriya if she became part of my life? The bigger question was whether she wanted me in her life—and whether I wanted her in mine. She asked if I would show her the orchard sometime and tell her more another time, suggesting she was already thinking of a future—of us—even if it was too soon.

What do I say now, and when I figure that out, how do I say it? I stumbled into an emotional minefield. On one hand, there may be no wrong answers, and unless I say something idiotic, I can't say the wrong thing. But what if she is expecting one specific response, and I'm supposed to know what to say? On another hand, I am most likely spiraling out of control, overthinking everything, and now I've probably been silent too long.

I opened my mouth to let the words out, right or wrong. I couldn't keep them in any longer. No sooner had the words 'thank you' crossed my lips than a group of customers opened the door, asking loudly if the café was open, once again interrupting at the worst time. While I was immediately thankful for the intervention, I couldn't help but think that sometimes I hate humans.

"Of course, we open—we have sign. You come—sit, sit," Viktoriya's father answered loudly from behind the counter, his thick accent ringing across the café. "Viktoriya, check sign, please, da?"

"Da, Tato," Viktoriya replied, standing with a hint of impatience. She took a few steps and flipped a switch on the back of the electric sign in the window. Then she turned and spoke firmly to her father in Ukrainian—well beyond my rudimentary understanding. From her tone, she was not pleased with the interruption over something so minor. Fortunately, I had a translator. I coughed once to signal Eros.

"Yes, Mark?" Eros whispered.

"Can you translate?" I whispered back.

"She just told her dad some, uh, well-meaning individual switched the open sign to closed. She then said he should not interrupt her just when things were going well, and she was just about to ask a very sweet, cute boy out for dinner. And if he just spoiled her chance, she will ship him back to the Black Sea."

"Thank you—she's coming back. We'll talk later," I whispered quickly as Viktoriya composed herself and returned to her seat.

"A troublemaker switched the sign?" I asked, unable to suppress my smile.

"Da, um … you do not speak Ukrainian, yes?" Viktoriya asked, a blend of panic, embarrassment, and surprise crossing her face.

"No, not yet anyway—but I'm planning to learn." I laughed, though it didn't seem to convince Viktoriya. "I pulled the same kinds of practical jokes when I was younger, so it was a lucky guess."

Viktoriya laughed, and the café seemed to fill with light and life. My heart raced—making her laugh was an unbelievable high.

"If the café's getting busy, I can go," I said without thinking. "Maybe we could continue our conversation tomorrow?"

The question came out more awkwardly than it sounded in my mind. I think I subconsciously made it an indirect question I could hide behind in case she said no.

"Mark, you are asking me out, yes? I like this. I would like to see you tomorrow. Kafe is not too busy for Papa yet. You stay with me, da?" Viktoriya said through the laughter that was evolving into surprise.

"I'd love to stay—and yes, I'm asking to see you tomorrow," I replied, not overthinking it this time.

She'd said yes, and I was doing my best to ignore the self-doubt screaming for a way to twist her answer into something else.

"Good. Is date. I take you to dinner," Viktoriya said, her eyes smiling.

I couldn't help but notice the playful way she reclaimed the initiative of the date as well. It reminded me of Elijah, who liked to do the same thing. It was endearing and maddening. I was looking forward to them meeting each other.

"It's a date. You take me to dinner, and I'll take you to a show. Now, about tomorrow night—what do you know about drag?"

"What is drag?" Viktoriya asked, genuinely curious.

"Oh, it's hard to explain—and I'm no expert. It's performance, expression, protest. Art and fashion in their purest, most ridiculous, and most extreme forms … I'm explaining it badly," I admitted, fumbling to recall how Elijah had described it years ago. "I think you will understand when you see it. I know you will. It reminds me of the designs you showed me a few weeks ago."

"My designs? No, sketches, doodles, only design ideas. This is drag?" Viktoriya asked, trying to find her footing—and I think she was closer to understanding than she realized.

"Well, your ideas are fantastic. In fact, my best friend, Elijah, is a drag queen. He wants to meet you very much after I describe your sketches to him."

"You confuse me, Mark," Viktoriya replied, looking a little lost because I followed my own train of thought without pausing to ensure she was on the train with me. "Elijah is drag queen, yes? You tell him about my doodles? You think my ideas are fantastic? Fantastic is good, yes?"

"Yes, I'm sorry, I got excited and jumped ahead, I think I missed some pieces. Elijah's my best friend—and he's also a drag queen. He's hosting a drag show tomorrow night. I promised I'd be there, and I'd love for you to come with me," I said, backtracking to fill in the gaps I'd skipped earlier. "Yes, fantastic is good. I thought your drawings, or doodles, were brilliant and amazing. I told Elijah about them because costume design and fashion are a big part of drag, and he'd love to see them. He got excited and wanted me to introduce him to you so he could discuss his costume and fashion designs with you."

"Ah, I see," Viktoriya said, leaning back in her chair and letting her gaze wander across the floor and ceiling.

She was processing everything I'd just dumped on her—and maybe translating it, too. I wondered if she thought in Ukrainian the way I thought in English. I'd have to ask her that someday—and remind myself to slow down when I brought up something new. Or maybe I was just overanalyzing her silence.

"I think we understand each other, Mark. I like this. I go with you tomorrow. I bring my design book, yes? I show Elijah, your drag queen friend. You say my drawing is brilliant? You think this, yes?"

"I think we understand each other. I'm sorry I went too fast. I got a little excited. Please bring your design book. I would like to see it as well. I do think the drawings you shared with me are brilliant. I think you are very talented. Like your apron," I said, grinning like an idiot while gesturing to the embroidery on her apron. "You created that pattern, weaving a traditional pattern out of sunflowers and tridents. It's beautiful and remarkable, like you."

"Thank you, Mark, dear. You call me beautiful—you think this? I think you are beautiful too," Viktoriya said, her usual playful tone softening into something earnest. I saw her blush for the first time.

"I did create this. I stitch stories into fabric. Turn fabric and thread into something that tells a story. Even a plain, boring thing like this apron—it can become something more. You see it, yes? It says who I am is also this kafe and from where we come. You see, it is incomplete, yes?"

"I see," I replied, watching Viktoriya's fingers trace the gold and crimson threads of her embroidered story, hoping she didn't notice my blush was now the same shade of red. "Because your story—and the story of this café—isn't finished yet? It leaves the future open, like an invitation to keep following, yes?"

"You are clever boy, Geralt of East Brunswick," Viktoriya teased, her flirtatious tone returning in full force—like a welcome embrace.

Viktoriya and I talked for another hour. I told her more about Elijah and the drag show we would attend together. She shared stories about leaving Ukraine. Her father, seeing unrest and danger on the horizon, worked tirelessly to bring them here in search of a safer, more peaceful future. Her dreams, as vast as they were, stayed rooted in her past, present, and future—strong but flexible lines connecting who she was to who she wanted to become. As her world expanded, so did her dreams. Viktoriya knew what she wanted and who she was. For her, hope wasn't passive—it was realization. She didn't wish for things; she made them happen.

When the Friday dinner rush hit its stride, I knew it was time to leave. While Viktoriya insisted her father was more than capable of managing, I sensed a hint of guilt in her voice. She was right— he could handle the customers with resilience and humor, though it was clearly hard work. I also understood he would struggle endlessly on his own before asking his daughter for help, and Viktoriya was similarly stubborn. That became clear when she refused to let me leave unfed.

Before she allowed me to leave, she presented me with her most recent attempt to perfect her Borscht Burger. It was actually delicious. Imagine a delicate meatloaf patty—a mix of beef and pork—with stewed beets, carrots, onions, and tomatoes, all topped with garlic-dill sour cream, cabbage, and sweet-hot mustard. She was absolutely right. This one burger could put the Sunflower Kafe on the map.

After watching me enjoy the burger she made for me, she bluntly told me to call her in the morning to make plans. With a surprising kiss on my cheek, she said it was time for me to let her return to work. I was standing on the sidewalk outside the café before I knew it. Beneath a sky glowing crimson and indigo, I walked home, replaying my conversation with Viktoriya for Eros—as if he hadn't been listening the whole time. I even let him take credit for the whole night. I was in too good a mood to argue.

Chapter 6

For brevity's sake, I'll summarize the next sixteen hours of Mark's life—and my own adventures. Though the details of my escapades could entertain audiences worldwide, only a few moments mattered to Mark's story.

Mark walked home that Friday night, practically dancing across the bridge like a happy fool. It was all thanks to me and the strings I'd pulled, but it wasn't the time to rub that in. In case you're wondering, I knew that because I tried—it went over like weak ankles on cobblestones. He said it was like taking credit for an avalanche when all I'd done was push a snowball downhill. He was so punch-drunk it wasn't even fun to point out that he'd just agreed. Avalanches start with snowballs. As an eternal cosmic consciousness, I knew when a snowball could trigger an avalanche. Mark didn't understand that the real trick was to get the proper snowball in the right spot at the right time.

I accepted that I wouldn't be entertaining myself with Mark for the rest of the night. I turned my attention to other problems—like Gale Barlow, who wanted to buy Mark's orchard and the Queen's Head Club out from under Elijah. The simple solution to both problems would have been to plant the idea that purchasing the club and orchard would be financially disastrous in Gale's mind. But that was only half a solution. It wouldn't give Elijah the down payment funds, nor would it help Mark's mother manage the orchard on her own.

Then there was the biggest problem of all—me. I was still behind the times. After centuries confined to that lamp, where I could only learn from what drifted into my limited sphere of awareness, and with civilization advancing exponentially, it took only a few years to become outdated. I needed to understand modern technology and society, or anything I tried for Mark might blow up in his face. Fortunately, I was as close to omnipotent as this universe allows. I only had to figure out how to navigate the internet efficiently—from inside Mark's pocket. I expected to solve that in a few hours while Mark lay in bed, wrapped in fantasies about the coming night.

That evening, Mark stumbled into his apartment after a leisurely walk home. He unpacked on autopilot—an act that might look haphazard to the untrained eye. Distracted as he was, it took several nudges from me to get him to power up his laptop and connect what he called an antique mouse and keyboard—tools easier for me to manipulate. After this, he pulled his phone out of his pocket and sent two text messages. The first went to Elijah: *'Big night tomorrow. What should I wear?'* The second was to Viktoriya. It said, *'Thinking of you, looking forward to tomorrow, goodnight.'* He didn't wait for a reply. He set his phone on the desk and retreated to the bathroom for an almost ritualistic level of grooming and preening, which was when he discovered I'd manicured his chest hair into the letter E—for Eros, naturally. I like to sign my work. Fortunately, Mark found it hilarious but declined to keep it, convincing me to restore his chest hair to its patchy former glory instead of shaving it off.

I began my expedition and preparations. I devoured everything I could about modern finance, real estate, social media, computing, programming, networking, and pop culture. It was quite an adventure. I even watched *Funny Girl*, as Mark insisted. I had to admit I got it; I really got it. For anyone unfamiliar with Barbra Streisand's brilliance, I can't recommend her enough. After a night of intense enlightenment, I was ready for the next evening—and everything it promised.

The Fixer, The Maker, The Drag Entertainer

****Mark****

It was a beautiful Saturday morning. Birds sang, the street below lay quiet, and the trains were running on time. The sky was clear and the sun was shining. Tonight, I had a date with a fascinating woman to watch my best friend put on what might be the best drag show on the East Coast—maybe even the country. I'd be naïve to say all was right with the world, but for me, more was right than wrong. My coffee was fresh and strong, its aroma filling the kitchen. I sipped my coffee and read the text replies from Viktoriya and Elijah.

Viktoriya's reply was brief: *I am happy to be on your mind. Call me in the morning.* Though short, it sent ripples of excitement through me. Elijah's messages weren't as brief. He was working through the same pre-show nerves he always had. I'd learned not to indulge his bouts of self-doubt or his subtle fishing for compliments. He didn't really want reassurance or validation. He only needed to air his nerves to the universe to exorcise them. Most of his messages focused on potential wardrobe options for me. He practically outlined the virtues of every shirt and outfit I owned. He ended his wardrobe dissertation with, *I'm sure whatever you choose will look fabulous and perfect.* That's how I knew he cared— he gave me all the information I needed to make the best decision. Then he trusted my decision to be the right one. He never liked to say outright what he thought. He liked to see me arrive, more often than not, in the same place he was.

I replied to both of them. I told Viktoriya I would call her a little later to make concrete plans. To Elijah, I reminded him he couldn't possibly be more prepared, and I had every confidence in his talent. I told Elijah I'd settled on a nice, casual dress shirt— no tie—and a pair of camouflage cargo shorts, just to keep him on his toes. I was setting my phone down when it alerted me to a new message. The message was from Eros. It said, *Headset, or I'll play with your brain.* It looked like Eros had figured out text messaging. That would be convenient. Still, he wanted to talk, so I walked to my desk, where my headset had recharged overnight, slipped it over my ears, and switched it on.

"Finally, I was getting bored. You're taking your time this morning," Eros chided through the headset. He sounded more confident today. "I've been working hard all night, catching up with the twenty-first century. There is so much I want to discuss—but tell me, how are you, Mark? Looking forward to tonight? I am."

"Good morning, Eros. Yes, I'm taking my time this morning," I said, pouring another cup of coffee and sitting back down at the kitchen table. "It's Saturday. You might've missed that detail in your research, but Saturday and Sunday are common days off work for many people like me. So, I can sleep a little later, enjoy my coffee, and spend most of the day not wearing pants. So, I'm good, very good today. I have a date, which you know, and Elijah's show, which I have been looking forward to for weeks."

"I'll have you know I didn't overlook that detail. I simply perceive and measure time in a way and on a scale that you do not. Besides, I didn't actually know what day it was. But never mind that. I have, among other things, been thinking about how to solve the Gale Barlow problem."

"I already objected to anything like manipulating his mind—don't forget." I slurped my coffee, testing its temperature.

"I didn't forget. Did you forget that I also object to any manipulation that would force anyone to do something against their will? That's why I stick to small nudges. Like, 'apples are pretty good—I'd like one.' See? But you distracted me."

"You're right; there are differences, and I don't object to ideas like that, but I still don't like the ethical implications. Sorry to sidetrack you. Back to solving the Gale Barlow problem."

"Right, aside from giving him the idea that buying your orchard and the Queen's Head would ruin him financially. I believe I can designate both as official historic sites, which can prevent future development and require preservation. It's complicated if they are going to continue operating as commercial entities, but it's not impossible."

"That actually sounds like a great idea," I interrupted a little too quickly. I hadn't finished swallowing; it hurt.

"Let me finish. It wouldn't completely solve the problem—it'd take time to make it work legally, and it wouldn't prohibit the sale, just complicate it and make it less financially lucrative. It's also something that could potentially get reversed in court. We must remove the motivation and any incentive to buy or sell."

"Don't forget Elijah's Plan B for Gale," I said, trying to steer away from complicated problems. "It's complicated, that's definite. I am a fan of the historical designation for the orchard. That one might clear the legal hurdles—the mill is already a landmark. The Queen's Head is not old enough to stand up to any challenges to its historical value. What do you think you could do to help Elijah come up with the money to make an offer to Bob?"

"Another simple problem that needs a complex solution. Complex unless I perform some transmutation tricks to turn lead into gold, which would not only raise suspicions but would also cause some legal problems and questions. Last night, I learned about the idea of raising money through online crowdfunding."

"Right, Elijah has one of those setups," I said, standing up, needing water and the bathroom. "I almost forgot about it. Keep talking, I'm going to the bathroom."

"I'll be going with you to the bathroom, remember, as usual. But thank you for the warning. Since Elijah already has a Donate-me page established, we only need to harness the power of social media and the audience at the show tonight to drive donations. And I can do a bit of behind-the-scenes encouragement to put a cosmic-sized thumb on the scale."

"That actually sounds like a good plan," I said, washing my hands in the bathroom. "I'll check in with Elijah, remind him to eat lunch because he always forgets before a show, and print out some signs for his donate-me page. Then I need to call Viktoriya to warn her that she doesn't need to get too dressed up, and I'll order a car to pick her up outside the café around six o'clock. That will give us both seven or eight hours to get ready."

"You're speeding up. Are those nine cups of coffee kicking in?"

"Yes, and it was only four," I said, walking out to my kitchen, where I left my phone. "We can keep talking while I get ready, but I'm making those phone calls first."

Eros

Mark flitted about his apartment completing various chores in no particular order. He called both Viktoriya and Elijah. I found Viktoriya's response to Mark's suggestion that she didn't need to get too dressed up endlessly hilarious. She told him in no uncertain terms that she would dress how she liked, regardless of where they were going. Still, she thanked him for the information and for considering her comfort. That disrupted Mark's train of thought, and I had to remind him to tell her when he would pick her up. After that call, I also had to talk him through a mild panic that he had accidentally told Viktoriya what to wear.

His phone call with Elijah was much livelier. Mark reminded him to eat lunch, print a few signs and flyers for his fundraiser, and remember to use a fresh glue stick because the older ones can get clumpy. I had no idea what that meant, but it sounded like good advice. Elijah reminded Mark to show up early, that he would have a table by the stage reserved, and that he expected tips. Mark explained after the call that it wasn't uncommon for a friend of one of the performers to start tipping by waving dollar bills in front of the stage as a signal and reminder to the rest of the audience. Whether they realized it or not, I had to admit—it made sense that humans in a crowd picked up on social cues.

Mark and I spent the rest of the afternoon covering various discussion topics. Some were related to ongoing problems we were attempting to solve, and others were what I should expect at the show. I was impressed with the breadth of Mark's knowledge of the subject, which made sense, given how close he was to Elijah. He mentioned that it was customary to use someone's drag name when they were in character rather than their given name. He assured me it was not at all confusing, and over time, you start to think of them as two different people.

I told Mark I planned to plant a small suggestion in the audience's minds. Nudging them to share photos and videos on their social media with the Donate-me information. He worried it might be too forceful. I tried to reassure him it would be more like whispering a recommendation to someone than exerting influence. He remained skeptical, so I offered to demonstrate. I planted a few ideas in Mark's mind. I started small—suggesting he wanted another cup of coffee and a frozen waffle. He declined the additional cup of coffee, but he did toast and eat a frozen waffle. Finally, I suggested he touch the hot iron with his finger while ironing his shirt. It was odd how long he thought about it before his common sense kicked in. After those demonstrations, he was relieved, and so was I.

Mark dressed in a nice, but not too nice, black button-down shirt. He debated wearing a tie. I suggested he wear a vibrant tie, which he showed me. I said it would add a splash of color and fun to his outfit. He decided against it, saying a necktie was a hazard at a drag show. So, he dressed in a nice shirt sans necktie and comfortable-looking matching pants. He spent an inordinate amount of time brushing, smoothing, and styling his hair, only to use his fingers to mess it up just a little before leaving. He said it was about finding the balance between looking like you put in some effort without looking self-obsessed—he spent about ninety minutes perfecting his hair.

Mark reminded me he wouldn't be wearing his headset, so if I needed his attention, it would be okay to prod his mind a little. I told him I'd probably pay more attention to the show than to him. I also wanted to leave him with the impression I wouldn't eavesdrop on his date. For the record, I would be closely monitoring every second of his date. While Mark was surprisingly competent as a human, he was still an unpredictable primate, and I was on guard to save him from a romantic disaster.

Mark

My phone buzzed—the rideshare had arrived and was waiting outside. They arrived a little early, which was nice. I felt silly paying for a ride to a place within walking distance. Still, a first date was about making a good impression and avoiding surprises. Besides, I couldn't be sure that Viktoriya would wear shoes that would be suitable for walking. I suspected she might, though she was usually insightful, clever, and resourceful. I decided I'd rather look like I was trying too hard than seem presumptive, unprepared, or unconcerned about her comfort. Yes, I actually had that internal debate.

"Okay, the car is here, Eros. Any last words of encouragement?"

"Oh, I know this one—I learned it during my research last night. Good luck, and don't fuck it up."

I could only laugh as I removed my headset and set it in its designated charging dock. I was actually impressed with how much Eros had picked up in a single night of research. I suspected he knew more than he let on—probably to put me at ease. Otherwise, talking to a partially all-knowing entity might've been overwhelming. With one last check to verify I had my phone, I sent Viktoriya a quick text to let her know I was on my way. I patted my pockets—wallet, cash, keys, and a mint tin filled with emergency anti-inflammatory painkillers, antacids, and adhesive bandages for Elijah. Satisfied I had everything, I left my apartment, headed down the stairs, and got into the waiting car. After a quick hello, I confirmed the driver knew the route to the Sunflower Kafe and then The Queen's Head Club before we drove off to pick up Viktoriya.

The car pulled up in front of the Sunflower Kafe. Viktoriya was standing out front on the sidewalk. The driver spotted her first and blurted, "Wow," then tried to cover it with a cough. I saw her a second later and had the same response. She looked impossible—an anachronism that somehow made the world bend to fit her. Her hair was styled in subtle 1950s victory curls framed by delicate pin curls that peeked from under a dark lavender scarf tied neatly on top. Her shirt looked like a tailored men's dress shirt, dyed the same dark lavender as her scarf. She wore a highly altered pinstripe vest over her shirt, with her signature sunflower and trident embroidered at the bottom. Those layers were a fascinating contrast to the black asymmetrical, loosely cut pencil skirt with crimson traditional hand-embroidered patterns running vertically down one side. Completing the look, she wore practical, broken-in black boots and a utility bag slung cross-body.

I'd never been so tempted to jump out of a moving car. The moment the car slowed, I pushed the door open and stepped out. I hadn't taken the time to compose myself and mentally rehearse my words. I almost panicked when Viktoriya spoke first.

"Mark! You look very nice, dear," Viktoriya said, smiling, walking confidently toward me.

"Thank you. You look incredible, Viktoriya," I responded as she gripped my arm affectionately without hesitation and pecked my cheek before she stepped into the car.

"Thank you. You are sweet boy," she said, shuffling across the back seat to the opposite side of the car, leaving room for me to climb inside next to her, closing the door behind me.

"Is that your design book in that bag?" I asked quickly, trying to regain my composure as the car pulled away over the bridge. "And your outfit is amazing. Did you make it?"

"Da, you say I should bring it along," Viktoriya replied, shifting her bag that looked heavier than it ought to be. "I design and tailor this clothing. It look nice, yes?"

"Nice? No, Viktoriya—it's stunning. Like you." I cringed inside, hearing how much it sounded like a bad pickup line. But it was entirely honest, and I meant it sincerely, and from the flushing in Viktoriya's cheeks, she knew that too. I even noticed our driver nodding in silent agreement, and I could feel my own cheeks begin to flush as we pulled up in front of the club.

I thanked the driver and pulled out my phone to add a tip before getting out. I wanted to ensure I didn't forget. I opened the door and stepped out, holding my hand out, offering assistance to Viktoriya. She accepted my hand and also turned to thank our driver, who couldn't help but smile back at her. When she stepped out, she didn't let go but shifted her hand in mine.

A shirtless man stood at the door of The Queen's Head Club. He wore a simple vest and a subtle nametag, which did little to conceal his well-developed muscular torso. He smiled familiarly as we approached, ready to open the door for us.

"Nice to see you again, Mark. Elijah, I mean Fanny, reserved a table for you," the doorman said, his voice far softer and friendlier than his physique. "Oh, Mark, who do you have with you? She. Is. Stunning."

"Good to see you too, Kareem. This is Viktoriya. Viktoriya, this is Kareem. The best and sweetest doorman and bouncer on the East Coast."

"Pleasure to meet you, Kareem," Viktoriya replied with a genuine smile before she looked at his vest, scrunched her nose, opened her bag, and pulled something out. "Your vest, it need color. Here, this is better, yes?"

She deftly pinned a handmade golden sunflower to Kareem's vest, opposite his nametag. Kareem looked down. His initial shock and surprise quickly melted into a genuinely overjoyed grin.

"Yes! Oh my god, I love it—thank you! Mark, I like her. You two go on in. The show should start in half an hour or an hour. You know how our host is tonight." Kareem smiled broadly as he opened the door for us, and we stepped inside. "Have a fantastic night."

Chapter 7

Inside, the club buzzed with energy—lively but not overcrowded, full of people enjoying themselves. We easily wound our way through the crowd to find our reserved table just to the left of center stage. The music was loud, so I leaned close to Viktoriya's ear to ask if she wanted to sit while I got her a drink. Or if she preferred, she could join me at the bar and leave her bag at the table. She decided on a third option. She was going to dance while I ordered drinks.

I watched Viktoriya glide toward the center of the dance floor, moving effortlessly to the pulsing rhythm built to make bodies move. I was in awe of her comfortable and infectious confidence. Within seconds, she made herself at home and invited everyone along with her. She laughed and smiled with everyone, dancing to songs twice our age, while I made my familiar trek to the bar. I caught the attention of one of the bartenders I knew. I ordered two of Elijah's signature cocktails with a few hand gestures and nods, signaling I'd be back soon to pick them up.

I weaved through the crowd on the dance floor toward Viktoriya. I caught her eye and reached out my hand. Instead of taking it, she grabbed me, spinning me toward her with a laugh. I whooped in response, spinning into her arms with a dramatic dip on the dance floor—she was impressively strong. We both howled and danced together for a moment before we left the dance floor together to retrieve our cocktails from the bar.

Returning to the bar, I was surprised to receive two large hurricane glasses filled with layered blue, red, and orange mystery liquor, garnished with an orange wheel. I was fairly certain these weren't what I'd ordered until I remembered the cocktail Elijah had been perfecting yesterday afternoon. I was positive it didn't matter what I ordered. Elijah had made arrangements. When I handed Viktoriya her glass, she eyed it suspiciously before giving me a questioning look. I shrugged and took a sip—it was delicious. Elijah had really dialed in his recipe. What did he call it? A Sex-on-the-Long-Island-Sunrise-Beach? We will need to workshop the name, but the drink was fantastic.

Viktoriya followed my lead and took a sip—her eyes popped open a little wider. She nodded, approving of the unusual cocktail. I gestured toward our table, where the music was a little quieter and we could talk without shouting in each other's ears. She nodded again, and we carefully danced our way through the crowd back to our table, where we sat to wait for the show to start.

"Is good. This, I like," Viktoriya said over the music, leaning close to me.

"It's from my friend, Elijah. I wasn't expecting them, but it is good. We can get dinner after his performance. I'm sure you're hungry," I replied, matching her volume, suddenly realizing the only thing I had eaten was a frozen waffle.

"Da!" Viktoriya responded, taking a sip of her drink while dancing in her chair.

The conversation was difficult, but not impossible. Still, we kept it to a minimum. While we were waiting for the show to start, she showed off her design book. It had more incredible clothing designs and costume ideas than I remembered, even the outfit she wore tonight. Her eye for fashion was inspired; her imagination boundless. Elijah was going to be crazy for these, and he was going to love Viktoriya, which made my heart leap to think about it.

About twenty minutes later, the dance music faded, leaving only laughter and conversation echoing through the club. The crowd gradually settled into seats near the stage, onto barstools, and at tables scattered throughout the club. The rest filled in amicably, standing wherever they could catch a glimpse of the stage, instinctively leaving a walkway down the center. The house lights dimmed, and the stage lights flared as Kareem strode onto the stage, microphone in hand. The golden sunflower Viktoriya had given him was still pinned to his vest.

"Good evening, ladies, gentlemen, they's in between, and them's on the outsides. Welcome to The Queen's Head. If you've been here before, you know the rules. If you haven't, we keep our hands to ourselves, are courteous to our performers, have fun, and tip generously. Now, please, show some love to your host, our own—Fanny Ryesand!"

The crowd cheered, and onto the stage stepped Elijah as Fanny Ryesand, dressed as a wrapped deli sandwich, complete with a skewered pickle hat on her head. Her makeup had improved since the last time I saw it. A pronounced cat eyeliner framed a classic smoky eye and subtle but effective pink lipstick surrounded by a shimmering silver glittered beard. She looked incredible—for a deli sandwich.

With a smooth gesture, she raised the microphone and began to sing—a half octave higher than I was used to hearing—the opening lines of "I'm the Greatest Star" from *Funny Girl* as the accompanying music rose in the background.

She was singing live instead of lip-syncing. I had no idea she was planning to do that. Elijah must have been practicing for weeks without my finding out. I was shocked. The performance started subtly, slowly picking up steam. As the song approached the first crescendo, the hat came off, revealing a styled Barbra Streisand-styled wig, the foam pickle hat flying into the cheering crowd. Fanny hit every beat, each punchline earning bigger laughs and louder cheers. Then, the sandwich began to unwrap as she hit the second refrain.

First came the tape of the sandwich wrap, which she ripped away on the beat. Followed by the first fold of the fabric sandwich wrapping. She pulled it away from her body, punctuating the word "nose." Then the second fold was pulled back, building to the finale. With a sung shout of "Wham," Kareem stepped on stage behind Fanny, and with one yank, the faux sandwich wrapping was off. Revealing Fanny in a low-cut sequined red blazer, with a string of matzo balls strung like pearls hanging low around her neck. A ruffled skirt of marbled, glittering blacks and browns, reminiscent of a good marble rye bread, hung gracefully to mid-calf, framing impressively tall black heels. There she stood—

center stage—belting out the final sustained lyric, "Here I am!" The crowd erupted.

I had no idea Elijah could sing like this, not in all the years we'd been friends.

I knew he could carry a tune, but singing along to musicals in a living room is a far cry from the performance we were getting tonight. Three-quarters of the way through the song, I finally stole my eyes away from the stage to glance at Viktoriya, who was also captivated, watching, mouth agape.

As my best friend Elijah, performing as Fanny Ryesand, hit the final lines of the song, perched on the edge of the stage, I remembered one of my responsibilities. I pulled a dollar from my pocket, holding it aloft as I cheered with the crowd. Like clockwork, moments after I raised that dollar, dozens of hands and dollar bills rose into the air. Fanny looked down, saw me, grinned, winked, and plucked the dollar from my fingers.

Eros

The club was far more entertaining tonight than it had been yesterday afternoon. I can't recall a time I had seen so many different people in one place. Everyone wore wildly different clothes and costumes—the color spectrum was off the charts. There was no uniformity or coordination, yet it all blended into a magnificent human harmony. It could have been my years of isolation speaking, or it could be that this was just that jubilant. Before Elijah's performance began, I made the rounds, hopping from mind to mind, planting the seed that this show would be worth capturing and sharing.

I was happy that Elijah had taken Mark's advice and printed some flyers for his fundraising website and had taped them to several tables. That made it easy to call attention to it and suggest that it was worth sharing, too.

When the performance started, I was pleased I had done that work ahead of time because the performance was incredible. Mark once described drag as subversive performance art—part gender play, part absurd comedy. His description was both a disservice and, paradoxically, remarkably apt. The juxtaposition of Elijah's masculine beard and feminine costume—being unwrapped like a deli sandwich—was glorious. I get it now. It takes the binary gender norms of society and mocks them in a way I didn't know was possible. I am so glad I came along.

I wanted to check in with Mark, but the performance completely claimed his attention—and by Viktoriya. I will be able to talk to him about this later tonight. I was also glad I'd watched *Funny Girl* last night; it made appreciating Elijah's—no, Fanny's— performance even more satisfying. Now, Fanny was collecting tips and waving to the audience, and I could already see people on their phones uploading videos and pictures, as we had planned.

"Oh. My. Gawd. You are such a beautiful and attractive audience," Fanny said, pacing the stage while counting the dollar bills she had collected.

"Although I have to say, some of you are a little more attractive than the rest," Fanny said, looking directly at Mark and then Viktoriya. "Did I see some of you filming that instead of enjoying it with your own eye-bawls? That's all right, sweethearts, just spell my name right, and come see me after the show so I can collect my royalties—HA! Before I say another word, can we show some love to our favorite bear, Kareem? Come here so these people can have one more look at your pretty face before you invite them to leave for the night."

Kareem walked back onto the stage, looking a little embarrassed at the whoops and playful catcalls from the audience.

"Kareem, what is that on your vest, darling? It is adorable," Fanny asked, looking at the sunflower Viktoriya had pinned to his vest while holding the microphone out for his reply.

"Thank you, everyone. That is my sunflower that this exquisite lady, Viktoriya, gave me tonight," Kareem replied sheepishly, gesturing toward Viktoriya before retreating off the stage.

"Oy, he isn't wrong. Viktoriya, you should be ashamed showing up looking like that, making all us girls look like corned beef by comparison." Viktoriya's responding laughter spread through the crowd, even catching Fanny off guard. "Oh dear, you are precious. I'll have to keep an eye on you. Now, as much as I wish it were true, you are not all here to see me. We have queens young and old, new and old, and one that is just old for you tonight. Because you were all so kind to me, I know you will be kind to the rest of my sisters. We even have a debut. You get to witness the birth of a drag-baby. Our homegrown Rutgirls Wawa will be up here for the first time ever. If you don't make her feel welcome, I will have the bar cut off your tabs. Roberta Johnson's Wood, another hometown hottie, is here, along with Sandy Leonardo, Lola Legs-up, Velvet Livingston, Bella Boudoir, Lizza Jest, and Wilmaton Sunset from across the Delaware Bay. Finally, Sassafras Eclipse and Sin-der Wisp—who still owes me seven ninety-five for half a pastrami on rye—are all here for you."

The crowd clapped, cheered, and whooped for each name. Fanny was a brilliant host—she roused the audience, reveled in the spotlight, yet shared it generously.

"Now, I'll be back after a few other numbers, so don't you worry. But first, please welcome the world premiere debut with pickles. Miss Rutgirls Wawa."

Fanny stepped off the stage as a new performer began a lip-sync routine—rough around the edges and lacking a distinct point of view, yet brimming with promise and passion. I would say she did an admirable job for the second drag performance I had ever seen. The audience was receptive and supportive, and in the end, they again followed Mark's lead, waving dollar bills in the air. She graciously collected her tips as she retreated from the stage to be greeted enthusiastically by friends and strangers. Mark and Viktoriya looked utterly absorbed in each other's company, their laughter rising easily above the din.

I couldn't hear what they were saying to each other over the noise of the club unless I moved closer, which I could. But I also thought Mark deserved a little bit of privacy. They held hands, leaning close enough that their words were private murmurs amid the noise. Not knowing what they were saying was torture, so I paid a brief visit to their table.

Viktoriya was on the cusp of feeling too much like an outsider, expressing to Mark that there were things that made him laugh that she didn't understand. Mark, determined to walk through the unknown land alongside her, was explaining the puns, jokes, and some of the origins of the various drag names. She would ask questions, and he would try to explain. Sometimes she laughed; other times, she admitted she didn't quite understand. Mark would reassure her and say there is a movie they can watch another night or something he can show her when they leave the club. He was patient and enjoyed the chance to share this with her.

She was appreciative and genuinely interested. They were clearly enjoying themselves, the space between them shrinking in both conversation and closeness.

Next came Roberta Johnson's Wood, storming the stage in a glamorous gown and a voluminous wig. They passionately performed a lip-sync to a four-decade-old aggressively masculine rock and roll anthem, and everyone in the audience sang along. They performed two additional numbers, with two wildly different songs from opposing genres. They grew more frantic as they went, driving the audience wild before collapsing dramatically on the stage. The next act was Sandy Leonardo, who sauntered onto the stage in a simple but revealing costume that would not help prevent hypothermia in the tropics. Their performance was a sensual and bawdy series of contortions and acrobatics to intense rhythmic dance music with no lyrical content. Based on their reactions and eagerness to wave tips in the air, the audience was titillated. Even Viktoriya was on her feet, cheering and waving a dollar in the air while Mark was laughing hysterically.

Before Sandy could finish collecting tips, Fanny Ryesand strutted back out—now clad in a garishly striped purple-and-green top, a tutu resembling a disturbingly realistic Reuben sandwich, and a large deli container perched atop her head.

"All right, Sandy, go on, collect those tips. I know it takes longer to collect them individually, and you are used to it being left on the nightstand. I'd rethink that outfit. It's always better to leave something to the imagination. The only thing you leave to the imagination is how much disappointment there will be for whoever you convince to take that off of you," Fanny said. They both laughed, making faces at each other as Sandy left the stage, and Fanny waved to her. "Love you—call me."

The audience laughed along with them, and then the laughter faded when Fanny sighed, and the introduction to "I'd Rather Be Blue" played right on cue. There was a hushed silence in the moments before she sang the first notes. For the first few notes, their eyes locked—his gaze mirroring hers with unspoken recognition.

Then she broke eye contact and began walking around the stage. Singing wistfully, almost mournfully, about a missing or unrequited love. Every few lines, her gaze returned to Mark. I was so entranced by the performance that I almost missed what was obviously happening. This wasn't a performance for the room—it was a confession meant for one person alone.

This was Elijah—not Fanny—singing directly to Mark, and Mark was staring back, enveloped in the performance of Fanny Ryesand.

As the last notes rang out, Fanny declared she would rather endure the sorrow of absence than the hollow happiness of another with as much fervor as possible. She tipped her head back, singing to the rafters, as the audience cheered, including Mark.

Then Mark turned to Viktoriya, who had been watching him the entire performance. The lyrics had reached her; the longing threading through her chest like a pulse she couldn't ignore. When Mark turned his head, she kissed him—and he kissed her. At that moment, Fanny looked down from the ceiling lights and bowed deeply as the audience erupted in cheers—everyone except Mark and Viktoriya. When Fanny lifted her head, Elijah saw Mark kissing Viktoriya. I watched Fanny Ryesand dissolve into Elijah Cohen for a single, devastating moment as he collapsed to his knees onstage.

The applause fell away, and all eyes, including Mark and Viktoriya's, were on Fanny Ryesand, on her knees in center stage. She rose, took a shuddering breath, and in one fluid motion tore away the green-and-purple sandwich tutu, revealing a sleek black gown beneath. She flung the deli container on her head into the audience in another instant, exposing another expertly styled and curled blond wig. This ensemble replaced every bit of camp and shtick with pure elegance. At that moment, she sang the first lines from "My Man" while she stared directly at Mark.

She sang tenderly of the love she bore for her man—a love he would never know—as the heart-rending melody rose to cradle her voice. As Fanny released Mark from her gaze, she turned her eyes to some distant point in the back of the room. Now she sang passionately to the universe—pain and heartbreak woven into every word. Right then, I believed only Elijah and I knew the truth. Mark and Viktoriya were watching this performance through clouded lenses. Seeing a heartfelt performance, hearing lovesick words, believing them to be naught but moving fiction.

If I possessed a heart, it would have shattered alongside his.

In that moment, Elijah—as Fanny—sang about her unwavering, unconditional love and devotion to a man who may not deserve it. My admiration and affection for Elijah and Fanny grew beyond measure.

Fanny took a final bow as the audience exploded with whistles and applause, many also wiping away tears. Fanny announced a thirty-minute intermission, then hastily retreated backstage. I followed, hopping from light to light through the walls until I was in a small closet where Elijah had collapsed in a chair, his body shuddering as he wept. I felt wretched for having missed something so obvious. Mark and Elijah were not only best friends. I knew that—I could sense it. But I let Mark convince me otherwise, and the only reason I could fathom that he did that is because he either couldn't see it himself—or he refused to accept it. I couldn't be sure, having only known Mark for a couple of days, but right now, I had the distinct impression he had unintentionally or subconsciously led Elijah on.

I could help Elijah. I could tell him Mark feels the same way—or convince him that he didn't actually love Mark. I could slip into his mind and rearrange memories until the ache vanished—but I couldn't bring myself to cross that line.

I wouldn't lie to Elijah or convince him to lie to himself, and I wouldn't rob him of what he felt. What he did next astonished me—and will, I think, until the end of time. He stood up, dried his eyes the best he could, took a deep breath, and spoke to himself.

"All right, Elijah, sometimes when we swing, we strike out. That doesn't mean we get to leave the game. Come on, Fanny, let's go meet Mark's date."

Mark

I cannot believe Elijah's performance. I've never seen that side of him before. It was raw and powerfully emotional. I can't guess whether he tapped into a deep well of past emotion or was an amazing actor conjuring that passion from his imagination. There were moments when I felt like he was singing to me, not as an audience member, but to me personally. I imagine I'm not the only one in this room who felt that, but it still left me feeling special. Clearly, Viktoriya felt it too—if that kiss was any indication of how deeply Elijah's performance had moved her. He walked offstage moments ago. It would likely take him a few minutes to come out and say hello. I looked around and caught the eye of one of the bar staff I recognized making rounds collecting empty glasses.

"Hi, Rhonda," I called to her with a wave.

"Hey, Mark, good to see you. Can I get you something?" Rhonda replied.

"Thanks. Elijah should be out in a minute. Could we get a drink and some water for him—and for us too?" I asked, swallowing the embarrassment of asking for something that may be a mild inconvenience.

"Absolutely—though it seems Elijah already called it in. Jim's on his way over right now with those."

"Thank you," I said, relieved and grateful for my friend. "Viktoriya, what did you think?"

"This is so fun! That was your friend Elijah singing, yes?" Viktoriya replied, buzzing with excitement. "So much emotion. I feel it—He loves someone very much."

"I think so too. I just can't imagine who," I said as Jim arrived with a tray of drinks. Three of Elijah's specials and three glasses of water. "Thank you, Jim."

"No problem, Mark, I'll see you soon," Jim said, walking away as Elijah stepped out from backstage.

His makeup was smudged, and his eyeliner had run. It looked like he had been crying a moment ago—most likely an after-effect of his heartfelt performance. I jumped out of my chair and walked over to meet him. As I wrapped my arms around him, he immediately returned the embrace.

"Elijah! That was the most incredible performance. I had no idea you could do that," I said. Letting go of him, I stepped back and to the side. "Elijah, meet Viktoriya. Viktoriya, meet my best friend in the world, Elijah."

"I am so happy to meet you. Mark talked of you—all night." Viktoriya hopped off her chair and embraced Elijah. "You sing beautifully. I'm very moved."

"Thank you, Viktoriya, that's too kind. It's good to meet you too." Elijah returned the hug. From the look on his face, he was touched to have received such a compliment. "Mark has talked about you, too."

"Oh, he has?" Viktoriya said, sitting down at the table, a glint of mischief in her eyes. "What does Mark say about me?"

"Okay, let's not—" I began to say, sitting down next to Viktoriya.

"Oh, yes, let's," Elijah said, sliding into the third chair, his eyes gleaming with the same mischief. "First of all, he completely undersold how gorgeous you are."

"Yes, he is not so observant," Viktoriya replied with a playful smirk that said she was deliberately holding something back.

"How right you are," Elijah laughed, lifting his glass and clinking it against Viktoriya's. "But let's not talk about Mark. Tell me about this stunning outfit you are wearing."

"You like? I made myself."

"Shut up. It's magnificent. Okay, I know Mark told you to bring your design book. Let's see it—show me your talent, girl."

Viktoriya sheepishly pulled out her design book and set it on the table in front of Elijah. I sat back and watched silently, knowing Elijah shouldn't be interrupted, like a dog with a bone. Elijah flipped through the book's pages, lingering a little longer on each page. He stopped on a page filled with sketches of theatrical asymmetrical dress designs. He stared at the page for a while before gesturing to Viktoriya to come closer.

"These are stunning. What are you doing with Mark? You are far too pretty. Far too talented, and far too good for him."

"Thank you. I think he is cute," Viktoriya replied with a shrug. She didn't argue the point. She didn't contradict him politely. She leaned into the 'yes, and' like a seasoned pro.

Elijah closed the book and handed it back to Viktoriya. Then he cracked and howled with laughter so hard his eyes watered, and he was gasping for breath. This made Viktoriya laugh, which spread to me like a glorious infectious contagion. While still laughing, Elijah stood and leaned down to pull Viktoriya into a hug. She hugged him back, and he held her close as his laughter faded.

"You are magnificent and way too good for my friend. If he hurts you, I swear I'll neuter him myself. You need to call me—I need your talent, and you need my embarrassing stories about Mark."

"Good. Mark will give me your number," Viktoriya said, flashing me a playful, goofy grin.

"Oh, this was a mistake. You two together are way too powerful," I said with a laugh, standing and looping my arms around both of them. In response, they both put an arm around me. I couldn't imagine being any happier than I was right then. "Elijah, I've got to take Viktoriya to find food to fight off your cocktails—and you need to fix your face. I love you. You were incredible tonight."

"Yes, Mark promised to feed me real food," Viktoriya added. "Elijah, you are wonderful."

"Oh, Mark, fuck your face. I love you, too. Hey, where's my tip?" Elijah laughed, stepping back out of the hug, snatching the last dollar bill from my pocket before glancing between me and Viktoriya. "You are wonderful too, Viktoriya. Don't let Mark send you home hungry. Now go on—get out of here. I've got a show to finish."

Chapter 8

Mark and Viktoriya stepped out of The Queen's Head Club into the cool night air, oblivious to the world around them. Hand in hand, they were focused on each other. As they reached the sidewalk, they briefly let go of each other's hands to look around. Mark leaned in to say something to Viktoriya—something I couldn't hear. I might have if I hadn't been preoccupied with what I'd just witnessed. Mark's best friend was in love with him—and had just made a brave confession that went unnoticed. Now, here was my friend Mark, quickly falling for Viktoriya, unaware of what was looming. I had to get his attention and speak to him immediately.

Mark had apparently suggested getting food down the street as they set off with intent. I took the opportunity to conjure a text message on Mark's phone, triggering a notification. The message said, *Mark, we need to talk. It is important. Your friend, Eros.* When Mark heard the notification, he nonchalantly pulled his phone out of his pocket and read my message. He furrowed his brow slightly and typed out a quick reply: *We can talk later. Viktoriya and I are picking up falafel,* then pressed send. He probably hit send out of habit—he knew it wouldn't go anywhere—or he was just keeping up the ruse. Playing along, I mimicked the vernacular from his other texts: *K, TTYL. ASAP. BBQ!* I wasn't entirely sure what that meant, but it was something he had sent in the past. It must have been amusing because he laughed, and I resigned myself to playing the spectator, a role I thought I had left behind when Mark set me free.

"Something is funny?" Viktoriya said, looking at Mark's phone screen out of the corner of her eye.

"Oh, yeah, sorry. Just a mutual friend of mine and Elijah's checking in about the show. I said I would tell them about it later," Mark said, tilting his phone screen toward Viktoriya slightly to show it wasn't an especially private message. "They just replied with a bunch of acronyms I don't think they understand."

"Ah, I have made this mistake as well," Viktoriya said with a giggle from some private memory.

"That reflects more on them than you. I think you speak marvelously. It is charming and uniquely Viktoriya. I can only imagine picking up that kind of shorthand communication in a new language wasn't easy. Did you learn English in school before you moved?" Mark asked warmly, empathetically understanding, and with genuine curiosity about Viktoriya's past.

"Da, it was tricky. I learned some English from books, movies, and television programs online myself before we move," Viktoriya said, a hint of pride behind her words. "I take class here to improve, but was not as good. They say I speak poorly but understand well."

"Let me guess—the professor was an American who probably spoke Ukrainian or Russian like an American."

"Da—like dirty capitalist pig-man," Viktoriya said, laughing openly. "He says Russia and Ukraine share language. Fool stuck in the Cold War."

"Capitalist pig? That sounds like something a Bolshevik would say. Oh dear, I'm an American sleeping with the enemy!" Mark said with sarcasm so thick it almost drowned the joke.

"Only if you stay lucky, silly American boy," Viktoriya shot back so quickly it caught Mark off guard.

She had caught an implication Mark himself hadn't realized he'd made. Even I hadn't caught the unintended double entendre in Mark's words until Viktoriya did. Her laughter shifted from self-amused to triumphant and mischievous as she caught Mark's stunned expression.

"I didn't—I mean … I didn't intend to imply," Mark stammered, his face flushed red, looking to regain his footing in the conversation. Then, with a sheepish but knowing grin, "You're teasing me."

"Da," Viktoriya said, obviously enjoying Mark's flustered reaction.

"Oh, hey—look, we're here. Falafel," Mark said, clearing his throat. "But it looks like everyone else had the same idea. It's packed."

"We get takeaway, yes? Then find somewhere quiet—just us," Viktoriya said, undeterred, a little hopeful.

"That's a great idea. My apartment is only a block away. It's quiet and warm. I even have chairs and a table," Mark said enthusiastically, equally hopeful. "Okay, it's not exactly a table—it's a countertop in my kitchen—but it'll serve as one."

Viktoriya nodded encouragingly in agreement. Together, they walked inside and ordered falafel and some kebabs to go. After hearing that it would take a little while for their food to be ready, they took a short walk down the street to a liquor store to pick out a bottle of wine. Mark shared his personal philosophy: any bottle of wine over twenty dollars is just for show, and there's nothing wrong with boxed wine.

While Viktoriya found this amusing, she redirected the selection by picking a case of Chernihivske beer, insisting it was far superior to any wine there. That was justification enough for Mark. He paid quickly, and they returned to the falafel shop to collect their food. I made a reminder for myself to ask Mark more about his personal wine theory because it sounded intriguing.

Mark and Viktoriya arrived at Mark's humble apartment in short order. Mark apologized for its plain décor and utilitarian furnishings, almost lamenting that the only other person he ever entertained there was Elijah. I could have screamed when he said that, newly aware of just how often he mentioned Elijah—and how prominent Elijah was in his life. I couldn't scream at him as a captive observer, but I would absolutely address that at the first opportunity. Mark rapidly cleared space on his kitchen countertop while setting down the takeout bag and the case of beer. He jogged to the cabinet and retrieved two mismatched pilsner glasses, setting them on the counter next to the beer.

"I'm sorry again. Pretty much everything here is mismatched. I guess it suits me; I'm a little mismatched myself," Mark said, vaguely gesturing to himself and everything in his apartment.

"Please, make yourself at home. The bathroom is through that door, and this is my kitchen, dining room, living room, and office."

"Thank you. It is nice, Mark, dear," Viktoriya said politely. "I will remove my boots if you don't mind. I use your bathroom. Pour beer for me, yes?"

"Absolutely I will, and I don't mind at all," Mark said, excising a pair of beer cans from the case and carefully filling two glasses with the golden liquid.

I took that opportunity to create another text, emphasizing my frustration and the need for us to talk.

"We will talk after Viktoriya leaves," Mark murmured. "Be patient—it's going really well."

I knew it was going well. That was part of the problem. I was glad it was going well, but Mark needed to understand what had just happened with Elijah, and his role, before anything went too far with Viktoriya. He may need to make a decision, and with each passing moment, that decision will be much harder. Or maybe it wouldn't be a hard decision at all—I couldn't say. I'd been thrust into this situation without warning or preparation, and just when it mattered most, I'd agreed to remain a spectator. To top it off, I was only now realizing that I didn't fully understand what Mark meant when he said, "Elijah's gay, I'm not." Maybe I was overreacting.

Viktoriya came back from the bathroom, holding her boots. On her feet, she wore colorful socks decorated with a cartoon rabbit and the words "What's up, Doc?" printed across them. She set her boots by the door and perched on a stool at the kitchen counter Mark liked to call his table. She lifted the glass of beer delicately and held it up in front of her.

"Za zustrich, to our meeting."

"Za zust … rich," Mark repeated carefully, mimicking Viktoriya's pronunciation before tapping his glass gently against hers. "To our many meetings."

They both drank. Viktoriya finished her glass quickly, and Mark followed soon after. Several moments after Viktoriya, Mark set his empty glass down. They both laughed while Mark refilled their glasses. As Mark refilled their glasses, Viktoriya unpacked the takeout containers, placed them in the middle of the counter between them, and opened them up. She plucked a falafel ball and a kebab from the container and took a bite of each, humming happily as she chewed. Mark slid the refilled glass toward her, then grabbed a falafel and a kebab from the container, eating both quickly. Viktoriya giggled and exchanged her kebab for her beer, raising it and waiting for Mark to swallow and raise his glass.

"Za shchastya," Viktoriya said as Mark raised his glass. "For happiness."

"Za sh … cha … stya," Mark repeated slowly, allowing the unfamiliar words to form correctly in his mouth. "To our happiness."

"Very good," Viktoriya said before drinking a third of her glass, and Mark did as well.

"Those are common toasts in Ukraine?" Mark said before taking another bite.

"Oh yes. Is tradition," Viktoriya said, between bites and drinks, finishing her beer and gesturing to Mark's half-empty glass. "Catch up, pretty boy," she teased.

Mark laughed and blushed as he finished his beer. Viktoriya plucked the empty glass from his hand and immediately refilled both glasses. I remembered the first time I'd witnessed a primitive version of this human ritual. Back then, choking down haphazardly fermented plant juice was a challenge of endurance. It seems much more enjoyable now.

"The third toast is the most important," Viktoriya said, lifting her glass and placing Mark's in his hand.

"Za lyubov." This time, she did not translate for Mark.

"Za lyubov," Mark replied without hesitation, smiling as he tapped his glass to hers. "For love." They both paused—Viktoriya's mouth slightly open—before draining their glasses.

"Mark, you have learned some Ukrainian, yes?" Viktoriya said, blushing slightly. It was less of a question and more of a statement of pleasant surprise. "You did that for me?"

"I did. I started months ago after we met for the first time. I had a feeling it would be useful," Mark said almost playfully, enjoying putting Viktoriya on her back foot for a change.

"You surprise me. What other secrets are you hiding?" Viktoriya asked, leaning forward, her eyes narrowing with playful curiosity.

Viktoriya was not the only one surprised. I was too, but I shouldn't have been. I remembered the Ukrainian language textbooks I'd found—I wondered how many times he'd rehearsed this moment. Perhaps he was more capable than I predicted.

"I'm a deep well of mystery. Why, even I don't know all my secrets," Mark said with a smirk across the counter at Viktoriya, leaning back into the upper hand in their flirtatious struggle.

Mark

Viktoriya stared at me across the counter. Seeing her flustered, as if her walls had dropped for just a moment, was exhilarating. I suspected she preferred—and was used to—controlling the emotional flow of her conversations. I was not an expert by any means, but in my experience, that was a sign there was pain in her past. I could understand that. There we were, exposing our vulnerabilities to each other, beginning to trust. In a way, we were both asking the same question: if I open myself to you, will you hurt me? It was a terrifying question because no one can honestly say no, or promise that it will always stay that way. To ask that question is to accept the risk of being hurt.

"Everyone has secrets, little things we can't admit or are ashamed of," I said, casually backing out of this subject. It was too soon for us to ask each other to reveal that much. "But let's slowly discover each other's secrets. The best things should be savored, after all."

"Da, I have secret identity—for your safety," Viktoriya said, giggling at her own ridiculous implication. "I have question about drag and Elijah."

I was happy she also stepped back from that vulnerable moment. While I wanted to dive into her with a burning desire, I was fighting the impulse. I couldn't be sure I was ready for the unknown consequences of unrestrained vulnerability. Now, my only concern was that she brought the topic of conversation back to Elijah. I was a little concerned she might start to feel jealousy emerging from my relationship with him.

"Of course, I can't say I'm an expert, but I'll try. What are your questions?"

"At the show ... those were men, yes?" Viktoriya asked, edging toward her real question. "I know this. These men are—I forget the word—men who like men?"

"Yes, generally speaking, they're gay men. I don't personally know everyone who performed, so that's just an assumption," I said, suddenly aware her question wasn't as straightforward as it sounded. "There are men, women, trans or cisgender, and non-binary individuals who perform in drag. Some are gay, some are bi or pansexual, and now and then, they are straight. But it originated with gay men."

"Yes, gay—that is word," Viktoriya said. It looked like she was working something out in her mind. "Elijah is gay, yes? Hm. He likes men how I like men? I know what that is, but not sure I understand—not sure of word. I don't like women like that; I don't know how it feels to like women."

"I understand. You mean it can be hard to empathize with feelings you can't feel yourself. Even if it makes sense, it can be hard to imagine," I said. I still had the feeling that there was something she was working out.

"Tonight, when Elijah sang—who is his man?" Viktoriya asked, finally arriving at her real question. "He loves some man very much. I hope he tells him soon."

"I don't know. He never told me about anyone. He tells me about all the guys he likes. I need to call him—" My phone rang, cutting my thought short.

I pulled it out of my pocket, and the screen was blank. It was not an incoming phone call. It could only be Eros. I tapped the screen and held the phone to my ear.

"Hello," I said, a little unsure.

"Mark, I know you're a little busy and distracted right now, but I need to tell you something about Elijah," Eros said, sounding a little panicked.

"Yeah, Elijah was brilliant tonight—it's a shame you couldn't be there," I said, standing and quietly excusing myself from the table. "Viktoriya and I left a little early to grab dinner. We were just eating. The shows run late, and sometimes they run the sets twice, so Elijah will be playing host for a few more hours."

"What? I was there—what are you ... Oh, right, covert conversation. Love it," Eros replied, momentarily confused.

"But seriously, you need to listen. There is something you need to know about Elijah."

"I'm sure it can wait until tomorrow—you know I don't like gossip," I said, irritation creeping into my tone.

I walked to the other side of the room, turning toward the window and my back to the kitchen. "If it's important, he will tell me himself, but I can get the message to Elijah in the morning; no need to interrupt … things. Unless it's something like life-or-death?"

"It's important. Otherwise, I wouldn't interrupt you and Viktoriya," Eros said. I could tell they were frustrated and agitated. "I have no reason to think it's life or death."

"I can tell you're excited. I am, too," I said, trying to calm Eros down before they did something drastic. "I will talk to you and Elijah tomorrow, I should get back to Viktoriya."

"Two days ago, you could barely talk to her, and now you're acting like she's some divine cosmic entity," Eros snapped, their mockery thinly veiling frustration. "I will talk to you after your *"goddess"* leaves."

"Thank you. Good night. Now, my goddess awaits," I said, throwing their mockery back before I could stop the words from escaping.

I was afraid to turn around. There is no chance Viktoriya didn't hear that. There is no way I will ever be that lucky. It would only get worse if I waited any longer to turn around.

I turned around, and Viktoriya was standing in the center of the room, staring at me with a hungry look and a wild smirk on her lips. Her vest was off and folded on the countertop, and her shirt was unbuttoned and untucked from her skirt.

Yeah—she heard me.

I couldn't fathom a way to explain how I did and didn't mean it. It sounded mocking, because it was, but the mockery was intended for Eros, not her. Yet, I couldn't have said it if I didn't think of her as a goddess.

"Goddess?" Viktoriya asked, slowly sliding her hands to her hips and pulling her shirt open a few inches. "You were talking about me, yes?"

She was going to toy with me now. Then, I realized what I was seeing; it hit me in the face like a snowball in winter. Her warm, flushed pink skin, exposed through her open shirt. From the waistband of her skirt, inches below her navel, up to her neck. The periphery of her breasts in violet lace was partially exposed. Under the delicate lace, her chest slowly rose and fell with her breath.

"I … um … that was … Viktoriya," I stammered. I could only stammer. For all the world, I don't know if I could have plucked a word other than her name from my mind.

"Mark, tell me," Viktoriya teased with a pout, shifting her weight from one hip to the other. "Who is your goddess?"

"I *was* talking about you," I admitted, waves of warm embarrassment and feverish excitement washing over me. "But, I didn't mean for you to hear that, I wasn't …"

"Oh, I hear you. Now, you tell me—do you see a goddess?" Viktoriya said, sliding her hands up her stomach, fingertips brushing the edges of her shirt. Her hands paused atop her chest, parting the fabric a little more, revealing a hint more of herself. "Like the Greek sculptures in ancient temples?"

"You're far more beautiful than any marble statue," I said, a wave of emotion dissolving my hesitation. I stepped forward, my phone slipping from my hand. "If the devotees in those temples could see you, they would question why they ever saw beauty in those mundane statues and ask how they might worship you."

Viktoriya froze, her playful smirk fading into a look of startled, bashful surprise.

Her lips parted, and the edges of her ears flushed red. She broke eye contact, looking at the floor for a moment. When she looked back up, she was smiling. It was a smile of hers I had only seen faint hints of in the past. It wasn't mischievous, flirtatious, or playful—it was raw and yearning. She was breathing deeply as she bit her lower lip, slowly drawing her hands apart across her chest and lifting her shirt away from her body. In one graceful motion, she freed the shirt from her shoulders and slid it down her arms and back, dropping it on the floor behind her.

I watched her hands vanish behind her back. Then, seconds later, they reappeared as her skirt dropped off her hips, landing on the floor around her feet like a delicate statue's plinth. She stood before me like a reflection of sunset on ocean waves, or snow-covered apple trees—radiant, delicate, alive.

Breathtaking natural beauty, but so much more alive and vital. Only violet lace lingerie interrupted the soft curve of her body. The unexpected revelation and the figure standing before me staggered me.

"You would worship this goddess, yes? But do you see me?" Then, Viktoriya posed, placing her arms and hands into the assumed positions of the Venus de Milo; her Bugs Bunny socks and her laughter only enhanced the exquisite evocation.

"Viktoriya, you are the most beautiful person I have ever met. I see you. The Bugs Bunny socks really complete the image," I said, pushing past the knot in my chest, unable to hide my grin. The reverence spell cracked, and I couldn't help but mirror her laugh.

"What?" Viktoriya said, raising an eyebrow and feigning indignation, her voice playful again. "Even goddesses like Bugs Bunny and socks."

I stepped closer, our laughter softening as I reached out my hands to her. She answered by stepping forward into my arms. Gently, I enveloped her in my arms, her face level with mine as I kissed her. As our lips embraced, her hands deftly unbuttoned my shirt, unclasped my belt, and unbuttoned my pants. Breaking the embrace just long enough to allow her to remove my shirt and pants. We laughed together again when we discovered my shoes blocked my pants, momentarily trapping me. She stepped back, giggling at my vulnerability and inability to run.

Before I could think of the best solution, Viktoriya knelt on the floor in front of me. She looked up, holding eye contact as she reached out, placing her hands on my thighs. Then, she allowed her gaze to drift down my body as if studying my anatomy. Looking straight ahead now at my red boxer briefs, which were noticeably tighter than they were minutes ago.

"I see," she smirked. "You rise to greet me."

With care, Viktoriya slid her hands down my legs and freed my shoes from my feet and my pants from my ankles. She set the shoes and pants to the side and gracefully stood up, using my body to keep herself steady. She held my face in her hands, and I did the same, cradling hers. We stood, seeing and holding each other. Her fingers stroked my beard and caressed my face. I cradled her face, brushing her cheeks softly with my thumbs. The thrum of desire was persistent between us, but it was now mingling with waves of comfort and connection. We kissed once again, living in the feeling of her lips on mine, her tongue dancing with mine. Then she pulled back and smiled.

"Mark, I like how you make me feel. With you, I feel safe— but also like I can never pull you close enough, no matter how tight I hold you. It is hunger—so much more than I have ever known. Hungry for you. I need you to feed me. But also, I feel something else—patience, like we have time to savor each other," Viktoriya said. Then she whispered. "But I am not patient."

"Viktoriya, I feel it too. I—"

"Sshh, Mark," she murmured, pressing her hand gently over my mouth. "Don't speak. Hold it—just as I do. Don't say what can't be taken back."

"There's an old song by the Shirelles—it's a classic, do you know it?" I said, humming a few bars of "Will You Still Love Me Tomorrow."

"How do they say it?—Can I believe your magic sighs? Yes, I know this song. Who doesn't know this song? Let's see if you'll still love me tomorrow."

Without a word, and without reluctance, Viktoriya and I agreed on restraint. We didn't need to rush into what we both already felt, yet we both needed to know if those feelings would last the night. Instead, we found an unspoken compromise.

While she was in my arms, our bodies were as close as possible without occupying the same space. I asked if she would like to sit and watch a film. She nodded eagerly and asked me if I would like another beer, to which I also nodded.

While Viktoriya carried the half-full case of Chernihivske to the couch, I queued up one of my favorites—*What's Up, Doc?*—its choice inspired by her socks. We settled, bodies entwined, onto the couch, still comfortably undressed. Throughout the film, we grew familiar with the feel of one another's bodies and the ways they fit together.

When the movie ended, Viktoriya ordered a car for the ride home, insisting it would be ridiculous for me to escort her home only to come back. I tried to argue that it was my duty to be her protector and ensure her safe return to her father. That argument met with eye-rolls and laughter, which I mirrored. We dressed each other as we waited for the car—an unexpectedly intimate act.

When her car arrived, I offered the leftover takeout kebabs to Viktoriya, which she declined, but she accepted one of the few remaining cans of beer to take home. I walked her to the street, kissed her goodnight, and watched as she stepped into the back seat and disappeared down the road.

I stood on the curb after her car pulled away, her kiss and touch lingering on my skin and in my mind. The night grew a little colder without her, but I didn't feel it right then. I felt only her absence, and the electrifying anticipation of tomorrow—and of what it might mean.

Chapter 9

I was both profoundly frustrated by Mark's idiocy and quietly impressed by how he handled himself with Viktoriya. Over my countless years of observation, I've witnessed both catastrophically disastrous and legendarily successful first dates. This might just be one of my favorites. Viktoriya and Mark shared a powerful, effortless connection. The night could have been spoiled had Elijah pressed his claim at the club, but he didn't, because I believe he valued Mark's happiness more than his own. Perhaps Elijah is right to let it lie, and Mark is right that I should leave it to Elijah to reveal. I could accept being incorrect, but I didn't have to like it.

After Mark ended our faux phone call, I settled into a fly-on-the-wall, voyeuristic role, ready to retreat to grant him a modicum of respectful privacy. I would have left as soon as it became clear what Viktoriya was initiating, but their awkward yet disarming affection held me captive. Before I knew it, I didn't feel the need to leave, so I settled in with Mark and Viktoriya to watch a fantastic film. I couldn't claim to understand all of it, but *What's Up, Doc?* was utterly delightful—I can't recommend it highly enough. I'm also beginning to realize that Mark has impeccable taste—though you'd never guess it by looking at him. I stayed in the apartment while Mark walked Viktoriya out, not that Mark would know if I was with him or not.

A few minutes later, Mark came back. After walking in the door, he walked over to his small, unorganized collection of vinyl records. He searched for a few seconds before pulling out a square sleeve featuring the image of a solitary woman. I didn't recognize her, but there was no reason I should—she seemed an interesting contradiction. But the title I remembered from my first night exploring Mark's apartment, Amy Winehouse's *Lioness: Hidden Treasures*. He opened his compact record player, gently set the black vinyl on the spindle, and flipped the switch. A moment later, a rich hum filled the apartment as a prelude to a soulful rendition of "Will You Still Love Me Tomorrow?" Hearing this song for the first time, I understood the deeper meaning and feeling of Mark and Viktoriya's brief reference earlier. I was losing count of the times I had been surprised by Mark, and humans in general tonight.

Mark drifted through his apartment, softly singing along as he tucked the leftover food and remaining beer into the refrigerator. He washed the beer glasses and set them aside to dry, and in an apparent need to keep moving, he wiped down the countertop. In truth, he was less cleaning than channeling his pent-up anxieties—keeping busy to prolong the lingering warmth of what had just transpired. I suspected he was also delaying the conversation he had promised me. On cue, Mark picked up his phone from the floor where he had dropped it around two hours ago. He looked at it hesitantly, then smiled at Viktoriya's message: she was home safe and, though what she felt scared her, she couldn't wait to feel that fear again in his arms. Mark replied, saying he was glad she got home safely, and he felt frightened too, in the best way possible. Finally, he promised to see her for coffee in the morning, and that he'd bring his arms for her.

"Eros, are you around?" Mark asked.

"Yes, I'm still here, Mark. Are you ready to talk?" I said through the speaker on the phone in his hand.

"I know I promised, but it was such a good night—I don't want to spoil it. I just want to sit with this feeling for now. Can it wait until morning?"

"I understand. I have no reason to think it can't wait. You really impressed me tonight, Mark. I know it was not your intent, but I also enjoyed myself more tonight than I have in a very, *very*, long time."

"Thank you, Eros. I'm glad you enjoy—wait, how much did you see?"

"Mark, I saw everything—and respectfully, you've got a great body and an even better ass."

"Jesus Christ, Eros. You, Viktoriya, and Elijah really are a matched set. But thanks for the compliment—and for keeping your distance."

"You're welcome, Mark. Before you call it a night, can you put on another record? I've missed really good music."

"You've got it. I know just where to start. Allow me to introduce you to Billy Joel."

Mark seemed happy—not just pleased, but radiating a hopeful kind of joy as he dashed to the records. He pulled out an album called *Cold Spring Harbor* and exchanged the record on the turntable, gently re-sleeving the Amy Winehouse album. He flipped the switch and introduced me to the rich musical poetry of Billy Joel. I thoroughly enjoyed the variety between songs and the surprisingly clever, resonant lyrical narratives. Mark moved around his apartment to songs so familiar they seemed knit into his bones. He flipped the record halfway through, then washed up and changed into clothes more comfortable for sleep. When the first album came to an end, he exchanged it for one called *The Bridge*, and I was treated to a new musical evolution. Halfway through "This Is the Time," there was a knock at the door.

"Shit, I hope the music wasn't too loud," Mark muttered, hurrying to lower the volume before opening the door—where a slightly worse-for-wear Fanny Ryesand stood waiting. This could be bad. "Elijah—sorry, Fanny—hey. Get in here before the neighbors think I've hired a call girl. What are you doing here?"

"Oh, Mark, I had to get out of there," Elijah said, dropping his Fanny Ryesand persona as he stepped inside. "I had to get out of there. Those new queens still haven't learned to share the dressing room, and I'm too dead-tired to wait for them to figure it out. And don't worry about your neighbors—they already know you couldn't afford me."

"I can't say I blame you. It looks like the rest of the show was a little rough. You forgot your bag," Mark said as he closed the door behind Elijah and walked to his fridge. "I've got a few beers and some leftover takeout if you're hungry."

"Thank you, maybe later. My stuff is hostage in the dressing room. You still have my spares here?" Elijah said, settling down on a stool at the kitchen counter while kicking off his heels. "And my backup clothes? I need to untuck and get out of this dress."

"Of course I do. Your spare clothes are still in my closet where you left them. And you have two tackle boxes under the bathroom sink. I replaced your cold cream and micellar water—you were almost out, and I finished the last of it." Mark said, closing the fridge. "I'm offended you even asked—as if I'd toss it out. Although that dress you left in my closet might be a candidate."

"Thank you, Mark. I knew I could rely on you—and trust you." Elijah said warmly, dropping his usual snark. I had to intervene to at least warn Mark what might happen. As before, I rang Mark's phone.

"Get yourself cleaned up. I put a bottle of adhesive remover that won't burn if you need it for the tape residue," Mark said while picking his phone up off the coffee table to see who was calling. "Hey, Elijah, you're welcome to the shower, I'm going to step outside to answer this."

"All right, thanks Mark," Elijah said, sliding off the stool and waddling into the bathroom.

"Eros, what is wrong?" Mark said, lifting the phone to his ear.

"I know we agreed to talk in the morning, but Elijah showing up changes things. There is something you need to know. And why does he need adhesive remover? Why do you keep his spare clothes in your closet? Also, I'm really enjoying the music—please don't forget to flip the record," I blurted out too quickly, afraid Mark might cut me off.

"I'm glad you're enjoying the records. Yes, I'll flip it. I keep some of his spare clothes in my closet because that's where I keep clothing. They are here in case of emergencies, and because we are less than two blocks away from the club, and he's my best friend, so of course. The adhesive remover is for the tape he uses to tuck. I'm not going to explain that right now," Mark said through a groan. "And like I said earlier—does this involve life or death? Is anyone in danger?"

"Tuck? Fine. I'll look it up later. No, no one is in danger, not physically. Maybe emotional danger—something that could, you know, feel like life or death. But no. No imminent danger," I said. "We were going to talk about it in the morning, but he is here now, and I don't want you blindsided if he says what I think he might."

"I can appreciate your concern. Tell me this: if you warn me—if you share whatever secret you think Elijah might drop on me—will it change anything? Will my knowing make anything better—or worse?" Mark asked, making a valid point.

"I don't think it would change anything," I begrudgingly admitted. "But I'm also worried about him. "I don't want either of you getting hurt. You are my friend; he is yours, and I'm fond of him."

"You are my friend too," Mark said calmly. "That means trusting each other. If there's something Elijah needs to tell me, he will, when he's ready. And then I'll deal with it the best I can. You and I just need to trust him. I appreciate you looking out for us. I'm going to go back inside to flip that record for you."

Keeping up the act, Mark tapped his phone screen to end the imaginary call. He was either committed to the bit or just on autopilot. He walked back inside as "Baby Grand" was ending. It sounded good—I made a mental note to ask Mark to play it again sometime. Mark walked over to the record player and flipped the record for me. With Elijah in the shower, Mark didn't have much to do, so he grabbed a beer, sank into the couch, and listened to the music with me.

Mark

Elijah showing up after a show wasn't unusual—but arriving still in full drag was.

The heels, the dress, the tuck—none of it was meant for walking two blocks to my door. Not unless something was wrong.

His story didn't add up. That was his club. Everyone on that stage knew it. They'd never push him out of the dressing room—and he'd never stand for it.

Something Viktoriya mentioned about his performance came to mind. Could that be what this was about? I replayed his performance in my mind: the way he seemed to crumble on stage, the raw emotion in his eyes as he sang. At the time, I thought it was just a stellar performance—but now, I'm not so sure.

Was it more than that? Did I miss something important? I couldn't help but feel like I was missing something. Regardless, when Elijah came out of the shower, I was going to get some answers—if he was ready to talk.

Here I was on the tail end of what might have been a perfect night, enjoying a Ukrainian beer, Viktoriya's presence still lingering in the apartment. I sat listening to "Big Man on Mulberry Street," caught in an unusual sort of cosmic awareness.

The brass instruments swelled as Billy Joel sang about a man caught between his dreams and his reality. Self-sabotaged by his worst impulses and insecurities. For some reason, the duality struck a chord tonight. Maybe it was because I couldn't shake the feeling that Elijah was wrestling with something, that he was carrying a burden he needed to share. The music fit the moment in a way I couldn't explain. Now I was waiting for my best friend to get out of the shower to tell me what's bothering him. Life can be strange—beautiful, complicated, messy, and wonderfully so. I don't know what Elijah's going to say when he comes out of the bathroom. Maybe he'll tell me it's nothing, that I'm overthinking things. But I know Elijah needs me. I want to be here for him, and I will be. That's why he's here.

The water cut off about the time the song reached the outro. Leave it to Elijah to be theatrically dramatic even when he isn't trying. I had to laugh as he opened the bathroom door and stepped out of the steam, dripping wet, wearing only a towel wrapped around his waist, to the song "Temptation." It just happened to be the next song on the album. Nevertheless, the image he struck with a sultry saxophone introduction was the right amount of fantastic for him. He walked into the kitchen, opened the fridge, and finally looked up at me.

"Does your offer of a beer still stand?" Elijah asked, retrieving a can of beer from the fridge.

"Of course," I said. "Always, you know you don't need to ask."

"Billy Joel—*The Bridge*. That date either went really well," Elijah said, dropping onto the couch beside me, "or it went very wrong. Which is it? Spill the tea, sweetie."

"Beyond very well. I don't even know how to explain it. It just clicked on every level. You saw Viktoriya, met her, she just draws you in," I said, feeling every moment of the night. "I should thank you. You encouraged me to bring her, and that performance of yours. She was really taken by your act. But come on, you don't really want to hear about my date. You're just being polite, so I don't feel bad about you wanting to talk about your show."

"No, Mark … I do want to hear about it. Honestly," Elijah said. There was something in his voice, as though for the first time, he wanted to talk about anything other than his show. "You seem happy, and I demand you tell me why."

"All right, we picked up some takeout and came back here. We talked, and she taught me these Ukrainian toasts. You'd love it. And we talked about the show," I explained, humoring Elijah, but I was growing concerned. "She's incredibly insightful. She asked if I knew who the man was that you were singing to. She said, 'He loves someone very much, I hope he tells them soon.' I said I hope he does too, and I don't know why my best friend hasn't told me about him yet."

"Shit … Mark. You found a good one, that's for sure. She picked that up. Maybe she picked up more than she said," Elijah said, hurt edging his voice. "You should keep her around—she catches the things you don't."

"Everything I miss? Elijah … that wasn't just a joke, was it? She's right, isn't she?" I said, more statement than question.

His crack about my "missing everything" stung—the kind that lands when it's too close to the truth. This wasn't Elijah teasing—it was a cover for something wrong.

"Mark, you don't want to hear it. You should let it go," Elijah said, then took a long drink from his can of beer.

"No, Elijah, I *really* do want to hear about it," I said, heat rising as I stood and turned to face him. "Talk to me."

He wouldn't meet my eyes. His thumb scraped at the can's paint, his shoulders drawn tight.

"Not now, Mark. Let it go," Elijah snapped. "How did your night with Viktoriya end?"

"Oh no, don't change the subject. I'll tell you how my date ended after you explain what I supposedly missed," I said.

He still wouldn't look at me; guilt flared, ugly and fast. My heart was pounding in my chest. He scraped the can to a patch of bare aluminum. "That performance was for someone. Who was it for, Elijah?"

"Why, Mark? Why won't you drop it? You think you can fix this? You can't fix everything, Mark. You're amazing, but equally oblivious and stubborn," Elijah snapped. Now he was staring daggers at me. "Stop being stupid! You kissed Viktoriya in the middle of my set and ruined—"

"Shut up and spit it out, you walking brisket! I don't care if I can't fix it. I still care. Put on the damn wig and dress if it helps you find the balls to say it!" I snapped back, matching his tone and meeting his stare.

It was harsher and meaner than he deserved—or than I'd intended. I was hurt and upset, so was he, and I still didn't understand why. He looked shocked and hurt. I had never said anything intentionally hurtful to him like that before. I immediately regretted it.

"Elijah, I'm sorry—"

"You're such a son of a bitch, you know that?" Elijah said, his voice trembling on the edge of collapse. He tore his gaze away from me and fixed it on his feet. His head hung between his shoulders as if the weight of unsaid words were crushing him. "It's you. It's been you all along. That entire performance—every word of it—was for you!"

His words passed through me, leaving me stunned like a gut punch. Shock swirled inside me, a tangled mess of confusion, panic, and recognition.

"That's why you wanted me there so badly," I said, more to myself than to Elijah. I was pacing in the kitchen now, searching for grounding. I couldn't believe what I was hearing. Instinct burned to argue, to push the question aside, lock it away. The confusion and fear strangled something deeper I couldn't touch. "Why did you tell me to bring—"

"When I told you to bring her along," Elijah cut me off, like he couldn't stop the flood pouring out of him, threatening to drown me. "I didn't think—"

"You didn't think?" I snapped, the words sharper than he deserved. Elijah flinched, but he didn't look away. "You know I'm not gay!"

My voice strained, and I hated how small it sounded. Small and terrified. My chest tightened, a vice closing around my lungs, making breathing harder and harder. My heart was pounding, a frantic rhythm I couldn't control.

"Don't kid yourself," Elijah snapped back, slamming his beer can down on the coffee table. He stood up, staring directly at me, looking through me. "Of course I know you're not gay. But I also know you—and you sure as hell aren't straight."

"Oh! You know me better than I know myself," I shouted at Elijah. Something inside me was afraid, something that whispered that Elijah might be right. "Then why didn't you just tell me, instead of turning it into a performance?"

"I didn't need the performance? You really are oblivious. Think, Mark. When I say 'I love you,' what do you actually hear? What do you feel?" Elijah was choking the words out through tears for the second time tonight. "And when you say it back to me—shut up—don't answer because you are going to do what you do. You will find the best way you can think of to fix the problem and avoid hurting me. I don't *want* you to avoid hurting me. If I get hurt, that's the risk I'm taking."

"Dammit, Elijah, why now? Why tonight? Why *me*?" I cried, confusion and anger and fear all fighting for control inside me. Was I asking Elijah, or was I asking myself, and what was I afraid of? And I heard in the silence between our words, like some cosmic joke, the record had moved on to play "Code of Silence." An impassioned duet with Cyndi Lauper about unspoken secrets.

"Mark, you colossal idiot. We don't get to choose who we love—only what we do with it," Elijah said. Slowly regaining his composure, he stepped closer until he was standing right in front of me. His words cut like knives into my heart, his questions seeping inside through the gash, looking for the answers inside. "God, Mark ... it's exhausting, loving you."

His words crashed against the rocky shores of my heart, wearing away the fear, confusion, and walls of denial. A small, insistent voice whispered somewhere deep inside, in a secret place I'd spent years trying to bury. The universe mocked me through the lyrics—songs about the secrets we keep even from ourselves and the fears they awaken.

The realization clawed its way to the surface, sharp and unrelenting. Elijah's words hung in the air like smoke, refusing to dissipate. Echoing in my mind, unrelenting, pressing down on me with the weight of something I wasn't ready to face, except he was standing before me, and I had nowhere to hide anymore.

"Elijah, I …" I faltered. The code of silence had been broken. My legs felt weak as Elijah stood within arm's reach.

His chest rose and fell, still faintly wet, the remnants of silver glitter in his beard catching the light.

His eyes pierced me.

"I hear *you*," I said finally. My voice trembled, threatening to strangle the words before they could leave my mouth. "When you say, 'I love you,' I hear your words, your meaning, and your heart."

I paused, regaining a measure of my own composure. Fear of the truth of these words slowly vanished as they left my mouth.

"When I hear you, I feel happy, and I feel a joy that frightens me. It feels safe and honest." The weight of the admission settled in my chest. I kept talking before I lost my nerve, the words spilling out like water through a cracked dam. "And when I say it back, sometimes it feels like the only true thing I've ever said."

Then I knew, like a shock through my chest. Elijah stood there, his lips parted, his eyes shimmering with tears that he wasn't trying to hide anymore. His soft black hair was still wet, dripping onto his exposed shoulders. Water from his beard, which still retained hints of glitter, trickled down his smooth, freshly shaved chest. The light-caramel color of his skin was growing flushed as he inched even closer to me. My own heart was thundering, my mind racing with a million questions I didn't have answers to. But for the first time, I wasn't afraid of the truth I saw reflected in his eyes. He reached out to me, and I stepped into his arms, and he kissed me, and I kissed him back.

Our lips met like old friends at first, but quickly became lovers. I could feel his beard against mine. His hands were in my hair and on my back. While the space between us vanished as our bodies pressed against each other, his towel threatened to fall to the floor. The stirring inside me screamed of long-restrained desire, newly freed from captivity.

His kiss was a revelation; fear and confusion flared, then vanished. The parts of myself I'd denied for too long stepped into the light—into Elijah's embrace.

It was always there. Buried beneath the surface, my love, stronger than fear, emerged triumphantly with a kiss. I pulled him closer, deepening the embrace, years of emotion crashing between us. Then, through the noise, shock forced my will to step back out of the kiss.

"Elijah?" I asked, uncertainty breaking through my voice. "What happens now?"

"For now, Mark," Elijah said, all his anger and pain washed away. "We go to bed and solve that problem in the morning."

"Elijah, I want to—but Viktoriya—and I don't think I'm ready for …"

"I know, Mark," Elijah interrupted, his expression tender and welcoming, though his voice held the slightest tremble. "As much as I want to, I won't push. I know you are not ready. Tonight, I'm content if you let me hold you."

Chapter 10

The sun was just beginning to cast its light on the legendary events of the night before, and I was still in a state of quiet shock. Mark had relegated me to the role of passive observer—and, unwilling to break our agreement, I accepted. It was difficult to watch Mark drift so near disaster so many times in one evening, but he had acquitted himself admirably. I didn't know what I would have done to intervene if things had gone wrong. Not to mention, there were intricacies and conventions of this modern world and culture still unfamiliar to me. I could easily make things worse instead of better.

This was not my first exposure to a love triangle, although it was much more like a love "V" than a triangle. It was clear that Mark had feelings for both Viktoriya and Elijah—and that they felt the same for him. In my experience, such arrangements usually end one of three ways: with one or two people devastated—or dead. Or there are secret affairs, which always result in devastation. Nothing can destroy a relationship like secrets and jealousy. Suddenly, I had a fresh fear for Mark. I didn't think Viktoriya would actually stab him—but of the three, she's the one I could most easily imagine solving this problem with a knife's edge.

Of course, as I reminisced, I recalled polycules of all variations and shapes that had flourished, so they didn't always end in disaster. It was possible, if that is what Mark, Elijah, and Viktoriya wanted, but it was too soon for that conversation. To be honest, it would be difficult for me to hide my personal preference here.

I was very fond of all three of these humans, but I knew I didn't get to vote here. Also, I needed to spend some time with Mark's phone and the internet to learn more about modern cultural conventions. I'd hate to advocate for something modern humans find culturally repulsive.

The dawn light crawled through the bedroom window, illuminating the intertwined forms of Elijah and Mark. I had agreed to stay out of Mark's bedroom—he called it a private space, and it was a boundary I didn't violate lightly. I just couldn't help myself after the emotional firework display Mark and Elijah had put on last night. I had to see the fallout for myself. I was surprised to see Elijah had attempted to sleep while wearing his bath towel, which he was no longer wearing, and Mark had stripped down to the red boxer briefs Viktoriya had been fond of. If I have the metaphors correct, Mark was the "little spoon" in the arrangement, which was slightly amusing because he was slightly larger and more muscular than Elijah. Still, I must admit, they looked sweet and happy.

Mark stirred as the sunlight brushed his face. With closed eyes, he rolled out of Elijah's arms and out of the bed. I watched as he staggered out into the kitchen and added ground coffee and water to the coffee machine—which I knew was his first love— by rote muscle memory that didn't require sight or consciousness. Once he set the machine to brew what he called the elixir of life, he retreated to the bathroom. Say what you will about Mark—his priorities were beyond dispute.

When he emerged from the bathroom, I was pleased to see him shuffle to his desk where he retrieved his headset, slipping the sleek and barely noticeable audio device around his ears.

"Eros?" Mark said quietly through a staggering yawn. "Are you here?"

"Of course I'm here, Mark," I replied, but not through his headset—he hadn't even turned it on. "I have to show you something—you can hear me without your headset now. But first, how are you feeling, my friend?"

"Coffee first," Mark said, reaching for the empty mug that always waited on his dish rack. "Coffee, then brain. You can't make coffee, can you?"

"No, I don't think so. I can push or pull physical things, but I can't lift them. So, the best I could do is switch your machine on or off, and it already has a timer to do that. Sorry—wish I could," I said, and meant it. "Of all my few limitations, not being able to lift anything is the most frustrating. Speaking of limitations—take off your headset."

"Understandable—but you'd be unstoppable in zero-G," Mark said, grabbing his mug the moment a cup filled the carafe. "If you wanted to think of a silver lining."

"Oh no—well, technically yes, but only in a quantum–Newtonian sense. In reality, we're helpless in space—it's easy to end up somewhere I can't reach anything but particles of what your scientists call 'dark matter' or 'dark energy' and while it can be quite useful and powerful, it can take ages to use it to gain momentum. But I think that's a conversation for after coffee, and another morning," I said, stopping myself from overwhelming Mark with information I wasn't sure he could follow this morning while decaffeinated. "I suspect that is not the topic on your mind, and you should try taking off your headset—it isn't even on."

"It's not? Then how can I hear you?" Mark said, draining his small cup of coffee after he had cooled it with cold milk. He finally took off his headset, setting it aside. "I'm curious—but wouldn't be able to follow any explanation without at least five more cups. So, we'll shelve that question for now."

"In that case, do I need to ask what's on your mind?" I asked while Mark refilled his coffee mug and carried it over to his desk, where he sat picking up his phone with his free hand. "Returning to my first question: how are you feeling?"

"That's … complicated," Mark admitted. "Honestly, I'm feeling a lot of conflicting emotions. Waking up in Elijah's arms felt intoxicating, but the second I left the bed, it felt as though I had betrayed Viktoriya. Yet …" Mark hesitated, casually dismissing a day's worth of notifications on his phone.

"I understand, Mark," I said, attempting to sound reassuring, although I could only imagine his turmoil.

"I want to climb back into that bed, as much as I want to call …" Mark froze as he flipped to a few new messages from Viktoriya, the first of which was a picture. "Oh—uh—you can't see that, can you?"

On his phone was a picture of Viktoriya that she had sent him. There was nothing inherently inappropriate about the picture, yet there was something about her pose, expression, and strategic arrangement, or lack, of clothing, that even I had to admit was deeply provocative. She had one hand grasping a ball of dough as though she intended to extract a confession from it. Her lips hung partially open, and her eyes looked slightly surprised, staring directly at the camera in her other hand. To top it all off, she was wearing only her apron.

"I can see it. I don't know if I'm using this term correctly, but is that a thirst trap?" I asked Mark, who was staring at the picture on his phone like a young man seeing an attractive woman for the first time. "I think that's what they are called on the internet."

"That's a thirst trap all right," Mark said, snapping out of his daze. "A good one too … What am I going to do, Eros?"

"There are messages too—you haven't read those yet," I reminded Mark.

He closed the photo to reveal two messages: *'Thinking on you. Wish this was you.'* Then another: *'I have day off after baking. Come to kafe.'*

"I suppose you'll need to go see her."

"Please, Eros—help me." Mark's voice cracked with panic. "I don't know what to do."

"Mark, listen to me—breathe. Just breathe. You're in a sticky situation, yes, but you haven't done anything wrong. I need you to understand that," I said, my tone turning serious. Mark teetered on the edge of panic when he should have been, absurdly, overjoyed. "Right now you're a lucky idiot. Two people are crazy about you—and you're crazy about them. The last thing you should do is burn it all down out of fear. I've been around for billions of years; I've watched hundreds of millions of relationships, good and bad. What you have right now is one of the rarest, most precious things in the universe. So just exist in this moment where things are good. I'll do everything I can to help."

"Okay—okay. I'm here. I hear you. Thanks." Mark inhaled and exhaled slowly, gripping his mug with both hands as if it were his only tether to reality, his phone forgotten at his feet. "You're right. Things are good—Elijah's asleep in my bed, Viktoriya's waiting for me, and it looks like she made bread. This is all alien to me. How do I avoid ruining everything?"

"Brace yourself—you might not like this. Two-thirds of this is out of your control," I said firmly. I'd shake him by the shoulders if I could. "You could do everything right and it could still explode in your face—that's love. All you can do is be yourself: honest and kind. When Elijah wakes, tell him what you want, even if you don't fully know yet. Then do the same with Viktoriya."

"Eros—this would be so much easier if you could grant me a wish. Make me stop feeling for one of them, and make them stop feeling for me," Mark said, halfheartedly. I couldn't blame him—he felt as if he were standing on the edge of the highest cliff he'd ever seen, terrified of the fall. "You can't do that, can you?"

"No, Mark. I can't—and I wouldn't even if I could." I paused for a breath. "What you want—or think you want—is magic. Magic isn't real."

"Walk me through it all," Mark said, stepping back from the edge; his voice still held panic. "I could use something different to occupy my mind. Start with how I can hear you now."

"Okay, Mark. That one is easy. As long as I'm close enough, I can use your eardrum the same way I use the speakers of your headset. I remembered how ears work while we were listening to music last night. As for your "wish"—ethics aside, the difficulty of that is astronomical," I said slowly. "Without getting into technicalities I couldn't explain sober— I could do real damage. Think of your brain like billions of tiny wires. I could touch, move, or even sever them. I can do it—but I won't. You don't want unintended brain damage, and I won't risk causing it. So, while it's technically possible, it's practically impossible. Ethically, I can't strip away feelings or experiences—or manufacture them. We've discussed this before: I have a line I won't cross."

"You're the shittiest genie I've ever met," Mark said with a chuckle. That was a good sign that he was snapping out of it. "I get it. Even if you found precisely the right wire to sever, what gives you the right? It would fundamentally change us. But hold on—you said you wouldn't cross that line, again? Again?"

"Shit. Mark, that's a story for another time. But in short, I crossed that line once for what I thought was a good reason," I said. I hadn't meant to let that detail slip. It wasn't something I'm ashamed of, but not something I'm proud of either—and I worried it might frighten Mark. Even now, his brow was furrowing the way it did before he was about to ask a question he probably shouldn't have. "Please don't ask right now. I promise I'll tell you everything another time. The short story is I went too far manipulating the mind of a human. And I was punished with that lamp."

"Okay, that's not unsettling at all, Eros. I won't ask, but I'm holding you to that promise. But, question," Mark replied, sounding back to normal now. "You told me you were imprisoned because you created the genie myths and fables. So, which is it? And while we are on that topic, you never explained how that worked if magic and wishes aren't real."

"I'd hoped you'd forgotten about that. Look, we just met, and I didn't want to freak you out more than necessary. I didn't want you to be afraid I'd treat your mind like a playground," I explained, doing my best to remain patient. This isn't where I planned to take this conversation. "The lamp's a bit harder to explain, so bear with me. It had a 'quantum dark matter and energy' fence wrapped around it. I can't explain it any better than you can describe the color blue to someone who's colorblind. This 'fence' had a rudimentary consciousness—like a smart lock—with one job: to listen for someone to make a wish to set me free."

"You're saying you were locked behind a cosmic smart fence that only opened with a secret password? Kind of like the fables?"

"More or less, yes."

"Well, that was surprisingly straightforward," Mark said dryly, undercutting the serious tone of the conversation. He picked up his phone from the floor, set it on the desk, and took his mug to the kitchen to refill his coffee. "You could've just said all that from the start. I would've managed—but I get it; you didn't know me yet. Still, thanks for telling me, Eros—and for the distraction."

"You're welcome, Mark," I said, once again impressed by Mark's resilience and adaptability. "Thank you for understanding. So, what kind of bread do you think Viktoriya made?"

The Fixer, The Maker, The Drag Entertainer

****Mark****

Eros did a good job distracting me from what felt like an impending panic attack. They even made a few solid points. A large part of the outcome was outside my control. If one thing was clear, it was that Elijah, Viktoriya, and I all had choices to make. I couldn't control or predict the choices of Elijah or Viktoriya. I couldn't even predict my own. Honestly, I hadn't even contemplated all the possible choices I could make; I didn't even know what I wanted. The best thing I could do right now was to embrace the moment honestly. I wish I felt better about that. No matter how hard I tried, I couldn't exile the fear, guilt, and anxiety milling in the back of my mind and churning in my gut.

The time on my phone taunted me; it was early for a Sunday—around seven-thirty. I expect Elijah will wake up in about an hour, then we'll have to talk. I had one hour to plan exactly what I was going to say. Maybe I should write it down or brainstorm with Eros. Then I should reply to Viktoriya. At least with a text, I could overanalyze my response before sending it.

Or I'd open her message, see that picture again, and forget how to spell my own name. I'm definitely going to need help from Eros.

"You know, Eros, I'm not sure I noticed the bread in that picture," I replied to the question Eros left hanging, trying to keep my voice down. "How about giving me a hand with the reply?"

"I can do that," Eros said. "How about, 'Nice buns,' or, 'I knead you too'? Or maybe just a thumbs-up emoji?"

"Oh, you're worse at this than I am," I said, making a mental note to save that kneading pun for another time. "What if I send a picture back? Is that too much?"

"Yes. Do that. Do you have an apron? You could recreate her picture," Eros was getting excited. "How quickly could you make bread dough?"

"Making bread is off the table, I don't have flour, and it takes hours," I replied, equally excited. This was actually a great idea. The apron I would have to borrow was Elijah's, and it was frilled with lace, pink, and embellished with sequins. "She won't notice the lack of bread once she sees the apron. It's Elijah's, so I'll have to sneak it out of the closet."

I walked into the bedroom as quietly as possible. Elijah was snoring softly, dead to the world. I thought about waking him to help me, and a pang of guilt twisted in my gut. Was this a good idea? Flirting with Viktoriya in Elijah's apron felt a little wrong. Maybe—but I knew Elijah. This is exactly the kind of thing he would do. I would just take the picture, but I'd wait to send it—at least until after we talk. I opened the closet door quietly and retrieved the apron before my decision paralysis could set in. Then I slipped out, closing the bedroom door carefully behind me.

"All right, Eros, help me out," I whispered, slipping the apron over my head and cinching it tight around my waist. Then, as a final touch, I grabbed the half-loaf of sandwich bread from the top of my fridge and tossed it on the counter, pulling a few slices out. "I'll need you to watch the phone screen, help me get the pose right, and take the picture. You can handle that, right?"

"Yes, I can. Open her picture again," Eros said quickly.

I opened Viktoriya's picture again and studied her pose. It was hard to focus without getting distracted by the glimpses of strategically bare skin peeking out from beneath her apron.

"Good, Mark—lose the underpants," Eros said. "Plant one hand on that bread, open the camera and hold it up."

"Right, pants off, hand on bread," I repeated, shucking my underpants off beneath the apron.

I opened the camera app on my phone, set my hand down on top of two slices of bread, and held the phone out. "Like this?"

"Yes, good. Turn your body a little to the left, tilt the phone slightly to the right. Look down a bit, good. Now, act surprised, like she just walked into the room," Eros directed. I followed their instructions—turned my body, angled the phone, looked down, then back up, acting surprised. I didn't have to fake the surprise—because right at that moment, Elijah walked around the corner into the kitchen, and the camera shutter clicked as Eros took the picture.

"Perfect! Got it. Oh, you're going to love—oh. Oh … oh no. I'm sorry, Mark."

"Mark?" Elijah mumbled, still half-asleep. He blinked hard, squinting at me. Then at the bread. Then back at me. "Is that my apron?"

"It's not what it looks like," I stammered through my desperate embarrassment. "I can explain—"

"Oh, Mark, I'm sorry, but I don't think you're considering what this actually looks like," Eros whispered in my ear while Elijah was crossing his arms in the flamingo kimono I'd forgotten he kept here.

"It looks like you borrowed my apron—one of my favorites, by the way," Elijah said, his theatrical tone building momentum. "And you are taking *naked* thirst-trap pictures … in your *kitchen* … behind *my* back."

"He has a point, Mark," Eros whispered again, then, to my horror, they snapped another picture, drawing our attention to the phone, which I was still holding in my outstretched hand. "OH! That might be the *BEST* picture yet."

"I … I … um … oh God," I stammered, my vision blurring. I dropped the phone like it was radioactive, watching in horror as it bounced, landing face up in front of Elijah, displaying my recent questionable life choice. "Is there *any* chance we pretend this didn't—"

"Not even the hint of a chance," Elijah said, picking up my phone from the floor and scrolling through the pictures. "Oh, the betrayal! This will not be ignored, Mark. Hm—that's a good angle. You took quite a few, didn't you? Oh, I see. Viktoriya. This was all for her then."

"… A *few* pictures …" I mumbled, directing my ire toward Eros. "Elijah, let me exp—"

"Explain? Let me try. You received this, frankly stunning, picture from Viktoriya this morning. Then you decided the *best* response was to recreate it in response. With *my apron*, while I was asleep in your bed," Elijah said with a dramatic flair, clutching my phone to his chest. "I've caught you … naked. Bread-handed, Mark Williams."

"BREAD-handed!" Eros roared, his laughter drowning out my rising embarrassment. The otherworldly, infectious cackle spread through me like wildfire.

My attempts to suppress the giggles were futile; within seconds, I was doubled over in uncontrollable laughter.

"I'm—sorry—Elijah—I just—" I gasped between laughs that nearly had me collapsing to my knees.

"Dammit Mark. You're too cute. Did you save me coffee?" Elijah said, dropping all pretense of being upset, offended, or hurt. Elijah set my phone down on the counter beside me, then grabbed his favorite mug from the cabinet and filled it with coffee. "You better send me those pictures. It's only fair, and that apron goes back into the closet, unscathed."

"Okay. Okay," I said, gaining control over myself and my laughter. A faint pang of guilt and uncertainty returned. I couldn't shake the worry that Elijah's lightheartedness masked a hint of hurt. I knew I had to do the thing I was dreading; I would have to have a serious conversation with Elijah. "I'll hang this in the closet. Then I guess we need to talk?"

"We do. Later. No serious talking before coffee. You know the rules. Now, give me a twirl before you put your pants on," Elijah said, nodding as he sipped his coffee, twirling a finger in the air. "Now, let me get a good look at you."

I laughed, feeling a sense of relief, and twirled, causing the apron hem to rise provocatively as I left the kitchen. The hard conversations would come, but not right now. There was no need to force it.

"That could have gone worse," Eros said. "I'm sorry I let that happen."

"It's not your fault," I whispered as I entered the bedroom and returned Elijah's apron to the closet, where it belonged. "We both got caught up in the moment. It turned out okay, I think. So … how many pictures did you actually take?"

"Oh, about fourteen. I found the filters and effects—I was exploring my artistic side," Eros said, almost bashfully.

"Good for you," I replied earnestly, picking out my usual nondescript, comfortable clothes and beginning to dress. "I'm looking forward to seeing—Oh, I didn't pick up my phone, it's still in the kitchen."

"Mark, are you sure Elijah's really okay? You know him better than I do," Eros asked softly. From the other room, I heard Elijah put on a record, filling the apartment with the acoustic energy of David Bowie's *Hunky Dory.* "What is *that?* Shut up—I have to hear this."

"That, Eros, is Bowie—another powerful cosmic entity," I said with a grin. If Elijah was playing Bowie, he was in a good mood—and he knew it always cheered me up. "You know, the world went wrong the day people stopped trying to become David Bowie."

I had no choice now but to dance my way out of the bedroom to "Changes," to meet Elijah mid-lip-sync on the coffee table. We danced together. Lip-syncing, laughing, reveling in the familiar comfort of each other, through the end of "Oh! You Pretty Things." When that song ended, we both retreated to the kitchen to refill our coffee and laugh together.

I picked up my phone from the counter. It wasn't exactly where Elijah had set it down minutes ago. I flipped through Eros's photos—mostly the same pose, each one dressed up in a different filter or effect. My favorite was a black-and-white vignette that had a timeless artistic quality. I switched to Viktoriya's text message to send her that picture—and, to my surprise, it had already been sent.

"Did you send this picture to Viktoriya?" I asked Eros and Elijah.

"No," Eros said.

"Yes," Elijah said at the same time. "I knew you'd overthink it and take forever. You'd already kept the poor girl waiting long enough."

"I was afraid you'd be upset—" I said, but Elijah cut me off midway through.

"Stop. Yeah, it stung a little. But I'm not that selfish," Elijah said, setting his coffee down and crossing the space to pull me into a hug. "Besides, she invited you to brunch—and you're taking me. We'll figure things out."

"It's really unfair how well you know me, and she didn't actually say brunch," I said, leaning into his arms, deepening my conflicted emotions. "You need to know this is confusing for me—having feelings for both you and Viktoriya."

"Focus, Mark. Brunch. Nothing stands between a gay man and brunch," Elijah said, kissing me gently on the forehead. "We can talk on the walk to my house. I understand it's going to be a minute for you. But please, let yourself enjoy a moment every now and then. I'm going to get dressed. I'm borrowing your suitcase to take my wig and pads home."

Elijah pirouetted out of the kitchen, a more eloquent and suggestively provocative mimic of my previous exit. I held my breath reflexively, watching the kimono rise and open, offering the briefest of glimpses of Elijah's body beneath the flamingos. I exhaled hard the moment the bedroom door closed behind him.

A tempest of tangled emotions churned beneath the surface, held in check by Elijah's quiet understanding.

I didn't know what I was going to do. Naturally, I made a mental list of every possible option and outcome. I ran out of imaginary paper fast. Clearly, I didn't understand all the variables yet. So, I started a new list—my top priorities: Don't hurt Elijah. Don't hurt Viktoriya. Try not to hurt myself. And eat brunch.

"Mark, Viktoriya replied," Eros whispered. I was so deep in thought that I didn't hear my phone's notification. "You're going to want to read this."

"Oh, I … shit," I gasped, staring at her response. *'Wish I was bread. Come here. I knead you.'*

"She. Used. My. Joke," Eros gasped. "Mark, you're doomed. She's going to eat you alive."

As unhelpful as Eros' commentary was in that moment, I had to admit they weren't wrong. I was in trouble. I just didn't know if it was good or bad trouble. I was admittedly eager to find out. Suddenly, a sense of urgency to rush out the door, with or without shoes, filled my mind. Mindful of the walk, I decided which shoes were the most prudent of options, and I had to wait for Elijah. I met Elijah in the bedroom; he was packing my small suitcase with his wig, pads, shoes, and dress. I tossed my phone down onto the bed. Viktoriya's message was still open on the screen, and I sat down to slip socks and shoes onto my feet. He glanced at my phone, and an involuntary squeal escaped him.

"She *KNEADS* you," Elijah said, snatching the phone off the bed. "Mark, you are in trouble."

"Shit. Shit. Shit," I cursed, fumbling with my shoelaces. "I didn't mean for you to see that."

"No, it's okay, Mark. I sent the picture, I deserve to see the response," Elijah said, scrolling through the messages. "Look, Mark, I know you have some things to figure out. I have my own hopes here, but I promise you now, I won't interfere with Viktoriya. I won't do that to you."

"Thanks, but I honestly don't know what I'm doing. It feels like I'm the passenger, not the driver," I said. For once, honesty came easy—Elijah made me feel safe. "I don't understand what I'm feeling, and everything is happening so fast."

"That is partly my fault," Elijah said, sitting down on the bed next to me. "I've felt this way about you for a long time. I had so many chances to say something, but by the time I did, I was late to the party—though I guess that shouldn't surprise you. A drag queen showing up late—classic. I know you want to argue, but just listen. I made assumptions—about you, about how you felt, how you'd react. It never occurred to me, in all these years, to ask. I assumed you were comfortable with your pansexuality."

"I'm not pansexual—or bisexual," I blurted out. "I mean … I don't think so. I don't know. Honestly, I just don't know."

"Oh—wow. Okay. I didn't mean …" Elijah said softly, his face a mix of shock, confusion, and disbelief. "I guess you're still working that out. I'm here, Mark. I wish I understood what you're feeling, but I can try."

"Thank you, Elijah, but you're not the only one who made assumptions," I said, resting my hand on top of Elijah's. "I'm not blameless. I always flirted back—I should've seen you, recognized the signs. Now, I'm between two people I care for, and the last thing I want is to hurt you or Viktoriya. I have to consider her feelings now too, and I have no clue how or when to talk to her about this."

"Stop thinking for now," Elijah said, standing and pulling me up. "Let's get brunch—we'll talk it out."

Once again, Elijah had pulled me back from the brink of an emotional crisis, but he inadvertently introduced an entirely new question. Was I pansexual or bisexual? It was a question I'd never really faced. At the moment, I wasn't even sure how I could know the answer to that question. While we gathered our belongings and left my apartment, I rolled the question around in my mind.

Did I feel differently about men and women, or was it the same? Was sexuality intrinsic, or was it a matter of preference— like choosing a favorite drink? Some people always wanted the same thing; I'd just never thought much about my own. And yet … I'd always felt like maybe I could choose. But that wasn't right, was it? No one chooses their orientation. So why did it feel like I could? How could I have never reflected on those feelings before? I had a thousand questions—and no idea how to ask even one.

Chapter 11

Mark and Elijah stepped out of the building into what they both agreed was a perfect day for a walk. The temperature was perfect—not too warm, not too cool, not too humid—with just the right balance of sunlight and drifting cloud cover. A slight breeze from the west carried a freshness from the nearby, vaguely rural farmland and parks, replacing the usual stale cocktail of suburban city air. Maybe it was the kind of day for a picnic by the river—or a drive out to Point Comfort. But no—Mark preferred the Sandy Hook side of Highlands; it was quieter. Elijah agreed. It was quieter there, and the air off the Atlantic always smelled cleaner than the bay.

Then came the grating sound of hard plastic suitcase wheels scraping and clunking against the sidewalk. Paired with their mundane chatter about nothing, it was enough to drive me mad.

The only saving grace? The moment right after they walked out of the building, when Mark paused for just a second on the spot where Viktoriya kissed him goodnight. A tiny, lingering smile flickered across his face. A sigh escaped him, so soft I almost missed it, but I didn't.

"Mark," I whispered in his ear. "Please—this conversation, on top of that damned suitcase, is going to drive me insane."

"I like it. Walking, idle conversation about nothing," Mark said out loud, mostly to me but also to Elijah. "When it's with someone you care about, it's like checking in. You're telling each other how you feel in the moment without saying it directly."

"Weird thing to say," Elijah replied with a sideways glance, sounding amused. "You're not wrong—it was just weird to say out of the blue."

"Yeah, I know, sorry," Mark said with a shrug. "It was just a thought that crossed my mind, and I think it might be good for me to practice letting a few of my thoughts and feelings out now and then."

"Okay, Mark," I said. "Good answer, and cover … Hey, you should talk about that Bowie musician. I want to know more about him."

"If you're trying to convince me you're too weird for me, it's not working," Elijah said with a chuckle, playfully bumping Mark as they walked side by side. "All right, if you're in a sharing mood. You never did spill the tea about how your date with Viktoriya really ended. I want all the details."

It wasn't the conversation I wanted—which was rude—but it was the one they needed. Mark shrugged and then smiled. He told Elijah everything. The simple walk for kebabs. How Viktoriya led him to pick out Ukrainian beer. And how something about her presence made everything feel just a little more magical. Elijah listened intently, occasionally reacting with amusement or approval. Mark recalled her gentle critique of his apartment décor, and how it made him like the space more. Then Mark recited the toasts Viktoriya had taught him, pronouncing and translating them almost perfectly. "Za zustrich"—for our meeting. "Za shchastya"—for happiness. "Za lyubov"—for love. Elijah sighed, saying he liked those and would have to use them.

The conversation shifted to Viktoriya's curiosity about drag, which Mark thought could easily become an obsession for her.

But she was also very curious about Elijah, particularly who he was really singing to. Elijah wasn't surprised this time. He mentioned that he remembered that part from last night. Finally, Mark recounted the "phone call" where she overheard him call her a goddess. And in the moments after, when she unraveled before Mark's eyes, he saw her. She was not just beautiful, but vulnerable, unguarded, taking the risk of getting hurt. And then, at the pinnacle of it all, "Will You Still Love Me Tomorrow?" came up, and Viktoriya stopped him from saying the words he couldn't take back, and together they restrained their impulses. Elijah, who had been nodding along, suddenly froze. His jaw nearly hit the pavement beside the suitcase.

"I don't know if I'm jealous, envious, or just impressed," Elijah said finally, dragging his gaze up and down Mark like he was re-evaluating everything he thought he knew about him. "I applaud your restraint—and hers, for that matter. I don't know if I could have … well, never mind. Those are inside thoughts."

"You *are* an inside thought, Elijah," Mark teased.

That … made absolutely no sense to me. But Elijah laughed, so apparently it made sense to him—and was funny.

"So," Elijah said after collecting himself. "After all that, then what? Did you stare at each other, half naked, for the rest of the night?"

"Not quite," Mark laughed. "We watched *What's Up, Doc?* before she went home."

"I mean, great choice, obviously. No arguments here. But, why?" Elijah said, blinking and staring at Mark.

"First, as you know, one never needs an excuse," Mark said, half-chiding. "But it was her socks."

"Her … what?"

"Her socks," Mark said, grinning. "She was wearing Bugs Bunny socks."

Elijah stared. Blinked. Stared again.

"Bugs. Bunny. Socks," Elijah repeated, exhaling a mix between a sigh and a whistle. "Mark, I might be attracted to a woman for the first time in my life."

"You do have good taste," Mark agreed.

"But you can't flatter your way out of explaining," Elijah said, steering the conversation back on track. "You came dangerously close to saying you *love* her?"

"Yeah, I don't know," Mark said, sheepish but unashamed. "In that moment, it was right there. If I'd said it, I would've meant it. I don't say it unless I mean it."

Elijah nodded, absorbing the information. He was sharp, as was Mark, and I'm certain he caught what Mark was really saying—and what it meant. He was quiet for the remainder of the walk across the bridge over the river. I could tell he was mulling over the events of last night, and what Mark had just revealed to him, putting the pieces together.

"It makes sense now," Elijah finally said, breaking the silence.

"What makes sense?" Mark asked.

"The way you reacted last night," Elijah said gently. "I mean. You were already on the edge—and then I crashed down on you."

Mark didn't react at first, then he released a long, slow breath. "... Yeah."

Elijah stopped walking, gently pulling Mark to a halt beside him.

"I know I already said it, but I need to be clear," Elijah said, meeting and holding Mark's gaze. "I won't come between you and Viktoriya—but I'm not ready to give up on you. On us. Not yet. I'm not pushing you to choose, but I won't lie and say I'm giving up. You need time, and you should take it. And I mean this—I'm not going anywhere."

"Thank you—"

"Besides," Elijah said with a smirk, ruffling Mark's hair, "if I have to lose you to someone, at least they've got fantastic taste in socks."

He gently smoothed Mark's hair back into place, then leaned in and kissed him softly. It was a genuinely tender, intimate moment beneath the old oak by the riverbank.

Both Mark and Elijah remained silent the remainder of their walk, but they did now walk hand-in-hand the last four blocks to Elijah's house. To be more exact, Elijah's apartment was above the detached garage of his family's house. In front of the garage was an old delivery van with "Zayde's Delicatessen" hand-painted on the side. Leaning against the van was a man who looked remarkably similar to Elijah, smoking a cigarette and wearing an off-white apron.

"Eli, Shabbat shalom," said the Elijah look-alike with a hint of irony.

"Shalom, Tevil. That was yesterday—you've got your Sabbaths confused again, brother," Elijah said, pulling his brother into a hug. "You remember Mark?"

"Of course that was yesterday, but I didn't see you. I have a proper job, remember—and the gentiles can't go without their Saturday bagel," Tevil said, releasing the hug to take a drag from his cigarette.

"I remember Mark, come here you get a hug too."

"Good morning, Tevil," Mark said, hugging Elijah's brother fondly. "It's true, we do love our bagels on Saturday."

"Speaking of proper jobs, why are you here?" Elijah asked.

"The van—I've got a delivery to make," Tevil said, jerking a thumb over his shoulder. "And you know how Mom and Dad hate smoking near the deli. 'The customers smell the smoke and think we're lazy and dirty,' plus I'm supposed to be quitting. Where are you heading?"

"Brunch," Elijah replied. "Up at the Sunflower Kafe."

"Ah, the Ukrainian place—nice café," Tevil said with an approving nod. "I didn't know they did brunch."

"They don't really, but brunch is what you make it," Mark interjected. "As long as there is coffee, and they make great coffee."

"I told you, Tev—brunch is a state of mind," Elijah said, landing a gentle slap on his brother's shoulder. "I am going to change and clean up. Mark, go on ahead, I'll meet you there. Go make your delivery Tev, before Mom comes looking for you, and change your apron or she will smell the smoke."

"Oi, good idea Eli," Tevil said, shrugging the apron off over his head after skillfully flicking his cigarette butt into a nearby trash can. "I'll see you later. Good to see you again, Mark. Have a nice brunch."

After exchanging another round of hugs, greetings, and farewells, the three men parted ways. Elijah dashed off up the stairs to his apartment, Tevil ran into the house to retrieve a fresh apron, and Mark turned around to continue the walk to the café. For now, Mark's spirits were high. He hummed Bowie's "Oh! You Pretty Things" to himself as he walked.

"Tevil seems nice," I said as Mark rounded the corner by Zayde's Delicatessen. "Not quite what I would have imagined his brother being like, but also exactly what I expected. I'd love to investigate this deli, but maybe now's not the time."

"He is nice, great guy actually," Mark replied. "Now is definitely not the time, but it's a great deli. We'll visit later. They have the best pickles."

"Right, focus on the mission," I said.

"The mission?"

"Yes, the mission," I answered. "For someone in the middle of a love triangle you are remarkably unstabbed so far. The mission is to keep you un-impaled."

"Okay, good mission," Mark chuckled. "I'm all in favor of avoiding impalement. How do we do that? I don't know what I'm doing here."

"I don't mean to alarm you, but I don't know," I said hesitantly. "That is, I can only do so much. You have to know how unpredictable humans can be. For liability reasons I can only offer limited guarantees of success."

"Worst. Genie. Ever."

"Not a 'genie' but I get your point," I said. "Look, I will watch out for you, Elijah, and Viktoriya. I want this to turn out well for all three of you. I'm letting you know now that if I have to bend a few of our ground rules to avoid another Hundred Years' War situation, I will."

"Good to know," Mark said haltingly. "What … do you mean *exactly* by a 'Hundred Years' War situation'? You're not talking about *the* Hundred Years' War in the 1300s and 1400s, are you?"

"Yes, *that* war—very messy affair. Loads of love triangles, a few love octagons, and at least one pentagram. Recorded history either glosses over them or omits them entirely. But specifically," I answered, doing my best to remain on-topic. "In the roughly 1360s I was involved in a messy little affair between Edward, the Black Prince; Joan, the Fair Maid of Kent; and King Jean le Bon that emerged after the Battle of Poitiers, ending with the Treaty of Brétigny. What the history doesn't tell you is this doomed love triangle is one reason those wars escalated."

"Eros, pretend I'm not a medieval European historian with an intimate knowledge of these people," Mark answered, sounding equally intrigued and frustrated. "Can you explain, briefly, the details and how it relates to me?"

"It's complicated, Mark. But I'll try," I said, dredging up the relevant memories. "In the Battle of Poitiers, Prince Edward of Woodstock from the House of Plantagenet—the Black Prince— captured King John II of France, also known as Jean le Bon, from the House of Valois. Edward brought John back to England as a prisoner, and the two became very friendly—if you catch my meaning.

"Now, Edward was planning to marry his cousin Joan, Countess of Kent—don't judge, that was a different time—when he returned. But, then John met Joan and, well … they also became very friendly. Suddenly, we had a diplomatic and emotional nightmare of a love triangle—albeit a passionate, wildly entertaining one.

"They kept their respective relationships secret from each other, which, shockingly, bred jealousy and resentment. When all three discovered each other's 'entanglements' Edward orchestrated John's escape back to France, choosing—with Joan's encouragement—to let him go rather than stab him, because, you know, love. But then John came back years later and mysteriously died shortly after. Years later, Edward also died from 'illness,' leaving Joan to pick up the pieces, so to speak. It was a whole thing—horribly messy, extremely complicated—and I've probably oversimplified it to the point of absurdity."

"It didn't sound too absurd," Mark said slowly as he chewed on the details I bombarded him with. "As curious as I am, I think that's a story for later. So, the point is … ?"

"The point, Mark, is this: don't hide the truth from Viktoriya or Elijah." I said, frustrated that the point was blatantly obvious. "You must tell Viktoriya about Elijah, do not wait too long, and try to be gentle about it."

"I don't know how, or when," Mark said, on the verge of panic. "I don't know what I'm doing, help me out."

"I know. You can't just blurt it out, we'll have to find the right time," I said, attempting to sound reassuring. "If I see the right time coming, I'll tell you. You don't have to rush, but don't drag your feet either. Viktoriya doesn't seem like someone who enjoys being left in the dark. Whatever you do, don't let indecision turn into dishonesty, and don't make it seem like you're hiding something. Viktoriya doesn't strike me as the *patiently wait in ignorance* type. That's how you get stabbed. Or worse, contract a mysterious illness historians will politely call dysentery."

"All right point taken, thanks," Mark said, pausing a block short of the café. "You know I'm worried about hurting Viktoriya—that's the last thing I'd ever want to do to her. But I think I'm a little more afraid of losing Elijah entirely, regardless of the outcome."

"Mark, no matter what happens, I don't think you'll lose him. "Some connections are stronger than romance itself. And you two—you're tangled together in something deeper," I said, secretly hoping I was not wrong this time.

Mark inhaled and resumed walking toward his destination, or his destiny, if you like a more poetic interpretation. Despite the chaos spiraling through his mind and heart, he remained surprisingly resilient. He was walking now as though he were embracing the greatness thrust upon him. It was hard to believe that his entire world had been upended twice over in less than three days, and I was only marginally responsible. Eons of existence—and yet the past forty-eight hours have taught me more than the previous forty-eight millennia. Mark Williams had single-handedly redefined my understanding of humanity. Finally, Mark exhaled as his hand gripped the door handle of the Sunflower Kafe and he stepped inside.

The café buzzed with late-morning life, filled with eager conversations rising from crowded tables. The mingled scents of fresh bread, coffee, and vanilla saturated the air, blending into the café's warmth. Sunlight filtered through the windows, casting warm, golden rays across the room. Viktoriya sat sketching intently in one of the armchairs where she and Mark had sat the previous Friday, two coffee mugs resting on the small table beside her. Sunlight bathed her in an enchanting glow. Her sketchbook lay open on her lap, her pencil moving with concentrated intensity that shut out the world beyond her page. Mark hesitated for just a fraction of a second. His heartbeat stuttered—I could hear it— and a quiet gasp escaped before he could stop it.

Mark

Viktoriya looked incredible bathed in sunlight. She wore what had once been a man's midnight-blue sports jacket and slacks, but she'd employed her ingenious talents to transform them to suit her. In addition to recutting the lines to fit her body exactly, she had inserted panels of golden houndstooth-patterned fabric that peeked through only when she moved. It looked like sunshine breaking through storm clouds. The effect was mesmerizing, though I'd need her to stand before I could truly appreciate it.

Viktoriya must have heard me gasp. She glanced up as I approached, her eyes locking onto mine. A familiar smirk curled her lips as her gaze drifted over me—slow, deliberate, assessing.

It's stupid, but after last night, after that text, after our exchange of pictures, something between us had shifted. The raw tension that once crackled between us—sharp and volatile, like a live wire—had changed. Evolved.

It was still charged, still unspoken, but now there was an ease, a comfortable certainty beneath it. It was new. Fragile. The bonds tethering us to each other hadn't yet been securely tied. The anxiety she once stirred in me had been the fear of rejection. Now, it was the fear of loss—and the hope for something more than tenuous, fleeting bonds.

"No apron?" she mused, tilting her head, eyes flicking over me. "Pity—you looked quite *comfortable* in it."

"I—uh—figured it wasn't really brunch-appropriate attire."

"Mm. A shame. You wear it well," Viktoriya said, nodding slowly, amusement glinting in her eyes.

She gestured to the seat beside her, tapping her pencil against the rim of a waiting cup of coffee. Viktoriya watched me sit down for a moment—not just flirtatious now, but genuinely pleased to see me. At least, I sincerely hoped.

"What is 'brunch'? This word—I do not know it," Viktoriya said, curious.

"It's somewhere between breakfast and lunch," I explained, suddenly wondering how Elijah would phrase it. "It's very popular with the drag queens, probably because they are never on time for breakfast. Elijah says 'it's a state of mind, not just a meal,' or something like that. He can explain it better than I can. He is coming too; he should be here soon."

"Oh, Elijah is coming." Viktoriya's expression didn't change, but something in her tone did—subtle, almost imperceptible, yet unmistakable.

"I should have asked. Is that okay?" I said, kicking myself.

"Da. Is okay. I look forward to knowing him—your friend— better," she said, shifting in her seat with the faintest hesitation.

There was a shift in her expression. Her warm smile had a hint of displeasure behind it I couldn't miss.

"Mmm. That was a look," Eros whispered in my ear. "She definitely wanted you all to herself."

"I'm sorry—that was stupid. I can call him and tell him not to come. He was there this morning when I got your message; I think I just invited him out of habit," I rambled, words escaping before I could consider the implications.

"Mark, be careful—that sounded like you're hiding something," Eros whispered.

"He was with you when you saw my picture?" Viktoriya said, confusion and embarrassment mingling in her expression. "And … your picture."

"Oh, no—he was asleep." I felt like I couldn't stop myself from talking.

"Da? You and Elijah have sleepovers often?" Her eyebrow lifted just slightly—casual curiosity, or something else?

"Not often, no. Sometimes after a show. My place is close by. He just didn't want to go home alone after that performance." I froze for a second, maybe a second too long. I expected chastising from Eros, or inquisition from Viktoriya, but received neither.

"Mm. Yes, this is understandable. Big night for him. Lucky for him you were alone." Viktoriya stirred her coffee.

Her gaze was lingering without pressing the subject further. Her expression was hard to read, as if she were processing something. Was she watching for a reaction?

"That wasn't just casual curiosity," Eros said finally as I gulped the coffee Viktoriya had waiting for me. "That was 'I suspect something, and I don't know if I like it.' Change the subject. Fast."

"This coffee is incredible … Sorry, I feel awkward—I'm still cringing over that picture I sent. I've never done that before—and it was nowhere near as breathtaking as yours. I could never look as stunning as you—" I said, hoping it didn't sound as awkward and unnatural out loud as it did in my head.

Viktoriya laughed, and every fiber of my body relaxed. She slapped my knee playfully and laughed again.

"A compliment, while fishing for another," she said, pretending to jot something in her notebook. "I must record this for history. So bold, Mark Williams. You were beautiful as well. "Perhaps there is hope for you yet."

"So, you have the whole day off after baking?" I stammered, feeling my blush reach my ears. I was sure my face and now ears were almost the same shade of red as Viktoriya's hair.

"Yes, all day—you have me," she said, slipping back into that inviting, easy tone she'd had last night over kebabs and drinks. "I hope I have you all day as well. Even if Elijah joins us—after all, I cannot truly know a man without knowing his friends. I want to know you, Mark."

My fear that I had made an irrevocable mistake—inviting Elijah and mentioning he spent the night—began to dissipate. But I knew that had more to do with her than any half-recovery I managed. Maybe I was lucky. Maybe she was just as determined as I was to solidify the fragile tethers between us. But that only made the weight in my chest heavier. The conversation about Elijah loomed larger now, not smaller. I had to tell her. But not yet. For now, I set it aside.

"Good," I said, allowing a goofy grin to spread across my face. "I want to know you too. It's a beautiful day outside. How do you feel about a walk by the river? There is a sculpture garden exhibit outside the art museum. Plus, there is this amazing unsanctioned, unofficial, open-air art gallery at the foot of the bridge on the way. Have you seen them?"

"That sounds wonderful," she said, her own grin mirroring mine. "I walk past sculpture garden, but not through it, and I did not see gallery by the bridge. You will show me your favorites, yes?"

Before I could answer, the café door swung open. I looked up to see Elijah stride in. He didn't exactly dress up for the occasion. Knowing him, he could look effortlessly runway-ready when he wanted, but somehow, he still managed to be acceptably overdressed. Then I did a double take, realizing how eerily coordinated Elijah and Viktoriya were dressed. Elijah wore a dark navy-blue houndstooth sports jacket over matching pants, paired with a faded gold shirt. It teetered on the edge of kitschy and garish, yet he made it work like a statement. Between the two of them, I felt like I belonged either in an orchard or a 1990s Seattle record store—just an old gray flannel over a thermal and worn jeans. Elijah's eyes flickered between us.

"Well, you two are quite the attractive couple," he teased, making a beeline for Viktoriya. "Stand up, beautiful, let me get a full look at this stunning outfit you created."

"Hello—Elijah? I did not recognize you. You look nice out of drag, dear, we nearly match!" Viktoriya beamed, standing up.

They both turned in slow, appreciative circles, admiring each other's outfits like two fashionistas who had just stumbled into their style soulmates.

"I adore this pattern on you," Viktoriya said.

"And on you. Oh. My," Elijah replied.

Elijah's and my eyes widened as Viktoriya turned, revealing the unexpected flourish of her design. A pleated tail flowed from the back of her jacket, cascading down to her calf like the trailing hem of a skirt. Within the pleats, she had inlaid the same golden houndstooth fabric—like hidden sunlight woven into her clothing. The illusion was even more breathtaking now that I could see the full outfit.

"Girl, lock up that jacket before I steal it. Oh my god, I love it," Elijah said, clutching his chest theatrically. "I knew you were talented, but this. This is almost enough to make me hate you."

"Hate me?" Viktoriya's expression suddenly shifted, looking alarmed. "Why?"

"Oh—no, no, no, not literally dear! God no!" Elijah quickly retorted, pulling Viktoriya into a hug. "Sorry, darling, it's an expression. It means I'm sick with envy over you and your talent."

"Oh, good," Viktoriya exhaled, visibly relieved. "I was afraid I'd have to ask Mark to castrate you myself."

They stared at each other in silence for a long beat.

Then, at the exact same time, they both erupted, bursting into laughter, remembering Elijah's promise to her from last night. And it is entirely possible that my heart exploded inside my chest at that moment.

"Sit, sit! I get us fresh coffee," Viktoriya said, waving Elijah toward the armchair across from me before collecting our empty mugs and vanishing into the kitchen.

"That, Mark," Eros whispered in my ear. "Is the best outcome I could have imagined."

"Yeah, that was fantastic," I said aloud, forgetting Elijah had no idea I had a cosmic relationship coach whispering in my ear.

"You can say that again," Elijah said, settling into his armchair with a grin. "I get it now. I mean I mostly got it last night when I met her, but now? I *really* get it. I love her!"

"That doesn't make this easier, you know," I said, feeling a familiar weight return to my chest.

"You're spieling to the shul, babe," Elijah sighed, slipping effortlessly into his Yiddish roots—as he always did when he got schmaltzy. "Let's just … put that on the shelf for now."

"Easier said." I exhaled a breath I didn't remember taking in—or holding. "But yeah, I'll try."

Because if I didn't set this turmoil aside, I would not survive the day without experiencing full cardiac arrest.

Chapter 12

Elijah leaned back in his chair, utterly at ease as he took in the café's ambiance. He had a gift for setting problems aside in favor of the moment. It was a quality I admired, envied, and, at that moment, resented. I often wondered if it was a product of growing up as a gay man in a religiously orthodox community, although his family wasn't exactly unyieldingly orthodox, and that community was more or less accepting now. Still, it couldn't have been an easy adolescence. And there was Elijah, basking as if he did not have a single concern. Either unaware of, or deliberately ignoring, the shift in the air his arrival caused. Maybe it was all in my head. Meanwhile, my mind ran frantic diagnostics, searching for faults before they became system failures.

"Mark," Elijah said, leaning forward, keeping his voice down. "I just wanted to ask, before Viktoriya gets back, you haven't told her anything yet, right?"

"Not yet," I said, matching his volume. "It's not a subject that makes a good conversation starter."

"Okay, understood," he said, relaxing back into his chair. "I'll try to follow your lead. This is a little exciting, isn't it?"

"Exciting is one way to put it," I replied, rolling my eyes, though his mood eased my nerves. "Here she comes—brace yourself; she's a force of nature."

Viktoriya carried a serving tray with three fresh cups of coffee, a small pitcher of cream and a bowl of light-brown sugar cubes, and a pile of freshly baked pastries. She set the tray on the coffee table between us.

"Here you are, Mark," she said, handing me a mug of coffee. It smelled of nutmeg, vanilla, and sweet cream, with a hint of cinnamon rising from the strong brew. It was an intensely comforting aroma that stirred memories of crisp fall mornings in the orchard with my family before a day of hard work. "I make it special, just for you. You will like."

"Thank you, it smells amazing."

"Elijah, for you I do not know how you like," Viktoriya said, handing Elijah a mug filled with unadorned black coffee. "So, I bring sugar and cream."

"That's perfect." Elijah smiled, accepting the coffee graciously. "I prefer mixing it myself anyway. Sometimes I like it sweeter, or with more cream, depending on the day. Ask Mark—never the same way twice."

That was interesting. He hates mixing his own coffee, and he always takes it the same way. Just a little cream, and very little sugar. He was being a little too polite. And the coffee Viktoriya brought me she prepared the same way she did for herself—like she wanted to share an experience.

"Oh, that was fascinating—they're staking claims, but politely. You got the special coffee, and Elijah got the do-it-yourself version. Then he subtly reminds her how well you know him. I've seen this before—brace yourself," Eros whispered, echoing my own thoughts.

I tasted my coffee, contemplating the charged atmosphere of rivalry between Viktoriya and Elijah. "She is about to probe the nature and depth of your relationship with Elijah."

"Elijah, Mark forgot to give me your phone number last night," Viktoriya said. She casually nudged her armchair a fraction closer to mine. Her eyes gleamed playfully as she met Elijah's gaze with a smirk and settled back into her chair. "I must have been … distracting."

"See, Mark—subtle, deliberate flag planting," Eros whispered unhelpfully.

"I'm sure he was," Elijah said with a wink intended for both of us.

"I didn't exactly forget," I said, more defensively than necessary. "I got … sidetracked."

"You did, I agree," Viktoriya said, unsubtly winking while she sipped her coffee. She turned to face Elijah. "Elijah, you tell me things about Mark he would never say himself. You know his secrets."

Elijah was mid-sip and froze, then almost choked on his coffee. He hesitated—longer than expected. His gaze flicked back and forth from Viktoriya to me, then to the pastries, like they might hold an escape. Searching for … what? Permission? A distraction? A lifeline? Or was he signaling that I should brace myself? It wasn't like him to hesitate when the opportunity to gossip politely arose. It must have been a reaction Viktoriya was expecting because she noticed it at once. She took a slow, indulgent sip of her coffee, watching Elijah like a cat watching a bird through a window.

"Ah, you guard his secrets well, don't you?" Viktoriya teased, sipping her coffee slowly. Her eyes never left him as she watched him stumble through his reactions.

"It's okay, Elijah, I can embarrass myself well enough without help," I said, tossing the lifeline Elijah needed. "Not even Elijah could guard me from myself."

"Now that's the truth," Elijah said, recovering from being on the back foot, which he was unaccustomed to. "Like when we hosted karaoke at the club, and you—bless your tone-deaf heart—thought it was a good idea to attempt Bonnie Tyler's "Holding Out for a Hero"? Sweetheart, I have never seen a crowd so confused and yet thoroughly entertained."

Both Viktoriya and Elijah erupted in laughter, watching me with something between endearment and pity in their eyes. I hoped it was endearment, but at this point did it matter? I groaned, sinking lower in my chair, laughing with them at the memory, halfheartedly trying to disappear behind a coffee mug.

"Well played, Viktoriya," Eros interjected, sounding almost impressed, as though they were commentating on a chess match or diplomatic negotiations. "She baited him with a loaded open-ended question and got what she wanted from Elijah's hesitation—you sacrificing yourself to save him. Now watch, Elijah will try to lighten the mood, to save you, but she's already preparing the next round."

"Da, da, this is good," Viktoriya said, setting her coffee down with purpose. She shifted her focus from me back to Elijah, less

playful now, investigating. "I could ask for *juiciest* of stories, but—
"

"Viktoriya, dearest. You ask a *dangerous* question," Elijah interrupted, setting his coffee down to bring both hands to his chest like the weight of those juicy stories was a physical burden. "The stories I could tell …"

"Instead, I ask basics," she continued. Her tone was light, but her eyes were sharp. "Tell me—you have known each other long? How did you meet? And you have seen Mark's orchard, yes?"

"Oh, it's been … fifteen years?" Elijah answered. He almost sounded disappointed by the seemingly benign question.

"Seventeen years, now," I corrected Elijah.

"Right. Seventeen years ago—this is interesting—Mark strolled into my family's deli looking for a pickle."

"It wasn't *just* for a pickle—they're great pickles—and he's exaggerating it's not that interesting." I interjected with a groan.

"Truer words. Anyway, there was this—thing—a pointless rivalry between our high schools, and I don't even remember—"

"It was a theater competition. I was a stage tech on a lunch break."

"That's right, you were dressed all in black, wearing a The Cure T-shirt. I asked if you were doing a 'pre-goth' thing. You remember what you said, Mark?"

"Yes, I said 'no, I'm not that cool.'"

"Which is still true, by the way," Elijah added unnecessarily.

Viktoriya snorted into her coffee at that, shaking her head as she watched our rapid-fire exchange. Her expression was curious and amused. She was enjoying the story. Her eyes glinted with something almost indulgent, her interest piqued at the mention of the band T-shirt.

"The Cure, I know this band. You both like them as well?"

"I did—or I do. A staple of teenage angst," I said, taking another sip of my cooling coffee.

"Ugh," Elijah added. "Who doesn't go through that phase? At least some of us grow out of it."

"I look forward to the day you finally do." I shot back, knowing neither of us entirely abandoned that angst.

"Oh, please," Elijah returned the volley. "Changing. Subjects. Yes, I have seen his orchard. He even talked me into helping harvest the apples—*once*."

"It wasn't that bad. And we paid you."

"Ever my faithful tipper," Elijah said, giggling into his coffee.

"You have known Mark so long. You must know him better than anyone, yes?" Viktoriya mused, tilting her head, her eyes fixed directly on Elijah. She didn't pose it as a question, but as a fact. Now she waited for confirmation.

"I have … I mean, I would hope I know him that well," Elijah said, but there was a slight pause. Just enough to notice, enough to mean something.

"Good," Viktoriya said, her smile meaningful. "I wish to know him that well. You will help me—yes?"

She patted Elijah's knee lightly, approvingly. Like she was rewarding him for answering correctly, because it was not really a request.

"Naturally, but should we ask Mark to leave first?" Elijah replied, leaning into the budding alliance, emphasizing his nonchalance by taking a large bite of one of the pastries, which he then realized was intoxicatingly delicious based upon his reaction.

"She's clever," Eros murmured, as though watching a chess match unfold. "First, she confirmed your history with Elijah. Now she's moving to recruit him. I can't tell if it's to test a suspicion, get closer to you, or seize control of New Brunswick—it could go either way."

"Oh dear, no," Viktoriya laughed. "Now Mark must tell me your secrets, Elijah."

She watched our reactions for a moment, absorbing the spark of chaos she dropped. Eros was right. She is a grandmaster, and we were just along for the ride.

"Mark, tell me about Elijah's deli," Viktoriya asked, smoothly turning her attention from Elijah to me. "Zayde's, yes?"

"Oh, yes, it's Zayde's Delicatessen, it's just down the street. Elijah worked there for his parents when we were in high school. Now his older brother, Tevil, is taking over, but I don't think their parents will ever give it up entirely." I answered almost obediently.

"True, my dear older brother must shoulder the burden alone. Fishing pickles from barrels for brooding, hungry pre-goth teens," Elijah added, with his particular dramatic flourish, which included a suggestive mime of manhandling a pickle. "Meanwhile, I fled the family business for a life on stage."

"Did you help Elijah with his drag, Mark?" she asked.

I wasn't sure where this line of questioning would lead, but I was absolutely certain she was probing for something. Or I might be picking up Eros' paranoia, and it may be simple curiosity.

"I did help actually. A little anyway, when Elijah was trying to develop a character. There were some we should never speak of," I answered with a sense of fond pride. I loved helping Elijah become Fanny Ryesand.

"That's true, if it wasn't for Mark I would still be Bernadette Peppers," Elijah laughed at the memory of his early drag disasters. "Fanny wouldn't exist without Mark. She owes you a debt."

"So much work, did you try it yourself with Elijah?" Viktoriya's eyes lit up with speculative wonder, like she was about to reveal a conspiracy. "It must be tempting."

"I would be lying if I said I was never tempted. I honestly considered giving it a try," I said. "But, no I never did. I've never been that brave."

"No!" Elijah nearly spat out his coffee. "You never once mentioned that!"

"Because you'd have me in a gown and halfway dragged up before I could protest." I laughed. Elijah looked like he was the one who had stumbled across a conspiracy, while Viktoriya looked on delighted.

"Fair!" Elijah shouted, waving an accusatory finger in my direction. "But, now I really want to see it. Don't you Viktoriya?"

"Oh, yes. Yes, Elijah and I are agreed. I would very much like to see this," Viktoriya said, maintaining eye-contact with me, and I shoved half a pastry into my mouth to avoid having to respond. "Elijah, Mark said you two had sleepovers."

Every function in my brain short-circuited—nothing but static and alarm bells. I must have looked like a deer in the headlights of an oncoming car with a mouthful of pastry. Five-thousand thoughts darted through my mind simultaneously. Why was she asking that? Why now? Was she watching to see how I'd react? What did she suspect? Is she simply teasing us now? How am I supposed to respond to that? Did I remember to swallow? Then Eros decided now was the best time to chime in.

"It's a very bold strategy. A surprise question seeking a deeper truth. Do they deny it? Defend it? Deflect with a well timed self-deprecating joke," Eros whispered like a sports commentator.

"… Sorry, Mark. I got caught up, but you should probably say something."

Elijah must have noticed and recognized my vacant decision-paralysis look, because he leaned over the coffee table and mock whispered to me.

"Should we tell the truth, Mark?" Elijah smirked, as though about to reveal everything. "About the pillow fights and the all-night Streisand movie marathons …" He paused, looking over to catch Viktoriya's eyes. "No? Our little secret?" Elijah sighed, leaning back dramatically with an air of resignation. "Ah well. Sorry Viktoriya, my lips are sealed."

He mimed zipping his lips shut, locking them, and tossing the key over his shoulder.

"Oh, god …" I moaned after swallowing hard, watching the smirk on Viktoriya's lips curl into a smile as she laughed.

"That sounds like great fun," Viktoriya said, her voice lighthearted. She looked at Elijah, then back at me. "Pity I was not invited."

Elijah erupted in laughter as I sat speechless.

"Oh, Mark. That wasn't just a joke. She was testing you—and Elijah. Now she's watching, assessing how you recover. A masterful stroke; I could learn from her," Eros whispered. Their commentary, insightful as it was, was becoming distracting.

"All right Viktoriya, it's time to turn the tables on this inquisition," Elijah said, reclaiming his composure with feigned seriousness. Leaning forward, he took a small bite of pastry and washed it down with a sip of coffee. "We are practically neighbors, and Mark has been selfishly keeping us apart. I need to know more about you."

"Is true—Mark is selfish," Viktoriya exclaimed, matching Elijah's feigned seriousness with her own exaggerated dramatics. "Ask your questions, I may answer."

I watched Elijah as he calculated his next move. Now I understand what Eros meant. As good as Elijah was, Viktoriya outmatched him. I was going to be a spectator for a while, so I selected another pastry and sat back to enjoy the match.

"Is it just you and your dad here?" Elijah asked with kind curiosity.

"Da. Just my papa for now," Viktoriya said, a hint of absence in her tone. "Momma is with my little brothers back home. She will bring them in summer. Is trouble with visas, so complicated and expensive."

"I can only imagine. I look forward to meeting them," Elijah responded thoughtfully. "Mark mentioned you are studying design?"

"Fine art design and marketing," Viktoriya said, sipping her coffee. "Marketing is a necessary evil. I do not enjoy it."

"I hear you. Marketing is the worst," Elijah nodded empathetically, sipping his coffee, preparing his next attack. "You and Mark have known each other almost two years now—if I remember that right."

"That sounds about right," I interjected. "About two years ago I delivered that troublesome laptop."

"Yes, a chance meeting," Viktoriya added, smiling at the memory. "I had no computer for class, Mark brought one to me."

"The University has a program," I explained unnecessarily. "They provide laptops for students who don't have computers and need them for classes."

"He showed up, was very kind to me. I find him funny—and very cute. I make him blush," Viktoriya recounted our first meeting, making me blush all over again. "I like this, so I call him when I have computer troubles."

"Oh, I agree. Kind, funny, and he blushes adorably," Elijah said, looking at me, growing redder by the moment, while he took an exaggerated sip of coffee. "Just like he is doing … right … *now.*"

I felt like I was on exhibit—*Blushing Man, in fifteen shades of crimson*—as both Elijah and Viktoriya stared. Identical smiles adorned their faces, watching me try to will myself into vanishing.

"Wait. You had a lot of trouble with that laptop. Did you *really* have such terrible luck with it?" Elijah said, leveling an accusatory glare at me. "Mark, did you let this sweet, precious woman live with a defective computer—just as an excuse to see her?"

"Okay, okay—maybe. Maybe I could've replaced the whole thing with a newer model," I said, holding up my hands in a feigned protest of innocence. "We don't have much better, but I absolutely would have … If I thought it was too much trouble. Or, if I minded fixing it so often. Okay. Maybe it was a little bit of an excuse. I enjoyed getting to see Viktoriya."

"Maybe …" Viktoriya said, blushing slightly. "Maybe I learn enough to cause … small problems."

"Oh, I see you two. Playing the same game," Elijah sat back, wearing a victorious smirk on his face. "Well done, Viktoriya. I approve and applaud your tenacity and ingenuity."

"Ahh, there it is—the end of a stellar match. Elijah just surrendered. If you were paying attention, that was him extending his approval to Viktoriya," Eros said, sounding thoroughly satisfied. "Notice now, how the victorious Viktoriya will decline the surrender and offer a gracious draw."

Viktoriya relaxed, her temporary embarrassment fading, replaced by her usual air of confidence. She finished her coffee and set her mug down with authority, looking at Elijah. She pulled her phone out of a pocket in her jacket and waved it in Elijah's direction.

"We are friends now," she said casually, yet with decisive friendliness. "You give to me your number."

"When you put it like that …" Elijah said with a chuckle, taking Viktoriya's phone from her. He began entering his name and number into her contacts. He even took a selfie for his contact picture.

"Look at that, Viktoriya didn't just win the match, she recruited her opponent," Eros mused in my ear. "This girl is a queen in every sense of the word. She would have ruled an empire had she been born centuries ago. Oh, I love this."

"I love this too," I said before realizing it had slipped out loud.

"What was that?" Elijah asked.

"Oh, I … love seeing you two get along," I replied, suddenly aware of the subtle shift in Viktoriya's posture and mood. Whereas before she'd carried herself with quiet competitiveness toward Elijah, now she seemed content—almost warm. And Elijah, who, although he hid it well, was all nerves before, was now happy and relaxed.

The bell on the café door chimed as a couple of new customers walked in, drawing Viktoriya's attention. She glowered and checked the time before looking up at me.

"We should leave before more customers come," she said, a mischievous urgency in her tone. "If I stay, Papa will find work for me."

"Right! We were going to walk to the sculpture exhibit and graffiti gallery," I said to clue Elijah into the plans Viktoriya and I had made before he arrived.

"You mean the graffiti walls under the bridge?" Elijah asked, leaning forward enthusiastically. "I love that—it changes every few weeks. What is the sculpture exhibit? I don't know about that one."

"Oh, it's at the art museum. It's a temporary exhibition. There's this one piece that looks completely different depending on the angle you view it from. You'd love it." I answered without a second thought, meeting Elijah's enthusiasm.

"Sounds amazing. I can't believe you didn't tell me about it before now," he said.

Elijah's voice was full of genuine interest and a hint of a question about his inclusion. I hadn't explicitly invited him, nor had I intentionally excluded him. When Viktoriya and I made this rudimentary plan, I simply neglected to factor him into the equation. Maybe I subconsciously hoped it would just be the two of us, or maybe I assumed Elijah would step back voluntarily. I could tell Viktoriya had a similar thought by the way she was looking at Elijah's enthusiasm. I recalled Eros pointing out how she had hoped to have me to herself today, and Elijah interrupted that. Now it was happening again. But this time, she seemed less disappointed. She glanced at me, and I wondered if she felt it would be cruel to freeze out Elijah after that conversation.

"Of course, Elijah, you are coming with us," Viktoriya declared, standing up, stacking the mugs back onto the serving tray. She picked up the tray and smiled at us. "I be right back."

She swiftly dashed away, carrying the empty coffee cups back to the kitchen. Elijah looked at me, a little surprised, before he grinned.

"So, Mark, is this like a double date for you?" he teased me, and I was awash with excitement and confused dread.

I'd expected to spend time alone with Viktoriya—to find a moment to talk to her, to resolve this tension. He wasn't wrong. It felt like a double date, like I was now attempting an impossible, forbidden balancing act. Of all the confusing emotions coursing through my body, disappointment was nowhere to be found. It was primarily exhilaration, and unsettling anticipation of the unknown.

The Fixer, The Maker, The Drag Entertainer

*****Eros*****

Mark was in over his head after that meeting, but he didn't know it at the time. He had thought that brunch was a test, but he had quite a surprise waiting for him. Viktoriya and Elijah met as unknowing rivals but emerged as allies. Neither Mark nor I grasped it then, yet Elijah had all but confirmed Viktoriya's suspicion—that Mark was his audience of one—without having to say it aloud.

She learned Elijah harbored deep feelings for Mark but believed her own position was secure. I didn't realize then that she still questioned Mark's feelings for Elijah. She seemed content with what she had learned about them both and their relationship, and where she fit in Mark's affections. Elijah projected confidence and ease, though I know now he was terrified. Mark was caught in a blissful panic, and I was too enamored with the three of them to see how swiftly they were all falling.

The three left the Sunflower Kafe, their easy conversation deepening the foundation of friendship they had begun to build. They revealed trivial details, such as that Mark had a truck he used so rarely that he kept it at the orchard for his mother to use. Elijah also had a car he used occasionally, mostly when he had to move storage bins of costumes between the dressing room in the club and his closet above the garage. Viktoriya hadn't yet found the time to get an American driver's license—and wasn't entirely sure she wanted to drive on American roads—prompting both Mark and Elijah to offer lessons, each eager to win her attention.

They stopped in at Elijah's family deli, where Tevil graciously made them a trio of simple turkey sandwiches they could eat on a riverside bench. Viktoriya made a point of asking for one of the legendary pickles, which she agreed was indeed worth the fanfare. While they ate in the shade of a tree on the banks of the Raritan River, Viktoriya asked Elijah where he found his clothes for his drag. To which he admitted to overpaying an underqualified tailor to alter thrift-shop and garage-sale finds for him, combined with his own use of hot-glue, safety pins, and determination. Just like that, she informed Elijah that he would no longer be using an underqualified tailor and would come to her for alterations. Then she demanded to see his closet at the earliest possible convenience. Meanwhile, Mark watched, a storm of conflicting feelings battling behind his eyes.

When they reached the graffiti wall, they were surprised to find half of it covered by a single satirical political mural. It declared that oppression grew in the soil of apathy, division, and ignorance. Hatred fed off fear, and resentment would destroy democracy only to breed cruelty. Buy it now because you deserve it before someone else does. The artwork featured military-uniformed, beer-drinking eagles in front of burning houses and buildings. I found it garish and heavy-handed, yet unmistakably well-intentioned. Viktoriya, Elijah, and Mark all noticed the heavy-handed approach, agreeing that it was a bold statement intent on being impossible to misinterpret. They appreciated the rebellious, dire warnings while understanding the underlying truth. They even noted that it had obviously covered many other pieces of inherently temporary artwork.

Along the rest of the walls, they found a collage of colliding, overlapping, and contradictory paintings. Each piece was compelling on its own, but together they formed a chaotic tapestry of expression. Viktoriya remarked that this was impossible to reproduce artificially; it requires organic and evolving expression of many minds, hearts, and hands working anonymously and collaboratively. I am not sure who was more impressed with her effortlessly profound articulation—Mark, Elijah, or me. They discussed the graffiti as though they were art historians leaving a museum. The walls stood as a mark of defiance—reviled by law enforcement, cherished by the community—a raw, unapologetic testament to human expression. I don't think I understand it at all, although I very much wish I did.

In the shadow of the fine art museum, the sculpture exhibition consisted of only half a dozen bronze, steel, and concrete works displayed on temporary plinths across the lawn. Viktoriya's favorite was a concrete form of a mother cradling a child, half of which had been deliberately smashed and destroyed. Elijah's favorite was a dancer made from a collection of repurposed steel pieces from all manner of industrial equipment that came together to form a singular expressive figure. Mark's favorite was an enigmatic bronze mass of shapes and voids—the piece he had described earlier, which took on different shapes depending on the viewing angle, allowing the viewer to find their own unique interpretation. They had each found pieces that, on the surface, appeared unimaginably different, but each spoke to themes of change, strength, and endurance. Three paths converged, forming a single road forward. I felt privileged to witness these three human souls learning to love—each in their own way.

Chapter 13

****Eros****

After what felt like days of debating each sculpture's meaning and worth, Viktoriya, Elijah, and Mark finally decided it was time to leave.

Mark confessed he hadn't planned that far ahead—he'd hoped inspiration would strike along the way—but he'd become so caught up in the moment that his usual foresight had slipped.

Viktoriya revisited her curiosity about Elijah's wardrobe. Elijah brightened at the idea, admitting he could use help reorganizing his closet. Mark—still eager to spend as much time as possible with both—immediately agreed.

Together, they crossed the bridge back to Elijah's house.

"What are you doing, Mark? You haven't even tried to talk to Viktoriya about Elijah," I said. "I know you can't answer me, but let me remind you—talk to her soon. The longer you bask in whatever this is, the harder it's going to be for both of you. And maybe—just maybe—bring it up with Elijah. It'd be better than saying nothing at all."

Mark seemed to mull it over. I felt guilty for breaking his reverie, but I suspected he was about to let it slip away. It wasn't deliberate—he just seemed to lose all rational thought whenever Viktoriya looked at him, or he at her. If she'd turned to him halfway across the bridge and suggested he jump into the river, I swear he'd have been halfway over before it even occurred to him to ask why. Elijah wasn't helping—he was openly delighting in the chaos, especially once he brought them into his apartment above his family's garage.

His "apartment" was really a retrofitted guest room. It lacked a kitchen but included a small refrigerator, sink, and counter with a toaster oven and microwave. His living space centered around a single couch, which he claimed folded out into a surprisingly comfortable bed.

His entertainment setup mirrored Mark's—complete with a small record player. Whatever wall space he had was adorned with framed vintage movie and musical theater posters. The crown jewel of the space was his "closet," though calling it that was misleading. He had turned the bedroom into his closet—meaning his closet had a closet—and it accounted for two-thirds of his overall living space. He liked to joke that he lived at home with his parents—just not *in* the house with them. The arrangement made sense for him; he didn't have to pay rent as long as he helped at the deli when they needed him.

Mark moved through the space with easy familiarity—because, of course, he was. He pointed out the *Funny Girl* posters—both the film and Broadway versions—as well as *What's Up, Doc?* Then he told her how he'd helped Elijah track down the originals, which had proved harder than it sounded.

Elijah was a gracious host, assuring Viktoriya she was welcome to anything in the fridge and should make herself at home. He even pointed out a small basket of feminine hygiene supplies in his bathroom—just in case a guest ever needed them.

Then he unveiled his "closet"—a modest bedroom converted into a closet, dressing room, and sewing space. One wall held a small sewing table and dress form beside a three-way mirror; in the corner sat an armchair likely older than any of them. The rest of the room was lined with rolling racks of loosely organized garments. Some racks held finished garments, others works in progress; one displayed secondhand finds awaiting alteration, while Elijah's everyday clothes occupied the small built-in closet from the room's former life. Around the room, shelves, and a bookcase displayed Elijah's growing collection of wigs in every imaginable style and color. Viktoriya's eyes lit up as she wandered, taking in the collection with open delight.

"If clothes could talk," Mark said dryly, rifling through a rack. "I'm sure a few of these would be screaming."

"How dare you, Mark," Elijah said, tossing a balled-up sock at him. "You're not wrong—but you don't say that in a man's closet."

"Be kind, Mark—these clothes have feelings," Viktoriya teased, glancing between them. "You have this organized, Elijah?"

"Loosely," Elijah admitted, dragging a rack from the wall. "This one's for new finds that need altering—some with potential, some only good for parts. The rack Mark's pawing through holds a few finished showpieces; others are still at the club. The one by you is a mix of completed and half-done pieces. The rest … well, chaos."

"I see," Viktoriya said, instantly assuming command. "Mark, sort finished pieces. Elijah, gather incomplete ones. I will sort rest—style, color, size. Go, my boys—work! Work!"

The cramped space burst into motion. Viktoriya, Mark, and Elijah kept bumping into one another as they shuffled clothes from rack to rack. Mark didn't seem to mind the collisions—if anything, he invited them. When he and Viktoriya brushed against each other, they lingered a beat—held by a magnetic pull neither could hide. When Elijah collided with Mark, they burst into laughter, effortlessly comfortable in their closeness.

Even I could feel the tension building like static electricity just waiting for a grounding to spark. Watching them whirl around the room, I saw how naturally they moved together—not as a single unit, but as parts of some living machine, fitting together as if by design.

The organization effort dissolved quickly as distractions took over. Mark would find a dress he remembered helping Elijah with years ago, and he would share the story with Viktoriya. Elijah would uncover an outfit he had found in a Newark thrift store and forgotten, and he would show it to Viktoriya for her opinion. Viktoriya would find an incomplete dress, and she would show Elijah where the seam was failing and explain how to fix it and make the seams stronger. All three of them would come together to share whatever thoughts or ideas were rising to the surface in their minds. Before long, organizing gave way to exploration— brainstorming costumes, swapping ideas, and critiquing designs. Viktoriya's sharp eye and designer's instinct lit a spark in Elijah— and that, in turn, clearly delighted Mark.

When Viktoriya began offering serious guidance, Mark stepped back slightly. He watched them with a quiet smile, his gaze moving between them—full of affection, admiration, and just a flicker of desire. Viktoriya turned to him for an opinion on how a color scheme suited Elijah. She had her arms wrapped around Elijah from behind, holding two garments to his chest. Mark startled slightly, blinking and swallowing hard—as if waking from a pleasant daydream.

****Mark****

Viktoriya caught me daydreaming. We'd all been moving around effortlessly. My mind wandered as I watched Viktoriya and Elijah together. The easy comfort they shared was familiar. It was the same simple comfort that Elijah and I shared soon after we became friends. It was confusing—the feelings that stirred inside me, seeing them bond in a way that didn't require me. Now, Viktoriya was calling me back to reality, her arms wrapped around Elijah, holding two different-colored garments against his chest. Something else stirred inside me—something I didn't quite understand—as I watched the two people I loved interact this way. I paused, realizing I was unsure when I'd started thinking of them both as people I loved—together, not separately.

"Sorry, you caught me daydreaming," I said, shaking my head.

"Oh, you daydream too, who do you daydream about?" Viktoriya giggled, peeking at me from behind Elijah.

"You know it's not fair to ask," I said, returning the giggle and adding a wink. "If I told you, it wouldn't come true."

"You can practice flirting later. We have fashion emergencies to solve," Elijah said. "How do these colors look together on me?"

"Is that fuchsia, or magenta, with lavender? I'm terrible with color names," I said, honestly trying to take the question seriously. "The combination isn't revolutionary, but it's a pleasing combination. With the right wig and makeup, it could really make your eyes pop. How about adding a turquoise accent?"

"Mark!" Viktoriya jumped out from behind Elijah. "This is perfect. Elijah, find some turquoise. I tell you, ask Mark—he has good eyes."

"Yes, ma'am," Elijah saluted, and began searching the racks for turquoise accents.

"Are we working on a new outfit?" I asked, joining the search.

"We have idea—you will see," Viktoriya said.

The goal of organizing the hanging garments was all but forgotten, replaced by the search for anything turquoise-colored. The way Viktoriya and Elijah worked together was a sight to behold. They had not yet achieved the symbiosis necessary to complete each other's sentences or anticipate each other's thoughts, but they were close. I couldn't help but feel like the odd one out in that crowded closet.

Part of me wondered how long it would take either of them to notice if I snuck out of the room. But it was only a tiny part. The rest of my entire being wanted nothing more than to remain as close to them both as possible. Then I realized I had yet to tell Viktoriya about Elijah and me, even though I wasn't sure what he and I had between us at the moment. And after that, I had to make an impossible decision, unless she decided for me by running far away. The cascade of thoughts battered my mind until nausea twisted in my stomach.

I gave up my search in favor of settling into Elijah's old closet armchair to watch them. It seemed they'd given up the search too, now taking turns pulling out dresses and holding them up to each other. The gold dress was lovely, but the cut would be unflattering on Elijah. Which was okay because Viktoriya said she could fix that. The mint-green dress would not look good on either of them and should be tossed aside to use as scrap. Then, they both pulled out identical dresses. Viktoriya laughed at the coincidence. Elijah laughed at the fact that he had bought duplicates without realizing it. They both laughed at each other. I laughed at myself, realizing I'd been keeping them apart in my mind.

It was as though the love I had for each of them was different somehow. But it was not different in any meaningful way. I loved them both in exactly the same way. The thought of giving either of them up was becoming agonizing, like a weight crushing my chest and eviscerating my stomach.

For the second time in this closet, I was torn from the grips of a daydream, this time when a balled-up sock bounced off my face. I looked up and saw Viktoriya and Elijah standing side by side, holding up a gold evening gown between them. They were both looking at me, obviously expecting a response to a question I never heard them ask.

"Mark, wake up. We need your opinion," Elijah said with a sense of urgency he only used when he was desperate for an opinion on his clothing.

"Yes, tell us. This dress—will it look best on Elijah or me?" Viktoriya asked, leaning on her words carefully, leading me to believe there was only one correct answer.

"Well, that's difficult to say," I answered, attempting to buy myself time to find the right words. "I mean, a dress looks very different on a hanger than it does when it's worn."

"He has a valid point, Viki," Elijah said, looking at Viktoriya. "If we want a fair opinion, he has to see what it looks like on both of us."

"This is fair; you go first," Viktoriya said, pushing Elijah and the dress into the closet within the closet, before turning around to look at me. "Perhaps we should see Mark wear dress too."

"I agree!" Elijah shouted from the closet.

"I don't know; I only object out of pure, crippling self-consciousness," I said, summoning everything I could to stop my face from blushing again.

"You say that every time," Elijah said, sashaying out of the closet. "Come on. If ever there was a safe space, it's inside a homosexual's closet."

"I'm with Elijah, Mark," Eros whispered in my ear. "I, for one, think you would look almost as nice as Elijah in that dress."

"You look amazing Elijah," Viktoriya said. "Don't you think, Mark? I will pick another to try—and one for you, Mark."

"Yes, Elijah, you do look amazing," I said, smiling at Elijah. "But your padding is so flat."

"Ah, you bitch! But thank you, Mark—and you too, Viki," Elijah said, clutching the imaginary pearls around his neck.

"Okay, I don't want to spoil the fun, but we can't all try on the same dress," I said, standing up. "Viktoriya, if you pick out something you think will look good on me, I'll try it on. Elijah, let's find something for Viktoriya."

"I will make you beautiful," Viktoriya said, her eyes lit with a fire of wholesome mischief as she began frantically searching through the racks of complete drag costumes and incomplete pieces.

Elijah sauntered over, giving a deliberate twirl so I could take in the full view of him in his gold ball gown. It hung loosely on his trim frame without the padding that would usually fill it out. I thought it looked much more alluring on Elijah than it did on the more artificial Fanny. From the way Elijah was looking at me, he knew I thought so.

"Tell me, Mark—what do you think? Really," Elijah said, slowly spinning again. "Is the dress wearing me? And will Viktoriya finally coax out the queen I know is hiding inside you?"

"Elijah, please," I said, pleading, aware Viktoriya could more likely than not hear everything. "No dress can wear you. You do look amazing, even better without the padding and clown face. And who knows, maybe Viktoriya is the woman who can do what you never could."

"You give with one hand and take with the other," Elijah said, smiling—hearing the compliment and catching the shade. "This is nice, Mark. Really."

"It is. It is also torture. Focus, please; we have to find something for Viktoriya," I said, turning away from Elijah to look through his collection of dresses and gowns. "Something black I think."

"I'm sorry, Mark," Elijah whispered softly, stepping closer, helping me look. "I have an idea. Yes—black but also …"

Elijah pulled a garment bag from the rack and unzipped it. Inside was a one-sleeved, floor-length black cocktail dress. The neckline plunged halfway down the dress, with translucent lace cut-outs. Loose corset ribbons held together the open side seams, which were open past the hip line. On the hanger, it looked less like a dress and more like a collection of hanging lace and ribbon around a few strips of satin.

"This. This will look stunning on her," Elijah held the dress with a grin hovering between pure evil and Dionysian glee.

"One, yes. Yes it will. Two, you are diabolical," I said. A confluence of desire, intrigue, and confusion tumbled through my mind. "I haven't seen this one before. Is it new? How have you never worn this?"

"I've had this over a year," Elijah said, zipping the garment bag closed. "I've never found the right combination of occasion and courage. I tried it on once, I've never been more attracted to myself. It's too much for the club."

"Mark! I found it. This is you," Viktoriya cried, prancing over with a hanger holding a pink sequined Western-style gown. The bodice had two embroidered pink ponies, with twisted Mylar string fringe outlining the cups. The skirt was stoned to make it look like chaps. It was garishly spectacular, unabashedly drag, and undeniably wonderful. "You will wear this for me."

"Mark. Mark, you know what that is," Elijah was jumping up and down, clapping me on the shoulder. "Yes, Mark, yes. I have never ever wanted anything ever so much in my gay life."

"Yes, Elijah, I know exactly what that is," I said, taking the hanger from Viktoriya, who was beaming with the satisfaction of someone who'd just discovered a delicious secret. "I will be the 'Pink Pony Club.' Elijah, get the hat. I'll be right out."

I took the dress into the closet and closed the door. This was one of Elijah's favorite pieces, one of his audience's favorites as well. It made everyone smile—even I was smiling as I undressed and slipped awkwardly into the pink dress. It was a simple one-piece that zipped up the back. Thanks to all the practice zipping Elijah in and out of his dresses—including this one—I didn't need help contorting to close it. Without a mirror in the closet, I didn't know how ridiculous I looked, but something told me without the boots and hat, I just looked silly.

I took one last deep breath, opened the door, and stepped out. Elijah and Viktoriya gasped in unison before erupting in mirthful laughter and applause. They were practically dancing as they ran to me, Elijah placing a bright pink spangled cowboy hat on my head, Viktoriya taking my hand and leading me to the mirror. Looking at myself, I was shocked. I didn't look bad. I also didn't look good. It was cute, but I was right; it looked silly without the boots.

I didn't hate how I looked. In fact, part of me loved it. Without realizing, I let Elijah and Viktoriya—standing at my sides—fade into the background of my thoughts. I was going to take this moment and live inside it. A moment in time where I didn't need to choose between Elijah and Viktoriya, or myself. I didn't care what would happen next. Lost in sequins, rhinestones, fringe—and freedom. I felt a sense of euphoria wash over me, but not like I was discovering a part of myself for the first time. I was seeing myself, unrestrained, unafraid, standing in a pink pony cowboy dress between two people I loved, who were both looking at me in the mirror with unrestrained affection.

"You need a drag name, Mark," Elijah said, the pride of a drag-mother gushing from every pore.

"This is great fun, but I don't think you're ready," I said, unable to hide my grin. "For A-Laddie Sane."

"A lady sane?" Viktoriya asked. She looked at Elijah and me, confused. "I don't understand."

"It's a play on David Bowie's *Aladdin Sane*—'Laddie,' not 'lady,' like a boy. But 'A-lady Sane' might be better. You're right, Mark, we're not ready for that," Elijah said with a laugh, handing Viktoriya the garment bag he was holding. "It's your turn, dear. This one is special, and a little tricky. I'll help you with it. Come on, into the queen closet. Mark, sit down before you hurt yourself."

"Ah! Bowie. Ziggy Stardust. Major Tom. Yes, I know this. Elijah—yes, you help me; I help you," Viktoriya said, nodding enthusiastically before holding up a red, modest-for-Elijah cocktail dress.

"I thought it was a clever name, and you look cute, Mark," Eros said softly.

"Thanks, Eros," I whispered back as I sat in the old armchair, which offered a direct view into the smaller closet—its door wide open. Neither Elijah nor Viktoriya closed the door behind them. I could only wonder whether that was an oversight—or deliberate.

Elijah opened the garment bag and extracted the dress, presenting it to Viktoriya. She examined it, noting the strategically placed lace and ribbons. She looked at Elijah and said something I couldn't hear, to which he nodded, and she nodded back in response. Then, Elijah examined the simple red dress she handed to him. It was not much more than a stretchable fabric tube with short sleeves attached to the neckline. To my surprise, they both shamelessly undressed in front of each other in plain sight of me. They had to know I could see them. Had they forgotten, did they not care, or did they want me to see?

I watched, transfixed and voyeuristic, incapable of looking away—or even blinking. I felt I *should* avert my eyes, grant them some semblance of decency, but they'd already abandoned any sense of privacy. The closet wasn't large enough for two people to dress or undress without their bodies brushing—but there were no accidents here. They were actively helping each other, like comfortable old friends. There was no shame, no spark of attraction, no hint of anything to justify the jealousy churning inside me.

But who was I jealous of? What was I jealous of? Elijah's hand on Viktoriya's back as he delicately unclasped her bra? Viktoriya's hands as she unzipped Elijah's dress and slid the straps off his shoulders? Or was it the hungry envy of sitting out here when I desperately wished to be in there with them both? I had become fixated, lost in thought and fantasy. I almost missed when they both glanced at me. Not together, but separately, independently sneaking a glimpse of me, watching them. It was almost too much to take. I could only imagine their motivations at this point. Were they both checking—in the hope I wasn't, or that I was—watching? Were they wondering which one of them I was looking at in that moment they were both standing next to each other, completely exposed?

I was dying, imagining myself rushing into that closet, stripping away the pink pony dress to join them. But I was frozen to that chair, transfixed, watching Viktoriya help Elijah step into the red dress she picked out for him. And watching Elijah slip that black dress of lace and ribbon over the curves of Viktoriya's body, finally adjusting and smoothing the lace and ribbons with delicate, trusted care.

They stepped out of the closet together, past the mirror to stand side by side in front of me. They paused, posed, and both slowly turned around so I could take them in from every angle. It was deliberate; they didn't glance at the mirror—they already knew exactly how they looked. Elijah's dress hugged his body sensuously, just tight enough to telegraph the outline of every muscle. Classy, but with a hint of trouble underneath, highlighted by the obvious bulge from his lack of a tuck. Viktoriya was every bit the goddess I saw last night, but now there was a domineering aura about her. The ribbons crisscrossing the open side slit of the dress revealed agonizingly powerful thighs beneath. The plunging neckline of translucent lace was like looking into a pool of calm waters concealing treasures or danger beneath the surface. This was for me. For the third or fifth time, I died. I also knew, deep down, I could never choose Elijah over Viktoriya or Viktoriya over Elijah. I wanted them both. I needed them both. I loved them both. It was bread and water. Pizza and wine. Beer and instant ramen noodles. Two different, completely complementary necessities.

"I ... don't know ... I'm ..." I stammered, grasping for words that refused to come. My mind was empty except for one burning thought: I'm in love.

Chapter 14

"Mark!" I whispered sharply in his ear. I needed him to snap out of it because he was dangerously close to running headfirst into catastrophe. "Get Viktoriya out of here. Talk to her now. This isn't how you tell her—and it's not fair. I'm almost sure she's figured out how Elijah feels about you. I'd wager the Library of Alexandria she suspects there's something between you two."

"That's no answer," Viktoriya teased.

"No, no, Viki. That is possibly the most diplomatically appropriate compliment our poor Mark is capable of. For now," Elijah said, resting his head playfully on her shoulder. "We are just too much for him."

"No, Viktoriya is right. You *both* look incredible. Viktoriya, that dress, you look … I'm a little … Please don't ask me to kill anyone, because never in a million years could I say no to you in that dress," Mark finally said, although it took half a dozen deep breaths for him to get the words out. "Elijah, tuck if you're wearing that in the club. Otherwise, you're eating. Not to kill the mood, but it may be time to call it a day?"

"What? You're kidding? It's barely …" Elijah said, looking around the room and at his empty wrist. "Daytime. I have no idea what time it is, but the sun is still up."

"It is four o'clock in the afternoon, on Sunday, September the seventh, if you want to know," Mark said, with a gruff vaguely British accent, for no discernible or logical reason, holding an extended shoehorn to his mouth like a pipe. It was clearly some inside joke between them—Elijah laughed and called him Gandalf.

"What are you doing? And what's a Gandalf?" I asked.

"Da, we are in the house of Elrond, yes?" Viktoriya smirked. "I do not remember wizards wearing pink hats in Rivendell."

"Viktoriya and I do not keep drag club hours," Mark said once he caught his breath from laughing. "And if you don't mind, Elijah, I would very much like to have Viktoriya to myself for a little while."

"You'd like that," Viktoriya and Elijah said in unison, and all three burst out laughing.

"Yes, yes. Elijah, I also would like Mark to myself," Viktoriya mercifully said, rescuing Mark from a situation I have no doubt he would otherwise lack the will to extract himself. "Sadly, we must change now."

Without hesitation, Viktoriya started slipping off her dress as she walked to the closet. Mark's face turned the same shade of pink as his cowboy hat. Elijah shrugged and quickly shimmied out of his dress, then slipped into a nearby pair of pants without replacing his shirt. Moments later, Viktoriya stepped out, fully dressed and holding Mark's clothes.

"Your turn now," Viktoriya said, that mischievous smirk Mark knew so well creeping across her lips. "My turn to watch."

Mark's pink face deepened to crimson, and Elijah's eyebrow shot up. To his credit, Mark stood, tossed the hat to Elijah, and reached behind to unzip the dress. He slipped it off, careful to keep it from crumpling on the floor, and handed it to Elijah. Viktoriya eyed Mark—standing in nothing but boxer briefs—and clicked her tongue, holding his clothes just out of reach.

"Disappointing," she said, shooting Elijah a sharp look. "Is this fair?"

"Fair is fair, Mark," Elijah said, making an exaggerated gesture toward Mark's underpants. "After all, you didn't even pretend to look away."

Mark was no longer a startling shade of red; instead, he was now ghostly pale. To his credit—again—he sighed, knowing there were only two ways out: the right way or the wrong way. He took one deep breath, and slipped out of his boxer briefs, offering them to Viktoriya. She accepted them, placing them on top of the rest of Mark's clothing. She stared at him—longer than necessary—

before finally handing over his clothes, a faint smirk tugging at her lips.

"I am no longer so disappointed," she said, locking eyes with Mark. "For now."

"Same," Elijah said, winking at both Mark and Viktoriya in turn.

Mark quickly dressed. He might have tried to say something, but none of the sounds he made qualified as actual words. Once Mark was dressed, he and Viktoriya helped Elijah return all the dresses to their proper places. Except for the black cocktail dress—he gave it to Viktoriya, declaring no one else on Earth could wear it as well as she did. Mark, on the other hand, was informed he should never again wear a pink cowboy hat due to his tendency to blush the same shade of pink.

Viktoriya and Elijah promised each other they would get together soon, so she could teach him a proper French seam. And he promised to take her to some of his favorite thrift shops. As they left Elijah's apartment, Viktoriya took Mark's hand in hers. Without saying a word, they turned the corner and walked toward the Sunflower Kafe and Viktoriya's home.

"Mark, I'm sure you've thought about how to broach the topic, and I don't know if you have a plan. But here's my idea," I said in Mark's ear. "You know she was intensely curious about who Elijah was singing to. I am almost positive she worked out it was you. But I'm positive she doesn't know that you know she knows—or that she knows you know … but who knows … I lost track. My point is it wouldn't be out of the blue or too unusual for you to bring it up. Especially after that exhibition in the closet—"

"Viktoriya, I'm curious," Mark said, rudely interrupting me. "Elijah called you Viki, did he ask you, or did you ask him to call you that? And do you like it? Should I call you Viki? I never really thought about it, I guess I just liked the way your name sounds when I say—"

"Da, he asked first. I do not mind it, but I do not prefer it," Viktoriya said, frowning slightly, as if considering it for the first time. "If you like, you may call me Viki too, but I like how you say my name. Is like you *know* me."

"In that case, Elijah can have 'Viki.' I'll keep Viktoriya."

Viktoriya stopped, pulling Mark to a halt beside her. They were nearly in front of the café. She looked at him as if he'd said something either profound or ridiculous. With Mark, it's hard to tell the difference.

"Our apartment is upstairs, I take you to the back stairs. We go upstairs without going inside kafe," Viktoriya said, an implication hanging on her words. "You would like to see my bedroom, yes?"

"Yes," Mark said, nodding like it was the first nod of his life. "I'd like that very much."

She led him by the hand around the back of the building to a staircase leading to an unassuming door. The kind of door you'd find behind almost any house—half window, half wood, complete with a well-worn pet flap. Viktoriya pulled a single key on a keychain from her jacket pocket and unlocked the door with practiced ease. Inside was a typical hallway—the kind people have seen thousands of times. I assume. It was my first actually, and only the third modern home I'd entered in a century.

The first doorway in the hall was Viktoriya's. I figured that one out on my own because she had hand-painted a navy-blue V superimposed over a sunflower. So, I couldn't feel too proud of my deduction. Her room wasn't much larger than Elijah's old bedroom-turned-closet. In one corner, she had a sewing form on a stand next to a desk that held her sewing machine, laptop, and a few textbooks. Next to one small chest of drawers, she had two clothes racks, very similar to the ones Elijah had in his closet. Her walls were an explosion of art, covering every available inch with hand-drawn designs, sketches, and even a few paintings and photographs. They were simultaneously chaotic and cohesive in their organic expression of Viktoriya. If I was simply impressed, Mark was flabbergasted.

Mark stood in the center of her room, slowly studying the walls—the same deliberate focus he used when examining graffiti or sculptures. But this time, there was nothing to interpret. It was literal. It was simply a literal representation. Lost in thought, Mark didn't notice Viktoriya close the door and slip off her jacket. She stepped closer to him while his back was turned.

"Mark?" Viktoriya said softly, and Mark turned around to find her only inches away.

"Viktoriya, what is it?"

"I must ask you a question," she said, reaching for his hand. Mark swallowed hard. I would have too if I had a throat or could swallow.

"Yes, go ahead," Mark said. The tremble in his voice was barely perceptible, but I could hear that he was terrified of what she could ask, knowing what we knew.

"Will you stay?" Viktoriya asked, pulling Mark even closer than he was. "Will you stay here with me tonight? Share—"

"Viktoriya, there is nothing I want more than to say yes," Mark said, wincing as he forced himself to take a step back. "I have to tell you something first. I wish this could wait until morning … This isn't how I wanted it to happen."

"What is it, Mark?" she asked, looking concerned.

"Last night … you asked who Elijah was singing to?"

"Mark …" she tried to interrupt, her voice uncertain.

"I don't even know how to say it," Mark said, covering his face as if to hide from her. "I'm afraid … it feels like I'm being torn in two."

"Mark, I—"

"It was me, Viktoriya," Mark interrupted. "I was Elijah's audience. I didn't know it then—"

"Mark!" Viktoriya interrupted, but Mark didn't stop.

"After you went home last night, Elijah showed up at my door." Mark turned away from Viktoriya for a moment, before he turned back but failed to meet her gaze. "He told me he's loved me for a long time," Mark said, the words spilling out.

He couldn't even look at Viktoriya, who was listening stoically. "Then he was standing there, asking me … how I felt. I didn't know how to answer him. He was just standing there waiting for me to say something … anything … and I don't know how it happened, or when … but … deep down … I knew. I mean, I know," Mark paused, finally meeting Viktoriya's gaze. "I'm in love—with you and Elijah. In love with two people … and I don't know—"

"Zamovkny!" Viktoriya shouted—Mark caught the meaning, if not the exact word, and he shut-up. Viktoriya's face cracked. She reached out and jerked Mark's hands away from his face, forcing him to look at her. "Perestan' hovoryty durnytsi i dai nam real'ni fakty, bud' laska … Sorry, I … Stop talking from your ass. Give me truth."

She stared at him, her stoicism collapsing, and he stared back, his confusion and fear dripping from his eyes. Viktoriya's unreadable mask gave way to realization.

"What do you want, Mark?"

****Mark****

I hadn't meant to blurt it out; the words escaped before I even realized what I was saying. The words left my mouth before I even said them to myself. The first time I said it aloud, the first time I told Viktoriya that I love her, was in conjunction with telling her I also love Elijah. Rather than break it gently, I let it crash through the window. Now she looked right through me, asking a question I'd only just asked myself.

"I … don't know … God … I mean … I don't know how to answer that now," I said, looking away because there was something revealing reflected in her eyes.

"I saw him sing to you," Viktoriya said, releasing my hands and stepping back. "I see you hear him, but not hear him. Today, I see you look at me and him the same."

"You? You knew?" I asked, the surprise clearing my mind.

"Not all … I … Ya pidozryuvala … unsure about you. Elijah is clear. This is why I feel … Yak hrim sered yasnoho neba … Like lightning from a blue sky," Viktoriya said. Her words tangled between Ukrainian and English. I had only seen her this flustered once before—over a term paper she accidentally deleted. "Last night … when I asked … you did not lie to me?"

"Lie? No. How could I lie? I couldn't even see it last night. None of this is coming out right," I said, stepping closer to her. This time, I took her hand. She saw what I didn't, and she didn't run. "I'm sorry, Viktoriya. Please believe me."

"American men lie," Viktoriya said, a shadow drifting over her expression. That wasn't about me—but it hit like it was. "But you did not. I know you. A little bit of idiot."

The Fixer, The Maker, The Drag Entertainer

Of all the times I've been called an idiot, this might be my favorite. Like the first glint of sunlight through a passing storm. It's not over yet, and I don't know what happens next, but like Eros said not long ago, I was remarkably unstabbed.

"I am an idiot. How long did it take before I asked you out?" I asked.

"Too long, because you missed when I asked you first," Viktoriya said, giving my shoulder a gentle shove.

"You asked … whe—oh God. I *am* an idiot," I said, recoiling as I remembered when she'd invited me for coffee a year ago—and I'd just shown her my full cup. "Viktoriya. I have a problem. I meant what I said. I do love y—"

"No. Do not say it again. How can you love two people? This is not possible," Viktoriya said, stepping back. For once, I'd pushed too fast. "You don't know what you want. You made a choice? Or you refuse? No … I think you make *us* choose. We … I … need time now I do not wish to say something that I cannot unsay. Please go."

"Okay, I hear you," I said, turning toward the door. With one hand on the doorknob, I asked, "Will you call?"

"Da. I will call," Viktoriya said. It was a short, unembellished, open-ended promise—and a clear end to the conversation.

I stepped through the door and left her apartment before I could second-guess myself and make matters worse. With each step, I replayed everything she said, and everything I said. She didn't reject me outright. That had to mean something, even if I didn't know what.

"Eros?" I asked, hopeful they were still listening and could help me understand what had just happened.

"I'm here, Mark. I'm sorry, that didn't go the way I hoped," Eros said. "She is just so …"

"Yeah, she is," I said, knowing exactly what Eros meant. "I'm sure you wanted to help. Thank you for not."

"I think she would have found a way to kill me if I had even tried. But you're right, I wanted to," Eros said. They even managed a sympathetic chuckle.

"Can I ask you something?" I said without thinking.

"You just did. But go on," Eros replied dryly. I should have anticipated that.

"Can you keep an eye on her? I mean, check in on her from time to time?"

"I can, now that I know the way. And yes, I will. Do you want me to check on Elijah too?"

"If you like, but I'm not worried about him. I think he's the only one of us that might understand what happened today." I answered. It was the truth. I thought about calling him, or turning at the corner to knock on his door, like he did mine. But I didn't. I didn't consciously choose not to. I only knew that seeing him now would only throw me into turmoil that I was unequipped to handle right now. Viktoriya was right. I was avoiding the decision, hopeful they would make the choice for me. Because in truth, I didn't want to choose between them.

It didn't make sense yet; it made perfect sense the way we complemented each other. Viktoriya and Elijah became friends as easily and quickly as Elijah and I had all those years ago. I think maybe I was even a little afraid they would choose each other over me, not that there was even a hint of romantic or sexual tension between them, as was blatantly obvious in the closet. They were both standing close enough to feel each other's breath on their naked skin without a single spark between them. Was I really avoiding a choice, or just refusing to accept the one I'd already made—a choice I couldn't make alone?

****Eros****

Mark walked home alone. I left him to check in on Viktoriya. She was in her room, as expected, texting with Elijah. She was telling him everything. She chose her words deliberately. She typed, deleted, and retyped her messages—each version softer than the last. Her hurt showed in the tremor of her breath as she whispered curses in Ukrainian. In that moment, she could not fathom how Mark could honestly say he loved them both, and Elijah was trying but failing to explain. Elijah at least had the benefit of knowing other bisexual and pansexual people. But then he had to admit he couldn't be sure if that was true about Mark, because Mark hadn't even come out to himself yet.

The Fixer, The Maker, The Drag Entertainer

The idea that someone could be unsure of their own sexuality baffled her. She admitted to Elijah that she didn't completely understand how anyone could be attracted to both men and women. How could someone not know that about themselves? She knew who she was attracted to and who she was not. Elijah, patient as ever, tried to explain. It was easy when it was black and white—when you knew what you found attractive and what you didn't. Mark never had that clarity. Because he rarely spoke about it, no one ever told him it wasn't the same for everyone. Society was often quicker to erase bisexuality than even to hide homosexuality, leaving little visibility for Mark to recognize himself in. Elijah pointed to the famously bisexual Freddie Mercury, whom most people thought of or talked about as simply gay.

I admired the grace they both showed toward Mark: Viktoriya's eagerness to understand and Elijah's drive to advocate for Mark. Then Viktoriya asked if it was possible for someone to be with a man and a woman at once without it falling apart. To Elijah's credit, he answered honestly. Yes, it was possible, and it happened. Sometimes it fails. Occasionally, it works—but rarely, since jealousy can surface easily when people aren't close. Viktoriya ended their conversation by asking Elijah to check in on Mark. She admitted she was afraid she'd overreacted and told Elijah she was glad to have him as a friend. Maybe it hadn't gone as badly as I'd feared.

I caught up with Mark quickly, hitching a ride or two on passing cars. He was just stepping into his apartment building. He shuffled toward the elevator, pale and hollow-eyed, like someone who'd just seen a ghost. And here I thought Elijah held the title for drama. Of course, he didn't know Viktoriya had been worried or that she'd already talked it out with Elijah. Elijah was a good friend. He was honest with Viktoriya about what happened—and, more importantly, what didn't—when he showed up at Mark's door last night. He told Viktoriya how Mark talked about her and their date. Elijah even apologized to Viktoriya for doing what he did. I didn't think he needed to do that. Viktoriya thought so too. She even said the only one who should apologize is Mark—to Elijah—for being so oblivious, and even that wasn't really his fault.

"Mark, I'm back," I said in Mark's ear, taking up residence in Mark's phone. "Viktoriya's fine. How are you holding up?"

"Hi, Eros," Mark said, moping into his apartment. "Thank you for checking. If you don't mind, I don't feel like talking right now."

"You're welcome. And yes, I mind—just a little," I said. I was disappointed in how defeated Mark was acting. "I spent the entire day, and a big part of last night, as a spectator or completely ignored. You could at least talk to me for a minute."

"You're right, I know. I'll be lucky if I can keep my mind off everything long enough to fall asleep. I don't think I can cope with talking about it," Mark said, wandering through his apartment on autopilot. "Is there something important you need to tell me? Or something else you want to talk about?"

"Yes, and there are hundreds of things I want to talk about, but not right now. But first, snap out of it, Mark," I said, a little louder than usual, while also making his phone vibrate in his pocket for emphasis. "Things did not go as badly as you fear. Did you forget how unstabbed you are? Viktoriya didn't even threaten to throw you out the window. And remember what Elijah said this morning?"

"Okay, I get it. But we humans don't exactly get to choose how we feel," Mark said, setting his phone on the charger. "But you're right. It could have gone much worse, and, except for those last few minutes, it was one of the best days. I guess that's why those last few minutes with Viktoriya felt like a kick to my chest. Best day I've had in ages—and it ends like that."

"All right, fair point. I'm sorry. We don't have to talk more than you want," I said, feeling a little embarrassed. Mark had reminded me—again—not to downplay human emotions. "I'll just say that Viktoriya is not mad at you."

"Thanks. I'm sure that'll feel more relieving in the morning. We'll have plenty of time to talk—and to distract ourselves—at work tomorrow," Mark said. "I'm going to take something and sleep—I'm exhausted, Eros. See you in the morning."

Mark, still despondent but a little more at ease, walked into his bedroom and closed the door behind him. That left me to my own devices for the night—which sounds more dramatic than it was. Remember, I don't sleep, so I have pretty much every night to myself. Tonight, I was going to make a list for Mark on his phone. I've noticed he keeps plenty of lists—mostly reminders. This one would remind him not to call or text Viktoriya—she'd call him when ready. Answer Elijah if he messages or calls. Call his mom, because he never called her back after they spoke on Friday. And a few things to keep him busy: go to the market, return Dr. Newell's antique oil lamp, and finally show me a map of the town. Then there were a few things I wanted to look up on Mark's internet—like what exactly a "Gandalf" is.

Chapter 15

Monday morning slunk into the apartment like an unwelcome houseguest, dragging Mark out of bed. His routine was a slow-motion disaster, made worse by the absence of leftover coffee to jump-start his barely functional brain. He cursed the innocent coffee maker for failing him. It begrudgingly dripped its life-affirming brew into the waiting carafe while Mark stormed around the apartment. He was preparing to confront a day he had no desire to face. Twenty minutes after it began, the coffee was ready, and Mark, now fully dressed, was drinking as much as he could, as quickly as the temperature would allow. As soon as he finished two cups, he shut off the coffee maker, leaving half a pot for later, and he dropped his empty mug into the sink.

The heavy ceramic bounced and rattled, sounding as though it should have shattered both mug and sink. Mark flinched at the sound, then sighed in exasperation. When he picked up and looked at his phone, the first thing he saw was the list I created for him. He groaned in irritation, and I braced myself for what promised to be a long, frustrating day.

"You made a 'to-do' list for me?" Mark asked.

"I did, good morning. I thought it might be helpful," I said.

"Did you think I'd forget not to call Viktoriya—or to call my mom? And why wouldn't I answer Elijah? Seriously?"

"Yes, I did. And you have a hundred lists on here full of things like this."

"Dammit," Mark muttered, closing the list and flicking through his phone to dismiss a stack of missed notifications. "I make those when I'm busy at work and think of something I can't do right away. Not because I need a checklist for my day."

"That makes sense. But, again, I was just trying to be helpful," I replied. "You seem a little crabby. Should I leave you alone today?"

"Sorry," Mark answered. "No, it's fine. Thank you for trying to help. And yeah, I'm not in the best mood today—can you ignore that and try to keep me distracted?"

"That, I can do. So, I found those books with that Gandalf—fascinating stories—but I don't understand something. What were you doing with that long shoehorn?"

"Oh, right. That's from the movie. In the film Gandalf was smoking his pipe in that scene. But not really in the book."

"They made that into a movie?"

"Yes—movies, three of them. I'm surprised you didn't find it if you were looking that up on the internet. It is extremely popular."

"I asked 'what is Gandalf,' and the first thing it said was that he was a character in a book, and I stopped reading that and went to your bookshelf, and found the book and read it. That answered my question so I just didn't read what else the internet said about the subject. I had other things to explore. Like this application that appears to list billions of songs—why would you want that? What good is a list of songs you can't listen to?"

"What do you mean? You can listen to them. Did you not press play?"

"Of course I did—do you think I was just born? Nothing happened when I pressed it."

Mark chuckled to himself as he picked his headset up off the desk and slipped it over his ears.

"Try it now. It needs to be connected to headphones or a speaker," Mark said, opening the app on his phone for me. I pressed 'play' and immediately heard music in Mark's headset.

"Wait—are you telling me we could have been listening to music this whole time? Maybe today is not going to be so bad after all," I said, immediately pulling up the playlist I'd assembled last night. "You're okay with this, right? Music in your ears all day?"

"I am. It's not unusual for me to listen to music most of the time—unless I'm actively talking to someone. Like you—so since you've been hanging around I haven't."

"Well, that changes now."

"Sounds good. Keep the volume low, please—and don't skip around too much. Come on, time to get to work."

"Don't forget my old lamp. You said you would return it."

Mark grabbed my old bronze oil lamp from the shelf and stuffed it into his bag before leaving the apartment. I spent the better part of the morning exploring and enjoying the vast library of music now at my disposal. Mark only objected to a handful of songs that were not to his liking. We even started to have fun together, and Mark began actively finding and suggesting songs for me. He spent part of the day in the office he shared with his friend and coworker, OT, who only pressed him once for details about the weekend. Mark told him he had asked Viktoriya out, and he had taken her to Elijah's show. They'd had an excellent time, but things got complicated and he didn't want to talk about it now. OT was understandably disappointed, but supportive and respectful. As the day progressed, Mark's mood improved slightly, but it was prone to shifting rapidly, especially if a song I picked reminded him of Elijah or Viktoriya.

Around lunchtime, Mark returned my old lamp to Dr. Newell, informing him it was harmless, and his problems had been coincidental, much to his relief. Mark left before Dr. Newell could launch into his newest complaint or philosophical theory—and I can't thank him enough for that. On our way out of the office, Elijah sent Mark a text message casually asking how he was doing. Mark read the message, and rather than tap reply and text back, he tapped on Elijah's picture to call him. The music paused, and the phone rang once before Elijah answered.

"Like clockwork," Elijah said with a laugh. "I text, you call."

"It's usually because my hands are full or I'm walking. Like now," Mark said. "I was just making a delivery and now I'm looking for something for lunch."

"I'd say come by the club, but I'm home today. "Hey, how are you holding up? Yesterday was … something."

"I'm not great, honestly. Yesterday was amazing, but it didn't end on the best note for me."

"I heard. I talked to Viktoriya after you left; she filled me in."

"You two talked …"

"Yes, Mark. We're friends now, or did you forget that part of yesterday? She was worried that she overreacted, and she told me to check on you."

"If she thinks that, why wouldn't she call herself?" Mark said, with a twinge of stress creeping into his voice.

"Because she's still not ready for that, Mark. Like it or not, you dropped a bomb on her," Elijah said patiently. "Not that it was entirely your fault—or within your control. Still, don't you remember how you reacted when I did the same to you?"

"Dammit, Elijah. I'm not ready to deal with this."

"Yeah, well, ready or not, Mark—you can't avoid it. Sooner or later, when it comes to me and Viktoriya, you'll have to decide what you really want."

"Like you said—bombs were dropped. Viktoriya wasn't ready, and neither was I. I don't really want to talk about it right now, and I'm not even sure I understand how I'm supposed to make a choice here."

"I was with you yesterday. I watched you. I think you already made your choice—and it scares you. You just don't know how to face it," Elijah said, letting the silence stretch. "I'll let Viktoriya know you're moping—but otherwise fine. Think honestly about what you want, Mark."

"I can't do this right now. I'll talk to you later," Mark said, ending the phone call. He exhaled hard, staring at his phone as if it had suddenly become too heavy to hold, regret etched across his face.

"Mark, you hung up on Elijah?" I asked. Mark surprised me by pushing Elijah away like that—not just that he did it, but by how abrupt and vaguely unkind it was.

"I know, I shouldn't have. I'll apologize later. I should've just texted—hearing his voice after yesterday was just too much," Mark said as he unpaused the music. "I'm not in the mood to talk. Let's just get through the day."

Aside from the passive background music we were both listening to, we spent the rest of the day and evening in relative silence. Mark grew progressively more irritable as time went on.

He started objecting more aggressively to songs, which devolved into accusations of deliberately choosing "break-up" songs just to torture him. Honestly, the way he was acting, I might have—if I'd even known what a "break-up song" was. As far as I was concerned, he was on the cusp of an unjustifiable tantrum. I decided it was time to leave him alone entirely when he accused me of meddling for simply reminding him to call his mother. We wouldn't speak to each other again until the next morning.

Tuesday morning kicked in the door and stormed into Mark's apartment like a vindictive ex-lover. Mark met the day with resentment and spite. We spoke very little that morning after he snapped at me again when I dared to suggest he should send an apology to Elijah. In true defeatist fashion, he simply announced that he wasn't emotionally prepared to find out how badly he'd ruined everything with both Viktoriya and Elijah. I tried to gently remind him that overall, Sunday had gone very well. He had no reason to write off Viktoriya, and needlessly pushing Elijah away was counterproductive. He wouldn't hear it, and he left for work without even checking whether or not I was with him.

I suppose I could understand—on a conceptual level—why Mark was avoiding Elijah. It wasn't about him; it was about what Elijah represented. If Mark talked to him, he just might have to face what he wants and either accept or reject it. And it didn't seem like Mark was in any way prepared for that. The fear was paralyzing. So, Mark fell back on familiar habits—he avoided making any decisions at all costs. So, as I saw it, the day's decision-making fell to me.

With my newly self-appointed decision-making powers, I sent Elijah a short apology text on Mark's behalf. I kept it brief. *'Sorry for hanging up on you yesterday, I'm just afraid right now.'* I tried to avoid overstepping too much. I saved the overstepping for when I sent the text message to his mother as well. I hadn't met her yet, but I had a feeling I'd like her. So, I took it upon myself to tell her Mark had meant to call her back, that he was sorry he hadn't, and that he'd had a very successful date he couldn't wait to tell her about. Then I added that we were working on a solution to the little problem she was having with that real estate jackass, Gale Barlow, and we would call her soon. Hopefully, those two messages would buy Mark some time—and a little space to breathe.

Unlike yesterday, Mark asserted his musical preferences while he worked, skipping most of what I wanted to hear. Yesterday, he couldn't stand "break-up" songs. Today, he was drowning in them—wallowing in heartbreak, lost lovers, and regret. It was depressing, even for me. Just when I thought I couldn't take any more of his self-inflicted punishment, an incoming call from Mark's mother rendered our conflict moot. I knew I should have told her Mark would call her when he could talk.

"Hi, Mom," Mark said, clicking a button on his headset to answer the call. "Is everything all right?"

"Of course, Mark, I was just calling you back to hear about this date," she said, casually dismissing his concern for her in favor of her interest in his news.

"Date? Wait—hang on," Mark said, muting his mic and checking his texts. "Eros, did you text my mother on my behalf?"

"Yes. I was trying to help. I should've said you'd call her later. I was going to tell you, but you were too busy sulking," I said.

"Thanks," Mark said—without a trace of gratitude—before unmuting his phone. "Sorry, Mom, I had my hands full. Yes, I had a date on Saturday, but now is not—"

"That is wonderful, Mark. Well, tell me about her!" she said, without letting Mark finish. "I want to hear all about it."

"Her name's Viktoriya. I took her to Elijah's drag show. You'd like her, but I don't know if it'll work out right now," Mark said with a sigh of resignation. It was clear that his desire to talk about it was at odds with his urge to push it far from his mind. "But I've got my hands full at the moment. Can I call you later?"

"Of course. I'm sure everything will work out dear. I know you don't want to hear it, but you need to have a little faith in yourself. You can call later; we're just getting the mill and cider press fixed up to process a few small test batches. We should have it fully ready for the first weekend of October," Mark's mom said, kindly respecting his wishes. "You'll come help with some of it?"

"Thanks. That sounds great. Of course I'll come help soon— before October, I hope," Mark said, finding yet another excuse to beat himself up. "Sorry, I haven't been there. I'll give you a call later."

"It's okay dear; I love you."

"Love you too, Mom," Mark said, ending the phone call. "Eros, please don't text anyone for me—especially my mother—unless I ask you to, or it's an actual emergency. Still … thanks. I think I needed that."

"Of course, Mark. Can I ask you a favor now?"

"All right, what is it?"

"Will you please stop skipping the songs I want to hear," I said. "Or at least keep it to a minimum."

"Okay, okay, I can do that. Sorry," Mark said, holding his hands up in mock innocence.

The rest of the morning went more smoothly. Mark's nerves had settled. His mood evened out after that brief call from his mom. He still gravitated toward sad songs, but was no longer actively drowning in them. We were coasting toward a sullen but peaceful lunch break.

Then, Elijah replied to the text I'd sent from Mark's phone.

Mark glowered at his phone, scanning both my message and Elijah's reply. In my opinion, Elijah's response was perfect—understanding, comforting, and irritatingly warm. He started by saying he hadn't even noticed Mark hanging up on him, and even if he had, it wasn't a big deal. Then he reassured Mark that fear was natural, but his real problem was not knowing what he was afraid of. Finally, he told Mark to call if he wanted to talk—otherwise he'd check in later.

Mark's face was a tempest of conflicting emotions—magnificent, in the worst way. One moment, he was on the edge of relief; the next, his expression curdled. Elation, outrage, embarrassment—then a sharp plunge into self-pity and revulsion. Finally, he settled into a particularly ugly shade of self-loathing, lined with barely contained rage. Seething, he muttered an excuse and left the office. The moment he stepped into the elevator, he lashed out.

"You texted Elijah." Mark's voice was low and sharp, vibrating with restrained fury.

"I did," I said, keeping my voice flat and unapologetic. "Because I didn't want to see you wait too long to realize you should have."

Mark jammed his fist against the elevator button for the ground floor. "I don't even know how to explain how angry I feel right now," Mark said, taking a sharp breath. "You know what? I don't need to."

"I'm not sorry, Mark." My voice stayed steady. "I won't watch you throw away something good just because it scares you."

"I need you to go." Mark's words were cold and cutting, almost unfeeling except for the shudder in his voice.

"You just can't help yourself, can you?" I sighed. "It's not enough to run away—you have to burn the bridge behind you. Fine. Suit yourself; take me outside and touch the first utility pole you see, and I'll leave."

Mark stormed out of the elevator, out of the building, and straight toward the first vertical object he saw. Technically, it was a streetlamp, not a utility pole—but I wasn't about to quibble. He slapped his hand against the pole—forgetting his phone was in his hand. The crack of breaking glass split the silence. Mark swore.

I slipped out of his phone, finding the veins of the streetlamp that would carry me away from Mark, away from his fear, away from his tantrum. I didn't have to leave. He wouldn't know the difference if I just ignored him. But right now? I wanted to go.

I wondered how many times Mark had done this to Elijah?

How many times had he pushed away the people who cared?

There was one way I knew how to find out. I'd find Elijah and ask him. And when Mark was ready to stop running? Maybe he'd learn something.

I could follow these electrical wires and go almost anywhere I wanted to go, but now I was going to find Elijah. He was most likely at The Queen's Head Club at this time of day on a Tuesday, so I only needed to find my way there. The web of underground cables was a dark, directionless maze. But I only needed to get across the street—once I hit the overhead power lines, I could see where I was going.

A few minutes later, I reached the club. It wasn't far, and once I had my bearings, I remembered the way. The hardest part wasn't the distance—it was the distraction Mark had left buzzing in my mind.

I had never been upset by a human before. They had annoyed, frustrated, and occasionally offended me—but none had ever hurt my feelings.

For the first time, I wished I really were the spiteful, wish-twisting djinn I once pretended to be.

I wormed my way into the building and slipped down to the bar. From the ceiling light above the bar, I spotted Elijah. A stack of glasses and a bar towel rested next to him, untouched. He leaned over the bar, engrossed in conversation with Viktoriya.

"I don't know. There is no perfect vehicle," Elijah said. "A touring bus or RV would have storage, dressing space, and a workspace—but unless you're traveling the country, it's overkill. You need something drivable, something parkable. I'd go with a mid-size cargo van if I had to replace the Honda Element I stole from my brother."

"You steal from your brother?" Viktoriya asked, emphasizing her exaggerated shock. "No, no. Elijah. You mustn't steal from brothers."

"Oh, stop—I didn't actually steal it," Elijah snorted, swatting Viktoriya's arm. "I claimed it. He replaced the old Honda years ago. It was—and still is—an ideal short-range drag-mobile. If he, Mom, or Dad objected, they would've said something. Besides, I still help out and let them borrow it."

"Good, good. You are not thief," Viktoriya laughed. "You only steal hearts."

"I. Never!" Elijah feigned offense, wildly clutching his heart. "And you're one to talk about stealing hearts."

"I am sorry, my friend," Viktoriya said, seeming to know exactly what Elijah meant by his playful jab. "Has Mark answered you?"

"No, no. You don't owe me an apology." Elijah waved away Viktoriya's words as though they were an uninvited pest. "You don't owe anyone an apology. No, Mark hasn't replied. He is stewing until he is ready to accept reality."

"I should call him," Viktoriya said, looking at Elijah's phone.

"Not yet, dear. Give him another day." Elijah's voice was soft but certain. "Trust me—I know his patterns. By this time tomorrow, he'll hit rock bottom. That's when he'll be ready to be honest with himself. Right now? He's still spiraling. He's in a self-pity tantrum, picking at the scab just to watch it bleed ... If you call him now, he won't hear you," Elijah exhaled, rubbing his temple. "He won't hear reason or love—only the voice in his head convincing him of the worst. That you're lying, or just teasing him. He's exhausting, but he is also the best man I've ever known."

Well, that was unexpected. I knew Viktoriya and Elijah had bonded, but this went beyond a bond of friendship. They were allies or co-conspirators, depending on your perspective. And to my relief, I didn't need to talk to Elijah. Which meant I didn't have to reveal myself to him or explain how I'd been watching and trying to help Mark for the past five days—had it really only been five?—*had it only been five days?* It felt much longer; so much had happened to all of us. It was a relief not to have to explain it all right now.

"Da. I will wait. You will check on him?"

"Yes, I'll check in on him, and maybe see if he is close to making a decision."

"I wish to help him. If he knows we won't force him to choose between us. Maybe that will help him decide," Viktoriya said. She made a wish—a wish I could grant. I could tell Mark what I just heard, or at least drop a few hints—enough to nudge him toward a decision.

"I honestly think he knows, somewhere in the back of his mind. I think that's what is scaring him. I know he seems oblivious to a lot, but he really isn't. He just doesn't always trust his intuition when it comes to people." Elijah took Viktoriya's hand and smiled. "We'll help him. You'll be the one to shake him. You're better at that than I am. In a day or two, you'll call him and pull him away from the edge. I think then, he'll be ready to talk with us."

"Elijah, you make me do your dirty work, da? It's okay—I do for you, and for Mark," Viktoriya said, patting Elijah's hand and returning his smile. "Excuse me, I have class soon. I must go."

"Okay, Viki. Thanks for teaching me those Ukrainian toasts. Show me more next time?" Elijah said, releasing her hand as she stood. "I'll let you know how Mark's doing."

"Da. Of course. Thank you, Elijah," Viktoriya said, adjusting her jacket as she slipped her backpack over one shoulder. She walked to the door, then glanced back with a smile and a wave. Elijah returned the wave as she stepped outside.

Viktoriya and Elijah had a plan—a good one, too. For the moment, we were all letting Mark stew. I felt better after hearing Elijah's explanation. Mark's outburst hadn't been about me after all—I hadn't overstepped. He was just reacting, running on fear instead of reason. That was a relief, but not enough to run back to Mark yet. Instead, I followed Viktoriya for a while. She fascinated me—so different from Mark, yet drawn to him all the same. I felt compelled to understand her better.

I tagged along with Viktoriya for most of the remaining day, watching and listening. I learned something interesting about her. She spoke and acted differently with most people than she did with Mark and Elijah. With them, she was comfortable, playful, teasing. With others, she was more reserved—her English slower, more careful, deliberately precise. There was no teasing, flirtation, or sharp wit, just friendly warmth, and distant politeness. Viktoriya wore a careful mask for almost everyone: polite, quietly confident, intelligent, foreign yet adaptable. But with those she trusted and cared for, she dropped the mask, revealing someone sharper, wittier, far more commanding than she otherwise let on. I had only been half-joking when I called her a queen and a grandmaster to Mark—but now, I think I'd underestimated her.

When I parted ways with Viktoriya, I spent hours drifting, exploring the area. I hadn't meant to take a road trip—I only hopped into a stopped car to listen to a song that caught my attention. Before I knew it, I was cruising southbound on the Garden State Parkway. My—well, the car's—first stop was the Jon Bon Jovi Service Area on the Parkway. That was my first chance to jump to a different car, one heading back north instead of further south. Unfortunately, my new host was not in the mood for music, but a dreadful talk show about conspiracy theories. I wouldn't escape that particular torment until Exit 129, when the car wound its way back into New Brunswick.

On the upside, I can now tell you in excruciating detail how the Jersey Devil differs from Bigfoot.

I found my way back to Mark's apartment much later that night, closer to dawn than to dusk. His apartment looked like the victim of a passing storm—books scattered on the coffee table, records stacked haphazardly in front of the turntable, movies in a heap in front of his television. Empty beer cans and half-eaten takeout containers littered his kitchen counter, abandoned and forgotten. All signs of a distressed mind on a restless search for distraction.

Morning arrived not long behind me, drawing Mark from his bed before his alarm. He moved even more lethargically that morning—carelessly dressing for work, pouring coffee into his body, gathering his daily essentials. He picked up his phone, tapping through the typical reminders and notifications with a sigh. Mark waited a few moments in silence before speaking, his voice hesitant.

"Eros?"

"I'm here, Mark," I answered.

"I was afraid you left me too." His voice nearly broke.

"Well, I didn't. No one has. Why do you assume you've lost before the battle is over? You just expect the loss before it happens. Never mind, don't answer that. Let me distract you with the tales of my recent adventures."

Throughout the morning and into the afternoon, I kept Mark distracted while he worked. I told him about my road trip up and down the Garden State Parkway. He was surprisingly interested in the differences between the Jersey Devil and Bigfoot. He was still morose, still defeated, but he was relaxing. Elijah's check-in didn't push him to either extreme. It wasn't until he left his office and returned home that he finally admitted out loud what was weighing him down.

"She's never going to call," he said quietly.

"Mark, give her more credit. She told you she would call. Have you known her to not do something she said she will do?"

"No … Not that I know of. But that doesn't mean—"

"It means she will. I know it's hard, but trust her. I do … So does Elijah."

"How?"

"You asked me to check in on her—I did, and I have been. So has Elijah. Take a breath, Mark. And as Elijah puts it, 'tell that bitch in the back of your head to shut the fuck up.' Trust them. Trust me. And for once, trust yourself."

"It's not that easy … You've been checking on them—what do you know?"

"I know you need to stop thinking so much. Use that dumb heart of yours, because—" Mark's phone rang, cutting me off mid-sentence.

He pulled his phone out of his pocket and froze, staring at the screen. His breath caught in his chest.

Viktoriya was calling. Once again, she was one step ahead—she and Elijah had a talent for that. I'd hoped for at least a moment to prepare Mark.

"Mark, I'm sorry. I should've told you sooner," I said, rushing the words out. "Viktoriya and Elijah have—"

"It's okay, Eros," Mark said, cutting me off. His finger hovered over the 'answer call' button. "We're in it now," he murmured.

Chapter 16

My phone vibrated in my hand; Viktoriya's picture stared at me just above her name. Reality blurred as my mind erupted with every conceivable outcome this call could bring. Eros had been trying to prepare me for something. In hindsight, it was probably this very moment. But it was too late for preparation now. The ship had left the dock. Time seemed to slow, the fog clearing from the harbor to reveal a single thought, standing defiant against the wind. Eros's words echoed—"trust them." I pressed the big green button to answer the call.

"Viktoriya?" I said hesitantly to the faint distant static coming from my phone.

"Mark, you are home, yes?" Viktoriya answered, always direct, to-the-point, as though conversational pleasantries were a waste of effort—one thing I adored about her.

"Yes, I am—"

"Good, good. I know what I want. I have made decision. You have had time—now, do you know what you want? Have you made decision?"

"I … um … Yes… I do—I have … I—"

"No, not yet, don't tell me yet," she interrupted.

There was a knock on my door, echoing over the phone call. She was here. She must have been standing just outside my door when she called. For a moment, the recent memory of the last time someone knocked on my door flashed in my mind as I reached for the knob.

I opened the door, and there she was—standing exactly where Elijah had stood two nights ago. The realization hit like a rush of hot summer air up my spine, tingling through me. Viktoriya was standing in the doorway, still holding her phone up to her ear. She looked like she might have come straight from work or class. Her hair was loosely tied back, and she wore a long jacket. It looked like it might once have been a dark blue men's trench coat. She looked at me, maintaining eye contact as she slipped her phone back into her jacket pocket, stepping inside without waiting for an explicit invitation.

"Viktoriya, you're here," I said, almost choking on the words between my surprise and exhilaration. "I'm ... sorry ... I just got home ... it's a mess."

"Shh," she said, holding up a finger. She turned, closed the door behind her, and locked the world out.

She turned around and dropped her usual backpack from one shoulder onto the floor. My mind was still catching up. Viktoriya was here. This was more than a casual visit for a face-to-face conversation. This was something else. Then, with slow deliberation, she reached up and opened her jacket, letting it fall from her shoulders. My eyes followed her jacket as it fell, rippling to the ground behind her.

My gaze drifted from the jacket on the floor to the black ribbons lacing the open side slit of her dress, where glimpses of thigh peeked through. Then, over the translucent lace of the plunging neckline that whispered rumors of the spectacular body beneath. Then to the single sleeve that left one arm and shoulder bare.

It took seconds to register the dress. I stared in disbelief, but there it was. The ribbons, the lace, the impossible silhouette—the teasing glimpse of skin beneath. She was wearing it once again, for me. *The* black dress. The one Elijah gave her. The one she wore that day in the closet, when I nearly drowned in my own jealousy and longing. The breath rushed from my chest. My heartbeat stuttered and pounded in my ears. I nearly unraveled, ready to collapse like her fallen jacket. I tried to find the words to say, any words. I groped in vain through the dark, vacant repository of my entire vocabulary.

She reached behind her head, pulled out the pin holding her hair, and let it fall from her fingers. The metallic clink of the pin hitting the floor seemed to echo through the apartment—and through me. Viktoriya stepped forward, her hair unfolding and cascading over her shoulders. She reached out to me, her fingertips gently touching the inside of my wrist. A delicate touch, enough to send a jolt of electricity up my arm. Her hand slid slowly up my forearm, tracing the lines of muscle beneath my sleeve. She stepped closer, brushing her hand over my shoulder, up my neck, finding my face. Her fingers slipped into my beard, her thumb tracing the curve of my cheek. Her gaze never wavered from mine.

"Shh," she repeated. "Just now—is enough; I know you have an answer—but I need you for myself first."

Her touch was soft; her gaze devastating. She was stripping away my last threads of doubt, unraveling me without a word. A tremor ran through me, and I exhaled sharply. At this moment, I was a captive in her hands. The last threads of my will strained and yielded as she closed the space between us.

"Mark—I am going to leave you for tonight," Eros whispered quickly. "Good night, and good luck."

Viktoriya kissed me softly, almost inquisitively, but it was not a question. Nor was it a plea. It was declarative, committing to a decision. She didn't pull or push; she simply opened the door and beckoned. I answered, kissing her back, wrapping my hands around her, holding her in place with me. I was entirely hers at this moment.

She pulled back from the kiss without stepping away. She looked at me with a question behind her eyes.

"Mark," she said breathlessly, nearly in a whisper.

She called my name, nothing more, but behind it was everything. I swallowed, understanding her meaning. She wasn't asking; she wasn't waiting for me to ask. She was opening the space for me to say no—but she knew I wouldn't. She didn't need me to say yes, but I nodded anyway, giving her my unwavering consent. She took my hand and stepped toward my bedroom without hesitation.

"Come," Viktoriya beckoned. Without force or hesitation, she led me into the bedroom, and I enthusiastically followed.

With each step toward the bedroom, my mind raced, like a pyrotechnic display of disparate thoughts. Had I fallen into an intoxicatingly vivid dream? No—she was here. Viktoriya was here.

In my bedroom. My bedroom—why hadn't I cleaned up my bedroom? Should I put on some music?

She stepped through the doorway of my bedroom for the first time, my hand in hers, following like a penitent worshiper.

What music would even be right for this? Otis Redding? Marvin Gaye?—did I still have the mixtape CD of sexy love songs I made years ago?

Viktoriya stopped at the foot of my bed and turned to face me. I must have looked panicked or terrified, because she looked at me and her expression flickered with just a hint of amused pity. She dropped my hand and brought both hands up to my face. She brushed my hair back with her fingertips and stroked my beard gently. Then, cradling my face in her hands, she closed the space between our bodies.

"Not yet," she said. Her breathless whisper, barely more than a sigh, brushed my ear, and the torrent of thoughts stampeding through my mind fell silent at her command.

"Not yet, what?" I asked, confused.

"No thinking—no talking, not yet … Just this," Viktoriya said. Her eyes locked onto mine—unrelenting sapphire depths pulling me in, looking into me, through me, devouring me whole. "Let me have this first."

Those few words tipped me over the edge into her arms. I brought my hands up to her face and drew her to me, kissing her. Our lips met once more. Through them, I felt our heartbeats collide—my frantic, driving pulse crashing against the steady, persistent meter of her drum. Our heartbeats fell into a rhythm wholly our own. She pulled me closer, tighter, her fingers finding purchase in my hair.

Her hips rocked forward, pressing into mine. My body answered instinctively, mirroring her movement. Our bodies drew together as if pulled by gravity, aching to become one. Our hands wandered up and down our backs—grasping, caressing, yearning. Together, we both moaned hungrily, pleading for more.

She broke first, stepping back from me as though it strained her will to force our separation. Viktoriya was nearly gasping, and she gazed at me as though she were starving. She reached for me, unbuttoning my shirt. I felt her fingers tremble against my skin— so slight it was almost imperceptible—as she freed each button. Her hands slid up my stomach, over my chest, easing my shirt open and off my shoulders. I dropped my arms, letting the shirt fall to the floor. Her hands caressed back down my chest, from my shoulders over my stomach, pausing at the waistband of my pants. She looked from where her fingertips danced up to me, wordlessly allowing me space to say no once again. I guided her fingers to the button and smirked, remembering to kick off my shoes first this time. She returned the smirk with a smile, recalling our first awkward undressing.

My pants fell to the floor around my feet. I stepped out of them, and Viktoriya turned, offering the zipper on the back of her dress to me. My fingers trembled as I reached for it, torn between the urge to tear the fabric from her body and the desire to treat her—and her dress—with the delicacy they deserved, savoring the moment. Slowly I pulled the zipper down, and with my fingertips lifted the soft fabric away from her back. I leaned forward and kissed the back of her neck, just between her shoulders, as I guided the dress down, off her body, to the floor.

Viktoriya pushed back against me with a soft, deep, involuntary hum of pleasure. She didn't turn around but reached up behind her, finding my head with her hands. My hands wrapped around her stomach, holding her tightly against my body. Her hips pressed back against me, rolling in a way that drove any conscious thought out of my mind. The more I kissed her, the more she moved and hummed, urging me to explore her body further. My lips on her neck, my hands rising to her chest, our heartbeats racing together.

From the other room, a wireless speaker I rarely used sprang to life. The sudden sound startled us, making us jump. I quickly dove for my pants, wrestled my phone from the pocket, and landed on my knees. I recognized the song just as I saw the music app open on my phone—confirming my suspicion. Apparently, as a parting gift, Eros had connected my phone to the wireless speaker in the other room and had created a playlist for us.

"I'm sorry—I must have bumped my phone with my foot—" I said, on my knees, ready to stop the sound of Amy Winehouse singing "Will You Still Love Me Tomorrow?" When I looked up, I saw Viktoriya smiling down at me.

"Leave it. Now this is our song," she said, popping a hip seductively. "Hm. I see you. On your knees already."

"I … am," I answered. Looking up at her, standing barely an arm's reach away. I glanced down instinctively and laughed, noticing she wore only her boots.

"Oh, what is funny, Mark *Geralt* Williams?"

"Your boots."

"Da. You are down there—take them off," she said, extending her boot toward me. I giggled while I untied her boots, slipping them off, one foot at a time. "You are good boy. You say you saw a goddess. Look, do you still see?"

Twenty minutes ago, I wouldn't have known how to answer her. I'd have stumbled, searching for the perfect words. But now my mind was clear; there was one thing, one person on my mind.

"No, Viktoriya. I do not see *a* goddess in front of me," I said without hesitation. "I only see *my* goddess before me."

Shock flashed across Viktoriya's face, melting in an instant into a blushing, exhilarated smile. She was only momentarily flummoxed, reclaiming control as quickly as she lost it. She took two steps forward, closing the distance between us. On my knees, at eye level with her hips, I exhaled—and felt the shiver it sent across her skin. The scent of her filled my nose, stirring carnal desire deep inside me, and my mouth watered.

"Good. Show me how you worship your goddess."

She reached down, entwining her fingers in my hair, drawing my face into her. I embraced her. I worshiped her with my lips and tongue, desperate, as though I might never taste anything again. I slid my hands up the back of her thighs, holding her tightly against my face. Her fingers tightened in my hair as she released a guttural moan, rising from deep inside her body where my lips and tongue indulged her. In this moment, I was Viktoriya's devout servant, reveling in the sweet nectar my goddess was blessing me with for as long as she would allow.

Her legs quivered, and she tugged me to my feet, panting desperately. She stared into my eyes, gently wiping my lips with her thumb. She kissed me passionately, pulling our naked bodies together as we staggered back and tumbled onto the bed.

Her legs wrapped around my waist, pulling me into her. We both gasped as the space between my body and hers vanished. The sound of Otis Redding singing "These Arms of Mine" floated in through the bedroom door. I pulled back from her lips and studied her face for a moment, reveling in her beauty and the shuddering ecstasy we now shared.

An hour later, Viktoriya lay with her head on my chest, tangled in the wreckage of my bed. Bob Dylan's "Lay Lady Lay," performed by a band called Magnet and Gemma Hayes, rang through the apartment. We were both still catching our breath. Every muscle in our bodies still trembled. I wasn't sure whether I couldn't move or just didn't want to. Beyond the soft music and our rhythmic breathing, the world was silent. She shifted, turning her head to look at me, a satisfied smile stretched across her lips and reached her glimmering sapphire eyes.

"Now, Mark," she said, only slightly out of breath now, brushing her fingers over my chest. "Now you can tell me. Do you know what you want?"

"Yes," I answered without hesitation.

"Have you made your decision? Tell me, what is it you want?" Viktoriya watched me, studying my expression. Confident as she was, I could tell she was nervous. I recognized that fearful look. I've seen it countless times in the mirror.

"Yes, although calling it a decision doesn't really fit. It was more like a realization," I said. I paused, reaching for the right words. Viktoriya waited, letting the silence linger, allowing me space to answer. Saying this aloud should feel terrifying, even impossible, but nothing feels impossible now. "I love you, but I cannot choose between you and Elijah. I can't choose any more than I could pluck my own heart from my chest and tear it in two. I love you both equally."

"This is what I thought," she sighed, as if it were not only the answer she expected but also the one she hoped for. She reached up, touching my cheek; her fingers brushed through my beard. "I love you too, Mark Williams. Even the parts I don't fully understand—yet."

"You do?"

"I do. I have for a long time now."

"Then, I have to ask—aside from making me take time until I could understand myself—why did you wait?"

"I needed to understand first … I was afraid, Mark. Not of you—of myself. I was afraid I could not accept it—of what I did not see before. What I did not wish to admit. So, I spoke with

Elijah. He helped me understand how you can love us both. And how I know from the moment he sang to you, but I would not admit it."

I held my breath, torn between fear and hope.

Viktoriya looked almost ashamed, as though she was confessing to me. I wanted to speak, to tell her everything was perfect, but I sensed she was not done yet, so I grasped the sheet next to me and held back.

"I did not know it was possible for me to love someone this way. But I know what I feel for you, Mark," Viktoriya said, looking at me, vulnerable and hopeful. "I will not pretend to know what happens next. But I know this—I do not wish to lose you."

"Me neither," I exhaled, releasing the shaky breath I was holding. Viktoriya sighed in response.

"Then perhaps … we are not so different," Viktoriya said, her lips curling into a small, knowing smile. "Tomorrow, we speak with Elijah. Don't overthink, Mark."

"I can try," I said, smiling back at her. She climbed up and pressed a soft, lingering kiss to my lips. I melted into her kiss, holding her close, settling into something new but comfortingly familiar. This was real. She broke the kiss and rested her forehead against mine. Together, we exhaled, embracing the moment, knowing neither of us had to do this alone.

"Sleep now, with me. We take day off tomorrow—together," she whispered, laying her head back on my chest, holding me close.

With a contented hum, she fell asleep before I could respond. I closed my eyes as the exhaustion of the past five days weighed down on me. Tomorrow, we'll begin something extraordinary.

I drifted into the deepest sleep I had ever had, filled with dreams of Viktoriya and Elijah, and what might be.

Chapter 17

Time is a strange thing for me. I don't experience its passage the way you humans do. Sometimes hours slip by like minutes, and other times minutes stretch into hours. That's what it's like for me, all the time, and I can't tell the difference. What I'm saying is the sun had risen a while ago. Mark and Viktoriya were still in bed, and I was bored.

Without Mark's phone, and his laptop still in its bag, I had nothing to occupy myself with—short of leaving the apartment, which I didn't want to do. I was trying to respect Mark's privacy, but there were limits to my patience and my curiosity. Mark and Viktoriya were in the same bed he'd shared with Elijah a few nights ago, and I was dying to know if Mark was the "little spoon" again. And so, I peeked in, just to be sure they were both okay.

I emerged from a light on the ceiling, and I hastily retreated. They were both very much awake in the bed, and Mark was not the "little spoon" this time. He wasn't any kind of spoon this time—more like a mandoline, with Viktoriya as the finger guard and Mark the sled. I'm not sure how well those similes work with modern cookware. I would say it was more like Mark was the sil, and Viktoriya the batta, of a South Indian ammikallu, but I don't know if those get used anymore. Let's just say there was a *lot* of visible skin. When they finally emerged, they'd need food, electrolytes, and a long nap.

I had three options: leave, interrupt, or wait. As much as it killed me to wait, it was better than leaving and possibly missing

Mark when he came out, or upsetting him. Still, I was eager to show him what I remembered I could do. So, I waited. I passed the "time" by practicing matter manipulation—it was still a little rusty. I turned a green banana blue. I cleaned out the inside of the coffee machine—though without hands, I couldn't empty the filter. And I fixed the broken kitchen drawer that always stuck open or closed, which drove Mark crazy.

I had just finished with the drawer when Mark staggered out of his room into the kitchen. He opened the refrigerator and pulled out two bottles of water. He was just close enough for me to reach him to get his attention.

"Mark," I said softly, directly inside his ear. Mark flinched, dropping both bottles of water.

"Eros?" Mark whispered so softly it barely made any sound.

"Yes, got a minute?"

"Not exactly," Mark said, still only just audible.

"Okay, will you at least bring your phone out here for me?"

"All right, where are you?"

"The sticky drawer."

Mark didn't respond. He just took the water bottles back into the bedroom and came back out with his phone. He set it down on the kitchen counter near the drawer. I slipped quickly through the drawer and counter, back into Mark's phone.

"Thanks. Let me know when you can talk," I said. "I'm inside—you can take the phone, unless you want to keep me out of the bedroom."

Mark nodded and set the coffee machine going. It hissed to life … and then died. The look of shock, betrayal, and grief on Mark's face could've fooled a casual observer into thinking an irreplaceable family heirloom had been destroyed. I guessed that was my fault—I must have damaged something when I cleaned it.

"Um … whoops. That might be my fault. Sorry, Mark. But silver lining—if you grab coffee from the convenience store across the street, we can talk on the way." I said as Mark glared at the now-dead coffee maker, as if he could resurrect a fallen friend by will alone.

He groaned, buried his face in his hands, then let out a resigned, desperate sigh.

"I will—kill you somehow. Let's go," Mark said through gritted teeth, more frustrated than enraged. Still, I believed him.

He disappeared into the bedroom. "Hey, Viktoriya—the coffee maker died. I'm going to run down and grab us a couple of cups. Sweet with vanilla cream, right?"

"Da. Large. One of your gallons. Please," Viktoriya replied, plaintive.

"No problem. I'll be back in a few minutes. Make yourself at home—there are towels in the bathroom if you want a shower. Elijah left a whole case of cleansers and body wash under the sink." Mark walked out of the bedroom, haphazardly dressed, slipping on his shoes as he went. He grabbed his phone and keys from the counter and dashed out the door.

"Mark, I'm really sorry about the coffee. I didn't mean to break it," I said the moment he stepped out the door. "I know it was like your best friend. I'm pretty sure I can fix it. That's actually what I wanted to tell you. While I had time alone, I remembered how to do things I haven't managed for centuries, and there's a blue banana on the counter."

"I—what? Hang on—what?" Mark called, jogging down the stairs. "A blue banana?"

"Don't worry about the banana, you'll see it. The coffee maker? An unfortunate victim of my unfamiliarity with its mechanics. But what I need is to teach you an old trick."

"You have no idea how hard that was to follow without coffee," Mark said, sounding exhausted—probably from a lack of sleep. "It's hard to feel excited about anything right now."

"I thought after last night you'd be positively giddy," I said. "Instead, you sound half alive."

"You don't understand how important coffee is to my people and our way of life," Mark said with a slow, self-satisfied giggle. "I've got two brain cells racing for third place right now. Giddy comes after caffeine."

"Mark, you are impossible. Listen—odds are you're not going to be on your own from now on. Unless you want me to reveal myself to Viktoriya and Elijah—which I wouldn't mind; I'm fond of them—you need to listen and focus."

"Okay, Eros. I'm listening."

"Good. When you speak to me, I don't hear you like humans do—I'm not human; no ears, remember? You don't actually have to make a sound ..."

"So I can just think at you ...?"

"No, it doesn't work like that. It's more like lip-syncing—try saying something without making a sound."

Mark mouthed a few extremely rude words.

"Mark! You kiss … nope, never mind, I know what you do with that mouth. Now do it again, but this time keep your mouth closed," I said, summoning all my infinite patience not to laugh as Mark silently formed his reply. "Good—you just said, 'This is stupid,' among other things."

"Ahrit, I mitt. This id gud schit," Mark mumbled silently, clearly needing practice.

"Keep practicing. Tell me everything I missed. What is it Elijah says—'spill the tea'?"

Mark's "tea" was scalding, but a bit muddled, thanks to his silent-speaking practice. He knew what he wanted, what Viktoriya wanted, and thought he knew what Elijah wanted. I was able to help fill in some of those gaps with what I knew from observing Viktoriya and Elijah. That set Mark's mind at ease, mostly. He still had concerns, which were natural when confronted with the unknown.

"Mark, let go," I urged. "You can't fight the current—it carries you where it will. Resist, and it drowns you. Yield, and it takes you exactly where you need to be."

"I don't know, Eros," Mark said aloud, balancing two large cups of coffee outside his building so he wouldn't be misunderstood. "It's like Dylan and the Beatles—Eros, you can research that later. Both were riding the first wave of their fame, carried along by a current they feared might drown them. One night in 1964, they met—fans of one another—and an idea was exchanged, among other things. What if we didn't let this current carry us where it wants to go, and instead took the oars and set our own course? After that, Dylan blew up the Newport Folk Festival, and the Beatles started truly writing for themselves. Both went on to create some of the most meaningful music of the 20th century—changing, in their way, the course of history. I think it's always got to be a combination of the two, Eros. You can't fight it, and you can't just be a passenger. You've got to take the tiller and oars and command your own destination."

"Compelling argument. I'd understand it better if I knew who Dylan and the Beatles were. I'll look into that," I said, resisting the urge to start researching immediately. I will have plenty of time while Mark, Viktoriya, and Elijah talk later. "But my point stands—you need to let go, just a little. Also, stop loitering outside your building talking to yourself, and take Viktoriya her coffee."

"Right. Coffee," Mark said, switching back to his improving silent speech as he dashed into the building and up to his apartment.

When we got back to his apartment, we found Viktoriya in the shower. Mark seemed to consider intruding on her shower, staring at the bathroom door before shaking his head and dismissing the idea. He set her coffee on the counter and drank his as if afraid someone might snatch it away. After half of his coffee was gone, he finally noticed the blue banana sitting on his counter.

"Funny, I don't even remember buying bananas. So, you turned this one blue?"

"I did, well, more accurately I adjusted the molecular makeup that reflects red and green wavelengths of light."

"Obviously, I'm aware of how light and color works—"

"Are you? Really? Or do you just think so?"

"Okay. I *think* I understand how it works. But what I was going to ask is: is it safe to eat?"

"Oh. Well, to be honest, I don't know. I don't think I did anything to alter it that much. Are you going to try it? You don't have to."

"Hell yes, I'm trying it," Mark said, peeling the banana. The inside of the fruit looked normal, and Mark didn't recoil when he gave it a sniff, so I assumed it smelled normal. But then he took one small bite, and reflexively he immediately spat it out. He didn't even attempt to spit it out in the sink or into his hands. Just a small bite of banana shot out of his mouth, landing with a dead squelch on the countertop. "Oh my God, Eros! That was vile—it tasted like a blue battery that barely survived an industrial accident. Why did it taste blue?!"

"That's one I can't exactly answer for you, Mark," I said, almost sheepishly. "I have no idea what anything tastes like. I'm sorry, Mark, I think I was so focused on changing the color I neglected everything else. Do you have another banana? I can try again."

"I didn't even know I had that one. You can try an apple. I've got some in the fridge. But maybe not right now while Viktoriya is here."

"Speaking of Viktoriya—here she comes," I said as the bathroom door swung open.

Viktoriya stepped out, wrapped in a towel just small enough to require one hand to keep it closed. Mark's eyes nearly popped out of his skull, saved only by the mercy of his human eyelids.

"Vik … I have your towel—coffee. I have your coffee," Mark stammered, reminding me of the first time I heard him attempting to talk to Viktoriya.

"Coffee! Thank Gods. My hero, Mark Geralt Williams!" Viktoriya exclaimed, carefully dashing toward him, with one hand clutching her towel.

To Mark's surprise, she made a beeline past him—straight for the coffee. Only after her first sip did she turn back to him, pressing a kiss to his cheek. Together, they drank in silence, as if coffee were the most important, the only important thing in the universe. At least for a minute. Then, without warning, they both erupted into laughter at absolutely nothing. And just like that, Viktoriya was wearing exactly that—nothing—the towel slipping from her fingers as she laughed.

The human body, I think, is one of the most beautiful things in the universe. I've been around a long, long time, and I must have seen millions of them—each beautiful in its own way. Maybe it's a touch of envy, or maybe just wonder at how delicate and vulnerable these forms are, willingly exposed to the world, trusting they will remain unharmed.

Of all the bodies in all the world that I have ever seen, right now, Viktoriya's is the most beautiful. Maybe it was the way she laughed—before and after the towel hit the floor. Maybe it was the way she looked at Mark—and the way he looked at her.

He looked at her like she was a sunset—not with lust, longing, or desire (though those simmered beneath the surface), but with awe.

Then there was Viktoriya. Her expression shifted from surprise to her trademark teasing smirk. She didn't hide. She didn't run. Instead, she calmly set her coffee down, stepped back, and held Mark's gaze.

"Whoops," she said with an exaggerated wink. "No ideas—I'm still exhausted … Okay, maybe ideas are allowed. But I'll get dressed now."

Mark blinked. "Ideas …" he echoed, like someone handed the key to a door they hadn't realized was locked.

Viktoriya laughed, scooped up the towel—and her coffee—and strutted into the bedroom.

She shot Mark a look over her shoulder—just to make sure he was watching—then disappeared behind the door with a giggle. Mark sighed, half-amused, half-defeated.

"Hey, Mark," I said, breaking his train of thought. "Want to put on some music while you wait?"

"Yes, Eros—great idea." Mark's silent speech was improving. "Older or current?"

"You pick this time."

"All right, let's try something new," Mark said, pulling out his phone to reconnect with the wireless speaker.

Mark introduced me to something he called *punk*—fast, chaotic, sometimes angry, sometimes defiant, always alive. It lit something in him, set him moving—not dancing exactly, but bouncing, shaking off the weight of the past few days. His energy was infectious. I almost felt it myself. Almost. But I wasn't him. I couldn't bounce, or thrash, or lose myself in music the way he could. And for the first time in ages, I ached with envy.

He was exorcising the tension and despair—cleaning his neglected space, tossing remains into the trash—as he waited for Viktoriya to emerge.

*****Mark*****

I'd nearly finished cleaning by the time Viktoriya emerged from the bedroom. In truth, the only reason I hadn't finished was because, somewhere along the way, my cleaning had turned into spastic half-dancing, and I forgot what I was doing. I probably would have felt embarrassed had Viktoriya not joined in, matching my chaotic dance. Honestly, I think that's the universal response to any Ramones song. You just have to move, sing, and rebel against the universe by throwing a blue banana peel across the room.

"What is this?" Viktoriya asked between songs.

"The Ramones," I replied, slightly out of breath as I fumbled with my phone to pause the music. "One of the most important bands in history. In fact—"

"I know Ramones—what is song?"

"Oh! I'm sorry," I said. "It's 'I Don't Wanna Go Down to the Basement.' They were pretty literal with their songs."

"I like. Will you play my favorite—'Beat on the Brat'? Is best for cleaning, dancing, good days, bad days, everything … except one thing—maybe," she said, laughing at herself, and laughing even harder when I took too long to catch her joke.

"… Oh my god, Viktoriya!" I laughed back, pressing play on Viktoriya's song request.

"I don't get it," Eros whispered, which made it even funnier.

Together, we laughed and danced around. Viktoriya helped me finish cleaning the apartment—without my asking or her offering. She just grabbed the trash can and started collecting the last few scraps. She paused only when she found a blue banana peel and stared at it like it was a blue banana peel.

"What?" she said, holding the banana peel out, with a mix of confusion, horror, and intrigue on her face.

"I know, it's the craziest thing. I don't know how or why it's blue, but it tasted horrible."

"Why you taste blue banana?"

"For science … No, just pure curiosity."

"Da. Da. Curious cat. Work, work. Finish then I call Elijah."

We finished cleaning the apartment—a simple task delayed by dancing and laughter. We took our time, reveling in the moment, delaying the complications we both knew were coming. I was equally excited and unimaginably nervous to venture into terrifyingly unknown territory. Unfortunately, my guide was more fellow traveler than reassuring navigator. Still, Eros was doing their best to help.

"Eros," I said silently. "We have to call Elijah soon. Any advice?"

"Yes, Mark. Stop thinking. Here's the plan: follow Viktoriya's lead. Trust her, trust Elijah—and yourself, for that matter. Oh, and I bet Viktoriya's hungry, since you ate her banana."

"Viktoriya, are you hungry? We should get some lunch," I said out loud, ignoring Eros' comment about the banana. "I don't have much here. Maybe we can meet up with Elijah."

"Yes, you read my mind," Viktoriya said, immediately pulling out her phone and tapping on the screen. "I call Elijah now … Pryvit, Koroleva Korolev, yak spravy?"

"Eros, can you listen in?" I said silently.

"Yes. She said, 'Hi, Queen of Queens, how are you?' Elijah said, 'Hey, Viki?—I'm fine, just heading out the door. What's up?'…"

"… Da. Mark is ready …"

"That was quick—you don't waste time …" Eros said, relaying Elijah's side of the phone call.

"We take day off …"

"Oh? Both of you?"

"Da. You meet us for lunch?"

"I can't today, Viki. I have to open the club for lunch …"

"Boo. We need talk and food."

"Well, yes ma'am. Come by the club—I'll open the doors early for you. The kitchen will just be firing up, but I'm sure I can get them to put something together. I *am* Koroleva Korolev, after all …"

"Da, da. Pobachymos'," she said, ending the call and slipping the phone back into her pocket before turning to me. "Elijah will meet us at the club for lunch. Come, we go."

Fifteen minutes later, Viktoriya and I stepped into The Queen's Head Club. I'd been here before while it was closed—it always felt half-alive in that state. Quiet, bright work lights overhead, just a few staffers moving around.

Moments after we walked in, Elijah came out of a back room, followed by the club owner, Bob Caldwell. Bob was a handsome, middle-aged Black man with a shaved head, wearing a comfortably flamboyant, androgynous top. They were both carrying large milk crates of new bottles for the bar.

"Thanks, Bob. You didn't need to help—I can manage," Elijah said, setting the crate on the bar.

"Of course, sweetie—but you have guests," Bob said, setting his crate beside Elijah's and meeting my gaze. "Hello, Mark. It's nice to see you again."

"Mark! Viktoriya!" Elijah exclaimed, genuinely surprised. He dashed out from behind the bar, wrapping his arms around both of us. "What took you so long? Mark, of course you remember Bob. Viktoriya, meet Bob Caldwell, the owner of this incredible venue."

"Of course," I said, returning Elijah's hug. "Good to see you too, Bob. How are you doing?"

"I'm good, honey," Bob said, walking over to meet us. "Viktoriya, it's a pleasure. Elijah is right, you are stunning."

"Thank you, Bob. Is very nice to meet you," Viktoriya said, extending a hand to Bob. "I like your club very much."

"You three are too cute," Bob said, shaking Viktoriya's hand, smiling at each of us. "I'd love to chat and catch up, but I have work to do, so maybe later. Elijah, take the table in the back corner. I'll try to keep everyone away. I'll bring you a couple sandwiches."

"Thank you, Bob, I owe you. Viktoriya, Mark, I'll grab us a couple beers once Bob leaves."

"Just remember to grab them from the case we haven't added to inventory, and I'll add those to what you owe me," Bob said, clapping Elijah on the shoulder before walking away.

Considering what we were here to discuss, the moment felt far too comfortably normal. I fought the urge to assess and overanalyze as we walked to the table. Viktoriya and I settled at the table. When Elijah sat down next to me with three beers, the reality of the situation hit me, and my mind went blank. I had no earthly idea how to have this conversation, let alone how to start it.

"So, um … I guess we should talk," I said, feeling suddenly self-conscious. "I don't know where to start."

"It starts by saying that no matter what, our friendship is safe," Elijah said, resting a hand on my shoulder. "Same for you, Viki—that's something I'm not willing to sacrifice."

"I agree, but we must also agree to be honest with each other," Viktoriya said, taking a sip of her beer.

"Okay, honesty. I guess there is no other way to say it. I love you both. I'm in love with you, Viktoriya, and you, Elijah," I said, looking at each of them in turn. As terrifying as it was to say, I felt safe with them in this space. "I think you've both made your feelings clear, and I can't choose between you. I want you both. I can't pretend to know what that means going forward, but I know I can't ignore it."

Something inside my chest loosened, like a muscle finally released after being held too long in tension. It felt different this time, saying those words out loud to both Viktoriya and Elijah. It was as if something captive had been released from its bonds. My world changed again in the blink of an eye.

"Thank you, Mark. It's nice to finally hear you say it out loud like that. So … what are we, then?" Elijah asked, taking my hand.

"This is—we all want same thing," Viktoriya said, taking my other hand in hers. "Except Elijah and me. We do not want each other."

"Viktoriya, you're so brutally direct—I love it, and I adore you too," Elijah squeezed my hand, smiling at her across the table. "So, we're talking about time, not ultimatums."

"How do you both do that—make something impossible so easy?" I said, looking from Viktoriya to Elijah, amazed at them both. I had built this up into an impossible conversation—pushing and pulling, searching for some unreachable middle ground. Instead, they met me with quiet certainty, like they'd already known, and were just waiting for me to catch up. "I was afraid I was being selfish, or reckless. That I was asking too much. "Tell me honestly—am I being selfish?"

"No," Viktoriya said.

"Yes," Elijah said.

They answered in unison.

"You are—just a little, Mark," Elijah clarified, chuckling. "Honestly, it's a good thing. Listen, a little selfishness is a requirement in the beginning of anything worthwhile. Especially relationships. You have to want something first; you can't love someone if you won't allow yourself to want them. If you're only ever selfless—always sacrificing—you'll disappear."

"Da. I see. Wanting is not wrong. Is honest. Is human. Be selfish in this," Viktoriya said, smiling back at Elijah. "What matters is—does your want become louder than ours? No, you, Mark, are never loud. I do not think you want too much."

"This is a big step for you," Elijah said, looking at me with warm affection. "You don't think of yourself enough. You might be the most selfless person I know. You're learning, growing. It's kinda hot."

"Da, da—more than kind of," Viktoriya added with her signature smirk.

We all laughed, and Elijah raised his bottle of beer.

"To selfish, honest beginnings … kinda hot ones."

"For friends and love," Viktoriya added.

"To a terrifyingly beautiful future for brave and broken hearts." I concluded the toast.

"You three are sickening," Bob said from the sidelines. He sat down at the table with a tray of sandwiches. "Sick-en-ing! I was going to stay out of it—but not now. Come on. Spill it. Spill it, darlings—Mother Bob wants every detail about this delicious little throuple."

Chapter 18

****Eros****

Mark, Viktoriya, and Elijah finished their light lunch while recounting everything to Bob, as he'd requested. He was already familiar with Mark and Elijah's friendship. The long-running flirtation between Mark and Viktoriya fascinated him, as if it were something entirely foreign. When they reached Elijah's show and the adventures in his closet, Bob kept jumping to his feet, shooting Mark impressed glances. By the end of the story, Bob had shifted from observer to an active participant. He freely offered his advice, drawn from decades of experience.

Bob's advice sounded like common sense—wisdom Mark might not fully appreciate; I worried he wouldn't. Bob counseled them to be patient, honest, and charitable with each other. He told Mark pointedly that acting on instinct would land him in hot water if he didn't learn to resist it. He'd need to form new instincts here. One such impulse—starting with a list of rules for each other— was a mistake; they wouldn't yet know which rules they needed. Start by figuring out what each of you needs in a relationship, and commit to open, honest communication from the start. It was exactly the advice I would have given—had Mark asked. He didn't, and that's okay. The important part: I'll have to remind him when he forgets.

Their meeting ended when Bob casually reminded Elijah that they should have opened a while ago and needed to wrap up and get to work. Mark said goodbye to Elijah with a kiss. It wasn't a big kiss—the kind that makes others uncomfortable—but it was impossible to ignore. Viktoriya definitely noticed. She shifted awkwardly. This was the first time she had seen them embrace like that, and she clearly was not entirely prepared to witness it. She looked away and took a deep breath, closing her eyes as if the sight stung—as if she were reminding herself of something she refused to forget. I wanted to reassure her somehow—but all I, or anyone, could do was watch.

After their brief kiss, Elijah watched them go with longing. I noticed a subtle change in Mark that I don't think either Viktoriya or Elijah did. He no longer moved as though the world were about to collapse on him. He stood just a little taller and seemed to be more sure of himself. I first noticed this slight change when he was at the table, when he spoke with Viktoriya or Elijah, he no longer broke eye contact as quickly as he could, like he was now more comfortable and didn't feel like wilting the instant their eyes met.

I felt the first inkling that my task here was complete—matchmaker duties fulfilled. I'll grant you I hadn't done much—just enough. And undoubtedly, my subtle nudging had been an incalculable key to this outcome. It was time to turn my attention to other problems. Like how to help Elijah secure the money to buy the club, how to create opportunities for Viktoriya's fashion ambitions, and how to help Mark save his orchard from Gale Barlow's advances—and from financial ruin.

But my mind was wandering, and I didn't realize Mark and Viktoriya were in mid-conversation outside the club.

"Da. A make-up date," Viktoriya said, nodding. "Our second date was interrupted by Elijah—he wasn't unwelcome, just uninvited—so, you owe me a make up date."

"That's fair. What do you have in mind?" Mark asked through a good-natured laugh.

"We have the rest of the day. You want I should teach you how to bake Yabluchnyk?"

"Yes, I'd love that," Mark said, genuinely enthusiastic. "What's Yabluchnyk?"

"Is apple cake. You will love. Come, come—we go to shop to get apple," Viktoriya said, taking Mark's hand and leading him away from the club. "Then I teach you to bake."

At the small market, Mark's deep knowledge of apple lore came in handy. He admitted the apples here were only acceptable—not the best, not by a long shot—but he knew how to blend varieties to achieve the right flavor and texture, since he couldn't get her any from his orchard that day.

Armed with their mix of apples, they spent the rest of the afternoon baking. Viktoriya showed Mark how she used lemon and lime juice to keep the apples from browning. Mark, of course, interjected—it was citric acid that prevented oxidation. She laughed with an exaggerated eye roll, hinting she already knew that particular apple fact. Then she moved on, introducing him to her secret spice blend built around cinnamon; I'm positive one of the others was nutmeg. It was a true lesson in baking, masquerading as an opportunity for Mark and Viktoriya to work together.

It took a while before Mark stopped offering unsolicited suggestions and random apple-related factoids. Fortunately, Viktoriya was patient, humoring his input—even the unnecessary bits. Still, she liked his idea of adding a bit of puréed apple to the batter to deepen the flavor. I think she enjoyed Mark's curiosity and enthusiasm for the process, and Mark clearly loved learning something new from her. They reveled in each other's company— laughing at flour-dusted mishaps, moving together in playful intimacy, exchanging tidbits of knowledge, teasing, and sharing meaningful, lingering glances.

For those few hours in the kitchen, nothing else mattered.

In the end, they produced a warm, golden apple cake— delicious-looking and, I can only imagine, intoxicatingly fragrant—and ate half of it for dinner. Viktoriya sent the remaining half home with Mark, along with the promise to teach him how to bake Palianytsia on Saturday. She made a point of emphasizing that it needed to proof overnight—just in case he missed the implication.

Mark

It was Friday afternoon when I stumbled into my apartment after work, juggling separate text threads with Viktoriya and Elijah. A week ago, I would have agonized for days before even *considering* making plans. Now I was casually arranging something last minute for tonight.

Viktoriya was working at the café tonight and had early-morning baking, so she was out. Elijah was performing at the club tonight, but he had time for me both before and after. That wasn't unusual. I'd helped him get ready and walked him home after his shows more times than I could count. But this time was different. There was a distinctly romantic tone—overtones, undertones, all the tones. It made me both nervous and excited—feelings that shouldn't have felt new anymore.

"Eros, you there?" I asked silently—more out of habit than necessity.

"I am. Rushing out to meet Elijah before his show, I take it?"

"That's the plan, unless he says no. Can you set a reminder to call Viktoriya tomorrow around noon while I get ready to go?"

"Yes, I can do that. But … so can you."

"If I do, I'll just forget. I get distracted too easily. Have you met me recently?" I said, kicking off my shoes.

"Fair enough. Just remember—I'm still not used to this human calendar. Who *designed* this monstrosity? None of it makes sense. I don't think those Gregorians could count. So, remember to double-check I get the date and time right."

"I'll bring that up to the Pope in our next meeting. Unless you can wish the world into using a sidereal calendar instead."

"Hm, that would be a good one. If only wishes were real. Say hi to the Pope for me … I knew a Pope once—Anterus. Talk about persecution complexes. Inadvertently starved himself to death, and they still tried to blame it on Emperor Thrax, who wasn't even *Rome* at the time."

"Oh my god," I said, laughing. "I'd threaten to lock you in the freezer for that—if it were even possible."

My phone chimed with a response from Elijah. He was home, getting ready—and judging by his unorthodox use of emojis, he was definitely excited for me to come over and help him. I wasn't sure exactly what he meant by *wear something cute*, but I would do my best to pick something from my wardrobe that I was now aware was disappointingly bland. Maybe I could borrow something from Elijah's closet. Did I dare go out in that pink pony dress? I think that might go a little too far, but I was still surprised the thought arose, and I considered it before dismissing it. Who was I becoming? I didn't know—and didn't have time to find out. But whoever he was, I liked him.

The Fixer, The Maker, The Drag Entertainer

Forty-five minutes later I knocked on Elijah's door wearing the cutest outfit I could assemble, which was admittedly a little dull—but nice. There was no answer, which probably meant he was in the shower. I checked my phone again—sure enough, I'd missed a text from Elijah while walking. He said he was getting in the shower, and I should let myself in.

As soon as I opened the door, I heard the shower running. He was expecting me, so I didn't announce myself—but I still wanted him to know I was there, so I walked toward the bathroom. I started to knock, then stopped. He'd left the bathroom door open, giving me a clear view of him through the glass shower door. There he was—back to the door, naked—rivulets of soapy water streaming down his body. I'd known Elijah for a long time. I'd seen him in the shower before—but this was the first time I was *really* looking at him ... all of him. The new person I was becoming, whom I was just getting to know, stared at Elijah, taking in the details of his back. From the nape of his neck to the backs of his knees—an indecent buffet of carnality. And then he turned around, and I was slow to raise my gaze to meet his eyes.

That was the moment the last thread snapped, revealing the side of myself that had always been hiding behind the curtains. I wasn't becoming someone new—I was finally discovering who I'd always been. *Here I am, Mark Williams, the bisexual standing in the bathroom doorway watching you shower, longing to help you wash your hard-to-reach spots.*

"You have terrible timing," Elijah said, shutting off the water and stepping out of the shower. "Ten minutes earlier, and you could've acted on those thoughts. Don't pretend. I know that look plastered on your face. I've given you that exact look a dozen times before. Now, be a dear ... hand me a towel?"

"I ... um ... yeah," I stammered, caught flat-footed by Elijah's perceptive call-out. I had to step into the bathroom to hand him the towel hanging half an arm's length away from him. That small step toward him set my skin aflame—I glimpsed my bright red face in the mirror. It wasn't fair. He knew it, I knew it, and we both had no choice but to accept it. "You did that on purpose, didn't you?" I asked, though my voice betrayed how flustered I was.

"Oh, Mark," Elijah said, drying himself slowly with the towel. "You've put me in a … difficult position. On one hand, I could let you believe I had a deliciously devious master plan. On the other, I could admit it was merely a happy—or perhaps tragically unhappy—accident of timing. Now, is *that* what you're wearing?"

I tossed my hands in the air and walked out of the bathroom. In one blink, as effortless as flipping a light switch, Elijah had gone from my best friend to my boyfriend—oh my God—Elijah was my *boyfriend.* My heart skipped like a scratched record, catching on the word again and again—boyfriend. *Boyfriend.* I couldn't take too many more earth-shaking personal revelations before my head exploded. Now, his critique of my outfit didn't frustrate me, but the fact he didn't like it did.

"I know. I know," I said, refusing to look back and expose my blushing. "It's the best I had. Come on, Elijah … Help your *boyfriend* pick something to wear."

"Boyfriend …" Elijah said, the word catching him off guard, as though that thought hadn't landed before I said it. "You—boyfriend—Mark—dammit you can't just say that. I had a plan!"

He had a plan. I had a plan. Everyone's got a plan until they're face-to-face with a naked queen in the shower. Now Elijah was chasing me into his closet, wearing nothing but a towel and a big stupid grin—and I planned to let him catch me. It wasn't much of a chase. The closet was only four or five steps from the bathroom. I'd made it two steps inside when he wrapped his arms around my chest from behind. He held me for a few silent heartbeats before gently turning me around to face him.

"Promise you're not joking this time?" he asked softly.

"I promise," I answered honestly, "no more jokes in the closet."

We kissed. Much like the first time, Elijah was still in a towel. Unlike before, this kiss wasn't a desperate, push-and-pull eruption of emotion. It was really our first truly mutual kiss, welcome, and self-assured, lingering on the cusp of escalating. Equally aroused, we both broke away from each other before either of us lost our senses. Elijah would never forgive me if I made him late for his drag performance—and he'd resent me forever if he missed it entirely. Even though we both knew it would be worth it.

Elijah shuddered, goosebumps rising along his shoulders as he closed his eyes and mouthed "later" to himself. He exhaled, opened his eyes, and smiled. It was time to get dressed. He handed me a shirt that was iridescent yet sheer, and pants that were almost so tight there'd be very little left for the imagination. I glared at the clothing suspiciously, but Elijah assured me I could trust him. When I said I wasn't sure I could pull it off, he scoffed and informed me, in no uncertain terms, that would be his job later. And an entirely new set of doubts flooded my mind, overriding my hesitancy about the clothing.

We joked and teased each other while he put on his second face. I checked the edges of his wig, gluing down the faux baby hairs and ensuring none of his natural hair peeked out. Finally, I fastened the safety pin securing the zipper at the back of his dress. These were some of his touring costumes and wigs. The kind that looked best from the back row, and wouldn't cause a single tear if lost in a dressing room fire.

We continued laughing as he climbed into the passenger seat of his own car after tossing me the keys. A lady never drives herself to the theater, he informed me. I tried to remind him that even if he were a woman, he wouldn't come remotely close to being a lady, and the club hardly qualified as a theater. He promised I'd pay for that slight. I wouldn't know where or when, but I'd definitely know it when I felt it. I couldn't be sure if the innuendo was unintentionally hilarious, or just accidentally euphemistic. Either way, I was pretty sure I'd be feeling something later that night.

The show was typical of a Friday night special. Old familiar lip-sync favorites, tired puns, and more genitalia-themed humor than you could shake a dick at. Everyone had a great time. Drinks flowed freely, and I proudly played my part in leading the tip parade. For the rookie performers, it was a catechism. For the veterans, it was just another Friday and a fistful of sticky dollar bills. The shining star—at least in my entirely unbiased opinion—was Elijah. He performed unrestrained, utterly fearless and exuding joy from the depths of his soul—so infectious, Bob nearly offered me three free drinks.

Watching him on stage, I realized I was not just seeing my best friend deliver a crowd-pleasing performance. I wasn't only enjoying my boyfriend's craft; I was watching someone light up a room. Making complete strangers feel seen and touched. Leaving an audience a little better than he found them and even stirring a little desire in them. I saw all of that and felt almost smugly satisfied that he wanted to come home with me.

"You look more than just a little satisfied with yourself, Mark." The voice of Eros slipped quietly into my ear, almost overriding the music still playing from the stage. "This is his last number, right? I assume you'll be needing some 'alone time' with Elijah afterward?"

"Yes it is, and yes, I do feel a little satisfied," I replied silently, smiling to myself. "We would like some alone time when he's done, if you don't mind."

"I don't mind at all. I'm happy for you, Mark, I really am. Tell Elijah he was amazing, for me. I think I'll hang around here and find you in the morning."

"Thank you, Eros, I will. I'll talk to you in the morning."

I couldn't tell whether Eros had left. If they left. For all I know, they never left and just remained a dead-silent voyeur. That might have bothered me a few days ago, but now it was just another new feature of my life. Like having a beautiful boyfriend, a gorgeous girlfriend, and the unsettling possibility that I might never be alone again.

As the last notes of Elijah's set rang out, he didn't bow or retreat to the safety of the dressing room—instead, he practically leapt off the stage into my arms. In front of the entire audience, he wrapped himself around me and kissed me, kicking up one foot just for show. It was a purely impulsive move—making us the spectacle, stealing the oxygen from whoever took the stage next— something Elijah would never intentionally do. With a mutual twinge of embarrassment, we both retreated from the crowd, escaping into the night.

Having had a few drinks apiece, we made the short walk back to my apartment, like we had many times before. Unlike before, electric anticipation sparked between our fingertips as we walked hand in hand down the crowded sidewalk. The streets were busy, filled with young college students experiencing the first sips of freedom. The rambunctious crowds either ignored our presence or enthusiastically commented. There was only one tense moment when a small, isolated group of pathetic boys foolishly decided to shout slurs at us. My stomach lurched. A strange fear tightened in my chest, flaring into outrage. My muscles coiled; my jaw locked. My hand gripped Elijah's tighter. Like a coiled spring, I braced for a violent defense. But then, before my blistering shock could ignite—before the rage erupted—Elijah's bright, defiant laughter shattered the night.

"Thank you for noticing—boys! I'm sorry, but he's mine tonight! Maybe try your luck at the petting zoo across the river!" Elijah shouted, silencing them effortlessly—ever the professional. If I hadn't fallen for him already, that would have clinched it.

We held each other even tighter after that, our synchronized footsteps on the pavement driving our bodies together. With each collision, the radiating heat between us swelled, crashing over us in waves. Every step carried us closer to my apartment door with breathless, silent, burning anticipation.

When we were only a few paces away from my door, Elijah slowly slid his hand into my front pocket. His fingers lingered against my thigh through the thin fabric before he wrapped his hand around my keys. Elijah glanced back, beckoning me urgently.

A reflection of earlier: I chased Elijah, and he fully intended to let me catch him. He stopped just far enough inside to let me close the door. The moment the door closed, he was upon me, erasing the empty space between us. His lips found mine; our mouths opened to each other. With my back against the door, Elijah pinned my arms and kissed me—desperate to quench his thirst. I yielded, welcoming him. His lips and tongue pressed, and in a rush, my defenses evaporated, my senses along with them. But neither of us wanted a surrender, especially so quickly. We both hungered for the fight—a drawn-out campaign of touch and tension until we breached each other's defenses and collapsed into a breathless truce.

I reclaimed my will and drove him backward, deeper into the room. He released my arms, allowing me to grab his hips, guiding him backward as we continued to kiss passionately. When we reached the invisible line between the kitchen and living room, we stopped and stepped back from each other. Breathing hard, we stared—desire, disbelief, and strained patience sparking between us. I looked at him, nodding my head slowly. In this moment, I needed him to know, without question, that I wanted this.

I—*wanted*—him.

"You need to de-drag, or you'll get glue all over my bed," I said with a smirk—thinking of Viktoriya.

"Oh, goddammit—I knew I should've skipped the glue tonight," Elijah said with an exasperated sigh. "This sexy illusion is anything but practical for action."

"Oh no! We might need to shower," I said, laying it on thick.

"Not in your tiny shower," Elijah said, crossing his arms and cocking his head. "There's no room for both of us in there. Didn't think about that, did you?"

"Shit! I forgot about that. Dammit—that was supposed to be sexy."

"Mark, sweetheart—you're sexiest when you fumble. Not because you try or fall on your cute ass, but because you don't have to try—and still do. Go on, pick some music; I know you're dying to. I'm going to wash this glue off quickly. And if I don't get this duct tape off soon, I'll cry."

We laughed—somehow, in our frenzy, we'd both forgotten that Elijah was fully tucked and taped. I understood how I could forget that detail, but surely he would've noticed the physical reminder at the first hint of arousal. I could only assume he was so used to the sensation that he no longer noticed it. That thought sent my mind wandering back to all the times I'd helped Elijah out of drag. I recalled every moment when a straight man might've looked away—averting his gaze instead of letting it linger, as I had. All those times—I remembered staring, watching, dismissing the desire I knew it stirred within me. There, alone in my living room, I nearly died of a decade's worth of compounded, cringing embarrassment. I'd been so oblivious. I wondered if I was the last person to realize what had been true all along—that I am, and always have been, bisexual.

I shook my head, breaking away from the retrospective self-assessment before I sank too deep into that pool of regret. I wrangled my thoughts and pulled out my phone to check the playlists Eros had made. If they'd made one for Viktoriya and me, had they also made one for Elijah and me?

Yes—yes, they had. A quick glance showed some expected overlap, but also a few unique selections. I almost wished Eros was around to ask them how they discovered some of the obscure show tunes on the list, a few of which I didn't recognize. As I scrolled through the playlist, the shower turned off. I looked up just as Elijah opened the bathroom door, wrapped in a towel.

"We've got to stop meeting like this," I laughed, pressing play and setting my phone down on the desk.

"Meeting like what?" Elijah asked, amused yet confused.

"You—coming out of the shower like that."

"That doesn't sound like the practical Mark I know and love—are you suggesting I skip the towel next time?"

"Oh, come on. You couldn't just let me have that one?" I felt the blush rush up my face, reaching my ears. I loved the new shape of our dueling flirtations but would never admit how much I enjoyed his riposte.

"Okay, you can have it," he said, pulling the towel from his waist and tossing it at my face with a single flick of his hand.

By the time I pulled the damp towel from my face, Elijah was inches away; my breath caught. Water dripped from his hair and beard, his turquoise eyes holding me. We stood face-to-face, frozen, until he reached out to unbutton my shirt. His soft hands slipped my shirt off, and he leaned in to kiss the hollow of my collarbone gently. His lips moved down my chest as he sank to his knees. With nimble fingers, he unbuckled my belt, then unbuttoned my pants.

"Stop me if you're not ready," Elijah said, but I interrupted.

"I want this. I want you," I said as plainly as I could.

That was all the encouragement Elijah needed. He knelt, lifted each foot, slipped off my shoes, and tossed them aside. Then he slid off my pants. I steadied myself on his shoulder as he helped me step out of them—and then out of my boxer briefs. He looked up at me, my hand on his shoulder, his face inches from my growing arousal. I didn't need to nod—yet I did. Our eyes locked. I wanted him to see—to know—I was granting him the permission he already had.

His hands and eyes explored me, lingering where he'd never looked so closely before. His hands ran down my stomach and over my hips. His fingers wrapped around me, feeling my response to his touch. Without releasing me, he leaned in, his lips pressing against me. His lips parted and drew me in. My body responded, shuddering, and a ragged gasp of pleasure escaped me.

His reaction was primal. His hands slipped around the back of my thighs, pulling me closer. His mouth, lips, and tongue grew eager, claiming me with hungry intensity. Every thought faded, replaced by electric ripples coursing through me, until he paused.

Elijah stood, pressed his body to mine, and we kissed with the same hunger. My hands roamed his back. Our hips rocked forward, pressing together. Without thinking, I dropped to my knees—nervous, eager, inexperienced, certain—acting on instinct. I took Elijah into my mouth. My lips surrounded him, my tongue caressing. For a moment I lingered on the unfamiliar sensation. Elijah's body shuddered in response. I let the newness of that unexpected act register for a heartbeat—then surrendered to it.

Chapter 19

****Eros****

While Mark enjoyed his time with Elijah, I was alone again. I considered another road trip after the club closed, but a nagging feeling kept me near Mark, so I stayed in town. Instead, I launched a small research and reconnaissance expedition to arm myself with the knowledge I'd need to help Mark, Elijah, and Viktoriya with their annoyingly unromantic problems.

Since I was already at the club, I started there. I clung to Bob as he directed the closing of the bar, doing everything he could to ensure everyone could make it home safely. He even paid for a few car rides, confiscated the keys from half a dozen patrons, sealed each set in a labeled envelope, and dropped them into the coffee shop's mail slot across the street for morning pickup. It was an ingenious and surprisingly compassionate arrangement. He wasn't sympathetic about the parking tickets they'd get; he called it penance.

After that, through a sequence of eavesdropping and systematic snooping, I learned a few things. Bob owned the building outright and had no urge to sell. Ideally, he wanted to sell the business and lease the building to the new club owner. He was absolutely determined to keep the club alive, and so he had no intention of selling the building to someone who wanted to tear it down and turn it into overpriced apartments, or soulless commercial space. This was great news for Elijah if he could raise the down payment, and last I checked his little crowdsourced fundraiser had exploded—though I didn't know whether it was enough yet at this point.

Still, not everything could be solved with viral crowdfunding and blind luck. Mark's orchard problem, for example, was unfortunately much more complicated. I offered to make Gale Barlow disappear permanently, but Mark said that was "unethical" or "murder" and wouldn't solve the problem of future financial stability. So, I made my way to the Alexander Library to research local municipal historic-site preservation designations and—hopefully—determine whether that might be a viable solution. Long story short: no—it wasn't the best solution. To make it stand up to scrutiny, it would take too long—and would mean manipulating township, city, and county councils. There was no way Mark would agree to that level of manipulation—or to fighting a battalion of lawyers. Plus, it might cause Mark and his family to lose control over the orchard and their home.

However, I could always get him a plaque that read, "George Washington ate apples here"—which would at least be something. In the end, I concluded that if Mark wanted to save his orchard, he—like Elijah—needed a brilliant business plan, and that's far from my magical wheelhouse.

Viktoriya's problem thoroughly stumped me. As far as I could tell, her biggest limitation was space. She had the motivation, creativity, ambition, and talent, but simply lacked the workspace she needed to act. I had only an inkling—the phantom of a concept that depended entirely on two men getting their acts together first. By then, the night had passed, the sun was high, and it was time to head back to Mark and Elijah—assuming they weren't still in bed.

When I reached Mark's apartment, they were awake in the kitchen with coffee. They were still waking up, so not much conversation flowed. Still, they checked in with each other about last night and how they felt. The shared consensus was that they were both pleased with how the night went and were eager to do it again. I wanted to pry, to ask Mark to fill me in, but I can imagine well enough. And I suspected Mark might want to keep that to himself. Also, I really would hate to interrupt a beautifully private moment between him and Elijah. So, I was content to observe until Elijah left to pick up his car and go home to get ready for a Saturday night shift at the club.

"I thought he might never leave," I said in Mark's ear moments after the door closed behind Elijah. "Good morning, Mark, did you have a *pleasurable* night?"

"Eros—good morning. When did you get back?" Mark asked with a hint of suspicion, deliberately ignoring my question.

"Not long ago, I think, an hour or two. I didn't want to interrupt you two."

"That was considerate. Thank you."

"So, Mark. How was your night?"

"I think I'm still processing it. But it was amazing—different, but incredible," Mark said with an introspective sigh.

"Say no more. I don't need details. I mean—I want details— but I don't need them."

"Good, because I wasn't going to share them. What did you get up to all night?"

"Oh, come on, just a few details, please? We can trade—I'll tell you what I discovered, and you tell me what you discovered last night."

"All right, fair. We can talk after I get out of the shower," Mark said as he walked into the bathroom, closing the door behind him.

Mark and I talked well into the afternoon. He gave me the highlights of his night with Elijah and actually ended his story with, 'and then, fade to black,' as if I'd understand—then explained the reference, blushing.

I followed by explaining what I'd learned about designating the orchard as a historic site—and why it wasn't practical. He was interested in the plaque idea—a little too interested. Suddenly, he wanted dozens for his trees, each naming local figures and celebrities who had supposedly done various things with apples. He made a list like a madman, arguing it would be a fun tourist attraction—and that the claims would be so trivial no one would care whether they were true. He might have a point—a very unusual yet savvy point. I had to rein him in before he went too far—and remind him he had plans with Viktoriya in a few hours.

Mark

I was running late—or felt like it. Viktoriya had said to come over around six, so there was no need to panic if I ran a few minutes late. Still, I kept checking the time and beating myself up for letting my conversation with Eros distract me. Our talk had planted ideas about the orchard and Elijah's club in the back of my mind. At first, I chalked Eros's eagerness to help up to a sense of indebtedness, but I soon realized it came from our deepening friendship. Those ideas sparked my imagination, and I wanted to linger on them. But tonight was Viktoriya's night, so I set those thoughts aside—shoving them into a mental box I swore I wouldn't open until tomorrow. It wouldn't be fair to her if thoughts of Elijah crowded in. I had to keep them separate.

So that's how I found myself jogging lightly down the street, trying not to think about how to help Elijah shape a business plan for the club he wanted to buy. His crowdfunding had taken off, and he almost had enough to buy the club from Bob—if Bob agreed to lease him the building. That was fantastic news, but Eros was right that Elijah needed a plan, and I wanted to help him with that. But I couldn't right now, and that was incredibly frustrating. I was so frustrated that I told Eros they could "hang around" on my date with Viktoriya—like a cosmic third wheel—watching her teach me to bake bread.

I walked into the Sunflower Kafe nine minutes after six and spotted Viktoriya in her favorite armchair, drinking tea as she waited for me. Her tea was still so hot she had to blow on it before she could take a safe sip. Suddenly, I no longer thought I would have any trouble keeping my attention on her. She was still wearing her practical yet distinctly personal work clothes, her hair just peeking out from beneath a headscarf. I laughed, picturing her outfit hanging on a costume rack labeled *"Sexy Ukrainian Baker."* She spotted me the moment I walked in. Her smile curled around the rim of her cup. A wave of butterflies radiated from my stomach, washing through me. Where there had been tension, there was now anticipation.

"Viktoriya, sorry I'm a few minutes late—later than I meant to be," I said, walking over and sitting down.

"Hm. You are here earlier than I expected," she said, giving me a little wink. "Is good—means you are excited to see me, yes? Sit with me. Have tea. Did you eat?"

"I'm always excited to see you, and yes I ate a little something on my walk over."

"Good, good. Then your stomach will not distract you from lesson," she said, sipping her tea. "Bread is serious business. I cannot have man who cannot make bread."

"I know. You have my unwavering attention," I said, pouring myself a cup of tea that smelled like a field of wildflowers on a summer evening. "I will be your devoted student."

She paused mid-sip, a thought flickering behind her eyes as she looked away. She smiled to herself. Whatever it was, she was not sharing it. I sipped my tea; it tasted just like it smelled, carrying me back to the fields around my family's orchard.

"This tea, you like it?" she asked.

"I do, it reminds me of sitting under my apple trees, watching the colors of the sunset in the sky through the leaves and branches."

"Da. It tastes of sunsets to me as well," she smiled at me over her cup. "Drink. We will go to work soon."

We sat quietly, enjoying the tea—simply existing near each other, separate but together. When the tea was gone, she picked up the teapot, and I picked up the two cups, and we carried them back to the kitchen. We set them by the sink beside a stack of unwashed bowls and utensils. Nearby, containers of ingredients waited beside a stack of clean bowls and measuring cups.

"You were baking today?"

"Da. Preparing breads for kafe. We bake them in morning too. But kafe bread is not what I teach, I teach to you my bread," Viktoriya said with no small amount of pride in her voice. "Put on apron and grab big bowl. You listen carefully to me."

I did. I listened very carefully. She slipped back into her accent a little, like easing into a pair of well-worn shoes. Viktoriya had always relaxed her English with me, more focused on what she was saying instead of how she said it. But here, English was an afterthought for her. I slipped the apron on and picked up the large bowl, which was next to the flour. She ferried the ingredients we would need to the counter and began her instruction.

Three flours went into the bowl in eyeballed amounts—wheat, barley, and oat—followed by a spoonful each of caramel-colored sugar and finely ground, mineral-rich salt, and finally a small bowl of loose, bubbly pre-dough.

"That's the yeast!" Eros whispered excitedly in my ear. "Amazing. I've never actually watched this before. That yeast is alive, did you know? You have to ask how long she's kept that colony going!"

"That's the yeast, right?" I asked, like Eros wanted.

"Da. We brought from home," she answered. "We bring small bottle from the big jar we started when I was four. It grows into big jar again—makes best bread."

To me, it felt like a mystifying blend of old-world alchemy, science, and artistry. She told me to mix with a large wooden spoon while she poured in a dark aromatic lager and water … until I couldn't stir anymore—which didn't take long. As soon as the dough just felt like pushing a squishy elastic blob around the bowl, we turned it out of the bowl onto the floured counter. She dusted more flour over the top and instructed me to use my hands to fold the dough over on itself until it was just 'a little sticky' then shaped it into a ball. Once it formed its slightly tacky shape, we transferred it back into the bowl, covered it with a damp towel, and set it aside to rest for an hour while we cleaned up.

While we washed up, Viktoriya told me how her bread reminded her of home. She was barely an adult when she came here. Her parents spent years arranging it so she and her brothers could get an education far from the growing conflicts—and have the opportunities they never did. She left behind the friends and life she was only starting to build. That carried-along yeast they've tended for years is part of that life, and this is how she kept it safe and alive in memory. I could understand the idea of keeping something alive like that. I felt the same way about my home and orchard. Except I could go back there anytime I wanted, but I chose to stay away. Now I could feel the yearning for home rising.

The proto-bread had to rest about an hour, which gave us enough time to finish washing the dishes and putting everything back where it belonged. After that, we rolled the dough—now nearly doubled in size—out of the bowl and back onto the floured counter. We kneaded out the larger air bubbles, stretching and folding to build chains of gluten. It wasn't enough to mix a few complementary ingredients; they had to be worked, stretched, and folded to come together and stabilize into bread.

"Like a relationship—a partnership," she said as we stretched and folded the dough. "A stable relationship takes work to come together and form strong bonds that won't crumble—unlike muffins."

We dropped the dough into a large square container, sealed it, and put it to bed in the walk-in fridge. I thought Viktoriya would die laughing when I said we were putting it 'to bread for the night.' Thus, cementing my lifelong opinion that a well-placed pun will always be the height of comedy. With the dough resting in the fridge overnight, it was time for us to go to bed as well so we could wake up at four a.m. to bake the racks of bread waiting in the fridge. She assured me her father was still inside, minding the counter, and that he'd lock up after the last customers left. When I asked why we hadn't seen him, she said he was giving us space, so he stayed out of the kitchen unless he absolutely had to, which he hadn't.

Viktoriya took my hand and guided me out the back door of the café. She wasn't leading me, but taking me with her. Together we walked up the back stairs to their apartment above, and into her bedroom. She pointed out the bathroom across the narrow hall, assuming I'd need it before morning. After taking turns using the bathroom and washing some of the flour off, we stepped inside her bedroom. At first glance, the room looked the same— but a closer look revealed changes. She had new sketches pinned to the wall, over the top of others in some spots. At least two paintings had been replaced, and the bolts and swatches of fabric were entirely different.

She closed the door behind her and asked if I was ready to go to bed. A lump formed and caught my voice in my throat. I nodded my head and watched Viktoriya undress, methodically folding and setting aside each article of clothing she removed. She wasn't undressing for me; she was simply getting ready for bed. It wasn't meant as seduction—but her unselfconscious ease made it all the more seductive.

"That happened quickly—sorry, Mark. I'll see you at four a.m.," Eros whispered. They could have slipped away quietly, but I think they knew I wouldn't have realized they'd gone unless they said something.

I followed suit, undressing and setting my clothes aside. For a moment, Viktoriya and I stood silently before each other—naked and vulnerable. She smiled, a smirk shimmering in her eyes as she climbed into her twin bed and held out a hand in invitation. I didn't need more than that one gesture to climb into bed, sliding under the sheets next to her. We lay down facing each other, our heads sharing one pillow. We studied each other, both searching for hesitation or restraint. She didn't need to say it; I could tell she was thinking the same thing I was—sleep or give in to each other? The decision was unanimous. Sleep would wait a while longer, and we kissed each other, drawing our bodies closer together.

Eros

Four a.m. rolled by—though I didn't notice; I can't wear a watch. I was deep into apple-tree botany in a university library archive. I had an idea for Mark's orchard, but I wasn't ready to tell him about it. Once we saved it from the immediate threat of redevelopment, Mark needed to worry about long-term viability and stability. My idea was to make that a little easier by working out a way to carefully and selectively 'mutate' his trees to make them far hardier, and increase both yield and quality with minimal resources. Ages ago I'd have experimented by blind trial and error, but that takes time and risks the trees. Humans had done this for centuries already. I just needed to learn from their work—figure out which cellular components to tweak to achieve the results I wanted.

That's how I missed the time. At five a.m. I popped out of the book I'd been absorbing and realized I was late getting back to Mark and Viktoriya. I knew Mark would understand. I was still annoyed with myself because I had been excited to observe the baking. I knew mechanically how bread went from goo to golden-brown keystones of civilization, but I hadn't ever watched it happen for myself. I retreated from the library and wound my way back to the Sunflower Kafe—which only took me a couple of seconds, probably—since I could move confidently at the speed of energy when I knew where I was going.

Back in the café kitchen, Mark and Viktoriya were in full production. There were racks filled with over two dozen trays of unbaked bread and pastries lined up near the large commercial ovens, awaiting their turn. I arrived moments before they slid the first batch of bread into the oven. Viktoriya was carefully explaining the elaborate timer setup she had created and was in the process of taping English labels over the Ukrainian ones for Mark's benefit. Four timer sets—two per oven, eight in total. A clever setup. I'm not sure I understood it, but Mark got it immediately and kept remarking how impressive Viktoriya was. When she finished, Viktoriya told Mark to start and began issuing orders.

Mark followed Viktoriya's directions with diligent obedience. He repeated each instruction before loading each tray onto an oven rack while Viktoriya marked the timer board and started each timer. In minutes, each oven was filled, and all eight timers were ticking away. Mark and Viktoriya refilled their coffee cups and sat in quiet contentment, sipping coffee until the first timer rang.

Viktoriya jumped up and walked to the ovens. She peeked into each, then reset the timers, telling Mark that everything looked good—no need to rotate trays or adjust temperatures— and that this batch would be ready in about twenty minutes. Enough time to brew a fresh pot of coffee and set out the cooling racks. I couldn't resist slipping inside one of the ovens to marvel at the transformation from a ball of goo into bread.

Over the next several hours I watched them pull fresh bread from the ovens, slide loaves onto cooling racks, and set them aside for the café. In addition to loaves, they baked tray after tray of pastries with industrious efficiency. Finally, they pulled the last tray—and the two loaves they had made together the night before. These loaves were special: slightly irregular, darker, more rustic, and—judging by Mark's reaction—far more aromatic.

Despite Mark's protests, they set the loaves aside to cool while they shut down the ovens and cleaned up. Once everything was put away, the fresh pastries went in the front case with half the loaves, and then Viktoriya said they could cut into one of theirs. Together, they reveled in an act I've come to understand as a nearly universal human joy—sharing warm, fresh bread.

They finished half a loaf before Viktoriya sighed that she had to help open the café and tackle the homework she'd been neglecting. Otherwise, she said, she'd have loved Mark to spend the day with her. Mark understood and asked if she'd mind his sharing some of their bread with Elijah. She didn't object. Instead, she sliced the remaining loaf in half and lovingly wrapped each piece—one for Mark, one for Elijah. She even packed a few fresh pastries for them before sending him home with a soft yet powerful kiss that nearly lifted him off his feet.

"Thank you, Mark," I said into Mark's ear as soon as he stepped outside the café. "I think I understand why bread matters now. Can you describe how it smells and tastes?"

"I was wondering when you were going to show up," Mark answered while almost skipping down the sidewalk. "I'm sorry. I don't think I could describe it in a way you'd really understand— not in the ways that really matter. They are somewhat foundational aromas and flavors, … like trying to describe a sunset to someone born blind. Abstractly, I guess it smells like life—soil, growing things, rain, basic nourishment. It kind of ticks the box for a deep instinctual need. The same for the taste in a way, but it's deeper. Like when you take a bite, part of your brain cries; 'Yes! We need this! We are safe now!' Maybe something deep inside us remembers what it takes to turn seeds, water, yeast, and fire into bread—into safety, stability, and abundance. But it's also home, hard work, and love—it's everything."

"Wow. I thought you said you couldn't describe it in a way that I could understand. I understand that, Mark. I almost wish I didn't—now I want to taste it even more. You, jerk."

Mark

My night and morning with Viktoriya left me borderline euphoric. So much so that it barely stung when Elijah told me he was feeling too burned out for company when I delivered the bread. I knew it wasn't personal; it still hurt a little. I think he saw that flash across my face because he quickly asked me to come over tomorrow night instead. He thanked me for the bread, kissed my forehead, forgave me for waking him at nine a.m., and went back to bed.

The next day—Monday—was a blur. I was unable to focus consistently on my work. My mind kept wandering back to my time with Elijah and Viktoriya. Everything I tried took two or three times longer than it should have, which was frustrating. A few times I tried to connect with Viktoriya to let her know she was on my mind. Her responses were brief—almost curt—she was having a difficult, distractible day as well. Eros wasn't much help either. They bombarded me with questions about everything they'd just read or seen, then insisted on scheduling dates with Viktoriya and Elijah—something I eventually, and perhaps unwisely, agreed to.

By the time evening came and I was knocking on Elijah's door, all I wanted was a quiet night. I can't quite describe the relief I felt when he suggested we just settle in and watch a favorite movie we'd both seen hundreds of times. We unfolded his sofa bed and climbed in with a box of cheap wine, a plate of deli meats and cheese, and the last of the bread I'd baked yesterday. Curled up together, Elijah and I settled in to watch the 1985 camp-classic *Legend*.

Luckily, we both knew the movie so well that we didn't need to pay attention. Once the cheap wine hit our mostly empty stomachs, our attention shifted to each other's bodies. Our clothes were exiled from the bed long before the Prince of Darkness appeared on screen. By the time the on-screen climax hit, it was the third in the room—and not the final one.

Tuesday morning I was late for work. I could've asked Elijah to drive me home, but I let him sleep knowing he had another long night ahead of him. I hated being late, even though technically I couldn't be—I didn't even have a set schedule. That feeling persisted throughout the day. Eros showed me the date-night schedule they'd set up; I couldn't focus and told them to handle it—something I soon regretted, since Eros can't tell time.

Case in point: Wednesday night. Viktoriya had a full day of classes, then an evening split between the café and a major design-term project—she was busy. Elijah had the night off, and we'd planned dinner; Eros added it to the schedule. That Wednesday afternoon, I glanced at the calendar Eros had made on my phone:

"Date with Elijah" was scheduled for the following week. I can admit it was my fault for not confirming—and for doubting my own memory. Still, I ended up ghosting Elijah. To his credit, he forgave me—but I still hate that I discovered the mistake only when he called (not texted) after I didn't show and hadn't called. Eros was mortified and apologetic, promising it would never happen again. Like the foolish, trusting human I am, I believed them—and failed to learn a crucial lesson: never trust a noncorporeal, eternal cosmic entity to manage your love life.

Chapter 20

Managing Mark's love life turned out to be harder than I expected—but not entirely my fault. The first thing you need to understand is that Mark is terrible at making plans. It's not that he doesn't make plans—it's that he makes them terribly. He plans countless details for every contingency—except the actual date. That's how he didn't notice my innocent mistake: I listed his date with Elijah for *next* Wednesday instead of *this* Wednesday. Thankfully, Elijah is forgiving and adapted his schedule to accommodate Mark.

Then there is Viktoriya, whose schedule is brutally inflexible. She hasn't had a free night since Saturday, which is frustrating—and makes her miss Mark more with each passing hour. Which means that when she finally has time for Mark, I can't afford any scheduling mistakes. I think she'd be as understanding as Elijah, but she likely wouldn't have the freedom to just swap nights. All of which is to say that after just two days, I'm—quite possibly for the first time—actually stressed out.

Thursday night, Elijah arrived at Mark's door with dinner. Nothing extravagant—just Hong Kong–style noodles with beef and his favorite cheap wine. What surprised Mark wasn't the dinner, but that Elijah had changed his schedule for him. He'd traded shifts last-minute with an understanding coworker, just to keep the mis-scheduled Thursday night date.

"It's not a big deal, Mark. We trade shifts last minute all the time to help each other out," Elijah said. "Didn't I say not to worry about it? I told you I would adapt. Meaning I'd meet you where you are—hungry, in need of noodles, and a movie I'm almost certain you've never seen."

"You just couldn't pass up the opportunity to be the better boyfriend, could you?" Mark said, clearing a space on his coffee table for dinner. "All right, what movie could you possibly have that you *think* I haven't seen?"

"Guillermo del Toro. Supernatural monster romance. *The Shape of Water*. And I don't care if you've seen it—you're going to be a good boyfriend and pretend you haven't, because I love this damn movie."

"Well, that'll be easy because I haven't seen it. Sit—should I get the good wine glasses or the cheap wine glasses?"

"Oh, this beauty deserves a plastic cup with ice. Cocktail umbrellas optional. Grab me a fork, will you? I'm not in the mood to fumble with chopsticks tonight."

Mark returned from the kitchen with two forks and plastic cups filled with ice. Elijah had queued up the movie, sat on the couch, and set the food on the coffee table. Mark sat down next to Elijah, checked his phone, and sighed before setting it down, face up, on the arm of the couch. Elijah glanced at Mark when he sighed, but didn't ask for details. He waited instead, giving Mark the space he hadn't needed to request. He also waited for Mark to signal he was settled with his food and wine—in a plastic cup— and ready to watch the movie.

What Elijah didn't see was that Mark was checking for a reply from Viktoriya. He hadn't heard from her all day, and I could tell she was on his mind. Now Mark was attempting to push aside his preoccupation with Viktoriya's absence to be present for Elijah. I wanted to nudge Mark to talk to Elijah about it, but for some reason, I felt apprehensive about interrupting. It felt like this was a larger conversation I needed to have with Mark. I'd noticed that Mark had stopped talking about Viktoriya around Elijah—and stopped mentioning Elijah whenever he spoke to Viktoriya. And if I noticed, surely they had as well—and that could become a problem.

The movie was excellent—haunting, beautiful, and filled with baffling nonsense I couldn't begin to grasp. Listening to Mark and Elijah dissect it made one thing clear: my grasp of modern media was so woefully inadequate that *The Shape of Water* was simply out of my reach. Whatever I was missing, it hit Mark hard; he struggled to hold back tears for the rest of the evening— even when Elijah gently led him to bed. Mark was in such a state that Elijah—through a display of tremendous willpower— declined Mark's enthusiastic, intimate advances. He said Mark wasn't in the right headspace for anything more conjugal than 'heavy petting'—and yes, that's exactly what it sounds like.

By Friday morning, Mark was in a much better state of mind. Elijah had a calming, grounding effect on Mark—like an anchor in a turbulent sea. He was often more clear-minded and calmer when Elijah was around. They said goodbye on the sidewalk outside Mark's apartment. Elijah reminded Mark that he was performing tonight, but added that he had no obligation to come, but was always a welcome sight in the audience. Mark was unusually noncommittal about attending, and I didn't understand why at first. Watching Elijah perform was among Mark's favorite things, and he didn't have any other plans; my guess was he was holding out hope Viktoriya would call with a last-minute date.

Halfway through Mark's workday, he received a phone call. His rising elation plummeted when he saw the call wasn't from Viktoriya but from his mother. He exhaled and answered, guilt written all over his face for not only feeling disappointed, but for repeatedly forgetting to call her back over the past several days. She was naturally understanding. Although I hadn't yet met her, I could tell she cared deeply for Mark. She was calling to check on him. Her curiosity about his dates—that she had heard so little about—was driving her crazy. She also had news: the cider mill was finally repaired. She needed to know when Mark would be able to come help process all the apples that were nearly filling the barn before they all went to waste. To Mark's credit, he didn't dodge the question about his dates, nor did he make any attempt to dodge the dozens of follow-up questions. He even agreed to ask both Elijah—who she already knew well—and Viktoriya if they'd like to come help mill and press thousands of apples. That seemed to be more than satisfactory to her for now, but she made it clear she expected Mark to call her again soon. The sooner, the better.

At first, I was frustrated; her call pulled Mark away from the mindset I needed him in for a serious talk about how he was isolating Viktoriya and Elijah. But then I realized it might be exactly what Mark needed to shift his perspective and potentially force the three of them together where they might work this out naturally. After all, they found their way together in the first place.

A few minutes before Mark ended his workday, Viktoriya called. He was so startled he fumbled to answer; it took him five tries to find the big green button and smash his finger on it.

"Viktoriya!" Mark said, his voice unusually unsteady.

"Mark, dear. Listen, please, before I lose my guts. I miss seeing you. It is not fair—I feel upset with you—but I do," Viktoriya said, sounding increasingly agitated and slightly nervous. "You have not tried to make time for me. Is not … um—shit. What is word? Rozumnyy … sensible. I know I had no time … I know … Are you giving all your time to Elijah? I'm sorry … I'm sorry, do not answer—Ignore that. I just miss you. So much. I feel like crazy person. Tomorrow—I have day, tomorrow. I will see you, yes? Please."

Mark froze, mouth agape, forgetting to breathe. Viktoriya sounded plaintive and unguarded, and he was completely unprepared for it. After a few heart-pounding seconds, he inhaled sharply and spoke, his voice surprisingly calm, almost monotone.

"That was … a lot, Viktoriya. I'm not sure how to respond—but I think I understand how you feel. So, what you're saying is that you'd like to go out tomorrow?"

"Yes, Mark, but more. I need to see you—and I do not understand this feeling," Viktoriya said, her voice a mix of frustration and relief. "I have to work now. You will call me in morning, yes?"

"Yes, I will call you and we'll make plans," Mark said, echoing her relief. "And I miss you too. Like a crazy person. I love you."

"I love you too. Do zustrichi."

"Pobachymos', Viktoriya," Mark said, and ended the call.

"Mark, I think you handled that well," I said. "Are you okay?"

"I think so, but I'm not really sure. I think I just defused a relationship bomb—my brain kinda short-circuited for a minute. We're going to refine that schedule you made tonight."

And that's exactly what we did. We spent the rest of the evening updating the calendar, adding reminders for Mark to check in with both Elijah and Viktoriya throughout the week.

Fridays, Saturdays, and Sundays were tricky to divide—Elijah's performances, Viktoriya's classes, and her café shifts all competed for time. That became one of my side quests—as Mark put it—covertly verifying their schedules the next time we saw them. I didn't entirely understand why Mark couldn't just ask them, but I think he felt like it was something he *should* already know. Whatever his reasoning, his mind was made up. Honestly, I accepted the mission because it sounded fun—and, after all, I am the ultimate spy.

Mark

Late Saturday morning, I called Viktoriya, as I'd promised, to make plans for that afternoon and evening. If she had the day free, I wanted to give her as much of it as I could. Between work and a major term project for her design class, she felt pent up. The only problem was that her craving for a night out to blow off steam clashed with her need for quiet, dedicated time alone with me. That made planning harder than I liked. My first idea was to take her to The Queen's Head to watch Elijah perform, but I dismissed that plan before I even suggested it. That would be anything but quiet, and after our call yesterday, I worried it might feel like Elijah was usurping her time just by being there.

We eventually settled on a small tavern-piano bar with simple food, live music, and mercifully small crowds. The band was a local acoustic Irish folk-punk trio. They were decent enough. Viktoriya and I enjoyed the performance, and she was excited to buy one of their handmade t-shirts. The print was slightly off-center, as if it had survived a decade in a drawer. We couldn't tell if that was an intentional design choice, but Viktoriya loved it regardless. She said it gave her an idea for the finishing touches on her term project, which was due in a week. I offered to help however I could—mostly manual labor or supply runs—and she accepted enthusiastically.

That added a few entries to my calendar, which Eros quickly supplemented with Viktoriya's work and class schedule. They claimed to have memorized it while she checked her phone during dinner. The calendar now looked like an incomplete, out-of-order rainbow of color-coded reminders. I could only hope it wouldn't hurt my eyes too much once Eros added Elijah's schedule. In the back of my mind, I questioned Eros's choice of color-coding. I'd meant to ask last night but had forgotten—and I wasn't fully confident in their consistency. But I couldn't do anything about that right now.

Our evening out ended with a friendly farewell to the three-person band who'd kept us entertained over pints of dark stout and deep-fried, cheese-covered food. We were still laughing about the band from New Jersey who sang using a fake Irish accent when we walked into my apartment. And after only a few minutes of settling in, Viktoriya said it was time I took her to bed. I'd say I caught her subtle hint—but there was nothing subtle about her undressing as she spoke. Even Eros picked up the cue and simply whispered, 'I'll give you some privacy. See you in the morning,' before leaving us—I assume.

Unlike our first night together, there was not a long, slow tease. Viktoriya had no patience for that tonight. Moments after I stepped into the bedroom, she ensnared me, removing my clothing with surgical precision, tossing the garments aside on top of hers. Once she had disrobed me, she pushed me back onto the bed. She pounced, landing on top of me with ease, giggling and apologizing for the abrupt ambush.

"I'm sorry, I couldn't wait any longer," she said through an intoxicating laugh that reverberated through her entire body—and, straddling me, through mine as well. "You're like bread, you know?"

"Bread?" I said, genuinely confused. She was either making a joke I didn't understand yet, or this was the most unusual dirty talk I'd ever heard—not that I'd heard much.

"Okay—how am I like bread?"

"You have a tough but delicate exterior. Inside, you're soft but strong. You are delicious, and I do not wish to go without you," she said, with a warm, almost embarrassed smile that grew into her signature smirk. "And when I knead you and make you warm ... you rise."

"Oh. My. God," I laughed so hard my eyes watered. "That could be one of the best things anyone has ever said to me."

"Good. Now, Mark, I show you how much I have missed you, and you will show me, until we cannot walk."

She leaned down and kissed me deeply, affectionately, nearly lifting me off the bed. When she released me from the kiss, she climbed off me, only to turn around and swing her leg over my head. Her knees were on either side of my head, my face embraced by her thighs. She leaned forward, lowering her body onto mine. The warmth of her kneading sent effervescent ripples of pleasure through my body—and I rose to meet her. As we enveloped each other, we dissolved and melted, tasting the passion and love dripping from our bodies, swathed by the muffled, hungry moans filling the bedroom.

An hour later, we staggered out of the bedroom into the kitchen, seeking water and anything to eat. Unfortunately, I had nothing worth eating, but it was still early enough on a Saturday night in a college town to get a pizza delivered. Twenty minutes later, we exchanged pleasantries with an embarrassed nineteen-year-old delivery driver and collapsed onto the couch with the best pizza either of us had ever tasted. Between the two of us, we demolished the pie before falling back into bed and dropping off to sleep in each other's arms.

Sunday morning was waning before we got out of bed, and it was almost too late for brunch by the time we left the apartment. As much as Viktoriya and I wanted to spend the rest of the day together, she had too much work, and we'd already stolen more time than we should have. I wanted to call a car to give Viktoriya a ride home, but she insisted on walking. She said it would be a good stretch after the night we'd had, which was way more fun than visiting a gym—and I couldn't disagree. By then, Eros had returned just in time to hear that and start pestering me for an explanation of the reference they didn't understand. I told them to run a few searches for it—they'd figure it out quickly.

I was right. Eros was downright disgusted by what they found in just a few searches. So much so that they forgot why I told them to run those searches in the first place. It took a few minutes to convince them what they found bore little resemblance to what transpired between Viktoriya and me last night. But it served as a lesson in not asking questions you are unprepared to hear answered honestly. I took pity on the timeless cosmic entity and spent the rest of the morning teaching them what eye bleach was, and how it wasn't just for biological entities. All beings, regardless of origin or divinity, can appreciate the soothing effect of baby goats on a playground.

Once Eros had settled down, I heard from Viktoriya that she'd arrived home safely—though she now wished she'd let me call her a car, because her legs felt unsteady. I commiserated and said I was contemplating sitting in an ice bath for a little while, but that would involve walking to the corner store and hauling several bags of ice up the stairs.

That was when my euphoric wandering mind was snapped back to reality. My phone chimed. Four unread texts from Elijah: three from last night, and one had just come in.

The first unread message from last night contained general information about his performance: the lineup, when he expected to go on, and what he planned to perform. The second and third messages were more direct.

'Going on soon. Don't see you, I'll look for you on stage.'

'You didn't come. Did you forget?'

Did I forget? I could feel my heart tearing itself in half as I read those words. I almost dreaded looking at the fourth message, but avoiding it wouldn't make it better.

'Mark, I know you didn't promise to come, but you could have told me. I looked like an ass in front of everyone, looking for my absent boyfriend. Maybe you were just too "busy" for me.'

Last night, I was too busy and didn't confirm plans with him. How could I have forgotten him like that? I had to call him back. Unprepared and unrehearsed, I pressed the icon next to his name, and the phone began ringing before I knew what to say.

"Mark," Elijah said, sounding mildly surprised. "I hadn't expected you to call so quickly, but I guess I should have."

"I am so, so sorry," I said, launching blindly into a default state of apology. "I didn't mean to ghost you."

"It's okay, Mark."

"No, it's not. I mean yeah, it will be. But I didn't mean to. I'm sorry. I swear I didn't forget—"

"Mark! Stop apologizing for everything," Elijah said, cutting my apology tour short. "Just ignore me, I was feeling needy and insecure—that's unlike me, I know—it's not rational at all. I just felt like you forgot about me," Elijah said. There was a barely perceptible wavering in his voice, as if he was fighting a sting that still throbbed. "You didn't promise to be there, you didn't even say you would, I made an assumption. So, if you think about it, I hurt my own feelings."

"Yeah, well, I still should have let you know."

"Hey, I'm your boyfriend, not your parole officer."

"That could be fun …" I laughed, but my instinctive deflection sounded hollow, even to me.

"Yeah … so, before you explain, know that I didn't ask, and you don't owe me an explanation—this time."

"This time," I said, echoing Elijah's words, hearing the implied limits to his patience and understanding. "All right, in that case, what are you doing today?"

"Laundry—and wig-washing. You don't want to help."

"Yeah, last time I tried to help, you almost strangled me for using the wrong soap, detergent, or shampoo. I still don't really understand."

"Exactly, that's why you are going to have yourself a self-care Sunday."

"Then how about tomorrow? Dinner, and we can talk about your business plans?"

"It's a date," Elijah said, sounding somewhat distracted. "I've got to go, I left a wig soaking in the sink. Love you, see you tomorrow."

"Love you too—go rescue that wig," I said and ended the call.

Elijah was right. I could use a self-care day to refocus and nurse this biting guilt. I'd dropped the ball with both Elijah and Viktoriya. They both forgave me quickly enough, but how many more chances would they give me?

I had a lot of thinking to do. Taking care of my laundry and cleaning my apartment should help clear my mind. Plus, I was sure I owed my mom a call, and I hadn't had the chance to talk with Eros in days. I always found it easier to work out problems while I was busy with mundane tasks, and Mom usually has some sage advice on offer.

So I caught up on personal care, refreshed my supply of clean clothing, and banished expired food from the refrigerator while chatting with Eros and checking on their progress helping Elijah,

Viktoriya, and my orchard. They'd made little progress since we last talked about it. Their ideas were more refined now, but their understanding of the complexities still needed work. I almost suggested they talk to my mom to tap her experience, but she would likely just tell Eros they should stop meddling.

Monday afternoon, I checked in with Viktoriya. I knew she had a busy week coming, and I had offered to help. She had most of the details for her project worked out and was down to execution. She said she could use my help on Thursday. Eros chimed in to say they'd put it on my calendar, so I told Viktoriya I would be there Thursday to help any way I could.

After work, I headed over to Elijah's with a bag of assorted Korean dumplings. I don't know why, but I thought dumplings were the perfect accompaniment to a business plan discussion. Miraculously, Elijah said the same thing when I arrived at his door. He eagerly unpacked the takeout onto his coffee table, skirting the blank yellow legal pad and pen that looked twenty years old.

"I hope that's not your business plan for the Queen's Head," I said, gesturing to the blank notepad.

"No, not yet anyway. But it will be, with your help," Elijah said with a wry wink.

"I knew I should have ordered extra dumplings—this could take a while."

It turned out we didn't need extra dumplings. Elijah had an entire notebook hidden under the table, filled with his ideas. Concepts that held kernels of great ideas mixed with ill-conceived fantasies. One was to turn The Queen's Head into a 100% drag club, including the staff in full drag, with every night a different theme. I suggested limiting themed nights to weekly or monthly and encouraging, not requiring, staff to work in drag. One practical plan was to close the kitchen and contract with a neighboring restaurant, which could benefit both. Ideas like that were perfect for a business plan proposal to highlight ways Elijah could both cut costs and improve service.

But the crown jewel of his vision was tucked under the heading: Drag Queen's Head Foster Home and Nursery for New and Motherless Queens. It was filled with half-formed ideas about a small membership fee to guarantee stage time and access to clothing. There'd be an on-site seamstress shop, seminars, classes, and mentorship opportunities. Much of that exists in the city, but at exorbitant prices and with limited access—a barrier for anyone starting out.

I helped refine these ideas, eliminating those that were unfeasible or too complex. I reminded him that Viktoriya was a magnificent designer and had dreams of setting up her own shop, so he should talk to her about this. Then, I had to rein him in before he got carried away with premature plans.

I laughed and made what I thought was an obvious observation. The club sits practically on a major university campus; it's basically Drag University. But that thought never occurred to Elijah. Elijah's face lit up as he scribbled a note to look up grants from the Department of Education. He said it never hurts to ask as he finished the last dumpling. He slapped his notebook closed and shot me a wicked leer, declaring the boring business meeting over.

"Why are you looking at me like that, Elijah?" I asked, feeling mildly vulnerable as his eyes slowly traveled up and down my body.

"Because I can't focus on anything else anymore. Something about you helping me with my business plan is irresistibly sexy. Like you could be my secretary or something horribly problematic and sexist. But deeply erotic," Elijah said, licking his lips and approaching me. "Why don't you take off your pants, darlin'—oh no. That killed it. How do people role-play that crap?"

"Oh. I don't know. But from you, it was kinda working for me," I said, laughing at what might be Elijah's first failed, yet somehow successful, seduction.

"In that case, come over here and let me show you what I learned from the Whoreton School of Business," Elijah said through a laugh while simultaneously unbuttoning his pants.

I shouldn't have, but I kissed him. Not only because I desperately wanted to, but because I knew if I didn't, he would escalate the puns.

"Elijah, there's something I've meant to ask you," I said, pulling away from our kiss. "Are you ever afraid you'll have to go into hiding when they outlaw clowns? Or will you just use less makeup?"

"You're only saying that because I can't chase you with my pants down," Elijah giggled. His giggle grew into a laugh that weakened his knees. "If they do outlaw us clowns, can you imagine a more hilarious prison *camp*? Picture it: *The Great Escape*, but with clowns. Theme song on bike horns."

"If you honk while we're having sex, I'm leaving you." I walked to the bathroom, trying to stifle my laughter until I was out of sight.

Chapter 21

By now, Mark has grown so comfortable with my presence that he sometimes forgets I'm even here. To be fair, I know I lack a physical form. As such, it can be easy for him to forget I'm there. Last night, I was there for Mark and Elijah's little business meeting. But they escalated so quickly, and I was so confused by their clown jokes that I kind of forgot to leave when I should have. I didn't linger—I just caught a glimpse of them together before slipping away. I'll just say I think Mark would be horrifically embarrassed if I ever told him how much I saw. Still, there was something magnetic about them together. I don't have any sense of what humans call "erotic," personally, but from what I've gathered, that would be an apt description.

So, after thoroughly reading Elijah's business plan and his entire notebook of ideas, I slipped out to practice my particular brand of "magic" on the flowers blooming in Elijah's garden. In a few days, I'll know whether my minor genetic manipulation worked—if the flowers bloom again with twice as many blossoms. If that works, I will be ready to tell Mark what I can do for his apple trees, and secure his help to ensure I don't ruin the apples. I am now almost completely confident I can improve the taste of the fruit without making them toxic. And from what I saw last night, Mark will be all too willing to put his body on the line as a taste-tester.

That is to say, Monday night ended on a high note for both of us, which made Tuesday even more distressing. The day quickly devolved into what Mark called a "shit-show"—I didn't understand the etymological origins of the phrase, but I grasped his meaning.

When he got to work, his mailbox was filled with 'emergency' requests for printer maintenance, and his friend OT was cursing as he frantically typed. Printers seem universally despised, yet frustratingly indispensable. From what I caught of their brief exchange, a recent printer software update had disabled the ability to print without a subscription. OT had spent most of his morning in triage only to discover the change hadn't been advertised, and he was already mired in customer-service negotiations. When Mark stepped in to relieve his friend, he was able to negotiate a reasonable solution—a common account for the university exempt from the monthly subscription fee. The only problem is that they would need to set up each printer on campus manually.

It would have taken both of them all day to accomplish this task, but they had me. I had only to whisper to Mark that I could help. I only needed him to show me what to do and where the printers were located. They were all connected with cables I could use to zip—like electricity—from one to the other in a fraction of the time it would take them. OT was skeptical when Mark told him he had an idea and could handle the set-up if he helped map out where everything was located.

The three of us made surprisingly quick work of the task. Mark showed me what to do on the first printer in the Alexander Library, and with OT's help, showed me a map with all the device locations plotted out. It still took most of the day, but I was able to fix almost every printer on the campus in five hours, making Mark look brilliant to his supervisors. Mark knew the praise was hollow—I'd done the heavy lifting, and we both knew he couldn't tell a soul. Still, he felt a rare moment of residual pride that tragically couldn't last.

Unfortunately, he didn't fare as well with the two people who mattered most to him. While I was busy saving Mark and his coworker, he was fumbling through a string of frustrated texts from Viktoriya. This problem with printers had interrupted her project, and Mark had missed addressing her emotional needs at that moment. She needed the problem solved, but more than that, she needed him to hear her stress and respond with compassion—

she needed her boyfriend, not IT support. Instead, he spoke to her as if she were just another student with a tech issue.

And when Elijah texted to check in and Mark vented, Elijah didn't respond with Mark's expected, or desired, level of praise. Instead, he told Mark it sounded rough, but that was something that came with the job, and this time he would need to stroke his own ego. Under normal circumstances, Elijah's quip about stroking Mark's 'ego' would have made him laugh—but this time, it deflated him. That evening, I helped Mark see that Elijah made him feel the way he'd made Viktoriya feel. Emotionally dismissed and unavailable. Elijah wasn't trying to make Mark feel that way; he just didn't clairvoyantly know what Mark's emotional needs were at that moment. I think I could have saved Mark from falling into those holes if I'd been there, but now all I could do was help him climb out.

That night, Mark sent an honest apology to Viktoriya. She said she understood and wouldn't hold it against him, but that he had to make it up to her when he came to help later in the week. And Mark decided it would be best if he just let Elijah off the hook for not responding the way Mark had hoped. He explained to me that Elijah had just learned the headlining drag queen for Friday night's show had canceled, so Elijah was filling the spot. As such, he suddenly had to put together a new number for the Chappell Roan-themed night, so he had his own distractions. That was when Mark told me he'd checked the calendar and made sure Thursday night was free before agreeing to help Elijah with rehearsal. In retrospect, I should have heard the alarm bells—the faint, rhythmic warning of something out of tune—but I didn't. I couldn't foresee how much chaos one slight mistake mixed with a lapse in communication could cause.

Wednesday played out like a rerun of Tuesday. The fallout from Printermageddon—as Mark and OT called it—was still lingering. Apparently, a dozen or so printers simply didn't accept the changes, or wouldn't come online, requiring Mark to venture out to solve those problems himself. At first I was afraid this was my fault, that I had made a mistake or forgotten them, but Mark assured me that printers were evil agents of chaos, and it was inevitable.

He and I spent the better part of the day traversing the campus to troubleshoot printers. Most were simple fixes—a reboot here, reapplying the same change there. A few were simply out of paper, which somehow prevented them from coming online after the change was applied. I asked Mark why. He simply repeated his earlier assessment: *evil agents of chaos*. While I understood the assessment, the rationale behind it was confounding. So, perhaps I can be forgiven for not urging Mark to double-check with both Viktoriya and Elijah, because we had no reason to suspect that I—of all "people"—might make an innocent human mistake. Even beings like me can forget—or confuse one day for another.

Mark

Thursday was shaping up to be a fantastic day. OT and I had survived Printermageddon and come out unscathed. By the end of the day, we'd cleared our inbox of every ticket and work request—not just the printer fiascos, but everything. It was the best feeling—knowing tomorrow would be nothing but light cleanup, and that we'd head into the weekend with no work hanging over our heads. On top of that, tonight I'd get an exclusive first look at Elijah's newest lip-sync routine before anyone else in the world. It might be just a rehearsal where I help fine-tune the performance, but still it's exhilarating every time.

The plan was simple: meet Elijah at the club after work. Our shifts ended around the same time in the early afternoon. He would drive us back to his place, we would clear space in his living room/kitchen/bedroom and get to work. We've done this before, blocking out the basic dance moves he could do in heels. We'd listen to a single song for hours until it was ingrained in our bodies. Depending on the song, we would either love it forever, or grow to despise it. It was surprising how few songs we could never listen to recreationally again. Eros was unusually excited, insisting something was going to happen. They didn't know what—only that they felt a strange tingle at the back of their mind.

When my shift ended, I headed over to the club to meet Elijah. On my way, I sent Viktoriya a quick message to check in, asking how the project was coming. She replied, '*hands full, plan on track, see you soon.*' I had '*can't wait to see you tomorrow*' typed out and ready to send when I reached the club—just as Elijah walked out the door. So I was distracted, and I never sent that response to Viktoriya.

"Hey, sweetie—perfect timing," Elijah said with a suspiciously wide grin. "Ready to go, or do you need to stop at your place for a toothbrush?"

"I'm all set—and unless you tossed it, there's been a spare toothbrush in your bathroom for a year," I said. "What's with the grin? What are you plotting?"

"I'm just happy to see you," Elijah said, twirling his car keys around his finger. "And maybe I really like this song, so this will be fun."

"All right, everyone's doing a Chappell Roan number, what's your song?" I asked as we both climbed into Elijah's car.

"It's 'Picture You.' Do you know it?" Elijah said, pulling out into afternoon traffic for the brief drive home.

"I do. Beautiful song. It reminds me of a modern Patsy Cline with the poetic framing of Paul Simon."

"See, that's why I need you—you get it on a level I can't reach."

"No, you get it. I just know how to say it. You're the one who makes everyone feel it."

"Careful, flattery like that'll get you everywhere," Elijah said as we pulled into the driveway of his family's home, in front of the above the garage apartment. "Come on, we've got furniture to move. You head inside and get started. I'll grab us some sandwiches from Tev."

"Say 'hi' for me," I said, stepping out of the car and heading for Elijah's door.

Inside, there wasn't much to do. I silenced my phone and tucked it into my bag, then dropped it by the door. The first step was to convert his bed back into a couch. Then the coffee table tucked into a corner, and the small table and chairs in the kitchen fit in the far corner of the kitchen. That cleared a space slightly smaller than the stage in the club. The last step would be to turn the couch around, which we did as soon as Elijah came in carrying two sandwiches from his deli.

"Okay, before we start, do you already know what you are wearing?" I asked, sitting down on the couch facing the makeshift stage.

"You haven't seen this one—it's new and unmodified, and there's no time for alterations. I'll show you later: a pretty tie-dye sundress, a soft gradient rainbow—red on top, violet on the bottom."

"Sounds nice, you wouldn't want to do too much anyway with this song. Do you already have ideas for blocking?"

"You might hate it, but I think going a little literal suits this song. You do know what this song is about, right?"

"I've got an idea what *I* think it's about, but what I think matters is what *you* think it means."

"Shit. You're going to make me say it. Fine—we don't have time to be coy. It's embarrassing, but … it's about you. To me, the song's about you."

"Okay … yeah. That makes sense," I said, unable to stop the blush rising like fire beneath my skin. "Say no more, please—I understand."

"So, don't laugh, but I'm thinking minimal. I think we can get the old fainting couch from backstage, but we should block with and without it. And the rest is like singing to a picture frame. It sounds kitschy and cliché saying out loud."

"It does, but most of it does. I think it'll work, but please promise it will be an empty frame, or a picture of someone like Chris Hemsworth."

"Empty. Actually, I'm thinking of a hollow frame—with no back. That way I can play with the audience, frame anyone, or anything I want."

"That's even better. All right, show me what you're thinking."

Elijah launched into the first of a dozen interpretations of the same song. The first run was straightforward—nothing over the top or dramatic, just a literal, honest take on the song. It laid a solid foundation, with flashes of earnest, desperate longing. It was a struggle for me to shove the subject matter to the back of my mind. Otherwise, it felt uncomfortably close to glimpsing Elijah's long-held, private yearning for me. On top of that, it was almost unbearably embarrassing to think of those moments on display.

The second round was much easier to handle. This version leaned into camp, with moments played for self-deprecating laughs. While it was wildly entertaining, it robbed the song of some of its power. The balance between honesty and comedy would absolutely need to land in the middle. I didn't have much to contribute, which was typical. Elijah's instincts were usually spot-on. He just needed reassurance and an eye from the audience to fine-tune. But there was one thing I suggested Elijah hadn't considered, for once. The number needed a reveal. The rainbow dress, concealed under a monotone dress or gown, then at the right moment, let it drop, revealing the vibrant rainbow—like the emotion unveiled by this song.

Elijah loved the idea so much that he immediately ran to the closet to find the right monotone gown that would work. A few minutes later, he came out in a slate-gray corseted dress that had been modified to move the zipper from the back to the front, with a simple hook-and-eye at the top. He unzipped it, released the clasp, and the dress dropped cleanly off his body to the floor thanks to the breakaway shoulder straps. Beneath it, he wore only a pair of novelty bikini briefs that read *"Here's Johnny!"*—so the reveal was, well, quite revealing. And possibly the funniest thing I had seen all week.

"Good, it works," Elijah said, gathering the dress off the floor. "You know, I might take that laugh personally, but I am a professional."

"Stop it. You knew that would crack me up. Go get the dress, and let me see it properly," I said, choking back my laughter, wiping the tears from my eyes. "And keep that trick in your pocket for another show, it's good. Really good."

He came back out of the closet a few minutes later in the same gray dress and stood in the center of the makeshift rehearsal space. He moved loosely to the music, gesturing toward nothing in particular. He casually unzipped the dress, then dramatically— on the first big downbeat of the first chorus—released the clasp and the drab gray dress hit the floor. The flash of color as the gray fabric fell away was spectacular—perfectly timed to the swell of the song. It will destroy the house. That was it. The performance didn't need any gimmicks, props, or tricks. Just one reveal sold the entire act.

I helped him get the first dress back on so he could run through the song to pinpoint the right moment and get the timing right. It took just two runs to lock in the cues and perfect the timing. We even planned a backup dress-drop cue, just in case he missed the first. Like I said, his instincts were good, and like he said, he was a professional. He changed again, putting both dresses away, ready for tomorrow night.

We took a break from rehearsal later than planned, but we both knew better than to interrupt when the process was flowing. Over sandwiches, we discussed a few ideas for improvisational moments. We ran through some basic contingencies—what to do if the dress didn't fall away or the zipper got stuck. Anything can happen on stage, so backup plans are essential to any solid performance. Elijah taught me that years ago, the first time he asked for my help to rehearse. As insurance, we waxed the zipper, loosened the clasp, and trimmed anything that might snag. We have spent hundreds of evenings just like this over the years—I had been so oblivious all those years, and he had been so patient.

Before we got back to work, I reached for my bag and pulled out my phone to check my messages out of habit. I wasn't expecting any messages, but my phone was still on silent from rehearsal. The instant I looked at my phone, my heart shattered—cold and brittle—as if it had hit the floor like ice. The screen blinked insistently, showing eight missed calls, nine text messages, and two voicemails—all from Viktoriya. Something was very wrong.

"Mark, I have a bunch of missed calls from Viktoriya," Elijah said, looking at me with concern. "Is something wrong?"

"I don't know yet, hang on—voicemail."

I listened to her voicemail before checking the messages. These days, if someone leaves you a voicemail, it's for a good—or bad—reason. As I listened, I felt my heart turn to ash. Something was very wrong, and it was me. I have just made a massive mistake.

"Oh no. OH NO. Mark! I'm so sorry. This is my fault," Eros muttered in my ear. "Call her back, now. You have to go. I can— I will—fix this, I have to. How did I get this wrong?"

"Elijah, I screwed up. Big time. I was supposed to help Viktoriya with her project tonight and got my dates mixed up, or something," I stammered, standing up. I scanned the room, desperately searching for anything I needed before running out the door. "I'm sorry. I love you. You're great. I have to go."

I bolted out the door, missing Elijah's response entirely. I was kicking myself for that already, but I'll have to deal with that tomorrow. Momentum carried me down the stairs, where I paused just long enough to call Viktoriya. I jogged down Elijah's driveway while the phone rang in my ear.

"Mark," Viktoriya answered. There was a wounded hurt in her lilting accent. "You forget me and remember too late."

"I'm sorry. I'm sorry. I got the date wrong. I didn't forget, I promise I didn't forget you," I pleaded, my voice wavering with each stride toward her. "I can be there. Running now."

"I am in bed. It is late now. Go home, call tomorrow. You say sorry and help then," she said, the edge faded from her voice. "Goodnight, Mark."

I came to a stop in the middle of the dark, empty street, a feeling of hollow sickness churning around inside me. I didn't know what time it was, but the sun was long gone, and it was silent. Glancing at my phone screen, it said one a.m.—then I recognized the depth of my mistake. Yes, I made a mistake, but this time it wasn't mine alone. That fact was anything but comforting, because only I would feel the repercussions. Only I could lose everything.

"Mark?" Eros whispered, guilt-ridden, tentatively concerned but cautious.

"Yeah." I said, resigning myself to the night, turning to walk home.

"I can't express how sorry I am. I just picked the wrong day."

"Eros. I know. As much as I *want* to lay the blame at your feet, I can't. Not just because you don't have feet, but because I missed it too. I didn't check; I got caught up. Can we just say this is as much my fuck-up as it is yours?"

"I can live with that—which I should remind you, is forever. So, that's *way* longer."

"I need to walk and clear my head—alone. Will you do one thing for me?"

"Of course."

"Can you send Elijah a message from me? Just say I'm sorry—I accidentally double-booked—and that I'll explain tomorrow?"

"Yes, that I can do, and I'll be here if you need me."

I walked home, allowing the cool, silent solitude of the night to envelop and embrace me. For a moment, I indulged in self-pity, asking the universe why these things always seemed to happen to me. But it was shallow and flaked away when I was able to answer easily—because sometimes I make poor decisions, and these things are called consequences. As I passed beneath the buzzing streetlamps standing sentinel over the shadows, I resigned myself to the company of whispering shades. These demons of doubt would haunt me all the way home. I could have dispelled them, but for now, I welcomed their company until dawn.

In the morning, a heavy blanket of guilt unrolled over my shoulders. What should have been an easygoing Friday became a brutal slog of a workday. It was hard to focus; every moment, I wanted to call Elijah and Viktoriya to find out whether this was the last straw, or if their patience would hold. To complicate things further, my mom wanted me to visit that weekend. When she asked, I didn't have any plans that would stand in the way, so I agreed. It wasn't until noon that I reached out to Viktoriya, a time I knew was between her classes.

I held my breath, waiting for her to respond, prepared for the worst, hoping for the best. My heart leaped when she replied, saying she understood my mistake and forgave me. She still felt hurt, but would get over it, and she had too much to do to afford to stay mad and dwell on yesterday. She gave me a list of things she needed me to pick up, which included a bottle of 'apology wine' and two empty garment bags from the dry cleaners. I should be able to pick up everything on the list between here and there. The list felt like a test, but at least a fair one. Which, in hindsight, was probably the point. A series of simple tasks that only require a basic level of care and attention I should be capable of handling without screwing up.

After three o'clock I set out to complete Viktoriya's side-quest for supplies. The side-quest's winding route more than doubled the walk to Viktoriya's place. I arrived a little more than an hour later with multiple bags from multiple stores and one bottle of 'apology wine.' She invited me inside warmly, gratefully accepting the odds and ends she needed to finish her project. Her room was an organized explosion of papers, patterns, and fabric scraps. There were two dress forms in the center of the room with what appeared to be partially complete gowns draped over them.

"Ah. Thank you, Mark. Just what I need. Come, we have much work," Viktoriya said, hugging me warmly after taking the bags from me. "Is good I know you take direction well."

"You're welcome. Just tell me what to do," I said, rolling up my sleeves and stashing my bag containing the wine by the door. "Seriously—I'll do whatever you need. I'm here."

"Good. Okay. First—this," she said, holding out a box of bent, twisted, and cut pieces of brass sheet, rods, and wire. "You know how to braze brass? Like welding, da?"

"Yes, I did quite a bit in the orchard, but it's been a few years. Usually, it was for utility, not ornamentation—I assume this needs to look good?"

"Da, it must be neat, for crown. No, not crown—tiara—yes that is word. Tiara. I show you," Viktoriya said, setting the box down on the floor and laying out the pieces of brass to show me how to assemble them. "You see, da? Tryzub—trident—goes in center. You can do this?"

"I can. Outside I assume? You have a torch? And files?" I asked, examining the pieces carefully, forming a plan in my mind.

"Da. Torch is outside, on the workbench under the stairs. What is 'file'?"

"A file, to smooth out the metal and the seam," I said, miming the action over one of the rough edges of the brass.

"Oh. Yes, a file. No, I do not have. This I forgot."

"All right, no problem. I've got an idea. Let me take this and I'll be back. Do you have a sketch, so I can make sure I assemble it correctly?" I said as we both put the pieces of brass back into the box.

"Da," she said, jumping to her feet, plucking a sketch of the trident tiara from her wall, and handing it to me. "You can do this, yes?"

"Absolutely. I can do this," I said, standing up with the box in hand. "I'll be back."

I walked out only a few minutes after arriving, already on another mission. I had two ideas, just in case the first didn't work. Under the stairs, I found Viktoriya's makeshift workbench with a few secondhand mismatched tools, including a basic propane torch and soldering kit. I pulled out my phone and did a quick search to verify my memory. An antique jewelry store with a repair shop sat just a block away—that was plan-b.

"Eros, are you here?" I asked barely above a whisper. "I think I could use your help."

"I am, and I think I know what you're thinking, and you're right. I can do this. I can stick those pieces together like they were—well, sticky."

"Hang on, I was going to ask if you could smooth it out after I brazed the pieces together. But you can just bond them? You're sure? You were watching when she showed me how it fit together?"

"I was, and yes. I was fusing brass together at a molecular level over five-thousand years ago—well, technically it was mostly bronze. Still, this will be no problem. Now, if you can find me some tin, I could turn that brass into bronze. Just think how impressed Viktoriya will be."

"I'm going to trust you here, and not just because I really want to see this metallurgical alchemy. It looks like there is some tin solder in the kit here, will that work?"

"I can make it work. First lay out the pieces and hold them together and I'll bond them."

"It's not going to heat up and burn my finger off, right?"

"I don't think so. Maybe let's just be careful."

Following Viktoriya's sketch diligently, I delicately held each segment of brass together while Eros worked their magic. I watched the metal change state at the joint and flash from solid to liquid and back to solid, forming a single seamless bond. We worked slowly, piece by piece, ensuring each was in exactly the right place. It grew warm, almost too hot to hold near the points of bonding, but as long as I was careful to keep my fingers away, it wasn't bad. After forty-five focused minutes, we'd assembled a tiara that looked like flawless, solid-cast brass—an exact match to Viktoriya's sketch.

"Step two," Eros said, sounding eager to show off their talents. "Take that tin—I won't need much—and wrap it around the brass in a few spots. And if there is any scrap brass or other metal you could set the tiara on, that will help too."

"All right. I think I can guess, in a very rudimentary way, what you're doing," I said, laying a few scraps of brass and a copper pipe on the workbench. After wrapping the brass tiara with the tin soldering wire, I set it on top of the copper and brass scraps. "But could you explain it—I'm curious."

"Forgive me if I don't explain atomic alloy alteration while I'm focusing—in easy-to-understand terms, that is, while I'm working. I'm cheating—finding the zinc atoms in the brass and replacing them with tin. I'm glad you found some copper that will be useful; I can use that to balance it out. All right, keep your fingers clear—don't try this at home," Eros said, sounding a little distracted. I watched the brass subtly darken, wisps of vapor rising off the metal. "Five thousand years ago, this was the real magic— not what I'm doing now, but teaching humans to do it so they'd think they'd discovered it themselves. Okay, this is about as far as I think I should push it. It's not perfect, but I think speed matters more here. Be careful, it's probably hot."

I held my hand over the metal and felt the heat radiating from it. It was definitely too hot to touch. I looked around and spotted a large coffee can full of water next to the workbench. I gently picked up the tiara with an old pair of pliers and dipped it briefly into the water—just enough to cool it safely, careful not to shock-quench it. I turned it over in my hands, examining it for any problems we might need to fix. Aside from a little cleaning and polishing, it looked amazing. The soft, bright brass was now a warm, tougher bronze alloy reflecting the setting sun. For a moment, it felt like I held an old-world, sacred artifact in my hands—something fantastical, ready to crown a hero before a mythic quest. I took another moment to dry it using my shirt and marvel at what Eros had done, and consider how to explain it to Viktoriya. Maybe I could get away with a wink and just call it magic—or say something closer to the truth: that a talented, conveniently nearby metalsmith had helped me.

"This is amazing, Eros. Thank you," I said, turning around to jog back up the stairs to show Viktoriya.

"It was my pleasure, Mark. Really, I haven't done anything like that in centuries. It felt good," Eros said, genuinely pleased with both the work and the result.

I rushed back into Viktoriya's room, ready to show off a crown fit for a queen—or a goddess. She'd nearly finished assembling the two gowns displayed on dress forms in the center of her room. If I had to guess, the tiara belonged with the one that shouted *Ukrainian goddess* rather than the one that softly whispered *Ukrainian-American from New Jersey*. The two dresses were complementary opposites, forming a unified statement.

The *goddess dress* was made of twisted and embroidered blue-and-gold linen, wrapped to resemble flowing robes. Beneath the drape of the blue-and-gold fabric was crimson lace, holding everything together yet peeking through the folds. The signature Viktoriya touch was a belt of satin sunflowers wrapping around the waist and draping over one hip.

The 'New Jersey' dress looked like it started life as an oversized black T-shirt, stretched from the left shoulder to the right ankle, leaving the right shoulder and left leg open. The left sleeve had denim fringe, and the left leg was wrapped in thin leather straps and silver buckles. Instead of the embroidery decorating the other dress, this one was adorned with spray-painted stencils of alternating Ukrainian tridents and outlines of the state.

Across the chest was a large gold Tryzub stencil layered over a cobalt-blue New Jersey outline. Above it read *DNIPRO*; below, *NEW JERSEY*—closely resembling the style of the band T-shirt she'd bought last weekend.

"Those look amazing, Viktoriya," I said, genuinely stunned by her craftsmanship and artistic vision. "I have your tiara. I think it belongs with the blue and gold. Really, these are incredible."

"Thank you, Mark," she said, hopping excitedly over to me from behind the dresses. She took the tiara from my outstretched hands eagerly, turning it over, thoroughly inspecting my work. "Mark, it is perfect. How did you do this?"

"I had help from a mysterious wandering master metalsmith—I think they might be a wizard. I'll introduce you someday if I can," I said, smiling at her while listening to Eros' pleased approval of their new title. "What's next?"

"Ah, I have list," Viktoriya said, returning to the reality of her task.

Together, we worked on her list, checking off each task as we went. Most were minor jobs—stitching in labels, cleaning up seams, taking a cigarette lighter to loose threads. The bulk of the work was assembling her presentation into a binder. We glued down fabric swatches to samples of her hand-cut stencils and her hand-drawn patterns. Then we added her printed essay on what the project meant and how she might adapt the designs for commercial production.

After three more hours of work, including a short dinner break, during which we nearly emptied the bottle of apology wine, we were finally almost finished. The sunset that had peeked through the bedroom window had long since faded into the open possibilities of night, and we both felt the familiar tingle of our spark returning. It felt as if my mistakes—even our mistakes— were only footnotes in our story, not defining moments; until my phone rang.

"Oh no," I said, in sync with Eros whispering in my ear. After last night, we both knew a ringing phone could only mean bad news—and we shared the gut-wrenching suspicion we'd messed up again.

I pulled out my phone, and my stomach seized into a knot the second I saw Elijah was calling. Immediately, I knew I had forgotten to follow up with him; to let him know I would be here and not with him at the club tonight. I closed my eyes and, for the briefest moment, wished this train would pass me by. I answered the call while Viktoriya watched, stone-faced.

"Mark! Where are you? You were supposed to be *here*," Elijah shouted, loud enough for Viktoriya to overhear before I could even say hello. "Don't tell me you blew me off again—for *her*. You promised, Mark."

"Elijah, I can only say I'm sorry," I replied, choking on the words as my panic rose to the back of my throat. "I thought I told you, but I must have been unclear … or I just plain forgot—like an idiot."

"Oh, you forgot. You missed one hell of a show—one of my best. I brought the damn house down because of your stupid help. And I can't even enjoy it, because you aren't here." Elijah's voice shook, anger and hurt dripping like venom from every word. "It's time you decide what really matters. Goodnight, Mark. Give my love to Viki."

He ended the call before I could respond, before I could apologize again. I sat on Viktoriya's floor, her project binder open in front of me, ready for the last page to be snapped into place. She sat down beside me, took the phone gently from my hand, and set it aside. I was in shock. My stomach had seized, and my heart was losing the will to beat. I wanted to scream or cry while running away to hide in the deepest, darkest hole I could find. Everything I'd felt the night before came crashing back, slamming me against the rocks of Elijah's words. This time, Eros couldn't even share the blame. There was no mix-up, no shared mistake.

Just me—washed ashore alone on an island of wreckage I built myself.

"You forget Elijah. You forget me. You even forget yourself," Viktoriya said, taking my hand in hers. "Finish work, then stay."

"I … you're not mad?" I asked, even more shocked. "I expected you to kick me out."

"Da. I am mad. You make mistakes, but one mistake alone can't break trust. This doesn't make me stop caring—for you, or us, or Elijah," she said, giving my hand a squeeze followed by an irritated slap. "We finish work now. Then sleep. Tomorrow, you fix it—or you don't. I hope you—we—fix it."

We finished the remaining work on her project in silence. Sealing the dresses in the fresh garment bags I collected from the dry cleaners, setting the completed binder on her desk. I could feel her unspoken, radiating disappointment as we both climbed into her bed. She'd wanted more from me tonight than she was now willing to take. Instead, she wrapped her arms around me, holding on to a moment that might vanish with the sunrise. I felt diminutive in her arms, undeserving of the grace in her touch, after what I'd done to her and Elijah. Not even the promise of dreams would spare me as I willed myself to sleep.

Chapter 22

An hour past dawn, sunlight filtered through the bedroom window, falling across the peaceful shapes of Mark and Viktoriya. They still held each other, just as they had when they drifted off. In this state, they looked comfortable and safe, like puzzle pieces perfectly fitted together. If I had a stomach, it would have collapsed like a dying star, bracing for what would happen when they woke.

I'd spent the night watching them, wondering how we'd all ended up here. I pushed Mark—gently, but I pushed. Then I kept interfering, naïvely believing I could shape the outcome. My motive was irrelevant now. Intentionally or not, I had contributed to the harm and hurt of the only three humans I cared about, and the only one who knew I existed. I suppose you could say I was feeling a little guilty and couldn't decide whether I should get more or less involved in the solution. The last thing I wanted was to make things worse, but doing nothing felt like giving up.

Viktoriya woke first. She looked at Mark, and a glimmer of happiness flitted over her face. A moment later, she pulled back as last night's memories returned, washing the joy from her face. She sighed and slid from his arms and rolled out of the bed, retreating from the room. I thought about waking Mark, but before I could act, he woke on his own to the sound of the bedroom door closing.

"Mark," I whispered. "Before Viktoriya comes back I just wanted to say I'm sorry, again. I'm here and I'll help any way I can."

"Thank you, Eros," Mark said through the silent speech he'd mastered. "I think this is a mess I have to clean up myself."

Just then, Viktoriya returned, balancing two cups of coffee in one hand. She acknowledged Mark with a calm, restrained distance, disappointment, anger, sorrow, and hope in her orbit. She handed him his cup of coffee, then turned to examine the work they had completed last night while silently drinking hers. There was something quietly dangerous about her air, like an executioner waiting for the order to strike.

"You did good work, Mark," Viktoriya said, without turning around to face him. "Thank you. I will call Elijah. We talk. Put this problem in ground. Face to face."

"It was no trouble. It might be a little early for Elijah."

"Da. But he will answer. This matters."

She picked up her phone from the nightstand and, with a few quick taps, called Elijah before Mark could object. I listened in as the phone rang three times before he answered sleepily.

"Viki?" Elijah mumbled. "It's early."

"Da. Sorry. It can't wait. We must speak, face to face—to face," Viktoriya said, pausing to take a breath, finally looking at Mark. "Will you come here, or do we come to you?"

"Give me a minute, love," Elijah said as his phone hit the bed and his footsteps faded. A minute later, the sound of returning footsteps followed, followed by the rustling of a phone being picked up. "Sorry. I'm awake now."

"Is no problem."

"So, here or there? Well, neutral ground would be best, but the Weehawken dueling grounds are too far away. You'd better come here. We might as well try to avoid our little relationship drama spilling out publicly. Bring coffee, please."

"Da. Da. We come to you with coffee. Mark will carry."

"Good. See you soon, I have to shower," Elijah said before ending the call.

"Come, Mark, we will go see Elijah. You will carry his coffee."

"Okay. That's fair," Mark said with a sigh, rising from the bed to his feet.

Viktoriya and Mark slipped shoes onto their feet and straightened their slept-in clothes. Mark collected his bag by the door, and they both walked out of the room, leaving behind two half-empty coffee mugs in the bedroom. They walked out of the upstairs apartment and down the stairs to the back door of the café. In the kitchen, Viktoriya quickly poured and prepared three large to-go cups of coffee, handing two to Mark. Within minutes, they left the café and headed toward Elijah's home.

Elijah answered the door in a plush lavender bathrobe and stepped aside, inviting Viktoriya and Mark inside. Mark walked through the door with slumped shoulders, a cup of coffee in each hand. He held Elijah's coffee out to him, trying to mask the awkwardness, but Mark was terrible at concealing his actual emotions. He leaked regret, remorse, and fear, but beneath it was hope and a burning determination to save three hearts. I recognized it because I felt exactly the same.

Elijah accepted the coffee, not begrudgingly or hesitantly—just with a smile behind a shadow of sadness.

"Thanks, Mark," Elijah said, taking a long sip. "Mmm, that is so good, Viktoriya. Thank you. Know what this really needs?"

"A fresh onion bagel," Mark replied without hesitating.

"Exactly. Toasted, simple, savory—with cultured salty butter," Elijah said, smiling at Mark, recognizing the bond still holding between them. He sat gracefully on his bed with a sigh. "But we'll have to make do without the bagel."

"I have never tried this bagel. You will have to show me," Viktoriya said, sitting beside Elijah. "Maybe we go after talk?"

"All three of us? I'd like that," Mark said, grasping the spark of hope from the air.

"I think that could depend on you, Mark."

"Yes, we resolve this first," Viktoriya said, bringing the talk back to the issue. "Mark, you have let us down."

"I know, I didn't mean to. But I know I did."

"Do you know how it feels to be forgotten? To feel like an afterthought?" Elijah asked, sharper than he probably meant.

"Yes. At least, I can imagine, and I understand," Mark replied softly, with humility. "It doesn't matter if I intended to or not. I know I haven't communicated the way I should have; I'm trying. This is more difficult than I expected."

"Da. I could do more too. So could you, Elijah," Viktoriya said, glancing between them. "You, Queenie, didn't tell me you had a show last night. Why no invitation?"

"Okay. You're right Viki, I should have invited you, I don't know why I didn't. It's not fair to expect Mark to suddenly get better without help," Elijah said, looking from Viktoriya back to Mark.

"Help that doesn't inadvertently confuse dates on a calendar," I whispered to Mark, apologetically.

"I appreciate you saying that, but really, this was my mistake, not yours. You all deserve better—and I will do better," Mark said, directing his words to all three of us. He held eye contact with Elijah and Viktoriya as long as he could. "Listen, I have an idea. I have to go home tomorrow to help Mom with the cider mill. Why don't you both come with me? It's been a while since the three of us spent time together. Viktoriya, I want to show you the orchard. Elijah, I know you've always liked it there. Maybe some time together—working, having some fun—can help us reset. What do you think?"

"I'm still a little mad—but more at the situation than at you. I'll get over it, and holding it over your head would hurt me as much as it would hurt you. And a day in that orchard of yours does sound nice," Elijah said, releasing a tense breath. "I'm willing to do minimal manual labor if it means I get to see you in a sleeveless flannel carrying a heavy bushel of apples."

"Da, I agree … carrying apples—da. I like to see this orchard with you," Viktoriya added, her mind seeming to wander just a bit. "I am surprised this is harder than I imagined. I have hope, or wish, still we try and we make it or we don't, but we try."

"Honey, did thinking about Mark doing manual labor scramble your words a bit?" Elijah teased Viktoriya's slightly more disorganized than usual English. "I get it, it's as good as you imagine, love. And I think we both understand what you're saying."

"You are rude—but I love you still." Viktoriya shoved Elijah with her shoulder, smiling at him, winking at Mark. "Yes, we go with you, Mark."

"Great! I'll give Mom a call to let her know. I was going to just take a cab, but Elijah would you?"

"Yes, I'll drive us, you carless bum."

"I have a car. A truck, but I left it for Mom to use. You know that."

"I know, I know. Of course this means we can't get bagels now, I have to get ready for a road trip."

"It's a twenty-five-minute drive," Mark protested.

"How quickly you forget about Jersey traffic. Go on, you two, I have work to do if we're going to drive in the morning."

"Da, I have work to do as well," Viktoriya added, climbing off the bed.

The three of them separated for the remainder of the day. They all had work to do, and I think they all needed time to digest that conversation. It wasn't as big a deal as it had seemed when it first arrived. The minor mix-up—my minor mix-up—had a slightly exaggerated impact, and seeing each other helped them realize it. Mark was walking home. The same path he walked two nights ago—once dark and ominous—was now bathed in welcome light.

"You know, Mark, this reminds me of another make-up conversation I observed. I think it was around 1590, in Norton Folgate—Middlesex, England. I was being used as an actual oil lamp on the desk of a charming writer called Kit," I said, attempting to recall relevant details. "He was writing something about the Queen of Carthage and had a disagreement—not too dissimilar to what happened with you and Elijah—with his boyfriend, Bill."

"Wait. Kit? Marlowe?" Mark interrupted.

"Believe it or not, Mark—we didn't exactly have introductions, but that sounds right. Anyway, his boyfriend, Bill—"

"Shakespeare? William Shakespeare?"

"Yes. Why is that surprising or significant? Kit called him Bill in that room, except when they were arguing. But as I was saying, Bill came in upset because Kit didn't show up to something he was doing at the theater, and Bill expected to see him there. Kit explained he was writing and got lost in the words, which Bill seemed to understand. Long story short, they talked, and the reconciliation was … devastating."

"That doesn't sound good."

"Oh, I see, I mean devastating to the room, not the relationship. They broke the chair, and the desk. Not from fighting, if you follow me. I always thought it was about unrestrained ego and pent-up lust, but now I realize there was more to it, and I understand something they said. "I expose my heart, and you wound me with a slight. Yet I cannot dismiss you from myself, for that would cut deeper." Or something along those lines—they argued in verse. Bill was hurt, because he loved Kit, and because he loved him, he could forgive him."

"You would be so very popular in the history and English departments."

"Are Kit and Bill historically significant somehow?"

"I think there's a few sections of the Library you skipped."

"Oh. My. God. I just did an internet search on your phone. That's who I was with? Oh—it makes so much more sense now. This is also very sad. I always wondered what happened to them. I'm going to need a few minutes."

"Sorry you had to find out like that. Take your time."

I withdrew from Mark for most of the day into the evening. That moment was the first time I truly felt my age. Maybe it was the shock of learning who Kit and Bill were, or realizing they were gone—especially Kit, so tragically and without explanation. They may not have known me, but I knew them—their private side: how they ran lines of verse together and made each other laugh. I watched in silent amusement and almost resented their joy and freedom. Of course, I had learned to come to terms with the fact that the humans I know will die and I would not. I think what I felt was the loss of a missed opportunity. Maybe I could have become friends with Kit, as I did with Mark—shared in their happiness—and maybe even saved him. I knew it was pointless to dwell, but after all I'd learned from Mark's friendship, I couldn't help feeling the sting—just a little. When I finally came around, Mark had already called his mom and confirmed plans with Elijah and Viktoriya to leave at nine a.m. the next morning.

The Fixer, The Maker, The Drag Entertainer

Sunday morning arrived, brimming with anticipation and hope. Mark was waiting by the door when Elijah sent him a text that he and Viktoriya were downstairs waiting for him in the car. He ran out the door so fast he nearly forgot to lock up behind himself. If I hadn't been along for the ride—hitchhiking on his phone—I'm sure he'd have forgotten me entirely. I didn't take it personally at this point.

He climbed into the back seat and leaned forward between the driver and passenger seats to kiss both Viktoriya and Elijah on the cheek. He sat back and buckled his seat belt, checking with Elijah that he remembered how to get there, which he did. The mood in the car didn't match. Mark was eager, Viktoriya tense and nervous, and Elijah quiet and simmering—all of them trying to hide it. At first, none of them noticed; it was just quiet, but after a few minutes Viktoriya asked if she could play some music. Neither Mark nor Elijah had any objections, so she leaned over the center console and fiddled with the old stereo. It began playing a thirty-year-old cassette tape, long fused into the stereo, now practically part of the car itself.

For the next several miles, they watched the urban landscape blur and shift past the windows while listening to a lightly distorted side B of Cyndi Lauper's *Twelve Deadly Cyns*. Halfway through "That's What I Think," Elijah laughed, and Mark and Viktoriya stared at him for an explanation. When he noticed their expectant looks, he reached out and turned the music down, letting it fade into the background.

"I just remembered the first time we hijacked this car and drove down to Asbury Park. That's when I put this tape in. The drive out was uneventful, and the day on the beach and boardwalk was great. But the drive home—Jersey traffic," Elijah said, growing more animated as he told the story. "We were stuck on The Garden State Parkway for three hours, and this tape got stuck—it's still stuck—"

"After two hours, and two miles, we opened all the windows and turned the music up as loud as possible," Mark interrupted, grinning. "And then we—and the six cars around us—ironically sang along to 'I Drove All Night. I still know all the words to that entire album—"

"Mark! You need to take Viktoriya to Asbury," Elijah said, cutting himself off. "She would love it … And I guess I could drive."

"I don't know. Viktoriya, do you think you are ready for a Jersey boardwalk?" Mark asked playfully.

"Please. I learn Skee Ball on boardwalks of Odesa on Black Sea," Viktoriya teased back, adding an exaggerated edge to her natural accent. "I crush you."

Mark and Elijah giggled. That giggle blossomed into a chuckle, then erupted into uncontrollable laughter, sweeping Viktoriya along with it. It was one of those rare, explosive, self-sustaining fits of laughter that erased every trace of tension. It rang through the car as all three wiped tears from their eyes and the landscape outside gave way to old homes shrouded by trees and preserved farms. They were still laughing when Elijah turned off the main road onto a long gravel driveway beside a modest sign: "Williams Orchard, Est. 1769."

Oak and elm trees, spaced naturally, bordered the gently meandering drive, suggesting the road had been carved around them rather than added afterward. Near the end stood a barn-like building with a large open space in front, presumably for several dozen vehicles. Mark called it a parking lot. And at the end of the drive was Mark's home. A modest two-story stone farmhouse, dating to the 1700s, had brick and wood additions from the 1800s and 1900s, giving it a slightly mismatched yet charming look. This orchard wasn't frozen in time like a museum; it had been honored through use, allowed to grow and change as it lived. It reminded me of Mark: a little anachronistic, with mismatched pieces that worked together—always adapting, always growing. It was beautiful. And waiting for them on the porch was Mark's mother, waving warmly.

Mark

We climbed out of the car, and I took what felt like my first clean breath of air in weeks. It's easy to forget we were just a few miles from where we'd been—and only a few more from one of the biggest cities in the world. Here, it always felt like that was an entire world away. I lived and worked twenty-five minutes away.

The Fixer, The Maker, The Drag Entertainer

That started as a convenience, and a small amount of room to breathe as I figured myself out. But after Dad died, it became a necessity, keeping that grief at arm's length. Soon it just became comfortable. Despite all that, this is and will always be my home, and I knew someday I would come back for good.

Mom cautiously descended the four porch steps, a radiant grin across her face. She didn't stop waving and was perilously close to looking like a lunatic before reaching us. I remembered something she said long ago: "Don't stop waving until whoever you're waving to waves back; that's how you know they saw you." Then another memory surfaced of me asking what to do if they never waved back, and Dad answering, "Then you become that crazy guy who never stops waving." I laughed and returned my mom's wave, and she broke her steady walk and jogged the rest of the way, throwing her arms around me.

"Marcus, it's so good to see you," she said, holding me tight in that unmistakable way only a mother can. "You don't visit enough. I know, I know. Still, I could stand to see you more. Okay, parental guilt-trip out of the way. Now tell me who you've brought along with you?"

"Hi Mom, it's good to see you too, and it's nice to come home," I said, returning the hug, noticing she was just starting to feel frail before I let go. "Well, Elijah, of course you know."

"Good morning, Mark's mom," Elijah said, smiling warmly. "How are you, Eileen?"

"Elijah, you're looking very well, a little thin. You don't visit enough either," she said, pulling him into a warm maternal hug. "We will catch up. You can tell me what trouble Mark is causing."

"Mom, that's not fair. You know he can't lie to you," I said, memories flooding back as I smiled at them both. "Mom, I'd like you to meet Viktoriya."

"Hello, Mrs. Williams, you have lovely home here," Viktoriya said, offering her hand to my mother.

"Good morning, Viktoriya. It's wonderful to finally meet you. Mark hasn't told me nearly enough about you—but he was right: you're gorgeous. Come here, give me a hug," Mom said, ignoring Viktoriya's outstretched hand and stepping into the hug herself. "Now, please, call me Eileen. Have you eaten? Or did you kids rush out. Come inside, I just started a fresh pot of coffee, and I'm sure we have something to eat."

She led Viktoriya into the house through the side-door, which led directly into the kitchen. Viktoriya insisted she needed nothing to eat or any coffee and couldn't possibly accept because she showed up empty-handed. My mom hand-waved Viktoriya's objections away. Offering us coffee was mostly an excuse to pour another cup for herself. We were, in effect, passively enabling a harmless habit. Once we were at the kitchen table, Viktoriya had a cup of coffee anyway, along with Elijah and me. We even nibbled on the muffins. Mom insisted she hadn't baked them first thing this morning. They just mysteriously appeared. Still, no one complains about blueberry muffins—no matter how mysterious their origins.

Over coffee, we shared news about the status of our relationship. Viktoriya was hesitant at first, but quickly realized that my mom's warmth and welcoming nature was genuine. Her acceptance reached to the very core of her being. If she judged you, it was probably because you'd just done something worth being ashamed of. In this case, she had two primary concerns— were we all happy, and was I treating Elijah and Viktoriya as well as they deserved? When both Viktoriya and Elijah answered "yes" to both questions, I couldn't hide my relieved sigh, even if my life depended on it. And that was as far as she probed into our relationships. The rest of her questioning revolved around catching up with Elijah and getting to know Viktoriya. As I watched, I silently whispered to Eros, asking if it was a bad sign that I could only remember a handful of times I had felt even close to this happy. Imagine my surprise when they dryly said, "Yes, you've led quite a sad life—until I showed up." That sent hot coffee streaming out of my nose.

I didn't even have a chance to feel embarrassed. Just the sharp sting of a scalded sinus, and the shock of how it happened. Thankfully, the pain was only momentary and faded quickly into an extremely unpleasant throbbing and one hell of a caffeine buzz. Snorting coffee is an alarmingly effective way to get caffeine—but I wouldn't recommend it. And of course, my boyfriend and girlfriend saw the whole thing and immediately started laughing while scrambling for towels and napkins. I couldn't hold it against them. I was laughing too. The mirthful conversation continued unabated until there was an assertive knock on the front door.

"That's probably Mr. O'Connor with the hay bales," Mom said, getting up from the table. "I'll be right back, dears."

Mom walked out of the kitchen, vanishing around the corner. Viktoriya, Elijah, and I refreshed our coffee, saving a cup for Mom. That's when we heard it. Raised voices at the front door. Whoever it was at the door was shouting—at my mother. We rushed from the kitchen to the front door. At the door, we found a wormy-looking man holding the door open with his foot and waving a large manila envelope in the air.

"Listen to me, Eileen! This place will be underwater by Thanksgiving. Do the smart thing and sign—"

"What the hell do you think you're doing?" I shouted, gently moving Mom away from the door and stepping into the stranger's personal space, forcing him back. "You've got thirty seconds to tell me who you are—and why you think you can raise your voice to my mother."

"I'm Gale Barlow. I am buying this place before your mother loses everything your father built," he said smugly, calm— infuriatingly presumptuous. "If she signs these now, she walks away with three times what this place is worth—"

"No. She isn't selling. Not to anyone. Especially not to you, even if she could," I said, suppressing the rage boiling inside me. "You should leave."

"Who do you think you are?" he shouted, arrogantly unaware of his miscalculation.

Viktoriya and Elijah pushed past me onto the porch, placing themselves between me and Gale Barlow. Standing shoulder to shoulder, they scowled at him until he shifted uncomfortably. Viktoriya launched a sharp, theatrical Ukrainian tirade, turning to Elijah, the professional performer, who picked up her cue instantly. He cocked his head to the side, appraising Gale before looking back at Viktoriya.

"No, I don't think so. Too much fat. Too buoyant," Elijah said with casual cruelty, glaring dismissively, like he was evaluating a brisket.

"Da. Too fat. You. Leave now," Viktoriya ordered intimidatingly—it wasn't even in the same ballpark as a suggestion.

Gale did the only smart thing he could—he turned and ran. We all stood on the porch watching him jump into his tacky pearl-white BMW and drive away as fast as possible. We waited until the car disappeared before doubling over with laughter.

"What was that you said to him?" Elijah asked Viktoriya.

"I thought I caught 'pigs' is that right?" I said.

"Da. Three little pigs—and big bad wolf," Viktoriya said, smirking and winking. "Silly American boys, so easy to intimidate."

I stopped laughing and simply smiled at Viktoriya and Elijah.

"Hey, Eros," I said silently. "Remember when I said I couldn't feel happier a few minutes ago? Well … now I've got this. I have to be the luckiest bastard in the world."

Chapter 23

Viktoriya, Elijah, and Mark stood on the porch, staring at one another. I know them well enough now to read not only their expressions but also the subtleties between them. Mark's assertive defense of his mother—and his uncharacteristic display of confidence in that confrontation—clearly impressed Viktoriya and Elijah. Viktoriya seemed to be seeing a side of Mark she hadn't known existed, while Elijah looked as though he'd just witnessed a once-in-a-generation geyser erupt. Their gazes radiated attraction, and their sidelong glances sparked faint, half-hearted flickers of rivalry. Meanwhile, Mark gazed at them like a smitten puppy, while behind him, Eileen watched with the indulgent amusement only a parent of grown children could manage.

"So, that was Gale," I murmured in Mark's ear. "I don't think I liked him very much. So … is pushing him into the Delaware Water Gap completely off the table? After meeting him, that particular red line of mine feels flexible."

"No, Eros, we can't do that—I mean, we shouldn't. That's a line I'm not willing to cross," Mark said silently. "Just be ready to make him go away just in case. It seems like he is getting desperate and might come back."

"What was that all about?" Viktoriya asked, breaking the silence. "Who was that awful man?"

"That was Gale Barlow, his firm buys up old buildings and properties. Burns them to the ground and puts up shitty, overpriced, soulless condos and houses no one really wants,"

Mark said, contempt dripping off every word. "An invasive parasite that only cares about turning a quick profit. Whatever he offers, he knows he can make two or three times as much selling it all off before the concrete dries on whatever he builds. He has no interest in long-term outcomes or the health of any community. Most of the buildings and homes are back on the market and vacant within a year of being sold. I'd sell this place to a seasonal Halloween costume company before I ever entertain a single offer from him."

"I agree completely—but you mean Eileen, right?" Elijah asked, tilting his head in mild confusion. "She'd have to sell it, wouldn't she?"

"No, Elijah," Eileen said, stepping forward to put an arm around her son. "After that son-of-a-bitch first showed up a year ago, we put everything in Mark's name. It was his brother's idea. If it weren't for that I might have worn down by now, but Mark, he can be as stubborn as they come."

"I still think we should've kept it in all our names. I don't love it being on my head alone," Mark said, shifting uncomfortably. "I know it makes sense—Jefferson and Lexie have their own lives and want to keep this in the family—but we were worried we'd start wearing each other down."

"It wasn't just Jefferson and Lexie," Eileen said, patting Mark's shoulder and glancing at Viktoriya and Elijah. "You gave us the idea, even if you didn't realize it. He's the one who said Gale seems like the type to never double-check anything—and to worry about legal details only if it ever makes it to a judge. So far, he was right. Mr. Barlow still hasn't checked. He just assumes everything came to me after Mark's father passed. But never mind about that now, come back inside, I'm sure Mark wants to show you around before we get to work."

Back inside, the four of them finished their forgotten coffee before Mark began showing Viktoriya around. As he pointed out pieces of his childhood, Elijah chimed in with memories of his own—each one, intentionally or not, stirring small flashes of jealousy in Viktoriya. With every reminiscence from Elijah, she drew herself just a little closer to Mark, which Elijah absolutely noticed. The undercurrent of tension between them eased once they stepped outside through the back door. Before them stretched carefully cultivated rows of apple trees. Beneath the trees, a small herd of goats peacefully grazed on grass and fallen apples.

"Goats! Mark, you have goats? You should have told me—I love goats!" Viktoriya exclaimed, shaking Mark's arm in delight. "They have names? What are their names? Introduce me."

"Yes—they clean up the fallen fruit before rats and raccoons move in. Yes, they have names. I don't think you want to meet them right now," Mark said, laughing. "They're mostly free-range here, so they aren't the friendliest unless you bring a treat."

"That's true. One of them—if it's still around—had it out for me," Elijah said with a laugh. "Do you remember that, Mark? It would charge me any time I caught its eye. I still have no idea what I ever did."

"I remember you gave it an unripe apple. I guess it held a grudge," Mark said. "They really like barley or oatmeal. I think they get tired of apples sometimes. We can feed them later—the ravens too."

"*RAVENS!*" Viktoriya gasped, her voice cracking with excitement. "You. Have. Ravens? Where? Show me."

"Kind of. It's more of a resident flock—a conspiracy, technically—that my great-great-grandparents coaxed into staying. They're smart—they taught their young that we'd let them eat fallen apples and feed them in winter when food is scarce. In return, they keep pests in check—birds and insects that would eat the apples. It gets noisy sometimes, especially when they squabble with the goats," Mark said, as if it were perfectly normal. "Some of them can be pretty friendly."

"Mark Williams, I may live here—with goats and ravens," Viktoriya said, squeezing Mark's arm like he might make her leave at any moment.

"That doesn't sound so bad. Elijah, did I tell you my plan for fictionalized historical markers?"

"Fictionalized? Like 'birthplace of James T. Kirk?' No, you didn't tell me about that."

"Not quite that fictionalized. More like mundane factoids no one can prove—or would bother to dispute. Like 'Bud Abbott and Lou Costello argued about apples under this tree in 1939.' Or 'Aaron Burr shot an apple off this tree in 1799.' A bunch like that, for local figures."

"That is clever. Is it for tourists—or your own amusement? I mean, the satirical folklore is weirdly brilliant."

"Both, Elijah. Both."

Mark continued his tour with what could only be described as a dissertation on the heirloom apple varieties they cultivated and their history. I was honestly surprised Viktoriya and Elijah didn't tie him to a tree and leave him there. Instead, they *listened* to him. I, however, had better things to do. I had trees to examine. I figured I'd finish my examination and learn everything I needed by the time Mark finished boring his girlfriend and boyfriend to death. When I got back, Elijah was interrupting—redirecting him to what they could do to help, which was surprisingly effective. Mark immediately changed tracks and led them to the mill, where they would work the rest of the day.

At the mill stood the large, barn-like structure we'd passed on the drive up. It was more than just a cider mill; it doubled as a production and storage facility, complete with a small area where visitors could make and bottle their own fresh apple cider using vintage hand-cranked presses. It was an impressively sophisticated setup. If Mark was to be believed, when fall set in, people flocked from the city for the quaint experience—and still made it home before sunset.

Mark took pride in the large mill and the press he helped create. It was fully mechanical, capable of obliterating apples at an impressive rate and pressing out twenty gallons of cider at a time. When running at peak efficiency, it could produce up to a hundred gallons a day—but that was midsummer, when most apples were just ripening. There were far fewer apples ripening in the fall, but, according to Mark, they were sweeter and had a more complex flavor. Of course, Elijah clarified for Viktoriya that it simply meant they tasted a little more "apple-y," and Mark didn't disagree.

By this point, I was struggling to pay attention. Not that I wasn't interested—but even my patience had limits. I simply couldn't fake enthusiasm for making apple cider—in large or small batches. Perhaps it would be different if I could even taste or smell it. But I couldn't, and therefore I was bored. Mark demonstrated how to sort apples from cold storage into buckets to feed the large mill. He paused to explain how to spot a bad apple, and I couldn't take it anymore. And if the side-eye and eye-rolls Viktoriya and

Elijah were exchanging were any indication, they were reaching their limits too.

"Mark, stop. Look at their faces," I whispered. "Look at them. If they didn't adore you, they'd have fed you to the mill by now. You're even boring me to death—and I can't die."

"Ah, right. You're both bored out of your minds—and you understood this ages ago, didn't you?" Mark asked Viktoriya and Elijah, taking my less than subtle hint.

"Yes, Mark, we understood pretty much right away. You just looked like you were having fun explaining it to us," Elijah said, smiling patiently at Mark.

"Da. You were cute. But now, you're starting to get less cute," Viktoriya said, her smile slipping into something slightly patronizing.

"I'm sorry, I got a little carried away," Mark said, looking a little embarrassed. "Why don't we start sorting apples. Then when Mr. O'Connor gets here, I'll call Mom, and I can show you how the mill and press work."

"Why do we need to wait for Mr. O'Connor?" Elijah asked.

"Oh, he helps us out with the forklift. Mom's not comfortable driving it, and I'm out of practice. Come on, let's move on to the next step—the apple bath," Mark said, motioning for Viktoriya and Elijah to follow him into the next room.

The next room resembled a Rube Goldberg–style water park for apples—tubs, hoses, and conveyor belts all culminating in a slide that led to the mill. The simple yet elaborate system fed the large mill, where I assume the apples got obliterated. This time, Mark kept his explanations mercifully brief. He pointed to the first tub. This was a weak citric acid and soap bath. A slowly rotating brush gently washed the apples clean of dirt and debris. From there, they floated onto a belt that lifted them up through a shower of water and dropped them into the next bath. This one was a slightly stronger citric acid bath, but no soap this time, just a gentle, swirling current. Finally, Mark described how apples from that bath were picked up by another belt and sent into the mill to be ground and dropped into the press.

Around this point, my mind wandered. Humans have reinvented this process a dozen times over the centuries, but it still came down to the same thing—smashing fruit like it had insulted your family and squeezing it as if it owed you money. I couldn't pretend to be interested. Still, he described the press: it squeezed the apple mash, which passed through a filter before the liquid was sterilized and collected in a large plastic tank. When he started on the options for what they could do next, I stopped paying attention. At least Viktoriya and Elijah were paying attention, watching Mark move through the space with a quiet reverence for the memories it carried. Unfortunately, I wasn't listening when Mark explained the side project his dad started with a small fermentation setup. All I know is everything was tested and ready—bottles labeled, racks in place. His dad just never got the chance. Mark was only a few signatures and a filing fee away from finishing what his father began.

A short time later, Mr. O'Connor arrived to drive the forklift, and Mark's mom came out, declaring it was time to get to work. Mark, Viktoriya, and Elijah began sorting apples into baskets, joking and bantering with each other. As they worked—filling baskets, hauling them one by one into the next room, dumping them into the bath—Viktoriya and Elijah took any chance they could to steal Mark away for a private moment. All the while, the mill and press rumbled and worked in the background.

These stolen moments were fleeting—a quick kiss out of sight, a lingering embrace behind a stack of barrels. But those moments did not go unnoticed by either of them. Viktoriya saw Elijah pulling Mark aside, just as Elijah saw Viktoriya steal Mark away. As they worked, their moments became less brief—and more brazen. It became clear Viktoriya and Elijah had unintentionally entered a fierce battle for Mark's time and attention. The work at hand, an afterthought.

Then the growing tension snapped—like a frayed wire finally giving way—and everything seemed to collapse in slow motion. Elijah whisked Mark outside and pinned him against the wall, kissing him as though the world might end. But Viktoriya caught them in the act. She must have had the same idea as Elijah, because when she saw them, she stopped cold. None of them said a word. The look on Elijah's face and the flicker in Viktoriya's eyes told me everything. Their own feelings startled them both more than what they saw. Before any of them could react, they heard a snap, several loud pings, and a crash—then Mark's mother screamed.

The Fixer, The Maker, The Drag Entertainer

My spirits were high—an understatement. Everything felt perfect. The day hadn't just gone well—it felt surreal, like a dream. I felt like I was growing even closer to both Elijah and Viktoriya. We had been working and laughing together, stealing moments here and there. Just outside, Elijah yanked me aside, pushed me into the wall, and kissed me. The world faded away. For that moment, the only thing I could hear was his heartbeat. Then, through the fog, a sound—a footstep grinding to a halt on the gravel—startled me back. Elijah and I both looked up to see Viktoriya staring at us. She looked shocked, like she'd just walked in on a moment she was never meant to see. But it was more than that. Her shock ran deeper.

There are moments measured in heartbeats—when the space between one and the next could stretch into a lifetime. This was one of those moments between heartbeats. We believed none of us had done anything wrong. There were no betrayals or lies, yet guilt swept through me all the same. We *had* all done something wrong, but none of us recognized it at that moment. The second I opened my mouth to speak, the next heartbeat thumped. Then came the sound. An echoing *snap* from inside, where the mill hummed. The gut-wrenching snap of chains under pressure—sudden, violent—and the world shattered.

We all felt the sound as much as we heard it. Before any of us could even flinch, we heard the *pings*—tiny pieces of machinery ejecting and ricocheting. Each reverberation sent icy chills down my spine. A wave of stomach-dropping terror washed over all three of us when the crash hit. The ground may have shaken, or it could have been my body trembling. From inside the building, the hum of the mill gave way to screeching metal—steel smashing into concrete. Then there was the scream. Rolling around the building, shooting out like a shockwave, rattling the windows of my very soul. My heart recognized it before my mind did. I was already running when the sound of my mother screaming finally registered.

As terrifying as the sound was, what I saw the second I rushed through the door nearly dropped me to my knees. Pure electricity shot through me. I no longer needed to breathe. The mill was crying out in agony. Somewhere in the back of my mind,

I recognized the sickly sound of my foot landing on a wet surface. I didn't dare look down. Mom was on the ground—prone, pinned beneath the holding tank and frame. Oh, God—she wasn't moving.

I slid to a stop inches away. I may have screamed. Whatever sounds I was making were jabbering nonsense. I fell to the ground, and everything caught up. Snapping into place. The fog condensed into focus. She was breathing. The wet floor was only water—no blood. Thank God. Instinct took control; I assessed the scene. Mom was unconscious, breathing, and not bleeding. The tank and frame collapsed, pinning her leg just below the knee to the ground. It was not as bad as it looked. She was already regaining consciousness.

Elijah and Viktoriya were only half a step behind me. I looked from them to the empty tank. Words weren't necessary. I jumped to my feet and grabbed the steel frame of the tank. Viktoriya and Elijah jumped to the opposite side and did the same. Together, we barely managed to lift the empty but heavy tank. My body screamed in protest as the metal frame around the tank scraped across the concrete. All three of us cried out from the strain as we freed Mom's leg. We were all lucky it was empty. I can't bring myself to imagine what would have happened if it had been even half full.

Everything still moved in slow motion. Mom stirred, whimpering in pain, as I took in the scene. What happened? The steel frame the tank sat on had collapsed. Half of it had just fallen apart, but hadn't broken. The chain driving the press lay coiled on the ground where it had fallen. Like the stand, it just came apart, but didn't break. Something was missing. Something wasn't right, but I couldn't see what I was missing.

"Eileen!" Mr. O'Connor shouted as he leapt out of the forklift and rushed to cut power to the mill. "I don't know what happened. Are you all right? Mark? Is she okay?"

"I don't know, I think so," I said, kneeling next to Mom. "Mom? Can you hear me? Don't try to move yet."

"Mark?" she said. Her voice was shaking. She was confused. "What happened? It hurts ..."

"The tank fell on your leg. We don't know why. Don't try to move yet. Where does it hurt—how bad?" I said, reaching out to rest a hand on her shoulder, gently encouraging her to stay still.

"My leg, foot, and head. I've had worse," she said, slowly pushing herself up into a seated position. "Help me up?"

"Not yet—let me check your leg and foot first. Sorry, this might hurt," I said, feeling her leg for signs of a break.

She gasped when I touched her leg, just below the knee, but she didn't cry out in pain. I didn't feel any obvious breaks. Mr. O'Connor handed me his pocketknife, and I carefully cut open Mom's pant leg to inspect the injury. No broken skin, no bleeding, no signs of broken bones. Relief hit me first, but guilt quickly drowned it. This could have been so much worse. This shouldn't have happened. I hadn't been paying attention. I missed something. This was my fault.

"It looks okay. I'm going to take you outside, get you off the wet floor," I said, carefully sliding my arm under her knees while she wrapped her arm around the back of my neck.

"Let me help," Elijah said, kneeling down.

"I don't need your help—or your distractions," I snapped. He recoiled.

"Let us help," Viktoriya said, firmly stepping forward.

"I said I don't want your help," I shot back. The anger wasn't just for them—it was for everything: the mill, the orchard, myself.

"Mark?" Viktoriya said, wounded and confused. I ignored her.

I gently picked Mom up off the ground. Doing my best to move slowly, I carried her outside. Viktoriya and Elijah followed closely behind, remaining silent. There was a bench just outside in the parking lot. I set her down carefully and crouched in front of her to take her shoe off.

"This is probably going to hurt. I have to take your shoe off to check your foot," I said softly, trying to stop my hands from shaking as I untied Mom's shoelaces.

I managed to slip her shoe off with minimal discomfort. She didn't cry out in pain, which was a good sign. Her foot, ankle, and leg were already turning black and blue as the bruising spread. Her ankle was swelling, but, like her leg, I didn't feel any obvious broken bones.

"Eileen, are you all right?" Elijah asked. I could hear the concern in his voice.

"I'll live, dear. Thank you," Mom said, forcing the pain aside.

"Good, I'll be at the house," he said. A mix of emotions wavered in his voice. He cared for Mom. She was practically a second mother to him. I could hear his concern, and the hurt my words caused. He turned and walked away without looking back.

"I don't think anything is broken, but I'm not a doctor. We need to get you to the hospital so someone qualified can check you out," I said, standing up on unsteady feet. "Will you be okay here for a few minutes? I'm going to grab a bandage from the house to immobilize your ankle."

"I'm fine—not going anywhere," she answered, doing her best to push the pain out of her mind.

I turned to walk back to the house, and Viktoriya reached out, not grabbing, just touching my arm. I flinched. My arm jerked, knocking her hand away. I still don't know why. I knew at that moment the last thing I wanted was for anyone to touch me. Without looking back, I started walking, focused on the task at hand.

"Mark, wait," Viktoriya called, hurrying after me. "Why are you angry with us?"

"Not now. I can't do this," I said without breaking my stride, refusing to look at her.

"You can—you just refuse. Coward," she said. I heard her, and she wasn't wrong. I just didn't care. "I don't know why I say this like that. Just speak to me ... please. I am sorry."

I tried not to react, but I stumbled. Her words hit me like a brick to the back. I didn't respond. I just kept walking. I didn't trust myself to reply while my mind was racing. As we approached the house, I saw Elijah sitting on the porch steps. I knew that posture; he was waiting for me. When I was close enough, he stood up and walked forward to meet me.

"Is Eileen going to be okay?" he asked. However hurt or upset he was with me, he still knew his feelings were not the priority.

"I think so. I need to take her to the hospital for X-rays," I said.

"I see. Well, good," Elijah said, apparently sensing it was now safe to ask what he really wanted to ask. "What was that, Mark? 'Haven't you done enough?' Then you tell Viktoriya—you don't *want* our help? I'm sorry, but—what the fuck?"

"I can't do this right now," I said—the only thing I could think to say.

"Say something else," Viktoriya said. She was angry, and her anger was cold. "We deserve more."

"Goddammit. All right, fine—we can't do this now. Maybe this was a mistake. Not just today, but us. Maybe this can't work," I said, desperately trying to avoid raising my voice or letting everything I was feeling overwhelm me. "I need you both to go. We shouldn't discuss this here, now. It's not the right time."

"What do you say?" Viktoriya asked, her cold anger softening into heartache. "Please, do not say I should go."

"Mark, what is this?" Elijah said. "What are you *really* saying? You owe me—us—a little honesty here."

"We need a break—for now. This isn't the time to decide anything. What we all need is time. I can't think straight, and if I try to decide now, I'll make the wrong choice for the wrong reasons. Please … I just need you both to go."

None of us said another word. Viktoriya and Elijah climbed into his car and drove away. As they pulled away from me, it felt as though the tether around my heart yanked it from my chest, leaving me hollow. I'd either just made the worst mistake of my life—or just the worst one today. But I couldn't afford a parade of self-pity and loathing. There would be plenty of time for that for the rest of my life.

I ran into the house and into the bathroom, where we always kept our first-aid supplies. We were never the most organized, so I was looking through the supplies for the right bandages.

"Mark, what happened?" Eros asked, startling me with the abrupt question in my ear.

"Weren't you watching or listening, Eros? Mom got hurt because I was too busy fooling around with Elijah and Viktoriya. And if she hadn't gotten hurt, I'm sure Elijah and Viktoriya would have blown up anyway."

"I don't think that's true, Mark. I was watching. Things were good, you just—"

"Don't give me that. None of this would've happened if you hadn't meddled in my life—if you hadn't pushed me. You play your games with people and never have to deal with the fallout."

"Mark. That's not fair—and you know it," Eros said, sounding too much like a disappointed parent for my liking. "I can accept blame where blame is due, but not here. I didn't push you anywhere you were not already heading. I didn't force your hand or make your decisions. I'm no god, I'm just as fallible as you. You're just afraid. Unlike Viktoriya and Elijah—who didn't deserve that—you can't push me away. You do what you need to—Eileen will be fine, by the way. I checked. One broken bone—I fixed it. I'll be here when you get back from the hospital."

I grabbed the bandages, snatched my truck keys off the counter, and bolted out the door. My truck was parked next to the garage, with a few empty apple crates in the bed. It was dusty. Mom clearly wasn't using it regularly, but often enough that it had no trouble starting—always a concern with a forty-year-old truck. When the engine finally turned over, I almost laughed—or cried. I couldn't tell which was trying harder to escape.

I backed away from the garage and turned down the drive. A few seconds later, I pulled up in front of the bench where Mom sat with Mr. O'Connor. I kept the truck running and jumped out—the bandage still in my hand. I wrapped Mom's ankle— imperfectly, but effectively—immobilizing it for the short drive. I realized I should've grabbed an ice pack from the freezer, but if I went back to the house, Mom would insist on skipping the hospital altogether, and I'd probably let her.

I picked her up and set her in the passenger seat of the truck. Then I thanked Mr. O'Connor for staying with her and for all his help. I didn't need to say it, but I reminded him he was welcome to stay and help himself to anything in the kitchen. He's a neighbor I've known my entire life. I could trust him to save us a beer. He thanked me and told Mom he would call to check on her later. I jumped into the driver's seat and pulled away, driving with careful urgency to the closest hospital.

The cab was silent. Mom was holding back tears. The radio had been dead for years, broken long ago, and I'd never fixed it. And Eros wasn't with me. I know I said I couldn't tell when they were absent, but now I could. They were never completely quiet. They had a habit of giggling or humming all the time. I'd gotten used to their presence. Now there was only silence—and my worst enemy: my own thoughts.

Chapter 24

The quiet drive to the hospital was mercifully short. If I had spent much longer in that silence, I would have fallen into ruminations about all the mistakes I had just made. It was inevitable. Still, I wanted to postpone that self-flagellation as long as possible. How does that saying go? Happiness is just the postponement of pain—no, that's not it. If you can't flagellate yourself, how the hell are you supposed to flagellate with anyone else? That sounds closer.

I really wish I could kick my younger self for never fixing the radio.

"How are you doing, Mom?" I asked, trying to sound calmer than I felt.

"I think I'll—OW!—live," she answered, pushing through the pain as we drove over a slight bump in the road.

"Sorry, I didn't see that one. We'll be there in a few minutes," I said, wincing at her yelp.

"I really wish we had fixed the radio. The distraction would be nice," she said.

"I literally just said that," I said, laughing.

"You did? I didn't hear you."

"Oh, no—just to myself," I said, a little embarrassed.

"So long as you don't get an answer you weren't expecting," she said, laughing softly. "How does that saying go? Only a fool argues with themselves and wins; a genius loses. I don't remember how it goes—I think it was George Carlin."

"Did Mr. O'Connor share his pain meds with you?" I asked, trying to make her laugh—to distract her, and myself.

"I wish, but he wouldn't share," she said, starting to laugh before gasping from the pain.

"I'm sorry, I shouldn't make you laugh."

"Please, you could always make me laugh without trying. Don't be sorry about that."

"All right—no apologies then. I think we're almost there—it's been a few years since I drove here. Embarrassing if I managed to get lost," I said, looking out the windows for familiar landmarks. "I don't remember the drive to the hospital taking this long. I guess it would be a bad sign to be overly familiar with driving to the emergency room—unless you're a paramedic; I bet they know all the shortcuts."

"You won't get lost—you never do, not really," she said, humoring me. "Or at least not for long."

I'd been away just long enough for the scenery to change—familiar but strangely foreign. I almost missed the turn. The hospital looked nothing like I remembered at first, and somehow I missed the massive blue sign. We were lucky there wasn't any traffic, because I had to cut across two lanes to make the turn. I chalked that up to rusty driving skills and a little stress.

I pulled up to the curb outside the emergency room and told Mom I was going to get her a wheelchair, and if she argued, I would ask for a gurney instead. It felt almost normal when she chuckled—but wrong when she didn't argue. I ran inside and asked the first person in scrubs for a wheelchair—and possibly a hand. Their brief blank stare told me they probably weren't the right person to ask—but they helped anyway. They rolled a well-used wheelchair out to the truck with me and helped gently lift Mom out of the passenger seat. I thanked the nurse—or doctor, or maybe janitor; I wasn't sure—and told Mom I'd meet her inside after I parked the truck.

I found a parking space easily enough and jogged back to the foreboding sliding doors of the emergency room. Mom was inside, in the waiting room, with a clipboard in her lap. Whoever decided ER patients should fill out forms in a torture-chamber waiting room before seeing a nurse deserves a special prize from Hell. Nothing like crippling pain and severe injuries to spice up writing your medical history with a ten-year-old ballpoint pen. I hope they have a special room in Hell—with bad fluorescent lighting, never-ending insurance forms, and bad pens.

I helped Mom finish her paperwork and handed the clipboard to a receptionist who had clearly learned to ask as few questions as possible. She hummed, glanced at me, then at Mom, and clearly decided she didn't want to ask any questions. She asked me to take a seat, and a nurse would call us back as soon as possible. So, I sat next to Mom and picked up an old entertainment magazine, thumbing through it. I asked Mom if she wanted to know how celebrities in 2014 were "just like us." She did not. I read the humanizing gossip article to myself while we waited.

After an hour—hospital time, twenty minutes in reality—we were finally called back to a small exam room. A friendly but obviously overworked nurse recorded Mom's vitals and then asked the question I had been dreading. "So, what happened?" Mom answered before I could. She told them there had been an accident and a large empty tank had fallen on her, pinning her leg briefly.

They hummed thoughtfully, inspecting her leg, ankle, and foot before coming to the same conclusion I had. It didn't look like anything was broken, but the bruising and contusions were severe enough that a fracture was possible. They asked us to wait for a doctor to verify everything they had just checked while they called a radiologist to take a few X-rays. They warned it might be *a while*, so they gave Mom a small shot of a painkiller to keep her comfortable. Unfortunately, they didn't have enough for me, so I was stuck staying uncomfortable.

"Looks like you're stuck in here with me," Mom said, sighing with relief as the painkiller kicked in.

"I'm not stuck in here with you—you're … wait, you beat me to it. Did Dad ever keep up with you?" I asked, laughing at our accidental synchronization.

"Not even once. Poor sweet man was always one step behind. I think he liked it that way," she said, the painkiller kicking in a little too well.

"That might be more than I wanted to hear. How did you two make it? You were so different," I asked.

"We weren't so different, and it wasn't always perfect. Far from it in the beginning. It came down to a matter of trust—

GREAT song—and listening. It took practice," she said, smiling to herself, surprisingly lucid despite the drugs. "You know, The Beatles were only half right. You need love to start, sure—but that's not all you need. The rest is a decision. To learn and grow. To accept the imperfections. Like dancing—give and take, together. I miss dancing with him; he was terrible—I mean, we both had to change a little … Oh, true apothecary. Thy drugs are quick … Mark, can you hand me some water?"

"Water, no problem," I said, filling a ridiculously small paper cup from the sink and handing it to her. "I remember the dancing. He had no rhythm, but damn if he didn't embrace it and dance anyway."

"Thank you, dear," she said, sipping from the tiny paper cup. "So, tell me. You're dating Elijah and Viktoriya—who is just the sweetest—at the same time? I didn't want to pry, but I'm high."

"This would be a fun conversation under better circumstances. Yes, I am—or was. We kind of left it in limbo. Surprise—guess this is me coming out," I said, not sure whether to laugh at the absurdity or cry at the reminder. "It all happened so fast I barely had time to process it myself."

"You don't really need to come out—we always knew. I mean, we knew what you weren't. It doesn't matter to me—as long as you're happy, your partners treat you well, and you treat them well. But if you want a party or something, I bet your sister would love that," she said with drug-induced honesty. "But what do you mean you *were* dating them? What happened? You three were so cute together."

"I don't know if I can explain what happened—I'm not even sure myself. I think I tried to balance too much—and badly—and ended up breaking promises, letting them down without meaning to. Or maybe they couldn't get past the jealousy. Maybe that was my fault," I said, sinking into the chair opposite Mom. "I would wind up focusing on one of them too much, inadvertently ignoring the other. Or maybe the three of us are just too different to work."

"Oh, my sweet boy," she said, giggling. "You sound just like your father at your age—so focused on what's wrong, you miss what's right. Think about the three of you. You're good together—so good. Remember how you all stood up to Gale— not separately, but together. While you were working the mill, you anticipated each other. And Mr. O'Connor told me how you all lifted that tank off me—you didn't even have to speak."

"Yeah, I guess so," I said, thinking about what she was saying. "But that was before I ..."

"Shush—let me finish. You made a mistake. We all do—get over it. You three are like ... I'm not sure ... magnets! Yes—like three magnets. They push and pull against each other on their own, but put them together and they move in the same direction," she said, waving her hands as if illustrating invisible fields. "You have to stop thinking of them as two separate relationships. One unit, not two. Like ... damn, I had an example, but I lost it. I'm going fuzzy around the edges. You get what I'm saying?"

"I understand. You're right. We do work when we're together," I said, feeling the weight of the obvious answer I couldn't see before. "Thank you. I wish we had this talk last week. Do you think we can get some of whatever was in that shot to take home—for the next time I need advice."

"Ha. Ha. Funny boy," she murmured, eyes already half-closed. "I'm close ... call your brother and sister, please, Marcus—so much like your dad. Love you."

She was asleep before finishing her sentence. I'd call Jefferson and Lexie when the doctor came back to take her for the X-ray. I didn't want to leave her—and there wasn't good reception in here anyway. Out of habit, I asked Eros what they thought, but was met with silence. Maybe that was for the best. I needed to work through this on my own.

About ten minutes later, the doctor returned, and we gently woke Mom. Together, we helped her into the wheelchair, and the doctor wheeled her to radiology. They suggested I wait outside to free up the room for other patients. When they left, I wandered out to the bleak waiting room and then stepped outside to call my siblings.

Once outside, the sight of the sunset surprised me. It was breathtaking, though the beauty was somewhat lost on me. Still, I paused to take it in and breathe before making my phone calls. My conversations with my siblings were brief and to the point. I told them about the accident, that Mom was getting a couple of X-rays, and that I'd update them when the results came in. I offered my opinion that she would be off her feet for a few weeks, but would be fine after that. To their credit, they trusted me to handle everything, keep them informed, and let them know if I needed them to come home.

Another long twenty minutes ticked by before the doctor returned, pushing Mom in the wheelchair. They called me over and delivered the good news. The X-rays came back clear—no broken bones—although they saw one hairline fracture that appeared to have recently healed. There was soft tissue damage that would take five or six weeks to heal properly. For the next few weeks, she should rest as much as possible, avoid putting any weight on her foot and leg for at least the next three or four days. After that, keep it to a minimum, use crutches, or a hard-shell protective boot. We could pick up both at the pharmacy, along with a small prescription for painkillers to help her sleep. Aside from a quick visit to the pharmacy, we were good to head home.

I called Jefferson and Lexie back to deliver the good news, and they said they would come to visit in a few days. I got Mom into the truck, and together we headed home. On the drive, I let her know I would put in for a leave of absence from work to stay with her until she was literally back on her feet. She was more interested in what I was going to do about Viktoriya and Elijah, but I didn't have an answer for that yet. As much as I wanted to, I still thought we needed some time to settle before I tried to repair the damage. She understood, but reminded me that if I waited too long, I would miss my chance—which I knew but could have lived without hearing out loud. She fell asleep a few minutes into the drive, so once again I was alone with my thoughts—until we were back home.

Eros

I watched Mark pull away from the bench where his mom was sitting with Mr. O'Connor. This wasn't the first time we'd been apart, but it was the first time it felt like a real separation. It didn't feel good. I should be angry. He essentially hung the blame for everything that had gone wrong around my neck—like a big dead seabird. The question swimming in my mind was: why wasn't I angry? It's not like I thought he might be right—did I? Did I push him into something he wasn't ready for? No, I could have, but I didn't. I encouraged him; I tried to help him. I was in the front row for his performance, waving dollar bills in the air. I just don't understand how he could blame me for what happened.

What happened? What went wrong? I couldn't have missed something so heinous as to cause this level of catastrophe. Not just with the mill—that was a mystery of its own—but with Mark, Elijah, and Viktoriya. Why did the accident push Mark over the edge? None of this makes any sense to me. It's entirely ridiculous. Is that it? Are humans just inherently irrational? Maybe that's the root of it all. Why couldn't they all just be more like me—capable of setting aside their egos and moving on past their own trivial mistakes? What really irks me is that I don't understand—though it feels like I should. I've been observing humans for thousands of years. I should be able to predict how they will act and react by now.

I doubted I'd unravel this mystery from the bench next to Mr. O'Connor. He hadn't left yet—just sat there, staring at the spot where Eileen had been. It was like he could still see her sitting there—and, with Mark not around, I had no one to ask about him. I'd just have to wait for Mark to solve that one. It was one more thing I'd have to accept not fully understanding—like the fracturing of Mark's relationship. When Mark comes back, we can talk about it all—and work it out together. We'd gotten pretty good at working things out together. He helps me as much as I help him. This is just so frustrating. It felt like I was so close to the answer. One mystery that I can solve is what happened to the mill, so that's where I will focus my attention.

At first glance, the wreckage looked more like piles of intact, disassembled pieces. It all looked like something Mark could fix in an hour or two without breaking a sweat. From what I could tell, the minimal damage was secondary—nothing that explained the accident. Now I wish I had paid closer attention to Mark when he was explaining how it all worked. By my deduction, the problem seemed to start with the chain—what had Mark called it? A long motorcycle chain. It looked like it had snapped off, though nothing seemed broken—more like it had simply fallen apart. Mark said it was actually multiple motorcycle chains connected. I examined one of the intact joints—it was a steel pin held in place by another, smaller steel pin. The pins were missing from the sections that failed. I'd have to look around for those, but from the sound it made, I can only assume they are long gone.

The tank stand was the same—the pieces had come apart, as if the bolts and pins had vanished. In this case, I'd expect to see them on the ground near where they fell out—but there was nothing. No sign of any bolts, pins, or nuts anywhere. They were simply … gone. Very strange. It didn't make sense, and now it was pissing me off. This was the one thing I was supposed to make sense of. Maybe I just need to expand the perimeter of my search.

I began searching the ground for any clues that might help solve this mystery. The immediate area around the mill revealed nothing unusual—mostly apple bits and footprints. But there was one unusual set of barely perceptible footprints that didn't match the others. They were smooth, like the soles of expensive shoes meant for sitting around, not working a cider mill. And those footprints ran only along one side of the mill—the side where the chain was and where the tank stand collapsed. It was unusual, but explained nothing. There could be a rational explanation, so my investigation continued.

Slowly expanding my perimeter uncovered nothing else unusual—until I reached the shelves near the door. On one shelf sat a box, and atop it, a small pile of steel pins, nuts, and bolts. They didn't seem to belong there. It was a very unusual—and not very useful—place for them to be. They appeared to be the very pins missing from the chain—and the bolts and nuts from the tank stand. And there was one more thing that absolutely did not belong: a sliver of manicured fingernail—painted with a matte, white-tinted translucent polish.

This little piece of fingernail was another anomaly. It didn't seem to belong to anyone who *should've been* here. It was manicured and polished. Everyone here, except for Elijah, works with their hands, and I haven't seen any of them wearing nail polish like this. Elijah comes closest, but his are artificial and removable. Between the footprints and this fingernail, there was only one conclusion: Gale Barlow had been here. And I believe he deliberately removed those pins, assuming it would be enough to cripple the mill. It was Gale, not Mark, who was responsible for this accident.

I was stewing outside the mill, back on the empty bench, imagining all the ways I could destroy Gale Barlow. That name was tainted—vile-sounding, like something too foul to speak aloud in polite company. I hated what I uncovered almost as much as I hated being alone with it. Just when I thought I might burst,

I saw the headlights of Mark's truck coming up the drive, and relief washed over me.

I raced across the open ground, catching the truck just in time and following it until Mark parked by the house. The moment he stepped out of the truck, I whispered to him.

"Mark, it's me. I'm here. Let's talk when you can."

"Okay, Eros, let me get Mom inside first," Mark replied as he walked around to the passenger side of the truck.

Mark carried Eileen inside and laid her gently on the couch. She was still asleep, barely stirring, when he set her down. He moved the surrounding furniture quietly to clear a path from the couch to the bathroom and kitchen. He tucked a blanket around her and made sure she was comfortable before stepping out onto the porch.

Outside, he didn't sit; he just leaned against the railing, staring at the trees and the glow of the light-polluted night sky. After everything that happened today, I decided to wait for him to break the silence. The silence stretched on until he tore his gaze from the dark horizon and finally spoke.

"Okay, Eros. I'm here," he said.

"First, how's your mom? Will she be all right?"

"Yes, she got banged up pretty good, but she'll recover."

"Good. And how are you?"

"Me? I'm surprisingly all right. I mean, I think my life just changed in ways I can't understand yet. I don't know everything I've just lost," Mark said, looking around. "Only what I was lucky enough not to lose—like Mom. And you."

"I'm sorry, Mark. For everything. I never meant to push you," I said, wishing I could physically sit down with Mark. "I should've listened and talked with you more. I took my experience for granted, I thought I knew more than I really did."

"I'm sorry too. You didn't really push me. Not anywhere I didn't already need one. What happened wasn't your fault," Mark said, uncharacteristically calm. "I had a chance to talk with Mom—she was a little high on painkillers but, honestly, kind of brilliant. She helped me see things a little more clearly."

"Now I'm sorry I missed that. So, what do you think went wrong?"

"With Elijah and Viktoriya, I never saw it as one relationship—I kept treating them like two separate ones. That made it impossible to hold on to either. Like I was unnecessarily juggling—so dropping everything was inevitable."

"I hope you appreciate the fact that I missed that too."

"You know, Eros, that actually helps. But I still don't know what to do ... if it's not already too late."

"I don't know—not yet—but I do know that together we can figure it out," I said, wishing I could offer a comforting, empathetic hand on his shoulder. "If it's not too much right now ... I need to talk to you about the mill."

"Thank you. I appreciate that. Yeah, now is as good a time as tomorrow. I assume you looked at it while I was gone. Did you figure out what happened?"

"Yes, I figured it out. First, you should know I think you can fix it easily—and I can help make a few improvements. The damage is minimal; in fact, not much is broken at all," I said, wavering between sharing the good and bad news. "But as for what went wrong ... there's something you need to see."

Chapter 25

Eros might have made their discovery sound a little less ominous. It was unnerving. I ducked back into the house and grabbed one of the flashlights we kept by the door. I'd forgotten how dark it gets out here—I'd grown used to the city's constant glow. The beam carved deep shadows along the short path, making the trees loom from the darkness. The crunch of gravel under my boots faded into silence, and the night—still heavy with the chill of a just-faded summer—wrapped its cold arms around me.

We entered the mill, the evidence of the day—and the accident—nowhere to be seen. Mr. O'Connor had cleaned up the mess we left behind. I needed to remember to thank him somehow. The silence was haunting; the shadows felt unnaturally deep. I shuddered.

"Okay, what do you need to show me?" I asked softly, out loud.

"The shelves by the door—on top of the box," Eros said directly in my ear.

I swept the flashlight over the few boxes on the shelves. At first, nothing seemed out of place. But if Eros wanted me to see something, there had to be something there. I looked again and immediately saw the anomaly.

"Those pins. Mr. O'Connor didn't put those there—he wouldn't do that. If he had found those, he would have put them with the other spare parts," I said, stepping closer to get a better look. "This isn't all you found—what else? What did you find?"

"Look at the chain—it's still coiled on the ground. Then look at the tank stand. I don't want to lead you to a conclusion. Tell me what you see," Eros said. I did as they asked and examined the chain and the collapsed tank stand.

"They … aren't broken," I said, looking from the chain and collapsed tank stand to the box. "This doesn't make sense—it's like they were … no. How could we not notice?"

The chain hadn't broken—it hadn't snapped the way it sounded. Someone had pulled the tiny cotter pin from the steel rivet linking it all together. All it took was time, tension, and vibration to bring it down. The tank stand had been sabotaged in the same way—just a few missing nuts and bolts—and the entire frame was left to collapse under its own weight. This wasn't wear and tear—it was deliberate. This could have killed someone … it almost killed Mom.

"There's more. You can't see it, but there were footprints—from smooth-soled shoes. Tire tracks from a nice car. And with the pins and bolts on the box … there's a sliver of fingernail," Eros said, sounding unnervingly upset. I jumped back to the box, leaning in close until I saw it.

"No … that's Gale's. Eros, tell me I'm imagining things."

"You're not. That is my conclusion as well. Gale came in here after your confrontation and sabotaged the mill. I can only imagine what his plan was, but those were his tire tracks, his footprints, and that is—"

"His tacky, brittle, manicured fingernail. That *fuck!*" I shouted, my voice ringing around the mill. I hurled the flashlight. It shattered against the wall, plunging the mill into darkness. "That shitting fuck-stain of a man—I am going to bury him! I'll—"

"Breathe, Mark. Breathe. We *will* get him. But I can't let you literally kill him. Trust me, I wish I could let you. Trust me—I wish I could. I've imagined doing worse. But you are *better* than that, and I know you don't really want to, you just feel like you do," Eros whispered. Their voice sounded strained, like they were holding back a dangerous, damned reservoir of rage.

"Okay. Okay. But I'm going to punch him. At least let me have that," I said, fighting back the instinct to explode.

"Once. Just one punch. Right in his smarmy, puffy face. Yes, I think that's reasonable," Eros said, matching my forced calm. "Otherwise, Viktoriya and Elijah would kill me if I let you go to jail."

The mention of Viktoriya and Elijah snapped me back to reality. The fury didn't vanish; it simply sat down in the waiting room of my mind, biding its time. We had to make a plan, and we had to calm down. There was nothing more we could do tonight. Exhaustion crept in. The weight of the day settled on me. I needed to sleep.

I made my way back to the house in the dark. I didn't even need the flashlight. A lifetime of walking this path had etched it into my legs. All the while, Eros and I filled each other in on the missing pieces of our day. In the morning, they would have a plan, and we would make Gale Barlow sorry he ever set foot on this farm.

The next morning, I woke up early. I didn't have to; I just always did when I was home. A life of ingrained habit meant that sleeping past six was almost impossible. I hadn't woken up in my old room in years, but I still knew every step between my bedroom door and the coffee maker in the kitchen. I met Mom at the kitchen table; she looked tired, staring mournfully at an empty mug.

"I didn't expect you to be awake," I said. "How are you feeling?"

"Tired, sore, mad. I couldn't manage the coffee with these," Mom said, shaking the crutches leaning against the table. "It's not as bad as it could've been ... but still.

"I've got the coffee, don't worry. I'll be here as long as you need," I said, preparing the coffee like I had a thousand times before.

"What if that's for good?" she said, a mixture of hope and regret in her voice.

"We'll cross—or maybe jump off—that bridge when we get there," I said, unsure myself how I felt about it. I asked myself the same question all night. "Right now, we take it a day at a time. For now, you just tell me what you need. No pretending you're okay. You can do that after you heal."

"All right, Mark," she said with a sigh. "I need coffee. Oh God, do I need coffee."

"Coming right up, Mom."

Eros

Mark made coffee with more care and diligence than I'd seen him use in his apartment. He wasn't doing it for himself; he wasn't thinking about his own needs. He was a caretaker, not just for his mother, but for this home and orchard, a role he stepped into as if it were a comfortable set of clothes. After yesterday and last night, I half-expected him to be a wreck this morning. But he was calm, focused, and almost like a man I didn't recognize—not someone new, but someone without a mask.

I listened while Mark sat with Eileen at the table drinking coffee. He told her about the minimal damage to the mill that he had seen last night. He left out the key details of Gale's sabotage and focused on what he needed to do to fix it. He told her it was just an accident, and he would absolutely make sure it could never happen again. I could tell she wanted to ask about Viktoriya and Elijah but sensed that was a topic he wasn't ready to discuss, so she let it go.

He cut her off after two cups of coffee and insisted on helping her back to the couch to rest. He left her a glass of water within reach and the small prescription bottle of painkillers, just in case. She looked a little annoyed when he handed her a book and her phone, instructing her to call if she needed anything. Otherwise, he expected her to stay put while he made calls and got to work. He reminded her of the doctor's orders—stay off your foot as much as possible for at least a few days—then he walked out of the house.

"Eros?" he said almost as soon as he stepped outside.

"Good morning, I'm here," I answered.

"Morning. It's going to be a busy day, I hope you're ready."

"Please. I was born ready—well, not literally. I came into ... never mind. Yes, I'm ready."

"Good. First, let's take stock of the mill in the daylight, figure out what we need to get it back up and running—you mentioned you had ideas for improvements. We'll put together a list and see what we need from the hardware store."

"Got it. Are you putting that list on your phone? I can help."

"Yes, thank you. After that, I have some calls to make. I need to let the university know I'll be on hiatus for a while. It probably means I'll have to clear out the university apartment—so we'll need a plan."

"That'll be fun. I've never helped anyone move before."

"It's not fun. Trust me. No one thinks it's fun. So, after I work that out—we get Gale. Do you have a plan?"

"Yes, I do. But I'm not sure how to find him."

"Don't worry about that, he left us enough business cards with his address we could wallpaper a house. Finding him is the easy part."

"Noted. Yes, I have a plan … how much do you want to know?"

"In this case, I have zero ethical reservations … well, almost zero. You were right, we can't kill him."

"Good. This might be hard to explain, and I'd rather not demonstrate. Basically, I'll talk to him—show him what he did, and what he almost did."

"You're going to *talk* to him?"

"In a manner. Do you remember the first time I talked to you?"

"Oh. God, that was uncomfortable. So, in his head?"

"Loudly, in his head. Right. I've been working it out all night. It will feel like the loudest thing you can imagine—right inside his skull—while he sees Eileen violently crushed as the mill collapses. It should scare him into wanting to hide in a cave for the rest of his life."

"I like it—I still get to punch him, right?"

"Yes. Just once."

"Perfect. Let's get to work."

The sun was just breaching the horizon when we entered the mill and began taking stock. First, Mark catalogued every part missing or removed by Gale, then listed everything that should be replaced. He didn't want to risk reusing anything damaged. Finally, he noted improvements: double the chain for redundancy, add a brake to the press so a loss of chain tension can't let the press fall, and build a solid tank stand with forklift access. And a solid stand for the tank—one that couldn't collapse but still left access for the forklift. My ideas needed no new parts—only time to modify pieces after repair—and Mark's trust, which he, to my relief, gladly gave.

After we took an inventory of the spare parts he had on hand, we had a reasonably short list, which Mark said should be doable with one trip to the hardware store. But something about the way he phrased it made me think he knew there would be at least two more hardware-store trips.

All told, we finished in under three hours. Mark sat under a tree to make his calls. For all the emphasis he placed on these calls ahead of time, I was expecting something much more dramatic. He spent a few minutes on a call with his department manager, explaining why he needed a leave of absence. His manager said he was sorry and asked if a week would be enough to know whether he could return. Mark said it would be enough time, and he would get the apartment cleaned out in a day or two in case they needed it. Then Mark called his coworker, OT, and had an even shorter conversation, but essentially said the same things.

The hardest calls were to his brother and sister; they were tense because, despite knowing better, he still felt responsible. He also thought he had forgotten to call them last night. They at least understood why he felt that way and reassured him that he wasn't at fault. They both said again that they would visit in a couple of days and thanked Mark for taking care of their mother. Twenty-five minutes. That's all it took for Mark to make four simple phone calls. And yet he looked spent, like he'd just finished a monumental task—like dragging the whole orchard up a hill.

After sitting under the tree for a few quiet minutes, Mark stood and said it was time to move forward. First stop: checking on his mom to let her know he was running to the hardware store. Back in the house, we found her sound asleep on the couch. Mark picked up her bottle of painkillers and counted the remaining pills. He told me she'd taken only one—a good sign she wasn't in too much pain. He left her a note and refilled her glass of water, and then we left.

In the truck, Mark seemed hesitant. I realized I hadn't seen him drive before—not that I doubted he could. He just looked a little rusty. He grumbled to himself about the roads, the other drivers, and the broken radio, which apparently made the silence worse. When I asked if he was okay, he admitted he disliked driving—didn't trust other people, and worried about making a mistake that could hurt someone. To help him, I looked at the broken radio for him.

Unfortunately, the radio looked beyond repair, its innards corroded or fried. Mark shrugged and said maybe he'd get lucky, and the hardware store might have a suitable replacement. They didn't, but they had everything else on our list, so Mark's disappointment was only mild. He loaded everything into the back of the truck and tossed a few straps over the small load to keep it in place. He said it was probably overly cautious, but at least worth the peace of mind. Strapping the load down was cautious—but probably easier than thinking about what came next: paying Gale Barlow a visit.

We pulled into a lifeless office park. It was a dismal space, the type no one would voluntarily visit. Six identical buildings designed to maximize misery and discourage lingering. Mark stormed into one, glanced at the directory, and climbed the stairs to the second floor. Each of the offices was identifiable by large numbers on the door and cheap removable plaques on the wall next to them. Mark found his target quickly and charged inside, where a secretary greeted him sympathetically, as if she too were sorry to be there.

"Hi, sorry—can I talk to Gale? Is he here?" Mark asked patiently. The office was small; we could see Gale sitting at his desk just a few feet away. Mark was playing along with their game.

"Of course—just a moment—I'll check," she said, turning to make eye contact with Gale, who was clearly pretending to be on the phone. He smiled and nodded, holding up one finger before hanging up his phone and waving us in. "He's ready for you—go on in."

"Gale Barlow, I need to talk to you," Mark said after smiling at the secretary and walking the four feet into Gale's office space.

"Yes, what can I do for—oh, it's you," Gale said, standing up from his desk, his wormy smile devolving into a smug smirk. "Why are you here? Come to make more threats? Forget your backup? Or did Eileen finally come to her senses and sign those papers accepting my very generous offer?"

"No—no backup today. Just me," Mark said, maintaining a non-threatening tone with great effort. "And no, Eileen—my mother—can't accept your offer. There was an accident."

"Oh, dear, an accident?" Gale said, unconvincingly playing dumb.

"Yes. Yesterday—the mill just collapsed," Mark said, playing along. The strain in his voice made it even more convincing.

"Oof. That's … unfortunate. Such a shame," Gale said, failing to feign surprise or concern. "That could wipe out the whole season. I guess that means she is rethinking her attachment to that old place. But, you should know … I might need to lower my next offer now."

"Oh, Gale. I think maybe you don't understand why I'm here," Mark said, taking one step forward, dropping the casual tone. "You can lower the offer if you want—it won't matter. Eileen—my mother—can't sign anything anymore."

"I think she—you said she can't … anymore," he stammered, retreating behind his desk and leaning on it for support. Genuine surprise and confusion crept into his voice, with just a hint of panic. "Wha—what do you mean? Why can't she sign?"

"Didn't you hear me? There was an accident, Gale. Yesterday. Not long after you left," Mark said, leaning forward over the desk. That was my cue—my chance to jump from Mark to Gale. I tunneled through the desk, up his arm, and into his mind, where fear had already cracked it open. Now, in his head, I listened and waited for Mark. "You didn't sound so surprised to hear there was an accident. Almost like you *expected* it. What did you think would happen?"

"I … I don't know what you're talking about," Gale stammered. I could feel his heart pounding.

"I know what you did, Gale Barlow. Do you? Do you know what you did to my mother?" Mark said, slamming his fist down on the desk, letting just a sliver of the rage out that I knew he was holding back. "Do you need me to tell you what happened to her when the mill *unexpectedly* collapsed on her?"

"On … her? ON HER?" he cried, finally picking up the false trail Mark laid, and now it was my turn.

I repeated Mark's words, screaming them into his ears—only he could hear. I echoed them in his mind. *"DO YOU KNOW WHAT YOU DID TO HER? WHAT HAPPENED WHEN*

THE MILL CAME DOWN ON HER?" Then it was time to add my own flair. I remembered the days when I carelessly played at being a god. I filled his head with my voice. It would be the only thing he could hear, think, or know. *"I KNOW WHAT YOU DID, GALE BARLOW! LET ME SHOW YOU."*

I plunged Gale into darkness. I was in control now. He saw only what I chose to show him, heard only what I allowed. And right now, he would feel exactly what I wanted him to feel.

I flooded his mind with visions of Eileen working at the mill, the machinery humming away, gentle vibrations flowing through his body. The scent of freshly pressed apples filled the air, and laughter rang through the building. For a fraction of a second, I felt Gale relax; it was a pleasant scene, a happy moment. Then, I brought the weight of the world down upon him.

The snap of the chain shot through his body, echoing in his ears. Then came the thunderous groan of metal straining and failing—the sharp crack as the first piece of machinery fell. I made sure he felt it and saw it crash into Eileen's fragile body. He felt the crushing weight, the shattering of bone, and the screaming. Pain flooded his mind as I forced him to watch the fabricated scene of Mark's mother—trapped, broken, bleeding, and crying out. She screamed in excruciating agony as the last piece fell on her, and I plunged him into abyssal darkness.

I held him there—in the void, absent of feeling. In silence, I made him watch his own hands: pulling pins from the chain, slipping bolts free, his fingernail snagging on the edge of the steel and leaving a fragment behind as evidence. I let him see the footprints of his cowardice as he ran for the door, carelessly leaving fingerprints as he fled the scene.

A moment later, I let his vision return. I restored his hearing. And I removed the traces of pain I had inflicted upon him. Then I left him, slipping back to Mark as he picked Gale up off the floor where he had collapsed.

"All done. It'll be like I was never there," I whispered in Mark's ear. "I showed him everything. Your turn."

"Thank you," Mark said silently. He stood Gale up on shaking legs, letting him lean on the desk. Mark gave him a moment to regain his bearings—to realize that nothing he'd just felt was real.

"What?" Gale mumbled, wiping the sweat from his face.

"We know, Gale. We know it was you—and what you did," Mark said darkly, delivering one heroically restrained punch to Gale's face. "You didn't know who you were dealing with, Gale. Maybe now you have an idea."

Gale recoiled—not just from the punch, but from the unseen danger standing before him. He staggered to his plush chair, clutching it like a lifeline, never looking away from Mark. But Mark didn't move. He took one punch, and that's all he would take. Now Mark waited for Gale to understand. And a second later, he did.

"Oh God. No. Please. I didn't mean—oh God—I never wanted to hurt anyone. I did it but I didn't mean for that ... What did I do?" He wept, holding himself up on the chair. "I thought it would just stop working! No one was supposed to get hurt—I only wanted her to take the deal! What did I do?"

"He believes he killed Eileen," I whispered to Mark.

I'd say I got the point across. He might actually feel sorry for what he did—good. We should let him fester with that. He hurt my friends. Leaving him with that is better than he deserves. But Mark won't. He is better than I am ... better than I was.

"You made several mistakes," Mark said, the malice draining from his voice. "And I showed you ... a trick. Mom—Eileen will be fine, as will the mill, and the orchard—my orchard, and my home."

"Trick? Who are you?" Gale asked, his voice unsteady, his expression dumbfounded.

"I'm Mark Williams, and that orchard is mine," Mark said, his voice carrying something more than pride. "It's all in my name, not my mother's. You've been chasing and harassing the wrong person—in more ways than one—all this time."

"I don't understand," Gale said, folding himself into his chair.

"You don't need to. What you do need to do is leave. Retire, find a new line of work, somewhere far from here. I have more than enough to ruin you—to make sure you spend years locked away after losing everything," Mark said firmly. "If you don't, or you come back ... well, I don't think I need to show you that. Do I?"

"No, I think I understand you," Gale said, the color draining from his face. "I'll go. Retire, I can retire. Please."

"Please?" Mark repeated, a trace of pity in his voice. "That is the word you reach for right now? You harassed—to put it kindly—my mother for the better part of a year. And then, you almost killed her. Please? Not 'sorry?' How pathetic are you?"

That was the last straw for Gale. He fainted, his face making a satisfying squelch when it hit the desk. Mark leaned over to check that he was still breathing—he was. Then Mark turned to walk out of the office and came face to face with Gale's secretary. She stared, but didn't seem angry with Mark.

"Is all that true?" she asked.

"Yes. All true," Mark answered.

"You left him alive?" she asked, remarkably unconcerned.

"He'll be fine. Passed out from an excess of conscience."

"All right. Go on. I'll make sure he keeps that promise before I quit on his sorry ass. Good luck, Mark," she said, smiling for real this time.

Mark walked out without saying another word. He didn't need to. It wasn't until we climbed into his truck that the full weight of the past two days crashed down over him. Mark sat behind the wheel of his old truck and wept with his whole body.

Chapter 26

The crash hit without warning. I sat behind the wheel of my truck, ready to drive home, when the specter of the past few days caught up with me and attacked. Elation, terror, anger, and grief collided all at once. My whole body shook as everything came pouring out. With Gale dealt with, the dam burst, and I was drowning in the flood.

A complete breakdown brings its own kind of clarity. For a few minutes, everything shuts down. It doesn't matter where you are. Your mind and body just stop until all that excess emotion you've been holding rushes out, leaving you empty for one euphoric moment. In that moment lies the clarity—like the eye of a storm.

In that moment of clarity, I knew it was time to make some decisions. It was a moment when I could feel that the choices I made now would alter my life forever. I knew I'd been standing at the crossroads for too long—years—unable to choose which path to follow. The same was true with Viktoriya and Elijah—I chose them, but I hadn't followed through.

I realized then that the orchard was my home; it was where I belonged. Mom would recover from the accident, but she was past the age to manage alone. It was time for me to come home for good. My days of having few real responsibilities had ended. It was also clear I needed both Viktoriya and Elijah in my life—they made me a better person. And, good or bad, I don't think I'd be here without Eros.

"Mark?" Eros whispered in my ear. "Are you all right?"

"Yeah," I said as soon as the body-wracking subsided. "Everything just hit me. Come on, Eros. Let's go home. There's work to do, and I'll need your help to set things right."

"With Elijah and Viktoriya too, right?" they asked.

"Yes, but not yet," I answered. "As much as I want to run after them, I have to fix the home I neglected first."

****Eros****

Over the next four days, I watched Mark grow into a changed man—not different, just evolved. I'd already glimpsed the start of that transformation this morning—he cared for his mother and faced confrontations instead of avoiding them. I've seen countless people face similar choices and run—but not Mark. He embraced it. That was something I never had to face—and, frankly, something I never stuck around long enough to witness.

Things were different at the orchard when we got back. Activity buzzed through the orchard more than before. A handful of people were there, working. Small tractors and other motorized vehicles moved between the trees. And Mr. O'Connor was there, coordinating the movements of everyone.

Mark explained that Mr. O'Connor was not just a neighbor. He was their oldest employee—one of the very few full-time employees they had. He was only a few years younger than Eileen and was Mark's dad's best friend. Mark said they didn't really think of him as an employee—more like part of the extended family. Mark suspected that generations ago their families had been related, so it was likely they were something like distant cousins. Mr. O'Connor was just as invested as Mark in keeping the orchard running.

Eileen had done an admirable job of keeping things running at a level she could manage, which kept everything just above water. As Mark explained the details, I wasn't especially interested in the business—not like Mark was. I caught the broad strokes; they supplied apples to several local markets, and even local elementary schools. The cider mill was originally how they dealt with the excess crop. They even had several of the original hand-crank mills and presses. The 'make your own cider' area was popular with visitors from the city—buy a bushel, put in a little labor, leave with fresh cider.

As we repaired the damage to the large mill, Mark and I discussed his plans for the future. It was one thing to fix what was broken today—another altogether to make improvements for tomorrow. He decided it was time to make his leave of absence from the university IT department a permanent resignation. As much as he found the work fulfilling and enjoyable, he knew it was safe and would never really challenge him. These were the areas where my skills could make a real difference.

I shared my idea of subtly altering the genetics of his trees to yield tastier, hardier fruit. He was skeptical but agreed to let me experiment with one tree—his oldest Winesap—first. Mark warned he didn't want another 'blue banana' incident. I understood his hesitation. A crop of purple apples might be novel, but bad for business. He was far more receptive to my mill improvements. I reminded him of the bronze tiara we crafted together for Viktoriya, and I fused many of the bolts and pins so we could never have another accident like the one Gale caused. I also smoothed out friction points in the machinery to reduce wear to nearly zero. In total, it took us just a day and a half to get it running better than ever.

The second half of the next four days was a blur of paperwork, permits, and invoices. Most of it, Mark only had to review to catch up on the years of operation he'd missed. I could tell it frustrated him because he found frequent excuses to leave stacks unread while he indulged in more interesting work. Things like creating or improving the "online presence" of the orchard. He insisted that while visitor traffic—people buying a few apples or a gallon of cider—wasn't the largest revenue source, it was the most profitable. So, by his logic, attracting more of that business could significantly improve the orchard's sustainability with minimal expense.

He envisioned creating a place people would visit for more than apples—for peace and memories. It was one of the few moments he mentioned Viktoriya and Elijah. Mark wished they were with him to help clarify and refine his vague ideas; they just knew how to make things real in a way he never could. I think he sold himself short, but arguing that point would be fruitless—and I liked hearing that he knew how much he needed them.

The hard day came on Friday. This was the day Mark chose to pack up his apartment, closing the door on that chapter of his life. It was also the day his brother and sister planned to visit for dinner. Since I was unfamiliar with the process of packing and moving, I asked if he was sure he didn't want to put it off for a day or ask his siblings for help. He reassured me it was not such a big job that he would need their help, and putting it off any longer would only make it harder.

Mark tossed a dozen empty cardboard boxes, rolls of tape, and trash bags into the bed of his truck, securing them with two heavy—but empty—apple crates and his "hand truck." He climbed into the driver's seat with a sigh and sat a moment before reaching for the ignition. I've seen that expression on his face before. He was talking himself out of running away from something difficult. He didn't say it, but he didn't have to. He was afraid of stepping into the unknown again.

"Eros, help keep me on track today—can you do that?" Mark said after turning the key. "I have a feeling I might lose my nerve."

"Sure, Mark, I can do that," I said. "How do I do that?"

"Stop me if I start reminiscing," he said. "And don't ask about anything you see or find—not until we get back."

"So, no having fun."

"You got it. That's moving, save that for unpacking. Let's get this over with."

Mark pulled into the spot reserved for his apartment. It was a vast space filled with vehicles of all types lined up in numbered spots. Mark pulled into the one he identified as reserved for him— or his apartment. He unloaded the collapsed boxes, apple crates, tape, and trash bags onto the "hand truck" and rolled it to the elevator.

Packing was procedural. In the bedroom, he unceremoniously stuffed his clothes into trash bags, tied them off, and tossed them aside. The same with his bedsheets, blankets, and pillows. For Elijah's portion of the closet, he assembled a box and carefully folded each dress and costume before setting them inside. When he finished, he closed the box, taped and labeled it, setting the sealed box beside the door. I wanted to ask if he planned to take it with him or give it to Elijah, but I promised not to question him.

The rest of his bedroom filled two more boxes, while the living room and kitchen occupied the remaining nine. I only had to keep him focused a few times when he came across something Elijah or Viktoriya gave him, or something that reminded him of them. It was painful to watch him go through this alone, but he wasn't really alone. I was there with him, but I could only talk to him. Which wasn't the same as physically being there for him, to help figuratively and literally carry the weight. Fortunately, he left the furniture behind as a gift for the next resident.

After five trips, Mark had shuttled all of his belongings down to his truck. At that point in time, he had a handful of tasks ahead of him before we could return home. First, he had to clean the apartment, so it was ready for the next occupant, which entailed disposing of any food he wasn't planning to take home. Then he needed to deliver the keys to his former coworker and friend, OT, who had some paperwork for him to sign. Finally, he would have to decide what to do with Elijah's box of stuff. So, it felt like a safe time to ask Mark a gentle question while he was arguing with a mop.

"Are you going to bring that box to Elijah?" I asked as Mark walked back to his former apartment building from his former office a block away.

"No … well, yes. I'll drop it off at the club for him," Mark said. "I don't feel ready to see him today."

"So you aren't going to see Viktoriya either?"

"No. I want to see them both, but if I do, I won't leave."

"Aren't you afraid of putting it off too long?"

"Of course, I am. But I'm more afraid of making the same mistake. Running to them again before I'm ready, or able, to give them what they deserve."

"In that case, when you drop that box off, I'm going to stay behind. I want to check on them."

"Okay, then how are you going to get home?" Mark asked. "It's a long way and I know you have trouble with long distances."

"Do you remember that unintentional road trip I took? When I wound up at the Jon Bon Jovi rest stop on the Garden State Parkway? It will be like that. Except now I know where I'm going. I'm not saying it'll be easy, but I can manage it."

"All right, just don't get lost," Mark said.

He picked up Elijah's box from the back of his truck and looked at it with the same expression he'd worn before he left home to pack up the apartment. That box was a tether. I could practically hear his inner monologue. *If I keep this, Elijah will have to come get it. But if I leave it, he'll have only one reason to come—to see me.* Mark was making the choice the entire walk from his truck to the club. Any moment before he lets go of that box, he could change his mind. He finally made his choice, and after a moment of hesitation, he knocked on the back door of The Queen's Head Club. Kareem, the resident bouncer and doorman, opened the door a few seconds later.

"Mark!" he said, surprised. "Nice to see you. Elijah's not here today, he took this weekend off. Is everything okay?"

"Hi, Kareem. Nice to see you too," Mark said. "Things are complicated right now. I hope they will be okay. I just had to pack up my apartment, and these are some of Elijah's spare dresses and costumes. Can you put them somewhere safe and make sure he gets them? I'm not ready to deliver them myself yet."

"Sure, Mark. I'll leave them with Bob—he'll make sure they're safe. Are *you* okay?" Kareem said, accepting the box from Mark without pressing for the details he really wanted to ask. "You're good for Elijah, you know, we've been rooting for the three of you. I'm sorry, I won't pry, but I hope you three work out whatever happened. Go on, before I get nosey. I hope to see you soon."

"Thanks, Kareem. I hope so too. I really do," Mark said, swallowing hard, then turned to walk away while I stayed behind with the box to track down Elijah and Viktoriya.

****Mark****

Walking away from the club shouldn't have been this hard, but it was. It felt like a gravitational pull, drawing me back to the familiar tables and dark corners. It shouldn't have felt like more than leaving a job and an apartment. But it was different because I wasn't the same as I'd been a week ago. I had changed—and was changing—in ways I was only starting to discover. Elijah would probably say, "It's about time you grew up," without hearing the irony. And I bet Viktoriya would say something startlingly profound, like 'only the dead never change.' I wonder what they are doing right now.

I'm sure Eros was disappointed I chose not to see them. They didn't say so, but how could they not be? I was disappointed in myself for not being ready after nearly a week without even a text. Maybe it wasn't that I wasn't ready. Maybe I was afraid of what they would say, or what they wouldn't say. Or most likely I'm just terrified they will reject me—the way I rejected them. I really regretted not fixing the radio in my truck when I had the chance. It was going to be a long drive with only myself to talk to.

The drive was not as rough as I had feared. I mostly ran through a list of things I hadn't finished yet for the orchard. I rehearsed imaginary conversations with Elijah and Viktoriya. I never got very far past apologizing. I kept thinking of new ways I might have hurt them. But when I got past that, I would explain how I made the mistake of keeping them separate in my mind. I shouldn't have been afraid to tell Elijah when I had plans with Viktoriya. Or tell Viktoriya I was busy with Elijah. And I should have at least tried to plan time for all three of us to be together. It all ended with me inadvertently hurting them both, and I looped back to apologizing. Clearly, I needed someone to talk to about this, someone other than Mom.

Just as my imaginary boyfriend was listing all the ways I'd been selfish, I pulled up to the house—which finally cut off that train of thought. I jumped out of the truck and began unloading before I started arguing with myself again. I ferried boxes up to my old bedroom one by one, stacking them on my bed. When the bed disappeared under boxes, I started unpacking selectively.

Books went back onto the empty bookshelves. Clothes were stuffed into empty drawers. Anything that belonged elsewhere, I set aside to be tomorrow's problem. I wished Eros were here with me. They'd be asking about every little knick-knack and memento I'd collected. Faded concert tickets, train tickets, even the receipt from a charity raffle I didn't win. I could look at each one and remember that day, night, or place. I pulled an empty can of Chernihivske beer out of the box—here's one that Eros would remember. Someone else might see trash, but I saw something different. I saw every moment of that magnificently chaotic night that turned my world on its head preserved inside it. From seeing

Viktoriya outside the café to Elijah knocking on my door later that night.

Then there was the handmade sunflower pin Viktoriya clipped to my shirt the night we went to that dive bar concert. I hadn't looked at it since that night. Only now did I notice it was not just a sunflower. It was a sunflower growing out of an apple, a delicately heart-shaped apple. It was such a subtle and beautiful personal detail. She never mentioned it—she just waited for me to notice how she'd tied us together in that tiny piece of art. My chest tightened as I set it beside the can on the shelf.

I kept going, picking up a stack of photos, programs, and playbills. The programs and playbills went on the bookshelf; the photos went on the corkboard. There was one picture of me and Elijah from the night he talked me into going out with him in drag. I didn't look bad, didn't look good either—but I've seen worse. The picture sat with a playbill from the closing night of *Kinky Boots*, April 7, 2019. I stared at it—signed by Cyndi Lauper: *'Mark, Eli, cute couple. I see you'*—I'd forgotten he tried going by 'Eli' that year. I couldn't believe I'd never noticed he'd given me the signed copy. I remembered him clutching it to his chest like a prize the whole train ride home. He never let me see what she wrote. He must've switched them when I wasn't looking. My chest burned and ached at once. I wasn't sure how much more reminiscing I could handle.

Luckily, I was running out of time. My brother and sister would arrive soon for dinner. I'd have a fresh set of memories to stir up even more feelings I didn't want. I really wish that can of beer weren't empty right now. Without thinking about it, I tucked the precious playbill into my pocket and headed down to the kitchen to prepare myself and the table for company. Step one: find Mom's stash of emergency social-interaction gin.

Around five in the afternoon, Jefferson and Lexie pulled up to the house. They came without their families, carpooling together. Both were signs they weren't planning to stay long past dinner. They carried a small stack of takeout containers with them, more than we would need for a single meal. A relief, since I'd planned to toss a frozen casserole in the oven. It had been a couple of years since we were all in the same room at the same time—not since Dad's wake. I slugged the shot of gin, stashed the bottle, and braced for the worst—but hoped for the best.

The Fixer, The Maker, The Drag Entertainer

They walked into the house and came straight to the kitchen, where I was standing, mentally preparing myself. They muttered a quick hello, balancing a dozen Styrofoam containers between them. Once they landed them safely on the kitchen table, they both turned their attention to me in earnest.

"Hey, Mark," they said in unison.

"You look good, how are you?" Lexie said, giving me a warm hug.

"Hey Lexie, you're looking good too. I'm all right. Holding it together," I said, hugging her back.

"Where's Mom?" Jefferson asked, looking around in case he had missed her.

"Oh, I think she is lying down upstairs. I think she got tired of the couch," I answered.

"I'll go get her. Is she okay on the stairs?" Lexie said.

"She seems to be. I worry, but you know her," I answered as Lexie walked out of the kitchen.

"Hey, we brought food … obviously. Mediterranean fusion—basically, lamb kebabs and lemon rice, with spinach salad. Anyway, we brought you some extra, and we weren't sure if it was just you and Mom or if you'd have … company." Jefferson said, spreading out the containers on the table.

"Thanks, just the two of us," I said, pulling four plates out of the cabinet. "The leftovers will come in handy—that was thoughtful. How are you?"

"Good. Work's fine—same old contracts,' Jefferson said. pulling a handful of forks out of the drawer. "It's not exciting, but it has its interesting moments. I like it for some reason, and it keeps the family fed."

"How's your family? I haven't seen Ann or the kids in a while," I said, grabbing glasses and a pitcher of cold water from the fridge. "I expected they would come with you."

"They're good. I didn't want to overwhelm Mom before seeing how she—and you—were doing. They'll come next time."

"Good, I'd like to see them," I said, pulling a dusty bottle of wine from the pantry. "Think I should open two?"

"I'll take just one glass … maybe two. I still have to drive back to the city later," Jefferson said, taking the bottle from me to examine the label. "But there's no telling with Lexie."

"Jefferson!' Mom called from the bottom of the stairs, holding the railing with one hand and Lexie's arm with the other. She wasn't wearing her protective boot, so she half-hopped into the kitchen with Lexie's help. "You brought too much food!"

"Mom, where's your boot? The doctor said two weeks," I said, moving to her other side to help Lexie guide her to a chair. "Especially on the stairs. Come on."

"It was getting smelly, so I took a bath. Don't worry—I was careful," she said, patting my hand. "I'll put it back on later."

"All right, all right. Just be careful. Please," I said, pouring her a glass of water and setting a plate in front of her. "They brought lamb kebabs, lemon rice, and spinach salad."

"Sounds good. Thank you both. Jefferson, come give me a hug. How are you, dear?" Mom said, holding her arms out to her eldest son.

"Hi, Mom," Jefferson said, stepping into her hug. "You're welcome. It's nothing special—I know we brought too much."

"Mark, how are things going?" Lexie said, sitting down next to Mom.

"Not bad—things have been going smoothly. I left the university, so I'm here full time now."

"Mark! You didn't tell me that," Mom said, smiling with surprise, but her tone held a hint of regret.

"I only decided recently—haven't had a chance to tell you yet."

"Well, that's a good thing, right?" Lexie said, serving Mom a skewer of lamb and rice. "Sit down, and fill us in."

I sat down next to Jefferson, and we all ate while I filled them in on the orchard. I explained the accident could have been much worse, leaving out the cause. I had finished the repairs, and things should be in shape to get back to normal next week. Operations weren't seriously impacted, and Mom's injuries weren't severe— she's obviously healing well. Dinner talk was mostly procedural. They cared, but weren't interested in the details—as long as nothing was wrong. I hinted at some of the plans I was working out, which they found more interesting. But not as interesting as my personal life.

"Mom says you're dating someone. She wouldn't say much else. So come on, brother—spill it." Lexie said, waving her wine glass in my direction.

"Oh, yeah. Um … well, it's complicated right now," I said, pouring myself the last splash of wine left in the bottle. "But, her name is Viktoriya. She's a student in her final year, studying design—fashion and costume. She's incredible. She came here from Ukraine about five years ago. She bakes for her family's café, the Sunflower Kafe. She's a force of nature—one of the most amazing people I've ever met … And I'm also dating Elijah—who you know … Surprise."

"Yeah, that part's not really a surprise, brother," Jefferson said, slapping my back.

"No kidding. You forgot we lived with you," Lexie said, laughing at my shock.

"Damn it—was I the last to figure it out?" I said, exasperated.

"Sounds like it," Lexie laughed. "But dating both of them at the same time. That is surprising. Didn't think you had it in you. They are both good with that arrangement?"

"They are, or were—like I said, it's complicated right now. And what do you mean you didn't think I'd have it in me?" I said defensively. I stood and went to the pantry for a third bottle of wine. "Viktoriya and Elijah became really good friends, and it was kind of their idea. But like I said, Things got muddled after the accident—then tense. I didn't leave things the best way. I'm not sure I want to talk about it over dinner."

"Good thing dinner's over then," Jefferson said, stacking plates with a grin.

"Don't tease your brother," Mom said halfheartedly, smiling, enjoying the kitchen filled with her children again.

"Oh, we're not teasing … much. Come on, you two, let's take that bottle to the porch so you don't have to spill the details in front of Mom." Lexie said, standing up, taking the bottle out of my hand.

"Will you be okay, Mom? Do you want a hand to the couch?" I asked, hesitant to abandon our mom.

"Yes, go on. Catch up with your brother and sister. I'm going to pick at this salad," Mom said, waving her hands at me like she wanted a little peace and quiet for herself.

I followed Jefferson and Lexie out onto the porch, into the comfortably cool October evening. Lexie popped the cork and offered Jefferson a refill. He shook his head, so she poured herself another instead. Without asking, she topped off my glass too. The three of us took a moment to breathe in the night air. The aroma of apple trees drifted around us on the porch of our shared childhood home.

I didn't need a prompt; I just started. Once I started, the story spilled out faster than I could think. I started with the background they knew about Elijah, and what they didn't know about Viktoriya. She and I had flirted for more than a year before I found the courage and the opportunity to ask her out. How that night exploded with dramatic irony—Elijah's performance and his arrival at my door. The twists and turns as we all discovered ourselves—what we wanted—and how the three of us might work. Then came my mistakes—how I almost lost them both—and our visit here was meant to mend those bonds. But then the accident happened, and everything fell apart.

"So that's when it clicked with Elijah?" Lexie asked.

"Yeah—in retrospect, it should have clicked years ago. Here, look at this," I said, pulling the playbill signed by Cyndi Lauper out of my pocket, handing it to Lexie. "That was his. He never showed me what she wrote, then quietly swapped our copies and left this with me. I only noticed it today while I was unpacking."

"We thought you knew all along," Jefferson said, reading over Lexie's shoulder. "He really never showed you that Cyndi Lauper called you a 'cute couple?' This was six years ago."

"He was *that* patient with you. Why are you so worried you messed up?" Lexie asked, handing the precious playbill back to me. "Nobody waits six years just to walk away after one bad day."

"True—but Viktoriya … she may not be so quick to forgive," I said, tucking the playbill carefully into my pocket. "She might be patient too, but I don't know if she gives second or third chances easily."

"From how you've described her, she sounds unwilling to let go of what she wants," Jefferson said. "I've seen it before with clients. CEOs are different, sure, but I've seen them take big losses to hold on to something they want. And it sounds like you're something she wants."

"Yeah, we know you, Mark. You're a good person. Speaking as a woman—not your sister, we aren't going to let the good ones just walk away as easily as that," Lexie said, finishing her wine.

"I don't know how good a person I am," I said, bracing myself. "There's more about the accident—and Gale Barlow—I haven't told you."

I told them the entire story behind the accident. After we confronted Gale on this porch, he sabotaged the mill as an act of desperate retaliation. Then I explained how my confrontation with him ended—violently. He didn't mean for anyone to get hurt—but that didn't make it better. One punch and a clear reminder of what I had on him—that was enough to make him walk away for good. I had enough to ruin him financially and put him in jail. I made sure he knew that if he ever tried to come after us again, he wouldn't be a problem anymore.

"Holy shit. I never thought you could do something like that," Lexie said, staring at me wide-eyed. "I mean, God knows we're all capable of worse. I don't know if I'm more impressed by you confronting him, or your restraint."

"Thank you for dealing with him," Jefferson said, looking at me through fresh eyes. "I wish you'd let me know how bad it was. I could've helped. You've got to keep us in the loop more. God knows Mom won't."

I promised I'd do better at staying in touch with both of them. We finished the wine; Jefferson accepted a final half-glass. Lexie advised me to call Viktoriya and Elijah as soon as possible. Apologizing would be a good start. But more than that, I had to be patient. They were learning how to navigate a new relationship, too. Making it work was as much on them as it was on me. Relationships—especially messy ones—only stay alive if you keep talking, like fire needs air. If we didn't talk, we'd suffocate the fire. They were right, of course. And I hated how right they were, and how obvious their advice sounded in retrospect.

When the bottle was empty and the talk faded, they decided to head out. They helped Mom upstairs to her bed and cleared the table before heading home. I sat on the porch, watching their car disappear behind the trees, wondering if it was too late to call Viktoriya and Elijah.

Chapter 27

I watched Mark walk away without looking back. I was on my own in the search for Elijah and Viktoriya. Fortunately, I had a good idea of their typical schedules—it wasn't the needle-in-a-haystack ordeal it could've been. It was a Friday afternoon, so the odds were good Viktoriya was working, or drawing in the café. Kareem mentioned Elijah had the weekend off, which meant he was probably home—likely tinkering in his closet—since he wasn't with Mark. So it really came down to my memory of how to get to Elijah's house from the club—and, just my luck, I had a marvelous memory.

It took some fumbling through the maze of power lines before I remembered my way to Elijah's house. I arrived at Elijah's above-the-garage apartment through a light fixture in his kitchen. My victory was short-lived when I realized Elijah was not home. I could've let that discourage me, but it was far too early in the search for one minor setback to rattle me. It was doubtful I'd find any clues to Elijah's whereabouts in his apartment, so I moved on to try my luck with Viktoriya.

I wove through the power lines several blocks down the street to the Sunflower Kafe. I popped out through the neon "OPEN" sign in the window—immediately confronted by nothing. Only Viktoriya's favorite armchair sat there—looking almost conspiratorial, as if mocking me. I wouldn't let one snarky armchair get to me; Viktoriya was probably in the kitchen baking.

So, I found myself staring out of a stand mixer at an empty kitchen.

It was fine—no way three dead ends were going to stop me. At least Mark wasn't here to see this. If Viktoriya was not in her armchair with a sketchpad and coffee, and she wasn't baking in the kitchen, she *could* be anywhere. But it was Friday afternoon; she didn't have classes past noon today, she wouldn't be studying in the Alexander Library, and she wasn't with Mark. She was most likely upstairs at her sewing machine.

I wound my way up the wiring to Viktoriya's bedroom and emerged in a lamp on a table next to her door. Jackpot! Both Viktoriya and Elijah were here—score one for me. It appeared that Viktoriya was showing off the design project Mark and I had helped her with recently. From what I could gather, she'd been telling him about it, and this was her first chance to show it off.

I spotted Elijah's phone on the table just beneath the lamp, thanks to my detective skills and keen observation. While Elijah was fawning over the stitching of the seams, I slipped down into his phone to peek at his text messages—yes, I know it was invasive. But I had to find out if there were any important details I should know. And I couldn't just *ask* them. Still, I whispered an apology to Elijah and Viktoriya for this invasion of their privacy.

I found out that Elijah and Viktoriya had been talking every day since they left Mark at the orchard. At first, they were commiserating over their confusion and bruised feelings. Then they took turns venting their anger with Mark to each other. Which then devolved into a brief flash of anger with each other— until finally they started being honest. They'd both let jealousy get the better of them, and seeing each other with Mark pushed them over the edge. At least they both agreed that Mark must have felt like he was being torn in two, and after the accident, it was all too much for him.

After two days of that, they apologized and forgave each other. Elijah was the first to ask what Viktoriya thought went wrong, aside from their pointless jealousy. She wasn't exactly sure, except that she was confident it wasn't entirely Mark's fault. Rarely was any such conflict one-sided—and this one had three sides. She called it a conflict triangle. Elijah agreed and made several triangle-related jokes that needed a lot of work. This was around the time they both realized they missed talking to one another and that they had stopped when they started dating Mark. But neither of them remembered deciding to stop. They just did. And then they didn't mention Mark again.

It took me only a moment to digest a week's worth of texts. By then, Elijah had moved on from admiring the stitching to taking in the work as a whole. He stood back, staring intensely at the two dresses, as though he was working his way toward a difficult decision.

"Nope," Elijah said, tossing his hands up before planting them on his hips. "I can't find a single thing I don't like. Honestly, Viki, these are abso-fucking-lutely incredible. I'm completely gobsmacked."

"Thank you, Queenie," Viktoriya said, blushing and beaming with pride. "You see my story? 'Viktoriya transformed'—is what I call this. You see, Da?"

"Oh yes dear, I see it," Elijah said, nodding enthusiastically. "It's crystal clear. No explanation needed. It's beautiful—like you, my dear."

"You talk too much. Thank you," Viktoriya said, beaming. "My professor said, 'theme was a little unimaginative—but executed flawlessly.' I'm not sure I understand."

"Oh, I think they mean there are thousands, or millions, of stories *like* yours. Almost everyone's families here have a similar story at their roots. What I think they missed was how you took that common—almost universal—theme and shaped it to be uniquely yours. Do I need to go rough them up for you? They didn't give you a bad grade, did they?"

"No, no. Is no need. I got an A-minus. They are fair, and said many more nice things. I think I understand 'unimaginative' now. Do you see tiara? My favorite part."

"How could I miss it? I've been thinking of a way to slip it into my pocket."

"Oh, no. For that, I would hurt you. It is mine forever. Mark made it for me. I mean, he put it together from my drawing."

"Mark? *Mark* did that?! How? It's flawless."

"I do not know. But I will make him teach me. He couldn't explain after you called."

"After I called? … Oh. Mark was here that night."

"Da … we remember."

"This is what he was doing. This is what he was helping you with. *This* is why he missed my performance that night," Elijah said, turning inward as the reality of what really happened unfurled in front of him. "I never explained it to you—I was too selfishly hurt—I would have understood. Mark helped shape my performance that night."

"So, when he was helping you … he was supposed to be here … helping me with this. I see," Viktoriya said quietly, looking between her dresses and Elijah. "He never said."

"It was as much his performance as it was mine—he was proud. That's why it hurt so much—like I'm sure it hurt you when he didn't show up."

"Da. I think we were hard on him for this. I did not know about your show. I would like to see it. I also would have understood," Viktoriya said, looking at Elijah with deep empathy. "I would have gone with him. Put off my work for my friend."

"We really were hard on him for this," Elijah said, guilt-ridden anguish washing over his face as he sat down on Viktoriya's bed. "He didn't really do anything wrong—just a few careless mistakes. He wasn't selfish; he was recklessly selfless."

"Reckless?" Viktoriya asked.

"Yeah, he cared so much about helping us that he forgot everything else," Elijah said. "Ironically, that meant he forgot us too."

"Da," Viktoriya said, nodding slowly, digesting what Elijah had just said. "We should have helped."

"Sure—it's obvious now that you say it. I missed you. Why did we cut each other off?"

"I don't know. I don't remember *deciding* to," Viktoriya said, scrunching her face up.

"Same. Whatever the reason, it definitely didn't help, us or Mark. We should have kept up with each other."

"Da. We are partners—you and I—partners talk. We were not good partners."

"This is new for all of us. It's only natural we would stumble a bit. But Viktoriya, do you still want this?"

"Do I?" she said, sitting on the bed next to Elijah. She fell silent for what felt like a long time, while Elijah fidgeted beside her, waiting. "Da. Yes. I do."

"Good," Elijah responded. "Me too. So, now is as good a moment as any. I want to go see Mark tomorrow. I want you to come with me. I mean, we should go together."

"I don't know," Viktoriya said, looking unusually doubtful. "He told us to go. What if he meant it? We don't know *he* still wants *us*."

Just when it seemed everything was finally falling into place, the moment turned. This could be a disaster for all three of them. If they only knew what Mark was going through. If only I could tell them—but I could. I spoke to Gale. Why couldn't I speak to Viktoriya and Elijah? There is no reason I can't or shouldn't. I was even inside Elijah's phone. This would be easy. I let the wave of impulsivity wash over me, and I made Elijah's phone ring.

"What? I thought I had that on silent," Elijah said, sprinting to his phone. He stared at it, puzzled—it was ringing, but no caller ID appeared. He answered. "Hello?"

"Hi Elijah—okay, this is going to sound weird, but please don't hang up. You don't know me, but let's just say I'm a friend of Mark's. I'm sorry this is a little awkward, but I need to talk to you and Viktoriya. It's about Mark," I said, trying unsuccessfully not to sound like an idiot. "I promise, it's important."

Elijah stood silent for a moment. Then, he took the phone away from his ear and looked at Viktoriya.

"You have to hear this," he said, tapping the button for speakerphone. "I'm sorry, who is this?"

"My name's not important—but it's Eros if you need to know," I said, hearing my own voice through the speakerphone. *Is that what I sound like?* "Mark doesn't know I'm calling you—and we should probably keep it that way. I know it's a lot to ask, but will you trust me?"

"We hear you. But trust comes after," Viktoriya said, louder than necessary.

"Fair enough, Viktoriya," I replied. "I've been helping Mark over the past few days—mostly by talking with him. You should know that Mark moved out of his apartment today."

"He what?" Elijah said, genuinely surprised.

"He moved back home and even quit his job. Don't worry, Elijah. He left a box of your stuff at the club for you. Kareem said he would give it to Bob to keep safe," I said.

"I'm not worried about the stuff," Elijah said. "I mean, I'm glad he was considerate enough to do that."

"Why did Mark move?" Viktoriya asked.

"The farm, and his mom—she's going to be fine by the way. Mark's been going through a lot, and honestly he is only *just* holding it together," I said. "Today, when he moved out of the apartment, he said he was afraid to see you—afraid he wouldn't have the nerve to leave—as though he was going far away. He misses you both. Deeply. But he's terrified—convinced, really— that he's messed everything up beyond repair."

"That sounds like Mark," Elijah said, looking at Viktoriya as if to say, *I told you so.*

"But who are you?" Viktoriya said.

"That's a little hard to explain. Let's just say I'm a friend. Someday, I hope I can tell you everything—and we can properly meet. I wish I could now; I really do," I said, struggling to hold back how much I wanted to spill everything. But I knew that would jeopardize everything right now.

"Okay, but why should we believe you?" Elijah asked, rising to meet Viktoriya's skepticism.

"You shouldn't. You don't know me. Go see Mark and find out for yourself," I said, watching Viktoriya and Elijah blink back their surprise. "I probably shouldn't say this, but he's making plans for the orchard, and he needs your help. He said you are both better at turning his ideas into reality than he is."

"What do you say, Viktoriya? Come with me tomorrow?" Elijah said, looking at Viktoriya hopefully.

"Da. Da, we go save Mark from himself," Viktoriya said, smiling at Elijah.

"Do me two favors—don't tell Mark we talked, and don't let him off the hook," I said, cutting the line before they could answer. I already knew they would.

"That was—" Elijah started.

"Strange," Viktoriya finished for him. "Do you know this Eros?"

"No, never heard of them. Do you think we can trust them?"

"Somehow, I do. But we'll find out in the morning."

"So, enough about Mark. There's something else I want to talk to you about," Elijah said, turning toward Viktoriya. "Do you remember me talking about buying the club from Bob?"

"Yes, you mention it many times. I remember you were saving money."

"Right. The fundraiser took off—it actually went viral—and I raised more than enough. Mark even helped me put together a business plan to pitch to Bob, and he just said yes," Elijah said, grabbing Viktoriya's hands. "In the next few weeks, I'll be taking over ownership of the club, and leasing the building from Bob."

"This is amazing, Queenie!" Viktoriya shouted.

"I know! It's going to take a little while for everything to work out with Bob. He is going to move out and retire in San Francisco. He said—and I quote—He's 'too old and too gay to keep putting up with New Jersey's heat and snow.'" Elijah said, getting more and more excited. "I thought about moving in, but I don't really need the space. So, I think that apartment would make a better workshop—for a seamstress."

"Do you mean … me?" Viktoriya asked, cautiously matching Elijah's excitement. "A shop? For me?!"

"For you!" Elijah confirmed. "If you want it. A partnership. There are countless queens who need a designer—plus me. There are details we can—"

"YES!" Viktoriya shouted, jumping off the bed. "Yes! I have many ideas!"

"Okay, don't get too excited—it's not official yet," Elijah said, standing and taking her hands. "We'll talk more about it when Bob and I work out the details, and you can tell me about some of your ideas. But I should get home so I can pick you up in the morning-ish."

Viktoriya squealed and threw her arms around Elijah, squeezing him within an inch of his life. She laughed, kissed him seven times on the cheek, then stepped back. She took three deep breaths to compose herself.

"You are best, my friend," she said, restraining a barely contained giggle. "My partner. Go on, get home, don't forget your jacket. I'll see you in the morning—with coffee."

"*You're* the best, Viki," Elijah said, giving her one more squeezing hug. "I'll see you in the morning."

Elijah grabbed his jacket and dashed out the door, with me still inside his phone in his pocket. Tomorrow morning, we'd all give Mark the surprise of his life when we showed up.

Mark

I woke up on Saturday morning feeling foggy after last night. I was a little hungover and a touch dissociated, but underneath that, I felt good. It felt like there was clarity just beyond a veil that might lift at any moment—clarity that hadn't been there before. There wasn't much to do on the farm, but I was afraid of sitting idle. So today was the day I was finally going to fix the radio in the truck. It wasn't much, but it was something I could do, something that would feel good. It felt symbolic, like I was going to be here using this truck for the foreseeable future. I owned it, but this made it mine.

Maybe when I finished crawling around under the dash, I'd finally call Viktoriya and Elijah. I could apologize like I needed to. Profusely. I could beg them to come back. I might be comfortable doing that; at least it would be honest. Maybe we could just try to put the pieces back together. But I knew I couldn't force it. I don't want either of them to leave, but that's not up to me. The more I thought about it, the closer I came to talking myself out of it. And the more those thoughts distracted me, the worse I got at keeping the wiring straight—it was only four color-coded wires, so how could I keep connecting them wrong?

I was finishing up the wiring for the fourth time when I heard a car pull up. I wasn't expecting anyone or any deliveries, but it wouldn't have been the first time I forgot something, so I didn't think much of it. I was getting ready to shimmy out of the awkward position I was in with my feet hanging out the passenger side door when a familiar voice rang in my ear.

"Mark! Mark, get out from under there," Eros said in my ear, making me jump and crack my head on the underside of the dashboard. "Oh, sorry, didn't mean to startle you. But you should climb out from under there. Someone is here to see you."

"Ow. Eros? What?" I said, sliding out of the truck, checking my forehead for blood. "How are you here?"

I looked up and saw Viktoriya and Elijah climbing out of his car. They hadn't seen me yet, so thankfully, they didn't see me roll out of the truck like a duck stuck on its back, probably with a welt on my forehead. I dropped to the ground, ducking behind my truck in full-blown panic. I don't think the clothes I was wearing had seen a wash for weeks, and I had no idea what my hair looked like. I was positive that if they saw me right now, they would turn around, pretending they'd never known me.

"Eros! What is going on?" I muttered under my breath.

"Oh, right. Well, Viktoriya and Elijah are here to help you out," Eros said, obviously not telling me the whole truth. "Look, just stop thinking for five seconds and go hear what they have to say."

"Seriously, you couldn't have given me a five-minute warning? Just look at me—I'm a mess," I said, reaching for the truck's side mirror to check my reflection.

"Okay, fair point—that one's on me. I can at least fix your hair," Eros said as I watched my hair smooth out in the mirror. "There, it's not perfect, but it's much better."

"Thank you," I said, slowly standing up, trying to think of what to say.

"Mark!" Viktoriya shouted, sprinting toward me the second she spotted me.

"Viki, what happened to playing it cool?" Elijah shouted through a laugh.

I must've hit my head harder than I thought. This couldn't be real—I had to still be under the dash, unconscious, hallucinating. Any second I'd wake up with pliers stabbing me in the ass.

"Mark, you should see the look on your face—like you don't think this is real," Eros's voice teased in my ear. I blinked and tried to shake the cobwebs from my head. "Well, it is. Surprise. Now snap out of it."

Viktoriya's arms wrapped around my neck in a hug so enthusiastic it ended in a tackle. We fell to the ground together, which made her squeeze me even tighter. I opened my eyes and saw Elijah standing over us.

"Hi, Mark. Do you two need a minute?" Elijah chuckled, taking in the ridiculous sight of us tangled on the ground.

"Elijah? Viktoriya? You're really here? I think I hit my head," I said as Viktoriya released her grip, and Elijah helped us both to our feet.

"Da. We are here," Viktoriya said. "To talk—no, to help. Well ... mostly talk."

"Well, I think the paper-thin pretense already crumbled. But yeah, we're here to help out. But—yeah, mostly to talk," Elijah said.

"Oh my God, I missed you both so much," I said, pulling them both into as strong a hug as I could muster. "I was going to call. I mean I wanted to. I just didn't know how. But you're here—wait, did you say you're here to help?"

"Yes. We were going to show up, play it cool, say we're here to help clean up the mess we left behind. Then work our way to talking. It was all going to be a dramatic display of teamwork wrapped in a romantic gesture. But then Viki tackled you before I could, and so here we are," Elijah explained in an overly dramatic fashion. I'm a little surprised he didn't include stage directions, too.

"That sounds exactly like you. Come on—you can help me feed the goats," I said, winking at Elijah.

"Oh no. Not the—"

"GOATS!" Viktoriya shouted, shaking Elijah. "Yes! We help feed goats, da?"

"Did I already say I missed you two—and that I love you both?" I said, my face hurting from smiling. "Come on, we keep the feed in the guesthouse garage—which I want to show you—because that's where I'm going to be living."

"In the garage of that old guesthouse? What, are you giving the rest of the house to those mean goats?" Elijah said, giving me a little shove with his shoulder.

There are plenty of things in this world I still don't understand—and how the three of us slipped right back into rhythm the moment they showed up is one of them. I remembered what Mom had said that night, drugged up in the hospital, handing out sage relationship advice like greeting cards. The three of us were like magnets—drawn together, as if we belonged. It was almost as if the past week had never happened. I knew we still had a potentially difficult discussion ahead, but I wasn't afraid of that anymore.

Together—not quite hand in hand—we walked to the small guesthouse. In the garage, we kept a large bin of alfalfa pellets, and some other assorted dried fruits and vegetables, which made a nice treat. We didn't need to feed them often—they foraged just fine—but it felt good to make sure their diet stayed varied and healthy. And honestly, it was just fun to interact with them. I guess you could say I thought of our goats as pets more than livestock. When I was younger, my brother, sister, and I named them all. I wasn't sure if any in this herd still had names, maybe Viktoriya and Elijah would help me name them.

We filled two buckets with feed in the garage and headed into the orchard where I'd last seen the goats. I whistled and shook a bucket, and within seconds, a dozen goats of different sizes, colors, and breeds surrounded us. One of the older goats kept its distance from Elijah, who was hesitantly offering handfuls of feed to the hungry goats. I warned Viktoriya not to set her bucket down or she'd be swarmed—an idea that seemed to thrill her. She squeaked, laughing as she made instant friends. Even Elijah started enjoying himself, finding common ground with his former nemesis over a large handful of raisins.

As we fed and played with the goats, the conversation flowed easily. I told them what had finally brought me home for good. It felt ridiculous to call it a birthright—but that's exactly what it was. The accident was just a sharp reminder that I had abdicated this responsibility for too long—which my family indulged. I knew that if I had decided this was not something I wanted, they wouldn't begrudge that decision.

Viktoriya shared the overwhelming success of her design project—the one I'd helped her complete. That filled me with a pride that had nothing to do with my minor contribution—and everything to do with her. Her drive, vision, and creativity—I felt proud simply to stand in her orbit. Plus, I was absolutely overjoyed at her success, not that I had any doubt about the outcome.

Then Elijah dropped the bombshell that his crowdfunding campaign had gone viral. He raised more than enough capital to buy the club from Bob, but also had a substantial reserve to kick-start operations. On top of that news, Bob had agreed to sell the club and—thanks to our business plan—had agreed to lease the building to Elijah at a reasonable discount. But that was not the only shocking news he had. Elijah explained that he'd offered Viktoriya Bob's soon-to-be vacant apartment as a workshop, and that the two of them were planning to form a business partnership.

Eros was humble enough to point out that they only played a minor role in facilitating those wishes. They helped get the boulder rolling down the hill, as they put it. Again, I was awash in joyous pride for their success, such that I could feel tears welling in the corners of my eyes.

I filled in the details of the accident they both witnessed. Starting with how minor Mom's injuries had been, and how she should fully recover in a few more weeks. Then I launched into the tale of how Gale sabotaged the mill, and my retribution. Both Elijah and Viktoriya stared at me with a strange mix of pride, admiration, and wonder—layered with a touch of shock, and beneath that, outrage and disappointment.

Not at me, but at missing the opportunity to participate in the dismantling of Gale Barlow. I couldn't dispute the fact that it would have been much more intimidating had they been there— as they should have been.

After we finished feeding the goats and catching up with each other, we carried the empty buckets back to the guesthouse garage. After putting the buckets away, I led them into the guesthouse— the place I'd decided to make my home. It was not a particularly large space, but with three bedrooms and a living room, it was three or four times larger than my old apartment. It needed some love and attention, but it was well maintained.

We congregated in the small kitchen. Elijah and I leaned on the counter, while Viktoriya sat on the island opposite us. I told them I had only decided to move into the guesthouse last night, so for now it was mostly empty except for a couch, table, and bed. Unpacking made it clear this was more than a move—it was proof I'd long since outgrown my old life. On a practical level, I had choices. I could stay in my old room, which would be comfortable, but would feel like being a permanent guest. I could have taken over a larger bedroom in the house, but that felt presumptuous. I would take up space that Jefferson's and Lexie's families use when they visit.

"I don't know why I felt the need to justify taking over this guesthouse. It used to be busy, but it's been empty for years. I think maybe I'm just dancing around the real reason."

"Da? What reason is that?"

"Well, I guess I was hoping this might be enough space— someday—for the three of us," I said.

"Mark? That's a big step," Elijah said.

"No—well, yes. I just meant, not right away … only if it ever felt right for all of us. I know I'm putting the cart before the horse."

"Sometimes you need cart first—to know how many horses you need," Viktoriya said, placing her fists on her hips with mock authority.

"Hard to argue with that logic, Mark."

"I guess that means we should address the horse in the room. I love you both. I want—with every fiber of my being—to make this work. I think we're all better together," I said. "I know I messed things up—badly. I made so many mistakes, but I—"

"Slow down, Mark," Elijah said, grabbing my shoulders gently, wordlessly reminding me it's okay to leave air in the conversation. "Viktoriya and I have been talking, too."

"Remember to breathe, Mark," Eros whispered. "Trust. Listen."

"Da. We agree. We both want this; we both love you. Da, Elijah?"

"Well, yes. I was going to lead up to that, but why beat around the bush?" Elijah sighed, grinning at both me and Viktoriya. "Because if we don't all want this to work, talking through all of our mistakes would just be a waste of time."

"Did I hear that right?" I said, my heart turning somersaults in my chest, hopeful I understood what I had just heard. "You both said you still want this—please don't tell me I misheard that. But you said, 'all of *our* mistakes,' just then?"

"Da. Queenie and I talked. You make many mistakes, and so did we. Elijah and I forgot to talk."

"We should have helped you. Elijah said you were … what was it?"

"Recklessly selfless."

"Da. That. Mark, you do not say *'no'* to us. You should sometimes."

"Not too often—only when you need to. But Viki's right. We stopped talking to each other. I forgot to tell her about my shows, and she forgot to tell me she needed help with her project. Making this relationship work isn't all on you—we let you take that on, and it was unfair."

"I'm not sure what to say. It feels almost redundant to apologize now—but I'm still sorry," I said, unable to hide my elation. "I don't know if I like to think of it as '*sharing*' each other, but I can't think of a better word right now."

"Yes, what Elijah said. Why beat a bush? We make mistakes. You make mistakes. We forgive each other because we love each other. Now—we share. Come Mark," Viktoriya said, jumping down from the countertop. She took me and Elijah by the hand. With a smirk of mischievous impatience, she tugged both our hands as she began walking out of the kitchen. "Show us bed. We practice sharing you now—together."

Chapter 28

Viktoriya led Elijah and me into one of the three vacant bedrooms. The only thing that made it recognizable as a bedroom was a solitary queen-size bed with pale-blue sheets and four pillows. My heart pounded, caught somewhere between excitement and fear of what might happen next.

"I think I see where this is going. I'll leave you to it," Eros whispered. "Pace yourself, Mark."

We stopped a few steps inside, and Viktoriya turned to face us. For a long moment, the three of us just stood there, silent and searching.

"I want this. Is okay, da?" Viktoriya asked softly.

"Viki, I don't know … I'd be lying if I said I'd never thought about it. But I'm not sure I'm ready," Elijah said, his hesitation obvious. "Still, yes, I'm willing to try if Mark is."

"I …" The words caught in my throat as secret fantasies flickered through my mind. I wanted to say yes, but fear held me still. "I've never … but I do want this."

"Good. First for all of us," Viktoriya said with a nervous laugh. She took a small step closer. "We go slow, da? Is acceptable to stop anytime."

"Here's to two firsts for me," Elijah said with a shaky smile, pulling off his shirt.

"I love you," I said, looking at them both, my voice trembling despite myself. I pulled my shirt off and dropped it on the floor.

Viktoriya stepped forward and, without breaking eye contact, unbuckled my belt, unbuttoned my jeans, and slowly unzipped them. When she let go, my pants dropped, pooling around my boots. We got the order of operations wrong again—pants before boots. Now I couldn't run away even if I wanted to. Before I could do or say anything about it, she dropped to her knees and began untying the laces of my boots.

"Now you take off Queenie's pants," she said, looking up at me. "I like to watch."

As Elijah stepped toward me, I could see his chest rising and falling. He was nervous. I reached out to him. I touched his chest and let my fingertips travel down his body. I fumbled with the button on his pants through trembling fingers. As I slid the zipper down, he winked and kicked off his shoes. Viktoriya smiled up at us and helped me step out of my boots and pants, before reaching up and helping Elijah's pants slide off his legs.

She stood and unbuttoned her skirt, letting it fall to the floor. She kept her boots on, which granted her an effortless air of power and authority. None of us had dressed for an occasion like this. We stood dressed only in unattractive underwear—the kind you wear when the possibility of being seen in them is unlikely. Yet there was something deeply human and moving in that unplanned simplicity—it made the moment feel honest. The allure of this mundanity, which illuminated this spontaneous act, was far more arousing than anything I could imagine. It wasn't rehearsed or planned—it was real. And that made it impossible to resist.

We hesitated, unsure and awkward, yet drawn together by something undeniable. Elijah exhaled sharply, as if a decision had just settled inside him. He stepped toward Viktoriya and kissed her lips tentatively. It was more than a friendly peck, but not by much. A flicker of jealousy caught me off guard, and I realized this must be what they'd felt last week. I held that spark for a moment, acknowledged it, and let it go as Elijah and Viktoriya broke away from their kiss.

"Hmm. That didn't feel quite right," Elijah said with a slight twinge of dissatisfaction. "Not wrong, just empty."

"Da. Nothing there. Nice, but no fire," Viktoriya said with a similar hint of disappointment. "But you have good lips."

"So do you, Viki," Elijah said with a smile.

"Why?" I asked, although I was sure I knew the answer.

"It felt right to try—to push past my discomfort. I was curious. It's like testing the water before a shower," Elijah said. "I'm comfortable with it now."

I stepped into their arms, pulling both Viktoriya and Elijah to me. I kissed them both deeply in turn, finding the fire that was missing from Elijah and Viktoriya's kiss. Our mutual exploration of each other's bodies began slowly, with deliberate touches. For the moment, the three of us remained in each other's arms as much as possible.

Their hesitation melted almost as quickly as it had come. We inched away from each other and discarded our uninspired underwear, taking in the soft vulnerability of each other's bodies. Elijah and I both knelt to help Viktoriya out of her boots. As soon as she stepped free onto equal footing, standing exposed before us, Elijah stood—leaving me kneeling, subservient, before them both. I've never resented having only one mouth so much in my life.

Hours later, we all collapsed onto the bed. Our sweat-covered bodies were entwined, glinting in the sunset light streaming through the windows. Physically spent and emotionally sated, we lay together, panting until sleep claimed us.

****Eros****

I left Mark, Viktoriya, and Elijah to their own devices when I saw the direction they were going. Okay, I might have lingered a little. There was something captivating about the way their bodies were entwined. They moved around each other like dancers learning a new rhythm—hesitant at first, then bolder, slowly drinking each other in, embracing the intoxication. When I left, I occupied myself with my tree project. Since Mark gave me only one tree to work with, I had to take my time. Killing it would be … inconvenient.

They lay tangled in bed beneath a single sheet. Both Viktoriya and Elijah were curled around Mark. Six legs entwined and arms embracing, they looked inseparable. As they woke, each had a moment of discovery, followed by a smile, before they closed their eyes again. It was as though none of them wanted to be the first to wake up. Eventually, each realized the others were awake—but no one wanted to break the silence just yet. Almost simultaneously, they all reacted to the physical strain they had put their bodies through the previous afternoon, evening, and night. The need for caffeine and a couple of painkillers quickly overruled any lingering desire for a morning encore.

"If this is what our future could look like, I think I could check that 'die happy box' now," Mark said, suppressing a yawn. "The only thing preventing this from being a perfect morning is the fact that there is absolutely no coffee in here. And no chance of it. Meaning we're going to have to leave this house for coffee."

"Two things," Viktoriya added. "You have no blanket. Is chilly. You let go, I freeze."

"Three things," Elijah added. "No curtains on your windows. Though it might make someone's day, it's still something to consider."

"I don't think there's much chance of us getting spotted through the window by a random passerby. At least not today," Mark said, laughing. "But I'll put curtains on the list for this place. As much as I hate to say it, we need to get up. There should be coffee in the house."

"Da … about last night—" Viktoriya said, hesitating, leaving her thought incomplete.

"Absolutely no serious conversation before coffee," Elijah said, rolling out of bed.

"True. I think we all want to talk about it," Mark said, crawling out from under the bedsheet. "But we need clear heads."

"Then coffee first," Viktoriya agreed, climbing off the bed.

For a moment, they all stood fully nude around the empty bed, temptation hanging in the daylight air. Whatever shame they'd carried the day before had burned away in the night. Still, they each stole glances at one another as they gathered their clothes from the floor. I noticed Mark's gaze linger on Elijah and Viktoriya as they bent to pick up their clothes. Of course, Mark's lack of subtlety did not go unnoticed.

"I've seen you look at a plate of pancakes and a cup of coffee just like that," Elijah teased. "Hungry, are we?"

"Oh? Hungry again already?" Viktoriya said, turning to face Mark. "But you ate so much last night. We look delicious, yes?"

"Mm-hmm … I—uh," Mark stammered, caught off guard by his own involuntary reaction.

"Yeah … you two … I mean—uh—"

"Coffee first," Viktoriya reminded him.

"I can't blame him," Elijah said. "Viki, you have a *deadly* body. If I were attracted to you—no offense—I'd be in heaven right now."

"Thank you, Elijah," Viktoriya replied. "You also have a … sickening body."

"Thank you!" Elijah said. "Mark never said anything so sweet. Mark, you can learn from Viki—and she needs to hear it too."

"Hey, I try. It just feels so disingenuous somehow when I say it. Or I end up thinking too hard, and then the moment passes while I overthink what to say—" Mark said, mounting an honest defense.

"Da. Is okay. I like to hear it, but Mark shows me in *other* ways I understand," Viktoriya said, stepping into her practical panties.

"Fair enough," Elijah said while slipping on his underpants. "Then it'll be my job to give you the compliments, our dear Mark, means to. You can do the same for me. And together we can compliment Mark and make him feel uncomfortably seen."

"DA! Mark, you look nice with no pants."

"Mark, you should wear shirts less—or never."

Mark slowly pulled on his boxer briefs, then collapsed in on himself dramatically. He made a show of swooning and falling to the floor. He groaned as though he had just been injured.

"Ah! Why do you like this? Compliments feel … like burning."

"Ha! Cute, Mark. Fine—your beard desperately needs a trim," Elijah said, laughing. "And your feet look weird."

"Honestly? That's better," Mark said through laughter, echoed by both Viktoriya and Elijah. "Oh, God, I haven't laughed this much in days. Come on, let's get coffee."

They laughed together as they dressed, and I witnessed one of the rare, fleeting golden moments in the universe. They were genuinely happy together. They belonged to each other. They earned this, not by overcoming or fighting adversity, but simply by opening themselves to the possibility of joy. I hated to interrupt, so I didn't, but as they walked from the guesthouse to Mark's childhood home, I quietly whispered to let him know I was there.

Mark

The aroma of freshly brewed coffee swam around the kitchen. The soft dripping of the coffee maker called to us. So intoxicating was that siren's call, all three of us failed to notice Mom sitting at the kitchen table, silently revering her mug of coffee. I picked three mismatched mugs from the dish rack next to the sink and set them on the counter. I poured coffee into each mug and set the carafe back on the warming plate.

"Cream and sugar are here on the table," Mom said.

"Mom!" I jumped. "I didn't see you there. Startled me."

"Sorry, dear," Mom said after taking a sip of her coffee. "Morning … you three. You look—well, it looks like you need coffee, and for me to not ask any questions. I'll give you some space. Elijah, Viktoriya, it's good to see you again … and to see you all together again."

Mom walked out of the kitchen gingerly with her coffee to the couch in the other room. I set a mug of coffee down in front of Elijah and Viktoriya before sitting down at the table with mine. They both hummed their gratitude and pulled the mugs toward themselves eagerly. Our mugs rang as we all stirred in our preferred quantities of sugar and cream. We all sat around the table, sipping our coffee, letting its warmth wash away the remaining morning fog from our minds.

"This is nice," Viktoriya hummed. "About last night, how do you both feel?"

"Amazing," I said.

"If memory serves, we all enjoyed ourselves. A few times," Elijah said. "I have no regrets."

"Da. I am glad," Viktoriya said, smiling. "I liked it very much."

"How would you both feel if it never happened again?" I asked.

"I would be okay," Elijah said. "Maybe a little sad. It was a good experience."

"Like holiday meal—it doesn't make holiday, it just makes it more special," Viktoriya said. "Good all year but is best because it's saved."

"I guess that's one way to put it. I could happily do that every day—not literally—but it feels like something to save for special occasions," I said.

"Da. Special, like cake," Viktoriya agreed.

"Hm. Well, sounds like we get to have cake and eat it, too," Elijah said with a perfectly straight face.

His straight-faced delivery didn't last long as both Viktoriya and I erupted in laughter that started as knowing giggles. Through the laughter, we all knew the question was settled. There would be many recurrences of last night in our future.

"It sounds like you've worked out whatever it was that kept you three apart," Mom said, gingerly walking back into the kitchen. "Don't mind me. I just need another cup."

"We don't mind at all, Eileen," Elijah said. "Sit—let us get the coffee for you."

"Thank you, dear," Mom said, sitting down at the table. Viktoriya took the empty mug from her hand, and I stood to grab the coffee carafe to refill it. "Thank you, Mark, Viktoriya. So, you made up?"

"Da. We made up," Viktoriya said, casting a smile toward me, and a wink to Elijah.

"It took a little time to understand," I said. "And a little good advice—thank you."

"Good. I hope that means I will see you, both, around here more," she said between sips.

"Yes, much more," Viktoriya said. "Mark said guesthouse has room for us all. I might never leave. I will name your goats."

"Oh, Mark used to do that—I think a few of them are still around," Mom said, gazing at the ceiling as if recalling a distant memory. "We never could keep collars on them. Mark, do you remember some of the names?"

"Oh, there have been a lot," I said, looking up at the same spot on the ceiling, searching for the memory. "Let's see ... there was Vincent—Van Goat, of course— The Great Goatsby, Balthazar, Robin Goodfellow, Rincewind, and Bottom. Then there were Rosencrantz and Guildenstern—though, fittingly, they're dead. There must be a dozen more I've forgotten."

"You can't remember? I think you're just too embarrassed," Elijah said. "How could you forget Mr. Tumnus—or Lady Ga-Goat?"

"I would never forget Lady Ga-Goat," I said adamantly. "She was very special."

"Silly names. I like them," Viktoriya said, squeezing my hand on the table. "We can name them together."

"Good, they need names," Mom said, sipping her coffee. "So, Mark, you have decided to move into the guesthouse? I guess I should get used to calling it your house from now on. You know there's room here—but I understand you need your own space, Mark. Still, I'm glad that old house is getting some use again."

"Yeah, I've outgrown my old room," I said, shifting a little awkwardly. "I know there's space here, but I want to leave room for Jefferson and Lexie when they bring the kids. And, yes, I got used to having my own space."

"That's sweet of you," Mom said. "You'll need some furniture, that space is pretty barren."

"These two can help me hunt for furniture," I said, smiling at Viktoriya and Elijah. "They know all the secret secondhand stores and thrift shops. Plus, that will make convincing them to stick around easier."

"Devious," Elijah said, slapping the table. "What do you think, Viki?"

"Da! I know where to find a couch!" Viktoriya said, slapping the table like Elijah. "Devious indeed."

"So ... you two might be ... roommates?" Mom said with a raised eyebrow.

"Mom, don't push, okay? We're figuring things out. And this is one of those things we don't need to rush."

"Okay, okay," Mom said, waving her hands dramatically. I wondered whether she'd picked that up from Elijah—or if he'd picked it up from her. "So, Elijah, how are your performances going?"

"Great—that's some news you'll like," Elijah said, taking Eileen's hands excitedly. "I'm buying the Queen's Head—the club. *And* Viki is going to open a shop upstairs—custom dresses, gowns, costumes, and my own *personal* fashion designer."

"Viktoriya, that sounds fantastic! Are you graduating soon, too?" Mom said, releasing one of Elijah's hands and reaching across the table to Viktoriya. "I would love to see your work. Next time you come over, maybe?"

"Da, da. I graduate soon, and will have a workshop of my own," Viktoriya said, squeezing Mom's hand. "I will bring some to show you."

"I can't wait," Mom said. "Mark, what about you, dear. What plans do you have brewing in that head of yours?"

"What makes you think I have ideas brewing?"

"Because I'm your mother."

"I've been thinking about hosting a small harvest festival— not this year; it's too late for that—but next year. We can have a band, some performances, maybe a few carnival games. And food, apples and apple-adjacent food, naturally."

"I can bake Yabluchnyk—Ukrainian apple cake. You will love it, da?"

"I can call in some favors—and I'm sure I'll rack up a few more by next year. We can do apple-themed drag. Oh, it's going to be amazing."

"See, this is why I need you two," I said, reaching across the table to squeeze Elijah and Viktoriya's hands appreciatively.

"That sounds fantastic—a lot of work, but if anyone could do it, it's you three." Mom beamed at us, sipping her coffee.

"Okay, that was dangerously close to a compliment," I said, standing up. "We should get going. These two are going to help me carry some boxes—and measure for a new couch."

"All right, I have a book to finish anyway," Mom said, waving her hands toward me as if she were shooing a dog out of the kitchen.

I led Elijah and Viktoriya out of the kitchen and upstairs to my old bedroom. The remnants of my childhood and adolescence fascinated Viktoriya, while Elijah was amused by his own memories of the space. And I struggled to contain my embarrassment at having the evidence of my younger self on full display. The relics of my youth felt absurd—needlessly shameful under someone else's gaze. I pointed out the boxes that were taking up the space, and the unpacked bags of clothes. Once we got those out of the room, there would be enough room to pack everything else up. The entire operation should take only a couple of hours—if I could keep Elijah and Viktoriya focused on the task instead of exploring every poster and knickknack.

"You have *so much*," Viktoriya said slowly, looking at each poster and picture tacked to my walls. "I want to know about it all."

"So much garbage, you mean," Elijah chimed in. "Mark has a long habit of holding onto junk out of sentimental attachment. It's sweet, but sentimentality should have limits."

"Uh huh, I guess I should get rid of some stuff. Like this old playbill," I said, casually picking up the autographed *Kinky Boots* playbill. "It's just silly to hang onto things like this—"

"Playbill? Mark ... is that—?" Elijah said, his voice dropping, eyes widening as he locked onto the papers in my hand. "*Kinky Boots*! You still have it—did you ever look at it?"

"Of course, I still have it," I said, handing it to Viktoriya, who was watching curiously. "I looked at it for the first time yesterday. You switched our playbills on the train, didn't you? What was your plan—to wait and see if I'd say something?"

"Honestly ... yeah. I was too scared to say anything back then. I hoped you would see it, and then ... we might talk about it," Elijah said, shuffling awkwardly as though he was ill-prepared to confront his old vulnerability. Viktoriya and I said nothing, holding space for his silence. "And when you didn't mention it, I assumed you saw what she wrote and thought it was a ridiculous joke ... or something like that. God. I can't believe you never even looked at it. I tortured myself for weeks—over nothing."

"Cute couple," Viktoriya said, reading the autograph out loud. "I agree. This needs a frame. We hang on wall. But empty Chernihivske can? Mark—is trash."

"Oh no, that can is a sacred relic. A memento from the night you two changed my life," I said, accepting the playbill back from Viktoriya. I reverently set it on the shelf, next to the empty beer can, and exhaled. "If this playbill gets framed, that can gets a shrine. Come on you two, we have plenty of time for show-and-tell of all my embarrassing adolescent memorabilia later. Let's get these boxes—and us—out of here."

"We will have to postpone the show-and-tell. I have to get back home to get ready for work soon," Elijah said, picking up the closet box he could reach. "I *really* need a shower."

"Da. I have class in morning," Viktoriya added, picking up a box. "We do show-tell soon."

The Fixer, The Maker, The Drag Entertainer

"Of course," I said, trying to hide my disappointment. Somehow, for a moment, I forgot they had lives outside me. When we were together, it only felt like time stood-still, time continued its relentless march forward. "I'm sorry, that should have occurred to me. Let's get these boxes to the guest—my—house before you two have to leave."

"Now I understand why you told me not ask questions while you were packing up your apartment," Eros said in my ear unexpectedly, making me jump.

"Shit, Eros, you startled me," I said out loud in front of Viktoriya and Elijah.

"Eros?" Viktoriya asked.

"Mark?" Elijah said, eyeing me like I was hiding a juicy secret.

"I ... uh, well ... I can't," I stammered, grasping for a plausible excuse. "Can't really explain."

"Mark, there's something I should tell you," Eros whispered.

"Eros is your friend?" Viktoriya asked, setting down the box and glancing at Elijah. "Mark's friend who called us?"

"They called you?" I asked, unable to conceal my shock.

"That would be the 'something' I should tell you," Eros admitted, their voice tinged with shame. "I'm sorry—they were wondering if you wanted them back. Please don't be mad."

I closed my eyes as conflicting emotions surged—relief and gratitude tangled with frustration and shame. I'd always known I couldn't keep Eros a secret forever—not that I wanted to— though this wasn't how I wanted the truth to come out. I braced myself for the worst and hoped for the best. I pulled out my phone, turning it over in my hand, unsure if this was a good idea. I set it down on a box and sat on the bed, bracing for a long conversation.

"This is an interesting story, and it's going to sound crazy coming from me. So, I think we should sit down, and my friend should do most of the telling," I said, glancing down at my phone.

"Is that a cue?" Eros whispered in my ear.

"Yes, that's a cue," I said out loud. "Viktoriya, Elijah, meet Eros."

"Your phone?" Elijah said, as though he thought I might have lost my grip on reality.

"Not his phone," Eros said. Their voice sounded thin through the weak speakers. "I'm currently inside Mark's phone. Hello again, Elijah and Viktoriya—I'm Eros."

Eros

This was another first for me—I had never been introduced to anyone before. The setting wasn't ideal, and there was absolutely no fanfare. No band, no grand hall—just a low-quality phone speaker carrying my manufactured voice. But Mark was counting on me not to make him look crazy, so I swallowed my disappointment. The conversation that was about to unfold would be a challenge. I desperately wanted to tell Viktoriya and Elijah everything, but I was now acutely aware that they had somewhere else to be soon—and I would not make the mistake of devaluing their time again.

"You're Eros. *Not* Mark's phone, but inside it," Elijah said, looking at Mark's phone skeptically. "You don't mean *on* the phone, right? Like, you aren't calling from somewhere?"

"No, not a phone call. I'm literally inside his phone," I said, realizing how strange that sounded. It had been much easier to explain when I was speaking from inside an old bronze lamp.

"You're like AI program?" Viktoriya asked, perceptive as ever.

"No, but I can understand why you'd think that," I said. "Mark, help me out?"

"Oh no. This is too much fun to watch after going through this myself," Mark said, laughing at my helpless discomfort. "You should start by explaining how we met, and what you are."

"Mark? This is joke, da?" Viktoriya looked at Mark with a furrowed brow, half-confused and half-concerned.

"It's not a joke Viktoriya," I said. "Mark's right, I should tell you what I am and how he and I met."

"Okay then, tell us," Elijah said, sitting down on the bed next to Mark, Viktoriya sitting on the opposite side.

"Right—no pressure. I won't be able to cover everything before you have to leave. So, I'm going to try to briefly explain my eternal and immortal existence," I said, employing every shred of restraint I learned over the past several weeks.

I recounted what you already know—how I found Mark from inside my old bronze lamp, which was stuck inside the office of a philosophy professor. Mark's initial skepticism when I revealed myself to him led to a series of questions and tests—which were unusual but clever—to better understand my motives. I didn't even recognize he was challenging me until he finished. Then, he compassionately granted me my freedom without a second thought of the possible consequences.

I gave them an abridged version of what I am. With much more truth and less self-aggrandizement and exaggeration of my abilities, I told Viktoriya and Elijah how I role-played as a genie. The mythology I'd invented—and even some of my mistakes. I hoped Mark didn't feel hurt now that he'd heard that I'd exaggerated and embellished what I could do. But at the time I thought I was arguing for my freedom, and I only hope he understands.

Then I briefly explained that I'd been tagging along with Mark. I tried my best to help him, though I occasionally—and unintentionally—caused problems. But I did my best to make it right without overt interference. I glossed over some of the finer details of my past, but left out nothing essential. I didn't mention the private conversations I had with Mark, or the intimate moments I'd witnessed—I wanted to respect his privacy. I couldn't tell whether Viktoriya and Elijah believed me. They kept exchanging glances with Mark that I couldn't read—was it doubt, disbelief, scorn, or pity? For the first time, I understood how Mark must have felt—nervous, exposed, and afraid of being misunderstood.

"Viki, you heard all that too, right?" Elijah said, looking at Viktoriya as though he were questioning his sanity.

"Da. All of it," Viktoriya said, nodding her head slowly.

"I know the feeling," Mark said. "It's crazy, but real. Eros is an incredible friend to have, I don't know if we would be here without their help."

"We do not beat a gift horse," Viktoriya said, nudging Mark with her shoulder. "Eros, thank you for helping Mark come to us."

"Beat a gift horse?" Elijah said, patting Viktoriya's hand. "But I agree. If you helped steer Mark in the right direction, I can't thank you enough."

"Oh, it was nothing. Really," I said, feeling as though I might cry—if only I had eyes and tear ducts. "It has been—and will continue to be—my pleasure. I really mean that; I've never felt so fulfilled."

"I have one question," Elijah added. "Can you help me with my heels?"

"Yes—and no. I can reinforce them, help mold them to your feet," I said, sensing the opportunity to cast a little shade that I had been waiting for. "But there's nothing I can do to help with your taste."

"Oh. My. God," Elijah said, dramatically clutching his chest as though he had been mortally wounded. "Mark, we're keeping them."

"I'm keeping you all," Mark said, pulling Elijah and Viktoriya into a tight hug. "Sorry Eros, I'd hug you too if I could."

"I understand, and appreciate that," I said, the phone speaker buzzing. "I don't mean to cut the moment short, but Elijah, you'd better get going if you want time to shower before work."

"Thank you. Where have you been all my life?" Elijah said, standing up. "Come on, Mark, you heard the cosmic entity. Time to get moving."

"Oh, now you can tell time," Mark said accusingly. "Where was that two weeks ago?"

Mark didn't expect an answer; he already knew I was still practicing. It was also apparent he didn't need a response as they were all picking up boxes and heading for Mark's house. The three-person parade carried boxes from Mark's old room, down the stairs, and out into his temporarily empty house.

They all set the boxes down in the middle of the small living room. They looked around, pointing out where they thought imaginary furniture should go. Elijah insisted the couch should sit by the window, facing into the room. Viktoriya countered—it belonged near the fireplace, facing the window beside the bookshelf she already planned to fill. Mark wanted a simple, functional square coffee table. Elijah had his eye on an antique oval glass coffee table. Viktoriya remained neutral as long as it could hold her coffee. But they all easily agreed that they looked forward to the challenge. After twenty minutes of planning and dreaming, Elijah said it was time for him to leave. Viktoriya agreed but said she wished she didn't have to go. Mark, pragmatic as ever, reminded them both that they made it through the past few weeks, so they could make it a few more. They'd found each other—and everything else was just details to work out in time.

"Look, Viktoriya, Elijah … Eros—I don't know what the future holds for us, and I don't need to. I only know what I hope it holds. I want us to find out together," Mark said, pulling Elijah and Viktoriya into another tight embrace, kissing each of them. "I love you … all three of you."

Elijah and Viktoriya reluctantly pulled away from Mark and stepped out the door. They said good night in a way that made it clear they didn't want to leave. As they walked to Elijah's car, Mark watched from the doorway until they were in the car, pulling away from the house.

After closing the door, Mark reached into one of the boxes and pulled out the autographed playbill and the sacred beer can. The playbill—proof that even the boldest queen fears heartbreak, and that a missed moment can still find its way back. The Chernihivske can—evidence that the unexpected can change your life, and that a simple toast can open a door. He held them up at arm's length, testing each wall of his empty living room until he smiled—finally finding the perfect spot. Somewhere within my intangible, indefinable soul—whatever that means—I was smiling too.

Epilogue

About eleven months later, near the autumnal equinox, the quiet three-bedroom guesthouse, a stone's throw from Mark's childhood home, was alive and bustling with energy. It was now the primary residence of Mark, Viktoriya, and Elijah. They moved in confidently, blending their tastes into a space that felt wholly theirs. Both Elijah and Viktoriya had claimed a bedroom each as their own private sanctums. Viktoriya's room was a less crowded echo of her former bedroom. Elijah's room was little more than a large closet with a futon. While Mark's room became a communal space, the queen-size bed replaced with a king, and the closet evenly divided into thirds, with three chests of drawers on the opposite side of the room.

Elijah's vintage movie and theater posters lined the living room, as did Viktoriya's paintings and sketches. Mark had shelves of knickknacks and mementos. At the focal point of the room hung an elaborate shadow box. It displayed an empty can of Ukrainian beer, which held a preserved sunflower. Next to the can sat the skillfully mounted autographed *Kinky Boots* playbill. Beside those was a new photograph of Viktoriya and Elijah kissing Mark on both cheeks while he held a milk crate of freshly bottled apple cider. And next to it all sat a tasteful transmogrified gold apple. I like to think of them as sacred artifacts, enshrined in gilded pine—hope and memory sealed behind glass.

Three pairs of boots sat next to the door, piled atop each other—distinctly different, like their owners, yet a matched set.

Viktoriya's favorite surplus military-style boots. Mark's practical logger-style work boots. Elijah's elegantly rugged ankle boots with a thick five-inch heel.

Light from the fading sunset filled the room with a warmth that might have been mistaken for firelight. The warm red-orange glow washed over the vintage floral-print couch reclaimed from the 1980s, which sat facing the fireplace. Mark lay stretched out, his well-worn flannel shirt hanging unbuttoned, his sock-clad feet resting on Elijah's lap. Elijah was still in drag, designed to make him look like a burlap sack of apples—complete with fake apple cleavage, and a sculpted red, apple-shaped wig. His nylon-covered feet were propped up on the simple coffee table, next to two bottles of Ukrainian beer, wet with condensation. Across from the couch sat Viktoriya in a well-worn armchair, stolen from the Sunflower Kafe. She watched Mark and Elijah, cradling a cold bottle of beer, the condensation dripping through her fingers.

They were all exhausted after the inaugural apple-harvest festival the orchard had just hosted. The sounds of laughter and the work of breaking down vendor booths and carnival games drifted through the open window. The smell of fresh-pressed apple cider and wood smoke from the marshmallow-roasting bonfires permeated the air. Mark's record player hummed quietly with Billy Joel's *Piano Man* album. The soft melody of "You're My Home" floated through the room as these three partners contentedly sighed, satisfied with the work they saw bear fruit that day.

The Queen's Head Club presented a wildly popular drag revue, curated and hosted by Elijah as Fanny Ryesand. Queens from all around the region had come out to support their friends. The crowd of families cheered as the queens danced and lip-synced for them. Viktoriya's theatrical apple-themed costumes dazzled the audience.

In the months before the festival, Elijah had transformed The Queen's Head from a humble part-time drag club into a premier proving ground. His themed nights became local highlights. The club was packed for every "Drag Is for Everyone" and "Newcomer Night," where every staff member performed in drag, and anyone in the audience was encouraged to join in. And the "Kings and Queens Ball" saw nights dedicated to drag kings owning the stage, supported by a sea of queens.

Viktoriya's upstairs business was booming, buoyed by the club's rising reputation. Word of her drag and high-fashion designs had spread, drawing attention from icons of New York's Garment District. Her eye-catching streetwear might soon appear at New York Fashion Week if she pursues that prospect. But as she told me, she is content with what she has now and wishes to let success come to her, not chase it.

As for Mark's orchard, if the festival was any indication of its prosperity, its future was secure. Thanks in part to the improvements I made, the trees now yielded three times the fruit with a fraction of the resources. Growing larger, longer-lasting produce with the perfect balance of sweetness and rich flavor. The trees now bore fruit up to three times a season; Mark's harvests, to say the least, were bountiful. And people hailed my apples as the best around—I couldn't be prouder if I had produced those solid-gold apples I joked about a year ago.

Viktoriya and Elijah had built a life with Mark, not around him.

Each could stand and thrive on their own, but together they created something far greater. And they even left a little space for me among them, allowing me to help where I could and simply observe as a supportive companion where I couldn't. I couldn't know what their futures held, or if this joy would stand the test of time—and that was okay. The past year hadn't been problem-free or even easy, but there were more beautifully perfect moments like this than not.

There were bread pans in the sink, glitter in the floorboards, and half-repaired gadgets in the closet.

This was enough.

The End

Acknowledgements

The soundtrack of this book draws inspiration from other people's art, to whom I offer my deepest thanks. Beginning with the Shirelles (Shirley Owens, Doris Coley, Addie Harris, Beverly Lee), Amy Winehouse, and Carole King and Gerry Goffin for "Will You Love Me Tomorrow." To Barbra Streisand for Funny Girl and What's Up, Doc? To Billy Joel whose music is ingrained in my life and the heart of this story. To Cyndi Lauper and Kinky Boots; and to Chappell Roan—"Picture You" was the seed that first inspired this story.

This book also leans on the work of The Beatles, Bob Dylan, David Bowie, the Ramones, Magnet & Gemma Hayes, and Otis Redding, whose songs and sensibilities wind through these pages even when they're only briefly named.

For the wider affectionate references: thank you to Bugs Bunny, Grace Jones, Patsy Cline, Paul Simon, Freddie Mercury, Omar Sharif, and Chris Hemsworth; to Legend (Ridley Scott, William Hjortsberg), The Shape of Water (Guillermo del Toro, Vanessa Taylor), and the worlds of J.R.R. Tolkien as brought to life by Peter Jackson and Ian McKellen; and to Edmond Rostand (Cyrano de Bergerac), William Shakespeare, and Christopher Marlowe—who will forever be the couple of my dreams (Kit & Bill).

Special thanks to Amber McClincy, who read the first, second, and third versions of this story and offered honest advice and feedback that helped shape this story. Also to Rose Hannel, who patiently created the fantastic cover art for this story—find them on social media under RosetheArtist24.

About the author

Kyle Steenblik is an award-winning, queer, neurodivergent writer whose work explores the complexities of identity and belonging. Based in Utah with formative roots in New Jersey, Kyle crafts character-forward fiction that blends humor, emotional intimacy, and the fantastical.

His debut collection, Tales of Weirderland, was awarded the 2025 Diamond Quill Award for Book of the Year by the League of Utah Writers. Drawing on his Shakespearean background, Kyle's storytelling balances wit and absurdity with a "quietly ferocious" emotional truth. He is particularly drawn to stories about people navigating systems not built for them—finding ways to bend rather than break.

Lived experience informs every page: from growing up with ADHD and autism to his journey as a husband and father of two. Whether he's in a library or a drag club, Kyle is an observer of beauty in unexpected places. He writes with a sense of generosity, hoping his work leaves readers feeling a little lighter, braver, and more fully seen.

More information about Kyle can be found at:
https://WastedWords.net

Other books by Kyle Stenblik
Tales of Weirderland: The Collected Volumes